Sweet Sweet Revenge Ltd

Sweet Sweet Revenge LTD

Jonas Jonasson

Translated from the Swedish by Rachel Willson-Broyles

HARPER LARGE PRINT

An Imprint of HarperCollinsPublishers

SWEET SWEET REVENGE LTD. Copyright © 2021 by Jonas Jonasson. All rights reserved. Printed in the United States of America. No part of this book may be used or reproduced in any manner whatsoever without written permission except in the case of brief quotations embodied in critical articles and reviews. For information, address HarperCollins Publishers, 195 Broadway, New York, NY 10007.

English translation copyright © 2021 by Rachel Willson-Broyles.

HarperCollins books may be purchased for educational, business, or sales promotional use. For information, please e-mail the Special Markets Department at SPsales@harpercollins.com.

Originally published as *Hämnden är ljuv AB* in Sweden in 2021 by Piratförlaget.

FIRST HARPER LARGE PRINT EDITION

ISBN: 978-0-06-324235-7

Library of Congress Cataloging-in-Publication Data is available upon request.

22 23 24 25 26 LSC 10 9 8 7 6 5 4 3 2 1

Patriotism is the virtue of the vicious.
Oscar Wilde

Tell Oscar I said he shouldn't think so much.
Aunt Klara

Contents

Contents

Prologue

Once upon a time, in the Austro-Hungarian Empire, there was a moderately successful artist. His first name was Adolf, and he would eventually be famous the world over for other reasons.

Young Adolf was of the opinion that true art depicted reality as it was, as the eye perceived it. More or less like a photograph, but in color. "Beauty is truth," he said, quoting a Frenchman he otherwise wanted nothing to do with.

Much later in life, when Adolf was not quite so young, he saw to it that books, art, and even people went up in flames, in the name of the correct worldview. This eventually led to the biggest war the world had thus far seen. Adolf both lost and perished.

And his worldview went into hiding.

PART ONE

Chapter 1

He had no idea who Adolf was and had never heard of the Austro-Hungarian Empire. Nor did he have any need to know. He was a medicine man in a remote village on the Kenyan savanna. He left so few impressions in the iron-rich red soil that his name is no longer remembered.

He was skilled in the art of healing, but his good reputation reached beyond his valley just as little as the events of the world outside reached in. He lived an unassuming life. Died too soon. Despite his great skill, he was unable to cure himself when he needed it the most. He was grieved and missed by a small but faithful assortment of patients.

His oldest son was rather too young to take over, but that was how it worked, that was how it had been throughout the ages, and so it would remain.

At just twenty years old, the successor had an even more negligible reputation. He inherited his father's relative competence but none of his good-naturedness. Being satisfied with small mercies for the rest of his life was not for him.

His transformation into something else began when the young man built a new hut in which to receive patients, one that had a separate waiting room. It progressed with his exchanging his *shúkà* for a white coat and was fully realized when he changed both his name and his title. The son of the medicine man whose name no one remembers any longer began to call himself Dr. Ole Mbatian after that fabled man of the same name, the greatest Maasai of them all, the leader and visionary. The original was long dead and offered no protest from the other side.

Tossed out along with all the old ways was his father's price list for treatments. The son drafted his own, one that did the great warrior justice. It would no longer do to drop by with a bag of tea leaves or a piece of dried meat as payment, not if you expected the doctor to have time for you. These days a simple matter cost one hen to treat; the more complicated ones required a goat. For truly serious cases, the doctor demanded a cow. If it wasn't *too* serious, that is; a patient who died got to do so for free.

Time passed. The medicine men of the nearby villages closed down their clinics, driven out by the competition on account of the fact that they still went by the same old names they always had and insisted that a true Maasai did not dress himself in white. As Dr. Ole Mbatian's list of patients grew, so did his reputation. His paddock of cows and goats needed constant expanding. The clientele on whom he could test his decoctions was so large that Ole became as skilled as people were starting to say he was.

The medicine man with the stolen name was already wealthy by the time he celebrated the arrival of his first son. The baby survived those critical first years and was, in accordance with tradition, trained in his father's work. Ole the Second spent many years alongside his father before the latter passed away. When the day arrived, he kept his father's stolen name but did away with the title of "Doctor" and burned the white coat, since patients who had come from far away had testified that doctors, in contrast to medicine men, might be associated with witchcraft. A medicine man who developed the reputation of being a witch would not enjoy many more days in his career, or even his life.

Thus, after Dr. Ole Mbatian came Ole Mbatian the Elder. His firstborn son, who grew up and took over from his father and grandfather, was, in turn, Ole Mbatian the Younger.

And it is with him that this tale begins.

Chapter 2

Ole Mbatian the Younger, then, had inherited his name, wealth, reputation and talents from his father and grandfather. In another part of the world, this would have been called being born with a silver spoon in his mouth.

His educational journey was overseen with care and, along with friends in his age set, he also got to take a detour through warrior training. He was thus not only a medicine man but also a highly esteemed Maasai warrior. No one knew more about the healing powers of roots and herbs, and only a very few could measure up to Ole when it came to spears, throwing clubs, and knives.

His medical specialty was the prevention of more children than a family wished to have. Unhappy women flocked his way from Migori in the west to Maji Moto in the east, several days' travel away. To have time to see them all he had an admission policy of at least five previously delivered children per applying woman, of which at least two must be boys. The medicine man never revealed his formulas, but it was easy to tell that bitter melon was an active ingredient in the cloudy liquid the woman must drink each time she ovulated. Those with extra-sensitive taste buds could also detect a hint of the root of Indian cotton.

Ole Mbatian the Younger was richer than everyone else, including Chief Olemeeli the Well-Traveled. Besides all his cows he had three huts and two wives. It was the other way around for the chief: two huts and three wives. Ole never understood how he made that work.

Incidentally, the medicine man had never liked his chief. They were the same age and even as children they knew which roles they would one day shoulder.

"My dad rules over your dad," Olemeeli might say to tease him.

He wasn't wrong, even as Ole Jr. preferred not to lose in an argument against him. Instead he solved the issue by whacking the future chief in the face with his throwing club, leaving Ole Mbatian the Elder no choice but to vociferously give his son a licking even as he whispered words of praise in the boy's ear.

Back then, it was Kakenya the Handsome who ruled the valley. He was secretly plagued by the realization that his epithet was not only accurate but in every meaningful way the sole admirable trait he possessed. He was no less concerned that the son who would one day take over appeared to have inherited his father's shortcomings, but not exactly his physical beauty. And it didn't help young Olemeeli's appearance that the medicine man's boy had knocked out two of his front teeth.

Kakenya the Handsome had an endlessly difficult time making decisions. He even let his wives decide for him now and then, but unfortunately he had an even number of them. Each time they were unable to agree on an issue (which was almost every time) he stood there with his tie-breaking vote and no idea what to do with it.

Yet in the autumn of his old age, and with the support of his whole family, Kakenya managed to accomplish something he could be proud of. He would send his oldest son on journeys; he would go much further than anyone had done before. He would, as a result, become well-traveled and return home full of impressions from the outside world. The wisdom he gathered on his journey would be a help to him when it became time for him to take over. Olemeeli would never be as handsome as his father, but he could become a resolute and forward-looking chief.

That was the plan.

Now, things don't always turn out the way one intends. Olemeeli's first and last long journey was to Loiyangalani, on his father's orders. The destination was chosen not only because it was almost further away than what was reasonably possible, but also because there were rumors that people had discovered, way up there in the north, a new way to filter lake water. Heated sand and herbs rich in vitamin C mixed with root of water lily had long been the known methods. But apparently, in Loiyangalani, they had come up with some new way that was both simpler and more effective.

"Go there, my son," said Kakenya the Handsome. "Gain knowledge from all the new things you encounter along the way. Then come home and prepare yourself. I feel that I don't have much time left."

"But Dad," said Olemeeli.

He couldn't think of anything else to say. He seldom found the right words. Or the right thought.

His journey took half an eternity. Or a whole week. Once he arrived at his destination, Olemeeli discovered that the people in Loiyangalani were advanced in many ways. Water purification was one of them. But they'd also installed something called electricity, and the mayor used a machine, rather than a pen or piece of chalk, to write letters.

Olemeeli really just wanted to go back home, but his father's words echoed in his mind. So he made a careful study of one thing and the next; he owed his father at least that much. Unfortunately, he tried out the electricity to such an extent that he got a shock and passed out.

When he regained consciousness, he took a few minutes to recover before tackling the typewriter. But there Olemeeli fared so poorly as to get his left index finger stuck between the *d* and *r* keys, frightening him so badly that he yanked his hand away with such force that his finger broke in two places.

Enough was enough. Olemeeli ordered his assistants to pack their bags for the arduous journey home. He already knew what he would say in his report to his father Kakenya: it was bad enough that electricity could bite you just because you stuck a nail into a hole in the wall. But the writing machine was downright lethal.

Kakenya the Handsome had seldom been accurate

in his prophecies. But the suspicion that he didn't have much time left turned out to be correct. His terrified and partially toothless son took over.

Newly minted Chief Olemeeli passed down three decrees on the very first day after his father's burial.

One: the thing called electricity must never, ever be installed in the valley over which Olemeeli ruled.

Two: machines for writing were not to be transported over the border, and

Three: the village would be investing in a brand-new water purification system.

So it came to be that for almost four decades, Olemeeli had been ruling over the only valley in Maasai Mara where electricity, typewriters, and by extension, computers, did not exist. It became the valley where not a single one of the six billion cell phone owners on earth happened to live.

He called himself Olemeeli the Well-Traveled. He was as unpopular as his father had once been. Behind his back he had a number of less flattering names. Ole Mbatian the Younger's favorite was "Chief Toothless."

The not-at-all-well-liked chief and the admittedly skillful medicine man may have been the same age, but that didn't mean they were of the same mind. It wouldn't do for them to quarrel as they had when they were younger. Ole Mbatian had to come to terms with the fact that the greatest Luddite of them all was also the one in charge. In return, Olemeeli pretended not to hear when the medicine man pointed out which of them had the most teeth left in his mouth.

The chief was a constant but tolerable concern for Ole Mbatian. His only true sorrow in life lay elsewhere: namely in the fact that he had had four children with his first wife and four with his second—eight daughters and no sons. After the fourth girl he began to experiment with his herbs and roots to make sure the next baby was a boy. But this was one medical challenge that proved beyond his capabilities. The daughters kept coming until they didn't come at all. His wives stopped delivering, even without any bitter melon or Indian cotton figured into the mixtures Ole Mbatian had tried.

After five generations of medicine men, the next man in line would be someone other than a Mbatian, or whatever they had been called before. Female medicine men didn't exist in the Maasai world. It's all in the name.

For a long time, Ole was able to find solace in the fact that Chief Toothless fared no better in the production of children. Olemeeli had six daughters right alongside Ole's eight.

But then there was this part where the chief had an extra wife to turn to. Before the youngest wife got too old, she produced a son and the heir to her husband and chief. Great celebration in the village! The proud father announced that the festivities would last all night. And so they did. Everyone partied until dawn, except for the medicine man, who had a headache and retired early.

That was many years ago now. Many more than what Ole expected he had left. But he wasn't ready to meet the Supreme God yet. He still had more to give. He didn't know exactly how old he had become, but he noticed he wasn't quite as good with a bow and arrow as he had once been and couldn't hit a target quite as accurately with his spear, throwing club, or knife. Maybe with the throwing club, now that he thought about it. After all, he was the reigning village champion.

There wasn't anything much wrong with his agility either. He moved with nearly as much confidence as always. If not as willingly. He was getting lazy. Had toothaches. And cures for toothaches. His vision was cloudier than it had been in his youth, but that didn't seem like a problem. Ole had already seen everything worth seeing and he could find his way to wherever he needed to go.

All in all, there were indications that one stage of life had made way for another. Or, alternately, that Ole Mbatian was depressed. When his sorrow over the son that never was got too tight a grip on him, he mixed himself up some St John's wort and roseroot in sunflower oil. That usually helped.

Or he took an extra walk in the savanna. He was out early each morning, thanks to his constant search for fresh roots and herbs for his medicine cabinet. He worked before the sun got too hot, beginning his walks while it was still dark. Alert to any noises from nearly silent lions that might be out hunting.

Was his stride getting shorter, perhaps? Ole had once gone as far as Nanyki. Another time he'd made it all the way to Kilimanjaro and on up the mountain. Now it felt as if the neighboring villages were far away. There was nothing to suggest that Ole Mbatian the Younger would one day, in the not-too-distant future, cause a considerable uproar in Stockholm, Europe and the world. The Maasai who knew so much about how to distill the healing powers of the savanna knew nothing of the Swedish capital city or the continent to which it belonged. And of the world he knew nothing beyond that it had been created by En-Kai, the Supreme God, who lived in the mountain Kirinyaga. Ole Mbatian called himself a Christian, but there were some truths the Bible couldn't change. One of them was the story of creation.

"Oh well," he said to himself.

The upshot of all of this was simply that he had to fight a little longer. And in good spirits, all things considered.

Chapter 3

Just over ten thousand kilometers north of the Maasai lands, in a suburb of the Swedish capital city of Stockholm, Lasse handed the keys over to the buyer of his life's work. It was time to retire.

This was no big deal for the former hot-dog stand owner. You were born, you pulled your weight, you retired, you died, you were buried. That was all there was to it.

But it was a big deal—and a terrible one at that—for one of his regulars. Just think, Lasse had sold his stand to an Arab. One who didn't know what Västervik mustard was. Or that the hot dogs go *on top of* the mashed potatoes. One who added kebab to the menu.

That sort of change would leave its mark on anyone. Victor was only fifteen when it happened. Hanging around outside the hot-dog stand with his moped was no longer what it had been.

His friends designated the new pizzeria across the square their new hangout spot, but of course that was run by another Arab.

There was something about those Arabs. And the Iranians. The Iraqis. The Yugoslavians. None of them knew what Västervik mustard was. They dressed weird. Talked weird. Couldn't they learn proper Swedish?

That was his first problem. The second was that his friends didn't see what he saw. They switched to the pizzeria from the hot-dog stand not because hot dogs had become kebab, but because it was so much warmer indoors. When Victor tried to make them see that Sweden was about to be transformed, they sneered at him. Wasn't life simply more interesting with a Yugoslavian or Iranian here and there?

Victor was alone in his ponderings. When his friends went to a disco, he sat home alone in his childhood room. When his friends played football on the weekends, he went to the museum. There he found comfort in what was authentically Swedish, like French Rococo and the Neoclassicism King Gustav III had brought to Sweden from Italy. But above all, he loved national romanticism: nothing could be more beautiful than Anders Zorn's *Midsummer Dance*; nothing more tinged with solemnity than the funeral procession of King Karl XII as depicted by Gustaf Cederström.

The opposite of kebab.

His upper-secondary school years were torture. The boys in his class thought he was strange for learning the succession of Swedish monarchs by heart, from the eighth century onward. For his part, he thought those boys were uninteresting. And the girls . . . well, there was something wrong with them. Some had a cloth wrapped around their heads; he wanted nothing to do with those ones. But even the ones who were real Swedes . . . it was hard to talk to them. What were they supposed to talk about? How did you get close to someone without necessarily letting her get close to you?

His military service came as something of a relief. Twelve months of rules and regulations in service to the nation. But not even the Swedish armed forces were spared from the foreigners. Or the women.

As a young adult, Victor considered a career in politics. He subscribed to *Folktribunen*, a newspaper published by Nazis that essentially clung to the same truths he did. He went to a meeting or two with what he assumed were like-minded people but didn't feel comfortable there. They wanted to bring about change with violence, but that presupposed that you were prepared to fight, which in turn might hurt. Victor had been quite familiar with the concept of pain ever since the time three hundred kronor went missing from his father's wallet. His father had no proof Victor had taken it, but he gave the fifteen-year-old a proper thrashing anyway. The point at issue was not something the son wished to rehash with himself afterwards.

The party Victor considered joining had both leaders and vice-leaders, but he himself was on the bottom rung. Within the group you were expected to obey and cooperate. Not just other men, but women too. How could you work with those? And how could you obey them?

His conclusion was that Sweden was lost, unless his temporary friends in the resistance movement succeeded in their revolution. Or unless he himself took charge of things—without getting beaten up or thrown in jail along the way. Although Sweden was in a state of general decay, it was still possible to find success in the country, unlike in the party, where you had to show *consideration*. That was just about Victor's least favorite word. *Consideration* for the party leader, his vice-leader, his wife and his cat. It was with determination, not consideration, that one would protect Sweden from the parasites.

The single twenty-year-old did not owe anything to anyone. He planned to fight his way to the top, whence he could allow his lack of consideration to blossom.

It could take time if it must, and it didn't matter a whit if it happened at the expense of other people. Precisely which top he fought to didn't matter either, as long as it was sufficiently high.

His climb began with getting a job with the most respectable art gallery in Stockholm. After all, he knew quite a bit about real art, and during his interview he managed to pepper art dealer Alderheim with lies about how much he appreciated the abominable modernism. To be on the safe side, he studied up on the topic before the interview, so he could say things like:

"It's not easy to sit here before the city's greatest art dealer and express the true function of thought."

Here he was alluding to the founder of surrealism, about whom his intended employer luckily inquired no further since Victor had forgotten his name. What he did recall was that he had been a leftist poet and the founder of an anti-fascist group. In short, an idiot.

His art-world plan was not a random one. Victor

had thought this out carefully: Anyone who wanted to enact change needed a *position*. Beating up a homosexual or scaring the daylights out of a foreigner might be a worthy act, but it wouldn't lead to any change to speak of. Except for that particular homosexual or foreigner.

And the way to rise to a position was to move in the right circles. Thus Victor needed to seek out money and power. Starting from the bottom rungs of industry would be as hopeless as doing so in politics.

The art gallery was a perfect springboard, for if there was one thing that united the members of the social-liberal power elite it was opera, theater—and art. And especially the modernist claptrap Alderheim sold. Victor would get to know the clientele, and it would only be a matter of time before he was offered something better.

The work itself involved taking on most of the client-facing responsibilities. Victor negotiated the right to call himself the manager. Alderheim had originally imagined more of an assistant, but the fellow was old, tired, and easily swayed. The manager's most important duty was to make the client like the art by liking him.

"I'm really a Cézanne deep down inside," he might

say with a smile that was confident and yet bashful. "But I must confess that I find myself drawn to Matisse."

And he would fill in a little nonsense, such as:

"Good old Matisse . . ."

He kept the rest of the sentence to himself (". . . may he burn in hell").

Perhaps the clientele imagined that the manager was caught somewhere between impressionism and expressionism, when in fact he was simply sticking to his plan.

Alderheim was dazzled by the manager's charm. This new guy was starting to feel more and more like the son he'd never had.

In those days, Victor's last name was still the extremely ordinary Svensson. Even so, a customer might occasionally invite him to a gallery opening or something else as excruciating as it was crucial. He made sure to be where he was meant to be when he was meant to be there. Biding his time, alert to every key that would lead him ever upwards.

He gave himself two years. If he didn't get a bite before then he would simply quit and reconsider. He never would have imagined that everything was going to work out on its own. The future came to him, no need to track it down. Her name was Jenny.

Woman was everything Victor despised. She was incomprehensible, weak, and emotional. He availed himself of what few advantages she did possess by visiting a high-end prostitute at one of Stockholm's finer hotels once a week. The benefit of high-end service was that he could pay by invoice. And that "sex" could be termed "frames," "oil cloth," or some other suitable item. He did not consider the opposite sex able to provide any other sort of happiness. Except . . .

Victor noticed that when it came to his daughter, Old Man Alderheim had got a notion in his head early on. She had hardly accomplished more than learning to walk when Victor arrived on the scene. He was nineteen years and nine months older than her. It would take patience on his part. And continued support from the old man, who was himself twenty-five years older than his own suspicious witch of a wife. Who might eventually have turned out to be a wrench in the works of this arrangement, if she hadn't removed herself from the equation along the way.

Jenny grew up, which is not to say she became attractive in the least. She crept along the walls. Radiated nothing. Dressed badly.

But she was an Alderheim. And one day she would inherit the place. A relationship between her and

Victor could bring him both a distinguished surname and, eventually, the whole business.

Yet there was the problem with the old witch. Victor suspected she was a member of the Left Party, because she believed it was up to Jenny herself to seek and find love. And she questioned the manager's emotional engagement and loyalty. She wasn't wrong, so it was a good thing she kicked the bucket.

It only took a few days. Cancer riddled her body. She hadn't said a word about being in pain, just stopped getting out of bed on Monday. Was carried off on Wednesday. Buried a week later.

Once the old witch was gone, the aging proprietor spent his days up in the apartment, grieving for days gone by. In the evenings he had Jenny light a fire in the library with its leather armchairs, his favorite works of art on the wall, and the big aquarium.

There he invited his intended son-in-law to share some cognac. It sometimes turned into quite a few snifters each week, but the drink was good and so was his objective. During the day, Victor dealt with the clientele, his lies and elegance ever increasing, as he bossed little Jenny around a sufficient amount.

Alderheim's daughter turned twelve, fourteen, and fifteen. She never complained and didn't seem to hang out with anyone at all. She approached new tasks with the same neutral expression as always. In time, she took over all the cleaning both in the apartment and the store. This way, Victor was spared from paying the wages of a part-time job. He used the savings to buy a little more sex without creating an obvious difference in the final expense tally. He also put Jenny to work in the boring archives in the cellar, which was where she preferred to spend time anyway. She even *smelled* like an archive.

Just as everything seemed to be smooth sailing, he was struck by a bolt of lightning in the form of one of the prostitutes from his past! All of a sudden she appeared in the store with a teenage boy at her side.

"His name is Kevin," she said.

"So?" said Victor.

The woman asked the boy to go wait for her on the sidewalk. Once he was out of earshot, she said:

"He's your son."

"My son? He's fucking Black."

"Perhaps if you take a closer look at me you'll understand how such a thing could happen."

The woman didn't blame herself. It wasn't in her job description to assess the character of an individual client before doing business with him. And there was only one rule beyond that: anyone who hit her was not allowed back; anyone who didn't hit her was welcome as long as they paid up. The man across from her had belonged to the latter category.

Victor had to close the store and get the lying woman and her son out of there before Jenny emerged from the archives. The old man was, as usual, up in his six-bedroom apartment and could neither see nor hear them.

With brand-new yet extremely debatable knowledge of his fatherhood, Victor herded mother and child to a café a few blocks away (it was ridiculous how much she'd gone downhill in just a few years). He asked what she wanted from him.

She wanted the worst thing of all. For him to take responsibility as a father. She hadn't said a word about Kevin's existence for all these years, but a hard life had taken its toll on her and now she needed help. Plus, the boy deserved a dad.

If only it had been about money.

"What do you mean, help?" he asked.

"I'm sick."

"What do you mean?"

The woman fell silent. Kevin's ears were full of music, but to be safe she sent him to the stand across the street to buy some candy. And said:

"I'm going to die."

"Everyone is."

More silence at the table, before the woman spoke again.

"I've got AIDS."

Victor shoved his chair back.

"Oh, shit!"

He wanted to deny it all, but it was possible that the plague-stricken woman had circumstances on her side. And she had shown up at the precise moment she shouldn't have, in regards to Victor's life plan.

He couldn't simply chase her off. For as long as she lived, she might pop up in the shop unannounced to spit blood or talk fatherhood with anyone at all.

As long as she lived, that is. Which, happily, seemed like it might not be very long at all.

Therefore, the key concepts would be "buying time" and "harm reduction."

In the ensuing negotiations with the dying mother, Victor promised to take responsibility for the kid until he was of age, given that the mother promised never to use the word "father" in earshot of the kid. Or any other time, either.

"The kid?" said the woman. "He has a name. Kevin."

"Don't split hairs."

Chapter 4

While Kevin's mother was busy withering away, Victor took a week's vacation. The increasingly decrepit Old Man Alderheim had to get off his ass and be useful for the first time in years. The manager rented a studio apartment in one of the most distant of all of Stockholm's southern suburbs, a place where he could hide his sudden problem. Eighteen square meters, a bed, a kitchenette, two chairs and a table.

He sat the kid down on one of the chairs, himself on the other, and informed him of the rules.

Number one was that Kevin must never get it into his head that Victor was his father. He had taken on this responsibility out of the goodness of his heart since Kevin's irresponsible mother was planning to die. *Guardian* would be a fitting title, but if that seemed awkward then "boss" would do.

The boy nodded, although he'd never had a boss in his life. Nor a guardian, for that matter. And definitely not a father.

Number two was that Kevin must never come track down Victor in the city. He lived here in Bollmora and would go to the nearby upper-secondary school every day, and then come home. If he did as he was told, the boss promised to make sure there was always pizza in the fridge.

Kevin wondered how his mother was doing.

"The hell with that, listen to me. This is important."

The immediate crisis was averted. And when the troublesome woman died a week or so later, everything could go back to normal. Kevin behaved himself, didn't make any trouble at school, didn't complain about the food. And above all: he never came to the art gallery. It was almost as if he didn't exist, which of course would have been preferable.

Jenny turned sixteen and then seventeen and eighteen, all as Victor couldn't come up with a single sexual reason to touch her. But nor was that the point. They only had to get married.

The old man was an excellent marriage broker. Each day he worked on his essentially apathetic daughter. Sometimes so vociferously that Victor could hear him from a distance. Alderheim's argument was that he wanted his life's work to live on after his death; that Jenny was too young and inexperienced to shoulder the responsibility; that Victor, on the other hand, was a mature and responsible man. A secure man, even. Did Jenny suppose she could develop any feelings for him?

Her response was not audible from the next room. To find any creature more taciturn than Jenny you would have to look in the old man's aquarium.

It would all work out with the girl. The problem with the bastard in Bollmora, however, was a thorn in his side. Time passed and the day approached when Kevin would turn eighteen. Once the boy was of age, Victor would no longer be able to control him. Then he would make a fuss. Victor had no faith in the inherent goodness of humankind; the only person he trusted was himself. There was no way of knowing whether it would be a month, six months, or a year; the only certainty was that Kevin would one day stand before him and demand Victor's money. First a hundred kronor for some minor thing, then more for a bicycle, then even more for a car, for study abroad, for a house of his own. . . . Once the boy learned that Victor was a fee-free ATM, it would never end.

Shit.

The manager needed to focus on charming the old man, pretending to flirt with and eventually proposing to Jenny, and making sure that fruitcake said yes. A *peep* out of Kevin in Bollmora would bring everything crashing down. Victor had known it for ages; it was only a matter of time before the kid would figure it out for himself.

Murder was out of the question. But what if the boy died anyway? That would be a different story. The problem was that eighteen-year-old boys don't just do that out of the blue. Kevin would need some help along the way.

Victor recalled the resistance movement he'd had dealings with many years before. You had to hand it to them for plodding on. At regular intervals, one or two of them would be locked up for assault, violent rioting, incitement to racial hatred, weapons violations, and a few other things. In between times, they honed their party platform. In many ways, they held the correct views. One of the first things they wanted to do once they'd quarreled their way to power was send everyone who didn't belong here back where they came from. Iranians to Iran, Iraqis to Iraq, Yugoslavians to . . . well, that one was trickier. But in all certainty, Kevin would end up in Africa.

That was a lovely thought. The problem was, he couldn't wait for the resistance movement's revolution. How many of them could possibly be working to make it happen? A hundred? Two hundred? And half of them were in prison.

No, as usual, he was on his own.

He thought about this Africa thing.

Then he thought a little more and took a respectable old atlas from Alderheim's bookshelf.

He ran his index finger slowly across the continent of Africa until it almost stopped of its own accord. And then he made up his mind.

A place for everything, and everything in its place.

Chapter 5

"Hello there, Kevin. I see you're out of pizza."

"Hi, boss."

Victor nodded, pleased. The boy knew the rules and was sticking to them. A well-mannered boy. Black, but well-mannered.

"You'll be eighteen soon."

"Today, actually."

"There you go. I thought we could celebrate with a trip next week. It must get boring, being stuck in Bollmora all the time."

A trip sounded fantastic. Kevin was happy here, though, thought it was nice, and after all the boss had said he was never to come into the city.

"Great, so you understand. But now it so happens I have business in Nairobi. Wouldn't you like to come along? Have a look around?"

"Nairobi?" said the boy.

"Kenya," said Victor.

In that moment, Kevin felt for the first time that there was something between them, almost like the boss was more than just a boss. He was prickly, and sometimes downright unpleasant, but deep down? They were going on a big trip together. To discover the world together. To *be* together.

"Thanks, Dad . . ." Kevin let slip.

Not that he thought it might be true, but he was lacking such a person in his life.

"Don't call me Dad!"

It took a few days to tidy up the most in-the-way pizza boxes and arrange for passports and tickets. Victor booked a round-trip ticket in business class for himself and a one-way in coach for Kevin.

Then he fooled Jenny and her halfway senile father into thinking he was going off on a jaunt to London to work on a potential client.

"I'll be back in a few days," he said. "You can take care of the gallery in the meantime."

"But—" said Jenny.

"Great. Kisses."

There was no way of knowing which country was Kevin's. Victor selected their destination on other grounds: enough civilization so nothing bad would happen to him—ergo, Kenya, not Somalia. And enough wilderness so the boy could never find his bearings—ergo, not a national park within walking distance of the nearest bus stop. In rough terms, this meant 550 kilometers from Nairobi and straight out into the middle of nowhere.

So far the trip had not been what Kevin had hoped— for instance, that he might discover a heart of gold somewhere inside Victor's tough exterior. They'd had the misfortune to end up in separate sections during the flights, which meant none of what the eighteen-year-old had dreamed of: chatting about life and the future. Getting to know one another. Learning to like each other.

A rental car awaited them at the airport; Victor invited the boy to sit in the front seat. Like an equal. Now, maybe?

The boy wanted the trip to be a long one; after all, they were seated side by side.

"Where are we going, Dad?" he asked.

"I told you not to call me Dad."

And with that, the conversation was over.

The boss continued to say nothing as he used the GPS to aim the Range Rover. Westward ho.

The boy was equally silent, for three hours. What was there to say? But in the end, he got tired of it.

"Can't you tell me where we're going? I'm curious."

"What's with all the chit-chat? Just enjoy the view, dammit."

A104 became B3 which became C12. The roads decreased both in width and quality. Asphalt turned to gravel as the sun went down. Victor and the boy had been on the vast savanna for some time now. And the shift from dusk to dark is fast, at the equator. Just as it turned pitch-black outside, Victor stopped the car.

"We're here."

"Where's here?"

"Where you belong. Get out of the car."

Kevin did, in contrast to Victor, who remained behind the wheel with the engine running. He left the boy next to an acacia tree and drove on a bit, to a spot where he could turn around. On the way back, he rolled down his window to say farewell.

"Don't be upset. I'm sure you'll be fine out here. I think it's in your blood."

"But Dad . . ." said Kevin.

"I'll be goddamned," Victor said, and drove off.

The kid had been repatriated. Nature would take care of the rest. Who could blame Victor if it took its course?

Just over twenty-four hours later, he was back in the gallery. One travel experience richer. One problem poorer.

"How was London?" Jenny wondered.

"Hot," said Victor.

It was the twenty-fifth of February.

The Tax Agency refused to declare Kevin dead. Following up with the police report regarding his disappearance, they demanded the completion of Form 7695, "application to have a missing person declared deceased." After that they would take the matter under consideration for a five-year period. *Five years!* Surely it hadn't taken the lions more than five minutes.

At least everything else was going Victor's way. The eternally grieving old man one floor up had, after all, turned over the entire establishment to him and his daughter, and Jenny said yes when he first took a deep breath and thereupon proposed. The breath was on account of his aversion, not out of apprehension for what she might say. She never contradicted.

Victor shared the happy matrimonial news with his father-in-law-to-be at the same time he told him he planned to take the daughter and father-in-law's name instead of the other way around.

"Out of respect for all you've done for me," he said, in accordance with the truth.

His father-in-law began to cry. To think that it all could have turned out so well for his beloved daughter.

The whole kit and caboodle was about to become Victor's. All that was left to do was get it in writing.

It was a difficult time, those few years it took for the old man to die on his own. He regularly returned, over cognac, to the topic of whether there might be a grandchild on the way. Victor skillfully dodged the question. To keep from falling into fleshly temptation he doubled his weekly visits to the high-end prostitutes. With condoms. He would not let any more bastards, real or made-up, get in his way.

Then it arrived, the best day of Victor's life so far. To think that it was on Christmas Eve that the old man told them the news. Victor could not imagine a better Christmas present!

"My dear Jenny, my dear Victor. I will soon be reunited with Hillevi."

"What are you saying, Dad?" Jenny said, upset.

"I am riddled with cancer, just like your mother."

Hallelujah, hallelujah, sing eternal praises, Victor thought.

"How awful," he said.

Now his path was free and clear. From nothing to everything in twenty years and eleven days.

Victor did wait until his father-in-law's body was cold, but barely, before he did what was left to do. He started a new limited liability company (Victory or Death Properties Ltd), protected the company with a prenup, got Jenny to hand over the art gallery, the six-bedroom apartment, and all her assets to him—at which point he sold it to the company for one krona. The operation gave his wife the formal right to fifty öre—half of one krona—in the event of their divorce. The rest would go to him.

It all went smoothly. As always, Jenny signed whatever Victor put in front of her. On rare occasions she had a question, but nothing he couldn't fend off. For instance, she wanted to know why they should have a prenuptial agreement tied to the new company. Victor said he didn't want to trouble her with administrative matters now that they would have children and everything (he assumed she didn't understand that children presupposed sex).

Sure, she could fight the arrangement in court later on, perhaps with some success. But only on a purely theoretical level. Victor knew that in practice, she didn't have it in her. And anyway, there wasn't much legal help to be had for fifty öre.

There was a lot to think about to make sure everything turned out right. After all his years in the antisocial world of art dealership, there was now one thing that was more urgent than any other. Victor sold twelve modernist works at a discount and tore up and threw out a thirteenth, an Erich Heckel with a price tag of 180,000 kronor. Or "Erich WRECK-el," as Victor secretly called him. The work featured a half-naked woman with androgynously chiseled features and green lips. The androgynous figure was such a gross affront to both beauty and society's rules and regulations that Victor didn't even want to hand that crap off for free, out of concern for the greater good.

After his initial art purge, he secretly listed Jenny's official residence as the apartment in Bollmora. He wasn't sure it was necessary, but in the troublesome world of jurisprudence, it was best to deploy both belt and suspenders.

And then it was *finally* time to get divorced.

———

"Salmon or chicken for dinner?" Jenny wondered one day.

"Chicken, please," said Victor. "And also I want a divorce."

That landed about as he expected.

"Chicken," said Jenny.

After all, her father was dead. What reason did she have to try to breathe vigor into a similarly lifeless relationship?

The divorce gained legal force in just a few weeks, because Jenny still kept signing everything. Victor figured this was because she was stupid. The truth was, she just wanted to be done with him. Get away from there.

She got what she wanted. And yet not. After a lifelong slumber, she woke up one day in a studio apartment in Bollmora, with hardly anything to her name but fifty öre and the clothes on her back.

Now, it so happened that Jenny was not as apathetic as Victor had thought. Early on in life she had made the choice to spend her time with art first and people second, assuming there was any time left over. And Victor and her circumstances made sure there wasn't.

It was true that she prioritized the care of her father first and the cellar archive thereafter. But she wasn't alone down there, among binders and documents. She had friends like Franz Kafka and August Strindberg in a small bookcase, and she adorned the walls with cheap but life-size paper reproductions of works by Vincent van Gogh, Max Beckmann, Isaac Grünewald, Marc Chagall, Ernst Ludwig Kirchner, Irma Stern, and a few others besides.

In the company of these artists, she herself painted with oils. It went so badly that with every passing day it became clearer to her just what geniuses her friends were. Archivist Jenny painted, and when she was finished, art critic Jenny lamented the results. On the whole, an agreeable existence. There, in the windowless cellar, she was content in her own misery. In this state she felt a kinship with her friend Kafka, who in turn felt that he had nothing in common even with himself.

On occasion she felt astonished that she could do so well with so little; she surfed around the internet to find answers and perhaps commonalities between her own life and those of the geniuses. She couldn't quite say she was mentally ill like Munch (who depicted his own anguish), Goya (who had hallucinations), or Chalepas (who first made a sculpture and then destroyed what he had just created), but she couldn't rule out a "neuropsychiatric disorder." That would have to do.

This very debatable disorder of whatever-it-was didn't stop her from detecting that the manager had begun to court her. And that her beloved father encouraged the arrangement. Victor was considerably older and didn't seem to understand a bit of the modernist world that meant everything to her. But he was her father's choice and he secured the future of their art gallery. Her father never went so far as to believe that she herself could do so. Until recently, she had only been a girl. Now she wasn't much more than a young woman.

And anyway, what was love? Aside from love for the eternally vivid yet sadly deceased modernists.

She said yes when he proposed. Or maybe her father did. She nodded silently in affirmation.

Before a civil servant at city hall, though, she had to say what she said for her father's sake. Because she couldn't muster any warmth for her new spouse, she felt anything but excited about the marital duties that awaited. It was strange that nothing came of that, but it was just fine with her. If there was anyone she would happily undress in front of it was Ernst Ludwig Kirchner. She would have loved to be Marzella in the painting at Moderna Museet in Stockholm. Or one of the five nude bathing women at the Brücke Museum in Berlin.

Kirchner was unrequited love personified. Born in 1880. Took his own life in 1938 in despair over what Adolf was about to accomplish.

Hindsight is 20/20. Her new husband asked her to sign—so she signed. He was always talking so much, and so awfully, and if she just did as he said she could go back down to her friends in the cellar, safe in the knowledge that her father was satisfied. As long as he was alive.

Hindsight indeed. About the part where they never had sex. Twenty-three-year-old Jenny still hadn't put any such knowledge into practice. She had had enough schooling and enough HBO to understand what it involved, though. Salvador Dalí's masterpiece *The Great Masturbator* made her empathize with the Spaniard. It was said that Dalí had been thinking of himself as he painted it.

She took the fact that Victor never forced himself on her for shyness and uncertainty behind all that bravado. After all, he knew almost nothing about art. Especially modernism. Never was he so small in her eyes than when he spouted his constant "good old Matisse" in front of clients. She had once shown him a picture of *Harmony in Red* in a book. "What's that piece of crap?" he'd said. "Don't tell me it's something you purchased?!"

Good old Matisse?

Now, however, she understood perfectly.

He was no innocent example of mediocrity. He had plans. They didn't involve her and never had, except for as a means to an end.

Bloody hell. No more real home, no art gallery, no cellar full of friends, no life.

Might as well walk into the sea.

She didn't know her way around the southern suburbs of Stockholm, had never been there before, but the capital city was surrounded by water. Surely all she had to do was walk; any direction would do. How long could it take? Fifteen minutes?

She walked slowly, feeling no urgency to reach her own death. She even spent time looking around. Why, it was getting on towards winter. The sun was shining and lots of folks were out pushing strollers. It must have been a weekend. Sunday, perhaps?

Way off in the distance was a shimmer of what looked like water. She headed in that direction, passing a field of kids playing football. They seemed to be having fun in the below-freezing weather. The first snow hadn't yet fallen.

Suddenly the ball came bouncing her way. She reflexively grabbed it in both hands.

"Nice catch!" said one of the football boys.

She smiled in return and tossed the ball back to him; he thanked her and threw it back into the game. And that was the end of that.

Nice catch? Why had he said that? Because it *was* a nice catch. By definition, a person who could catch a ball in the air was not incompetent. That was all it took to set Jenny's mind on a fresh path.

The only thing that would happen, if she drowned herself, was that she would have done Victor Alderheim a favor. Now that she thought about it, she didn't want to give him the satisfaction. How the hell could he sell off the finest pieces the gallery owned for next to nothing? And where had that Erich Heckel painting gone?

Chapter 6

Victor was pleased with the circumstances. The witch had been dead a long time. The old man had followed her. The make-believe marriage had been dissolved and the worst specimens of artwork disposed of. The work of building a collection of real art could begin.

And it would soon be five years since the bastard got eaten up by lions. The Tax Agency had promised to deliver the declaration of death by post.

Kevin spent the first minute after Victor left him alone on the Kenyan savanna standing still in the dark, unable to comprehend what had just happened.

During the second minute, he still didn't understand but was starting to grasp a different fact: if he stayed put, he would soon be dead. During the last leg of the car ride he had seen with his own eyes that there were wild animals everywhere. Not least lions.

But that didn't mean he had anywhere to go. Perhaps he could climb? If things were so bad that his boss and guardian wanted Kevin dead without making it happen himself, perhaps he shouldn't have dropped him off right next to a tree?

It's not always easy to climb an acacia, but Kevin was both young and limber. Soon he was sitting in the branches almost three meters above the ground. There he planned to sit until dawn. It was imperative that he stay awake.

Anyone who has ever spent a night alone in an acacia on the Kenyan savanna knows that it's easy to become discouraged. It took Kevin no more than twenty minutes to question his own rules. *Why* must he stay awake? After night came day, and he'd still be in Kenya. Just a few months earlier, his science teacher in Bollmora had been kind enough to teach the class about the wild animals of East Africa. The very hungriest of them hunted at night, while the angriest slept. At daybreak, they switched off.

If Kevin climbed down when the sun came up,

what would he encounter? A buffalo? A rhinoceros? A female elephant who was dead sure he was a threat to her baby?

And if none of those happened to be around for the moment: Which direction should he go?

No, he might as well just fall asleep to escape it all. But first he had to try to figure out how he had ended up here.

A few years earlier, his mother had introduced him to a man who was, shortly thereafter, appointed as Kevin's guardian. This man wanted to be called "boss." The boy accepted this arrangement; he'd never had a dad, after all. The boss might be the closest he'd ever get to one.

In retrospect, Kevin thought he understood. Mom had probably been way up in the hierarchy of prostitutes when he was little but fell down the ranks as she grew older. When she died, freed of her immune system and all its whims, only Kevin and the guardian were left. Mom had been the very embodiment of love and generosity in the midst of everything, which was more than you could say about the boss.

So why had he accepted this assignment? Kevin guessed money was involved. Mom must have paid him so her son would have security even when she could no longer be there for him. This plan didn't turn out so great, there was no denying that. She probably hadn't had very many stand-in moms or dads from which to choose. So Victor it was. He *was* an art dealer.

Then came Kevin's eighteenth birthday. The boss was formally relieved of his job. But instead of ceasing the pizza deliveries and asking the boy to take care of himself, he had brought him to Kenya.

Why?

Apparently so he would die. *But why?*

Did his contract with Mom state that he would support Kevin all the way through university? Or was the boss up to something illegal, something he was afraid Kevin would discover? In which case, how? They never spent any time together.

The whole situation was impossible to understand. Much like life in general.

Did he hear something rustling out there in the dark? Kevin listened intently.

No, it was probably nothing.

Anyway, life. Which was about to come to an end. At least his early years had been pretty happy ones. Mom was around during the daytime, or starting around lunch, at any rate, when she woke up after a long night of work. She bought him things. He was the first in his friend group to have his own tablet. On his fourteenth birthday he received a laptop. That was right around the time Kevin began to understand his mother's career, and what all her vitamin shots really were.

He loved her no less for it. But it did make a mess of his social life. Kevin knew he got along well with others. He joined them in kicking a ball around the playground, and that was fun. So was school itself. He liked group work the best; it was all give and take and included the occasional laugh. It made him feel normal.

But then the school day ended. Kevin learned the hard way not to go home with any of his friends. There he was subjected to their parents. Who is your father? What does your mother do? Lying was the only option to stay ahead of the game. He tried that, but it didn't make him feel good.

While he lived with his mother, of course, he could have brought a friend over to his place. But to answer his friend's questions, he would have had to say something along the lines of "Dad doesn't exist, Mom is asleep because she has to work tonight, as a prostitute. Also she has a bit of a cough. We suspect HIV. Would you like a sandwich?"

Perhaps it was the laptop that spared him from becoming a complete outcast. Online he could play games with people his own age all over the world. Just how "his own age" they really were was impossible to say; everyone had a different name than in real life, and made up both age and sex. That was fine with Kevin. He wanted to be called Lonelyplanet, a rather solitary and poetic handle he'd gotten from a travel guide to France that Mom had given him along with the promise that one day they would visit there.

Instead he ended up in Bollmora. And had to choose the name Lonelyplanet47. Apparently there were forty-six other lonely planets out there.

There he sat, with a guardian who wanted to be called "boss" but not "Dad," and who came to visit once a week at the most, to fill the cupboards and be extra sure not to accidentally utter any words of encouragement. All this, immediately after the one who actually had love to give gave him away so she herself could die.

But Kevin managed, satisfied with what little he had. He still enjoyed school. His classmates left him alone on afternoons and evenings. His weekends consisted of the laptop, pizza boxes, and . . . well, that was it. It would be nice to become an adult. His grades would get him all the way to university when the time came. Or maybe he would get a job. In France, even? What kinds of things did Frenchmen do? Picked grapes, probably. Maybe not all of them.

Then there was this issue with the lack of parents. Kevin didn't want a new mother to replace the one who'd done such a good job, given the circumstances. But there ought to be a father out there somewhere, if his biology teacher was to be believed. For the time being, this father had a peculiar proxy in the form of art dealer Victor Alderheim.

It would be an exaggeration to claim there was any chemistry between Kevin and Victor. When the latter arrived with the weekly pizza delivery, conversation consisted of a "hi," an "everything okay?" a "here's the food," and, on rare occasions, a "Jesus, what a downpour." Followed by a "see you next week, later."

Kevin wanted so badly to prolong those moments. He made his way to the school library, where he found a hefty book that claimed to give an overview of all of art history in its more than four hundred pages, starting with the cave paintings of the Stone Age. His plan was to browse through it to find topics of discussion for the next week.

This book fascinated the seventeen-year-old; it was

chockablock with full-color illustrations. A world he'd had no idea existed opened before him. He found that he had firm opinions about most of it.

He gave the Renaissance an immediate thumbs-down. It all seemed like one big advertisement for the Bible. The Romantic Movement had more interesting traits. Eugène Delacroix even depicted two bare female breasts when he illustrated the July Revolution of 1830.

But things didn't get truly exciting until the nineteenth century was about to give way to the twentieth. Kevin was utterly taken by Claude Monet and his dawn painting with a red sun and a rowboat holding a helmsman and a single passenger. For a long time the boy thought his fascination was rooted in wondering who the passenger might be. Something told him it was a woman, but it was impossible to tell. Where was she going? And who was at the helm? A poor fisherman, up with the sun to earn a bit of money? To safely transport the woman to . . . well, where was she going? And why? So early in the day.

Then he realized that the painting had grabbed hold of him for a different reason. It was the dawn light itself that was the true art. The way the red sun was mirrored in the water. The mild fog that suggested early autumn and . . . Kevin found himself speculating about how warm the air might be. Or, rather, how cold. Eleven degrees?

Victor had hardly made it through the door with the week's pizzas before Kevin eagerly showed him the page with the painting that had moved him so.

"Look, boss. Isn't this beautiful?"

Victor cast a glance at the open book. And was annoyed.

"Watch out for that rubbish."

This was the very kind of art that led to homosexuality. That questioned authority. That muddied societal ideals.

"Jesus, what a downpour, right? See you next week. Later."

Then came his eighteenth birthday. Victor dropped by, and for the first time, his arms weren't full of food. He thought he and the boy should discover the world together. For the hundredth, and last, time, hope for something that at least *resembled* a father-son relationship was kindled in Kevin.

There was no calling it anything other than attempted murder. Victor wanted the lions to do the job. And very soon, they would.

Must. Not. Fall asleep.

Might as well fall asleep.

That's when he spotted them. Two lionesses under the tree; they'd already discovered him. Dead-tired Kevin was suddenly wide awake. His will to live was greater than his will not to. And after all, being eaten up by carnivores could not be the most comfortable way to meet one's end.

In general, lions are not great thinkers. They live more on instinct. Like the one that told them the smell from the creature up in the tree equaled food for half the family. Not great thinkers, and essentially useless climbers. Unlike the leopard, who was waiting his turn nearby, until he had waited so long he forgot what he was waiting for and wandered off.

The creature in the tree didn't give up. When the morning sun appeared, the lionesses slunk off, in a bad mood after their fruitless night. Time to locate the pride and lie down in the shadows somewhere to sleep off their hunger and the hot day. Neither of the lionesses realized that if one of them stayed put while the other gathered cubs and males, their daytime rest could be spent right under the acacia which contained the yummy-smelling creature, until their food fell down right under their noses. Table service!

———

Kevin, who was not supposed to fall asleep under any circumstances, did so anyway as soon as the lions vanished and all the adrenaline he'd been feeling did the same. He lost his grip and hit the soft slope beneath the tree with a dull thud.

Chapter 7

Medicine man Ole Mbatian the Younger liked to converse. To exchange ideas with others. Learn new things. Unfortunately, life in the Maasai village was not optimal for his needs. From his wives he learned only to be ashamed of himself. The weekly meetings with Chief Toothless were anything but intellectually stimulating, and neither were his conversations with the villagers in general. There were many positive things to be said about the typical cow- or goat-herder on the savanna, but anyone seeking deeper insights to the meaning of life would do well to speak with someone else.

Which left the smith's sister. In her youth she had accidentally boarded the wrong bus in Narok and ended up in Nairobi by mistake. It took her three years to find her way home again. The advantage to that was that she knew better than anyone else in the village how life worked on the outside. The disadvantage was that she could never shut up about it. Ole Mbatian was envious, but since he wouldn't admit it to himself, his feelings stopped with believing that he couldn't stand her chatter.

His dawn walks on the savanna brought a suitable escape. There the medicine man could talk to himself while, for instance, he searched for amaryllis to treat snakebites. To keep these conversations as interesting as possible, he switched between Swahili (which he got from his mother), the Maasai language Maa (from his father), and English (which the colonizers had long ago bestowed upon his people along with Christianity and left-hand traffic).

Amaryllis grew everywhere except where Ole happened to be looking on this particular day. But it was a beautiful morning and the birds were welcoming it at full volume. There was something religious about the whole experience. Ole Mbatian had great faith in God. Thanks to his faith, he wasn't frightened, only happy, when a nearly full-grown man fell from the heavens and landed at his feet.

"Thank you, Lord," he said, picking up the black-and-blue boy.

Kevin was half out of it with exhaustion and dreamed that someone was gently lifting him up. Or was that for real? A person? Who was saying something Kevin didn't understand.

"What did you say?" he managed to produce, in English, despite his daze.

"Oh, so you don't speak all our languages yet," said Ole Mbatian. "Well, the ways of the Lord are unfathomable. You're just as welcome anyway, my dear, beloved boy."

The medicine man, who had been starting to think that he was getting too old for just about everything, gently arranged the boy on his back and set off briskly home to his village. It was only seven kilometers.

Kevin was suffering from exhaustion and dehydration, but now he had been admitted to the medicine man's clinic. Ole Mbatian dabbed his forehead with cool banana leaves and managed to get some water with a mild dose of cayenne pepper and ginger into him.

Then he thanked the Lord once more, and said to the boy:

"What shall we call you, my son?"

"Kevin?" Kevin suggested.

Ole Mbatian smiled. Kevin sounded lovely. Kevin it was.

Three years and eleven months later, Kevin was no longer a boy but a full-grown man of almost twenty-two years. He had developed talents he'd never even imagined. He had an ear for languages, and now he spoke fluent English and could get along in both Swahili and Maa. And ball sense! His father the medicine man had put him in warrior training early on, under the tutelage of both himself and his brother. For God had seen fit to send him a son who knew absolutely nothing about spears, clubs and knives, one who wouldn't last a day out on the savanna.

Ole and his brother taught; Kevin nodded, understood, practiced, and absorbed. By the time he was nineteen, the heaven-sent boy was nearly fully versed in how to survive under the open skies, hungry gobs of wild animals notwithstanding. Around the same time, he felled his first lion with a spear (out of sheer necessity); as a twenty-one-year-old he swam the Mara River and back after having first spotted nine crocodiles with his bare eye and noting their exact positions and whether they were looking for food or just lying there taking it easy.

Kevin loved his new life. The first real life he'd had. And no one could be prouder of his son than Ole Mbatian the Younger. He had no doubts in the face of the crucial year-long test Kevin must undergo before he could be sworn in as a full Maasai warrior. The youngster was six or seven years older than the other candidates, but his journey from the heavens had, of course, begun so much later.

However, no one told the boy what awaited them after he and five others spent twelve full moons in a row on the savanna and in the bush, with nothing but the clothes on their back and their spears, clubs and knives. On the day after the twelfth full moon, they were all in one piece and back in the village where a feast was being prepared.

In the first hours after the completed ceremony, it dawned on Kevin what remained.

Circumcision!

Better the long rains, the short rains, and another twelve full moons on the savanna than *that*.

Papa Ole, the most understanding person you could imagine, couldn't see the problem. He explained to his son that you were born, learned the art of war, got circumcised, got married, and regretted the marriage. That was just the way it was. And there was no need for Kevin to fear that by way of the circumcision he would be tying himself to En-Kai or any other god he didn't feel he knew well enough. The medicine man had heard that there were tribes to both the north and the west that made such a connection. In the Maasai view, circumcision was a test of manhood, full stop. All the son needed to worry about was not making a sound during the process. Ole was sure he could manage.

And he believed that was the end of the discussion.

But Kevin withdrew from the festivities. He sat down in his father the medicine man's hut to think. Naturally he could handle the ceremony; it wasn't that. But what business did anyone else have with his willy? How exactly did it work? Did they take half off, or just a little bit? And what did they do with the leftovers? Toss it to the chickens?

Kevin didn't want to know more, but he didn't have much time. Papa didn't understand and never would, no matter how hard his son tried to explain. The medicine man himself was the one who held the knife.

Suddenly everything happened very fast. The young man took his Swedish passport and changed into the clothes he hadn't used for five years, but which still fit, if badly. Then he stuffed his shúkà into his backpack, grabbed two of his father's valuables to use as payment on his journey—and took off. He fled in the name of his own willy. Without saying farewell.

From the day the medicine man plucked Kevin from the ground beneath the acacia tree, Kevin had enjoyed five years of love from his adoptive father and everyone else around him. The son received constant praise for being a quick study from his father's brother, Uhuru Mbatian, the prominent Maasai warrior and Kevin's private tutor in the art of surviving on the savanna. Of course, it was about much more than that; it was about respect for animals and nature. And about patience. Integrity. The art of using all your senses.

The Maasai education started when a child was four, with exams beginning later in the teen years. Kevin began when most of his age set were already finished. But he caught up in less than half a decade.

Except for the circumcision part.

Sticking to one's principles was another thing Uhuru Mbatian had taught his nephew. The student was practicing this to its fullest when he decided to flee. The second most important thing in Kevin's life was his adoptive father Ole. The most important was his willy. Not that he had used it for anything besides passing water yet, but that might change one day. God willing.

He had to go back to Sweden; where else could he go?

Chapter 8

I t took a few days, but now Kevin was standing out-side the door of his apartment in Bollmora. Should he unlock it and step in, or ring the bell first? What if someone answered!? Who would it be? Certainly not Victor.

The nameplate said "Alderheim." It seemed rea-sonable to assume that the studio was empty, meaning it would be a place he could rest up after his long jour-ney and ponder his next step in life.

He unlocked the door and opened it—and found himself facing a stranger.

"Who are you?" said Jenny Alderheim.

"I could ask you the same thing," said Kevin.

"I live here," said Jenny.

"Me too. I think."

Kevin looked both kind and surprised, and he had his own key, which was enough for Jenny to ask him to come inside instead of calling the police. Anyway, she had no phone from which to call.

They each took a seat on a wooden chair in the eighteen-square-meter apartment and told one another about themselves and their relationship to the man who had done them so wrong. When Jenny got on the topic of her former life and how she had been happiest in a cellar, where she preferred to talk to various works of art on the wall, she heard how silly it sounded. Kevin consoled her by saying that he had once spoken to two people in a rowboat at the entrance to the harbor in Le Havre.

"Monet," said Jenny.

Her new acquaintance had just described the prime example of impressionism. With reverence, it seemed.

Kevin nodded. And told her about the book he'd borrowed from the library in the hopes of sparking a conversation with the great art dealer. And how poorly it went. But the silver lining was that he had become friends with Claude Monet. And BFFs with Marc Chagall.

Jenny was bowled over. Not because Chagall was one of her absolute favorites, but because she was sitting here talking about art with an actual human, one who wasn't even dead or an artist himself or both. One who responded. Then she heard herself say:

"What would you say if I said 'Harmony in Red'?"

Kevin smiled.

"Good old Matisse."

Jenny was in love.

Before Jenny and Kevin had even known each other for one hour, they had managed to share the short version of each of their life stories and discuss the impact Matisse's mother had had on his artistic development.

But it was starting to get dark outside. Reality was crowding in. Jenny had been living in the apartment for almost three months. Kevin had lived there for several years, several years earlier. Neither of them wanted to claim right of occupancy ahead of the other. They would simply have to share.

In his eternal kindness, Victor had supplied Jenny with a few thousand kronor when he ditched her in the apartment. He said she was welcome to come by if she needed a few thousand extra to really get back on her feet. He made no promises, times were tough, but he would try. For the time being he would cover the rent and the high-speed internet. These were not free, he wanted Jenny to know.

There were a few hundred-kronor notes left of Alderheim's alms; Jenny lived on the cheap. The pot would soon need replenishing. What could Kevin contribute?

It looked promising for a moment, as he placed a couple of wrinkled but colorful notes on the table. Four hundred Kenyan shillings. About thirty-six kronor. Minus forty in exchange fees.

When Kevin asked directly, Jenny stated that she would rather drink poison than track down Victor Alderheim and stand there with cap in hand. What that man did not need was to be made to feel generous. He ought to be tormented, as he tormented others. And then he should be tormented a little extra, just for being the person he was.

Her voice was quiet but firm. Hearing it, Kevin felt an affinity for Jenny, for he carried similar feelings. He wasn't exactly proud of it, but he'd had plenty of time to think during his years in Kenya. One image that recurred in his mind was dropping his former guardian off on the savanna in front of a pride of lions. "Why, what are you doing, my son?" said Victor in Kevin's fantasy. "Don't call me that," Kevin responded as he drove off.

Did Jenny and Kevin have this in common as well? The thought of revenge?

"What would the Maasai have done with him?" Jenny asked.

The art dealer had swindled and ruined his wife. And tried to take the life of a young man he'd likely been paid to protect. No sense in arguing over which was worse; in fact, in Maasai society, it would have led to the harshest punishment from the village council: his head stuck in an anthill for a slow death.

Jenny didn't think they needed to go quite that far. Anyway, there weren't any anthills in the immediate vicinity of the art gallery.

Victor Alderheim would get what was coming to him—Jenny and Kevin shook on it. Kevin thought, but didn't say, that Jenny's hand was soft, warm, and pleasant. And Jenny didn't say that she thought the same thing but the other way around.

"Come on," she said, pulling her new cohabitant to his feet.

There was a second-hand shop not far away, one that sold just about everything. Kevin needed something warmer to wear on his top half and the household needed an extra mattress to put on the floor.

Bollmora's second-hand shopkeeper recognized Jenny and offered a friendly greeting. She had been there a number of times before. She wasn't one of his best customers; she was far too cautious about price tags for the shopkeeper's taste. But he knew she was hard up. For fifteen kronor he had sold her a table lamp he could have easily gotten twenty-five for. And when she'd gazed at a scrub-brush for long enough, he threw it in for free.

Now, in any case, he got to sell a mattress and a Norwegian wool sweater. Two hundred kronor into the accounts, no receipt.

"Come back anytime."

Just before a blood-pudding dinner, Kevin sat down to compose a long letter to Ole Mbatian in which he explained himself, asked for forgiveness, and proclaimed his gratefulness and love for the man who had first saved his life and then given him a new one. Unfortunately, he could never, ever return. Uncle Uhuru had, in his sunrise-to-sunset lessons, preached that a true Maasai warrior armed himself with his club, spear, knife, and principles. Without all four, you were not complete. Kevin had had to leave his club, spear and knife behind, but he still had his firm principles. The highest of which was that he would allow no one to cut into his genitals. So that was that. Kevin apologized again and closed his letter.

Jenny read it and said she thought Kevin was brave.

When it came to the principle in question, she supported it. Especially since the reasoning wasn't religious in nature. It was another matter that art history was full of circumcisions, a symbol of Abraham's covenant with God. According to the Scriptures, the latter wanted a minor portion of the willies of Abraham's descendants (which turned out to be quite numerous); in return, Abraham would be given the land of Canaan and become the ancestor of nearly everyone and everything. An honorable agreement, Abraham thought, and with that it was done. This had, as far as Jenny was aware, nothing to do with the rite of manhood that Kevin had fled from, and even less to do with *female* circumcision, which ought to be labeled aggravated assault.

And so it was that the newfound friends, also virgins both, came to discuss during their simple dinner the value in keeping one's own genitals intact. Both were additionally conscious that the person across the table had soft, warm and pleasant hands.

Chapter 9

Jenny enjoyed having Kevin as a sudden cohabitant from the very start. For years she had been certain that she wasn't like other people, and that she therefore must be content with the small things in life. Now she lived with a person her own age who wasn't like other people either; the two of them were more like each other. Even as their collected financial assets shrank, their sense of solidarity and the need to take revenge upon a common enemy grew.

No killing. Only tormenting. A Swedish version; head-in-an-anthill-lite. But they needed to be able to afford food on the table to have enough strength to give Victor the punishment he deserved, or even to figure out what that might look like. Even if they stuck to blood pudding breakfast and dinner, with no fried eggs, jam, or lunch in between, their money would run out in a few days.

This conflict meant that their irritation about Victor only increased. Jenny taught Kevin her mantra:

"Fucking Victor."

As therapy, it was effective. For any other purpose, it was not.

Income first. Revenge second. The order of operations was set.

"What can you do, that could earn us money?" Kevin asked.

Jenny considered this.

"I'm good at archiving."

"Archiving what?"

"Whatever you want."

Kevin didn't know what the market looked like in Stockholm for archivists of whatever. Nor did Jenny.

"How about you?"

"I can't do anything. Except stare down a lion. Do whatever I like with a throwing club. Swim across a river full of crocodiles without being eaten. Hit my target every time with a spear or bow and arrow. Speak Swahili and Maa. And a few other things."

"Do whatever you like with a throwing club—what might one want to do with one of those?"

"Hit a buffalo in the head from sixty meters away. Or at least fifty. Papa Ole could do seventy, but he's extraordinary."

Kevin's résumé was longer than Jenny's, but none of his talents were Stockholm-suitable. For instance, there were no crocodiles in Nybroviken, and all of the city's buffalo were safely behind fences at Skansen.

"I can survive on the savanna for a year as well, with nothing but a knife, club, and spear."

"So you ought to be able to keep the two of us alive at least through this week?"

Sure, but there was just this issue with a lack of wild animals. One prerequisite for successfully taking down an antelope, butchering it, and grilling it on a campfire was, of course, that there be at least one antelope at hand.

"Maybe we should reconsider Skansen, then," Jenny said.

Skansen was Stockholm's noble open-air museum with its zoo full of bears, moose, wolves, lynx and other creatures that wouldn't feel at home in East Africa.

"And enjoy free food in prison afterwards," said Kevin.

They smiled at their miserable circumstances. At least they still enjoyed each other's company.

It occurred to Kevin that both he and Jenny were by definition unemployed. If he knew his Sweden, that meant unemployment benefits.

In principle, it was a lovely idea: getting paid for not working, while they worked full-time on getting revenge on Victor Alderheim.

Jenny knew it wasn't that simple. For instance, in order to be considered job-seekers they must actively look for jobs. Anyone who didn't was classified as lazy and that wouldn't get them any money at all.

How this worked in greater detail was something the employment agency would have to figure out. They had an office in downtown Stockholm.

But there was no point in hurrying off. If they were sloppy with the details, there was a risk that one of them would actually be offered a job. That would mean more money in hand, but not much time left over for what was truly important.

Kevin knew what he had to do. All of his belongings were in the backpack he'd had with him five years earlier, when Victor tried to get him killed. They included his passport and a few other things, most importantly: his *shúkà*.

The Swedish Maasai's entrance into the employment agency was a grand one. Kevin had practically frozen to death on the way, but now he stood there in his proud, red-and-black checked cloth, sandals on his feet. The counselor at the agency had nothing against dealing with Kevin and Jenny as a unit. This initial meeting would be all about registering them as jobseekers and communicating the general guidelines. In the future they might talk about job-hunting classes or professional development training. Out of sheer curiosity, the counselor elected to begin with the man in the red-and-black checked cloth. So, he was looking for work as a Maasai warrior? Even without taking a closer look at the placement files, they could probably assume that the demand for those was limited. Perhaps he would consider something else? Taxi driver, for instance?

Kevin had learned to drive a car on the savanna. In the village there was nothing but a moped here or there, but a Range Rover criss-crossed the valley; it belonged to the World Wildlife Fund. They were there to save the leopard from extinction. That particular effort wasn't going great, but Kevin had become friends with one of the WWFers, a Norwegian woman who was extremely surprised when one of the young

Maasai began to speak Swedish with her. This contact led to Kevin tracking down leopard families for the Norwegian in return for driving lessons.

"Shall I interpret what you just told me to mean that you don't have a driver's license?" said the counselor.

"Do you need one to drive a taxi?"

The effect was as intended. The counselor turned to Jenny. Who made the mistake of saying she had worked in an art gallery all her life and was a real hot-shot when it came to archives. The culturally well-rounded counselor happened to know off the top of his head that Nationalmuseum had just put out a job announcement that might be a good fit.

Although their goal was to *not* get a job, Jenny's face lit up. Nationalmuseum wasn't her favorite; they administered, among other things, the world's oldest portrait gallery, almost five thousand paintings whose common attribute was that they prettified the subject's outward appearance and ignored what was on the inside. Altogether, almost five hundred years of faces that said nothing.

But, of course, Nationalmuseum was more than that. Not as much modernism as Jenny would have liked; but that was not part of the museum's mission.

Just as Jenny was starting to get really excited, the counselor brought out the job notice. The museum had a list of requirements not even Victor Alderheim could lie his way to: certified proficiency in both English and French; three years' academic study in archival and informational science.

"Who spends three years at university to learn how to archive?" Kevin wondered.

Jenny was back in reality. They were there to get money, not jobs. She asked the counselor how much they were talking, and whether it might be possible to get a small amount in advance.

The response was not at all what Jenny and Kevin would have liked. For one thing, that money didn't come from the employment office but whichever unemployment fund one was affiliated with. There were funds for the unaffiliated as well, but to access these took forms, statements from former employers, and a few other things besides. As far as the employment counselor understood, you also had to start by paying an application fee of 130 kronor for the unemployment fund to even take on your case.

"Per person?"

"Um, yes. Per month."

Jenny and Kevin realized that they would be financially ruined several times over before they could even claim any money. Paying in order to get paid? What had happened to the Swedish social safety net?

The counselor suspected that these clients were out for money rather than work; he'd run across their type before.

"Perhaps you should set your sights on income support instead. Or social welfare, as we typically call it. The annoying thing is that you won't get a single krona along that avenue either, if you aren't at the disposal of the job market."

The new friends stopped off for a far-too-expensive consolation coffee in the city while they turned over a few more rocks.

If it wouldn't be possible to get paid for nothing, perhaps they should aim for employment for one of them while the other focused on Alderheim. Was archiving really the only thing Jenny could do, if she placed her humbleness aside? Couldn't she rightfully call herself an art expert?

Yes, if she put her mind to it. But that wasn't a get-rich-quick sort of avenue. Even being an artist was bad enough. Vincent van Gogh managed to slap together two thousand paintings in his day, and even so he was destitute by the time he shot himself.

Kevin thought there might be a connection there but had to let it go because Jenny passed the question back to him. Same humbleness aside: What could

Kevin do better than anyone else, that could also be leveraged into money?

Well, there was that issue with the swimming among crocodiles and the lack of crocodiles in Greater Stockholm. Not to mention the ice on the water.

All he could come up with was that they could have brought home some bacon from the local amusement park, Gröna Lund, if it had been open in the middle of winter. There you could win stuffed animals simply by hitting a target, and that was within Kevin's skill set, presumably no matter the projectile. He expected he could amass ten or twenty teddies before they were kicked out.

"To sell to whom?" Jenny wondered.

Kevin didn't know. In any event, it was off the table.

Ninety-six kronor for two cups of coffee and one shared bun wasn't really a treat they could afford, but they were screwed anyway. Whether they began to starve in three days or two didn't really matter.

They sat at the table in silence as Kevin drained the last of his coffee.

"Fucking Victor," he said, digging his civvies out of his backpack.

The coffee was gone; time to change clothes in the café bathroom. If only he had the oomph to get up.

Jenny was gazing distractedly out the café window.

"Sweet, sweet revenge," she said.

Kevin noted that this might be something to put on their wish list. But was Jenny thinking of Victor Alderheim or the employment office in this case?

"No. It says 'Sweet Sweet Revenge' in the shop window over there. 'Sweet Sweet Revenge Ltd.'"

Kevin looked where Jenny was looking.

"What kind of name is that? It makes it sound like they're selling revenge in jars."

"That would be perfect," said Jenny. "Do you think four jars, two each, would be enough for Victor?"

If only life were that simple. But if perchance they were packaging and selling revenge across the street, one could only imagine that they must want payment.

"In general, businesses don't work for free," said Kevin. "How much revenge do you suppose we could get for two hundred kronor?"

"Minus the hundred we just drank up," Jenny corrected him. "There's no way to know in advance. Go get changed now, and we'll head across the street."

PART TWO

Chapter 10

It never actually occurred to him, but broadly speaking, the ideologically driven art dealer in Stockholm shared his view of society with the moderately successful artist Adolf of the Austro-Hungarian Empire just over a century earlier.

Other young artists had left naturalism behind for something new. What was the point of spending months on a painting if the result was no different to what a photographer could produce given an hour in the darkroom?

Many of those among whom the new ideas caught on came from Paris. The most important factor they had in common was not that they were all named almost the exact same thing (Manet, Monet, Morisot . . .) but that they had a passion for expressing reality in an entirely subjective manner, as they *felt* it was. For that reason they came to be known as impressionists. The true impressionist experimented with color in a way that would cause any realist to become short of both breath and temper.

The movement spread to the rest of Europe and to the United States. In Holland, it was taken up by Vincent van Gogh, who built an artistic bridge to the next -ism that awaited. All while he went crazy, cut off his ear and was locked up. Before this he managed to relocate the motifs of impressionism from rural life and nature to his own inner world, where such chaos reigned that the critics didn't know what to do. In order to place the Dutchman somewhere along the long timeline of art history, they had to invent the concept of post-impressionism. Vincent had no thoughts on the matter. He had already taken his own life.

After France and Holland, it was Germany's turn to serve as representative of the new ways. Thus expressionism was born as one big thumbed nose to Adolf the naturalist. While an impressionist preferred to paint beautiful things, the expressionist captured what moved in the soul of the subject, no matter that subject's beauty.

Among its precursors were Ernst Ludwig Kirchner, Max Pechstein and Emil Nolde, all inspired by the

Norwegian Edvard Munch, who had placed a woman on a road and filled her entire being with his own angst.

Nolde, for the record, was a dedicated Nazi, but that was of no help to him when Adolf became party leader and went to battle with the degenerate art world. In Adolf's eyes, all the new -isms had transformed what was true and good into something despicable.

He and his like-minded friends took a purely scientific view of the matter. Expressionism was objectively atrocious, and thus it was exhibited in Munich so people could outdo one another in their laughing and crying at Nolde and his ilk.

But the Munich exhibition did not have the effect Adolf had intended. Young art students made their way to Bavaria to get their first and last look at what would soon be destroyed (or secretly sold off—after all, money was money). Influenced by what they saw, they scattered in all directions, out of reach of the future stomping of Nazi boots. And so it was that expressionism survived, unlike the man who wanted more than anyone to kill it dead.

Chapter 11

Irma Stern was five years younger than Adolf and remained off his radar, since she was born in a dusty little town two hundred kilometers west of Johannesburg. There were no cars and no electricity, but there were plenty of farmers around.

Irma's father Samuel was an adventurous man from the third-largest city in the world, Berlin; he had brought his brother and his young wife along with him to South Africa.

Samuel opened a shop where he sold fruits and vegetables, cooking oil and sugar, needles and thread, paper and ink, wine, cognac, and the occasional cow.

When there was unrest in the region, he took the side of the Boers in the Second Boer War with the British, which was fought over rule of land that in fact belonged to neither party. The Brits won, placed the

Boers in concentration camps, and chased the native people out into the bush.

Counted among the Boers, Samuel was locked up too, until he declared his loyalty to His Majesty the King in London—a man he had hardly even heard of.

Meanwhile his wife Henny fled to Cape Town with little Irma. There the girl began preschool. To her delight, she was given pens and crayons to write and draw with. She drew faces and more faces. All with fiery cheeks and sparkling eyes.

"Why?" asked her teacher.

"I don't know," said Irma.

The schoolteacher wanted to correct the child; that wasn't what people looked like. But she refrained. The girl was so little; surely she didn't know any better. And the drawings . . . no matter how poorly made . . . the teacher couldn't quite bear to throw them out.

Chapter 12

Irma's father's restlessness didn't fade as the years went by, and the family commuted back and forth between Berlin and southern Africa.

His daughter was no longer a little girl but a young woman with a dream of one day being a real artist.

The world war, the first in the series, broke out and, for a time, kept Samuel from traveling south again. Their postponed Africa trip gave Irma's mother Henny the chance to enroll her daughter in art school in Berlin.

It was hard for the young and unruined art student not to be influenced by the fact that the world was on fire. Until this point she had been more conventional in her creativity and had taken only cautious steps into the modern. But then one day, on a tram in war-torn Berlin:

Across from her sat a child with skinny arms, her braids hanging straight down on either side of a bare forehead, her frail fingers clutching tight to a bouquet of meadow flowers, as if she were trying to reassure herself that there was still some beauty in life.

The child was in no way one of the worst victims of the war, but in that moment Irma understood that she had to express the suffering that war brought to all.

She called the painting *The Eternal Child*. When her mentor of several years saw it, he threw his brushes to the floor.

"Tasteless," he said, and went on his way, never to return.

He was an impressionist and had just had the future thrown in his face.

Irma probably would have sunk into depression from all the lack of encouragement, if it weren't for her newfound friend Max Pechstein, the symbol of everything Adolf didn't stand for. Pechstein was fully German; Irma was a mix of Germany and South Africa. When they couldn't meet, they exchanged letters. They developed such a personal relationship that Pechstein once dared to open a letter with "Dear I. Stern." Young Irma blushed.

Chapter 13

After Irma Stern's mentor left her in a rage, she was filled with doubt. Who was right? Her mentor, or Max Pechstein? What was art? Wasn't *The Eternal Child* a mirror reflecting her feelings? What gave anyone the right to judge her heart of hearts as tasteless?

She knew she wasn't alone, and yet she was lonelier than anyone else. The conservative, colonial South Africa was as yet spared from the stunts of the expressionists; the leading social class was still stuck back in romantic realism. Both people and influences traveled slowly in the early days of the previous century.

Certainly there were rumors in Cape Town about new greats like Gauguin and van Gogh. But the revolutionaries of German art never became as famous as their opposite, the increasingly categorical Adolf.

The true expressionist felt that the industrialism of the previous century had a negative effect on people's spiritual lives. As a counterbalance to black machines in a smoky gray environment, the expressionists filled their works with bright colors that at their very height should clash with one another. Most of all they clashed with all the brown that was spreading through Europe, along its streets and across its town squares.

Max Pechstein was fired from the art academy in Berlin when the most prominent representatives of the brown trousers discovered that he had painted naked, orange women frolicking under a tree. Much later it was said that no one had ever seen Adolf so angry, with the possible exception of the time he was presented with the results of the Battle of Stalingrad. Three hundred and twenty-six of Pechstein's works vanished from German museums; many of them haven't been seen since.

But before he was banished from his own country, Pechstein managed to get Irma thinking along the right lines. For her part, she managed to return once more to her beloved Africa.

Which didn't immediately love her back.

Chapter 14

Irma painted and painted. Most of all she loved to paint Black men and women in all imaginable colors. They were Malay couples, housekeepers, Zulu women, Xhosa girls—everything she saw, sensed, and felt. Now certain that she was good enough, she exhibited her art in Cape Town. The most tactful critic confessed that he didn't understand what he was looking at. The least tactful said that his strongest inclination was to vomit. In between she was accused of being an insult to human intelligence. As if that wasn't enough, she was reported to the police for general indecency. In the name of decency, the report didn't lead anywhere.

By this point, the artist took her setbacks with aplomb. Max Pechstein's kind words had hit their mark and taken root. She didn't need the narrow-minded art-world circles of Cape Town. She turned up her nose at them and packed her bags.

This time her journey didn't lead her back to her old homeland, and that was just as well. Adolf probably still didn't know who she was, but she had just about every fault there was to have. Not only was she an expressionist, she fraternized with Black and brown people. And was herself a Jew.

All that was missing was Bolshevism.

PART THREE

PART THREE

Chapter 15

Irma Stern was about to march decisively into Jenny and Kevin's lives, long after her death. They had no idea that this was the case as they left the café, which had just taken almost half of their joint assets, just by demanding honest payment for two cups of coffee and one bun.

In the office across the street sat the CEO of Sweet Sweet Revenge Ltd. He too had no idea what awaited: that the German–South African artist was about to fundamentally change their lives. With plenty of help from a medicine man–slash–Maasai warrior.

The CEO in question was called Hugo Hamlin. He was born and raised on Lidingö, a wealthy island suburb of Stockholm. He was the younger son of physician couple Harry and Margareta Hamlin, and the little brother of Malte.

The only thing more important than Saturday dinner at the Hamlins' was Sunday dinner. From the time he could sit by himself on a chair without falling off, he partook of appetizer, main course and dessert in what was nearly a ritual form. His mother handled the food; his father was in charge of conversation and wine. He preferred to sample the latter starting in the early morning, to make sure it was correct.

Their topics of conversation were always of a scientific nature. When the children were small they heard all about the Polish girl who grew up to win the Nobel Prize in both physics and chemistry. And how she discovered elements so dangerous that they became the death of her. Big brother Malte wanted to know more about her discoveries; Father and Mother told him. Little brother Hugo was more interested in how much money and renown a Nobel Prize would bring you.

Their conversations grew more advanced as the children matured. Their parents made no bones about their desire for their sons' sons to follow in their footsteps. And preferably surpass them. If Marie Curie could win double Nobel Prizes, it wasn't unreasonable to imagine that their double sons might scrape together one between them.

Malte was on the same page. At the tender age of fourteen he said he was considering becoming an ophthalmologist. He chose the specialty that was hardest to pronounce in order to tease his little brother.

"Do you know what ophthalmology is, Hugo?" he asked.

"All I know is, it sounds boring."

Their father Harry warded off a fight about nothing. He said that ophthalmology was the same thing as an eye doctor, but in doing so he made the mistake of mentioning how many years of study it took to land at a somewhat reasonable salary level.

"Twelve?" said Hugo, who was just that. "Not on your life."

The brothers were only eighteen months apart in age, and they liked each other a lot, but deep down inside they were different. Big brother was a scientist like his parents; little brother was . . . well, no one knew what he was.

Harry and Margareta had met during their specialist training in geriatrics, and they worked side by side on age-related illnesses and disorders up until they began to feel the effects of the same themselves.

Then they quit and moved permanently to their summer home in Vaxholm, where she took a part-time position at the local clinic and he sat on the veranda to drink red wine full-time. The parents gave the Lidingö house to their younger son and transferred the equivalent amount of money into an account for their older son's twelve-year medical education.

While Malte headed off to Uppsala to immerse himself in neurobiology, homeostasis and intervention, the eighteen-year-old homeowner Hugo stayed put and delved inside himself to see what talents he might possibly have. Something, anything at all, that would bring him financial success in some life-affirming way.

He had shown promise in drawing early on but was never really encouraged in that direction by his parents. Especially not after the time he secretly drew his father in the shower, enhanced certain elements, and showed the result to his evangelical high school art teacher.

Drawing might be fun, but it brought him no advantage—only lambasting from two directions. Still, he didn't drop the idea entirely. In his general searching he occasionally ended up at the local book café, where Lidingö's most prominent starving artists regularly gathered to convince each other how torturous life was and how little they cared about financial success. That never stopped each of them trying to get someone else to pay for their coffee. Hugo felt left out. What he wanted from his artistic tendencies was—first of all, last of all, and all the alls in between—to have a good time. A prerequisite of which was, in his view, that he earn money.

Hugo and Malte spoke over the phone now and then. The tone of their conversations was loving and just brutal enough.

"How's the homeostasis going?" Hugo might ask, without even knowing what that was.

"It went fine, thanks. We're doing clinical anatomy now."

"Do you have time for any rectified spirits between lessons, or do you all just sit around with your noses in your books?"

Malte explained that rectified spirits weren't handed out freely to medical students, but he understood what his little brother meant. He'd enjoyed the occasional glass of wine in the cheerful company of medical students of an evening, but they did have to get up at six each morning so he had to be careful.

"And you intend to live like this for twelve years?"

"Just ten and a half to go now."

"Idiot."

"I love you too."

With that, it was Hugo's turn to report on his current situation. He said that he had left the depressed paupers at the book café behind, but that there was still hope. He had just discovered and been dazzled by a French-American artist who placed a bicycle wheel on a pedestal and in doing so became both rich and famous.

Malte smiled at his little brother's ambition to find shortcuts in all things. But by all means.

"Mom's bicycle is still in the garage, isn't it?" he said.

"Idiot," said Hugo.

"Your words."

Hugo knew no more than was necessary about the artist in question, but anyone who could make money on bicycle wheels, urinals and snow shovels was worthy of both admiration and attention. That didn't mean, of course, that someone else could find success in the very same way. But, something along those lines?

Thus encouraged by his big brother, Hugo reconsidered. When he was ready he spray-painted a potato peeler gold, called his creation *Laid Bare*, and set the price at five thousand kronor. The used peeler had cost him two kronor, and he'd found the gold paint on a shelf in his very own garage.

With that, he dressed in black, practiced the art of looking complicated in front of a mirror, and went all the way to downtown Stockholm to hawk the work outside the Royal Dramatic Theatre, immediately following a performance of Ibsen's *Peer Gynt*.

The result was that all but three members of the audience looked away as they passed the artist. Two stopped to scoff at him and express hateful conjecture about his social standing. One, who had been forced to attend the theater by his wife and had understood nothing about the play he'd just seen, realized that the youth with the potato peeler possessed something different, perhaps even something special.

"Do you want a job?" he asked.

"Peeling potatoes?"

"No, I work in advertising and PR and all that. I think you've got that special something."

Never, during the endless weekend dinners of his upbringing, had Hugo been told he might have anything but a lack of manners.

Advertising, PR, and all that? Didn't sound so bad.

"How much does it pay?"

Chapter 16

Eighteen years later, big brother Malte had long been an established and popular specialist at one of Europe's leading eye clinics, which was located in Stockholm. Little brother Hugo, thanks to the potato peeler outside the theater, had been hired as an assistant at what would one day be one of Scandinavia's leading advertising firms. After three months he was given a permanent position, after six months he was a project manager, and for a decade and a half now he had been the brightest star at Great & Even Greater Communications.

His commute was no longer undertaken by bus from suburb to city. These days he traveled to Hong Kong, South Korea, Japan, Germany, France, Spain and Italy at least once a year, to the United Kingdom more often than that, and to the United States so often he'd lost count. In this context, "the United States" meant New York and Los Angeles. That was where it all happened.

Hugo devoted the time between his trips and coming up with all his ideas to counting the money that poured in. Mostly it was a result of his creative genius, but also no adman was better than he was at expense accounts (which was, itself, a form of creativity).

He had long planned to start his own business, but he earned what he deserved and, for at least the first fifteen years, it was a lot of fun. To be sure, he hadn't won a prize in three years; the younger generation was hot on his heels. Perhaps it was time to set his sights elsewhere before they started to lap him?

Hugo and Malte were as much friends as they were brothers. They had lived in close proximity for years, ever since Malte sold his flat in Vasastan in order to move in with his girlfriend in her Lidingö villa. She was a doctor too, of course. Rather wooden of manner, Hugo thought. But Malte was happy with her, and that was the important thing.

The adman himself was careful never to become too emotionally involved. The risk of a girlfriend was that kids would follow, and Hugo had a hard time seeing the joy in that. Changing the smelly diapers of someone who would keep him up all night as thanks—in what way did this stimulate creativity?

He was different from the rest of the advertising crowd in that he neither lived in nor dreamed of a penthouse in downtown Stockholm. And he seldom drank to excess with other advertisers while they showered each other with affirmation. After a day's work, he got in his Volvo (a Volvo?!) and drove back out to his residential neighborhood, where he acted as if he were a perfectly average person.

The house was larger than he needed, but the neighborhood itself was only mildly impressive. The neighbors thought he was one of the masses. What they didn't know was that he secretly studied them, figured out their thought patterns, what they liked, what they disliked, and why. He often plucked one of them from his memory when it was time to birth a fresh idea. How would he get Mrs. Levander to buy chicken an extra day each week? What could convince Runesson's teenage boys to switch data plans?

Perhaps the only one of his neighbors who functioned neither as a neighbor nor as an object of study was the occupant of the corner plot adjacent to Hugo's place. He was grumpy, curt, and generally suspicious. Never satisfied with anything, except for when he was crawling around on all fours in his carrot patch and talking to himself. Or maybe he was talking to the carrots.

Hugo wondered how to package advertising messages to a man who conducted the better portion of his intellectual exchanges with a carrot. He arrived at the conclusion that it wasn't possible.

Thus the international adman had the full palette of consumers on his street, including the one who fit in for the sole reason that he didn't.

If only it hadn't been for the garbage-can incident.

The grumpy man's name was Birger Broman, and he was a widower, a government workplace safety inspector, and impossible to reason with. Broman had begun placing his garbage can on the wrong side of his driveway for pickup every other Thursday. It was overfull and the garbage bags were improperly tied. It smelled bad, attracted flies, and was generally unpleasant to look at.

He could just as well place the cans on the other side of the driveway. It wouldn't cause him any extra trouble, create any extra work for the garbagemen, or make any difference to the flies.

But it would be better for Hugo.

The adman spoke with him, but Workplace Safety Inspector Broman stood his ground. The road did not belong to Hugo Hamlin, in contrast to the mailbox thirty centimeters away.

"The property line runs here," Broman said, pointing with his crooked index finger. "If you want that to change, you'll have to talk to the municipality."

Hugo responded that he had no desire to move the property line, he just wanted to be spared the stench and the swarms of flies when he got his mail.

"So instead you want *me* to have the stench and swarms of flies when I get *my* mail?" said Broman.

Here one should bear in mind that Broman's house was on the corner; his mailbox was safely around the other side, far away.

"Well, that would be more fitting, considering that this is your garbage, your can is the one that's too full, and you never tie your bags properly. But your mailbox isn't even there."

"Are you trying to tell me where to put my mailbox?"

Hugo talked to his brother about the neighbor and asked whether Malte wanted to lend a hand by giving Broman a nice kick in the ass, or, even better, beat him to death.

"*Primum, non nocere,*" Malte replied.

"Huh?"

"From the Hippocratic Oath. Doctors are meant to keep people alive, not the opposite."

Hugo had the sense that from that day forward, the can got a little bit fuller and the bags were tied even more sloppily. But he wasn't sure. The only thing he knew for sure was that Broman hadn't changed his mind.

It went so far that one day Hugo himself moved Broman's can to the correct side of the driveway. He pulled it with one hand and held his nose with the other.

At which point, Broman called the police.

"Criminal conversion!" he said to the two unfortunate police inspectors, who felt that there were better ways than this to serve the public. Instead of issuing a caution, they asked Hugo to grow up.

"*I'm* the one who needs to grow up? This is the idiot who puts his can right next to my mailbox out of sheer cussedness!"

"Illegal defamation!" said Broman.

"There's no such offense in the criminal code," said one of the inspectors. "Now, here's what we're going to do: you there, stop moving your neighbor's garbage can, and you, don't even think about calling the police again. Okay?"

Workplace Safety Inspector Broman was on the verge of asserting his legal rights, but the officer looked so stern that he didn't dare.

Once the long arm of the law was gone, Hugo tried one last time.

"Please, Broman, can't you just . . ."

"Call the municipality and share your opinions there. And you heard what the police said: once more and they'll lock you up!"

As his neighbor again suggested he turn to the municipality, Hugo felt the urge to strangle him. Or shove him into the bin. Or force him to eat up his own rubbish.

Fortunately, he never did any of this. He resigned himself to the fact that he had one of the worst neighbors in Sweden. That is: He resigned himself in *action*. Not in thought.

During the weeks and months that followed, as Hugo drank his morning coffee and looked out at his neighbor, his yard, his garbage can and the driveway, his mind turned somersaults about the garbage-can conflict.

About how best to get revenge.

His first idea—strangling in a public place—wouldn't work. It would come with ten years to life and that wasn't worth the trouble. Assault and force-feeding were even more out of the question, because they would land Hugo in prison and once he came out, the workplace safety inspector would exist just as much as he ever had. He couldn't stand the thought of the smirk that would grace Broman's lips.

A simple solution might be to give him a taste of his own medicine and then some. There were no rules about how many garbage cans you could order from the municipality to be emptied every other Thursday. What's more, small households could request a pickup just once every four weeks.

Five cans in a row along the property line he shared with Broman? All equally stuffed? Improperly tied bags—no, *untied* bags—with a pickup once a month?

This would be delightfully frustrating for the workplace safety inspector. But at the same time, it would be even worse for Hugo and—worst of all—Broman would know it. Revenge that bounces back is no revenge at all.

Hugo entered a new mindset, the mindset of an adman. His latest stroke of genius at work was the rebranding of a formerly leading orange marmalade that had lost ground. It had long been in decline, languishing on store shelves, but now it took up half the prime shelf space in those same shops. Thanks to Hugo, all of Europe was now munching on marmalade made of well-pulped, half-rotten, unpeeled oranges. It was the same marmalade as always. The only difference was that the Swedish adman had made it indispensable on the kitchen table by changing the flavor from "orange" to "orange-umami."

"But it doesn't have any umami in it," said the sales director of the marmalade company.

"So?" Hugo replied.

"We can add it, of course. I'll talk to the product division. What is umami, exactly?"

A man who could make anyone at all experience something fresh about old marmalade certainly ought to be able to take down a crummy old workplace safety inspector. All he had to do was find the inspector's weak spot and hit him there.

Inspector Broman loved his garden with a passion. He puttered in it from early spring until the first snow fell. It would have been a pleasure, in Hugo's eyes, to see his neighbor's garden destroyed. Killer slugs? Where could he buy a few hundred of those? And how could he instruct them to torment the neighbor, but not the neighbor's closest neighbor, that was, Hugo himself? There was nothing in the pest-control literature to indicate that slugs could demonstrate loyalty towards their owner. Talking sense to a killer slug would be no easier than doing so with Broman.

Where might that bastard keep his bottles of fertilizer? If he could just get his hands on those, he could exchange their contents for glycol, chlorine, or something else just as ruinous. And then take a front-row seat on his veranda to watch the inspector walking around, humming and slowly killing his own rhododendrons.

Or perhaps he should become a beekeeper. Ten thousand bees might not be enough. Twenty thousand? There had to be a limit to what his neighbor would stand for. Although the same probably went for worker bees as for killer slugs: tough to reason with. "Okay, ladies, same thing again today: Everyone to Broman's! Okay?"

Rabbit husbandry, however, sounded more doable. Fifty rabbits who were never given any food would quickly find their way to Broman's carrots, right?

For a while, Hugo was counting on planting a juniper hedge as close to Broman's property as possible. The downside was that his garbage-can revenge would go on for a decade or two before the junipers really took off. The upside was that the hedge would be thick and, when fully grown, up to twenty meters high. It would also block the sun for the neighbor and his garden plots for at least five hundred years. Junipers were long-lived little rascals.

Considerably more so than Inspector Broman, it turned out. For one day he dropped dead, his nose in the topsoil, at the age of sixty-five—and Hugo never had to lift a finger. After a while, a young couple moved into Broman's place. They put the garbage can where it belonged and were generally pleasant folks.

Faced with all these changes, Hugo felt empty. It was as if Broman had won the battle by forfeiting before the revenge caught up with him.

There was no such thing as perfect satisfaction.

Chapter 17

Peace and quiet settled upon Hugo Hamlin's neighborhood. No one argued with anyone else. The annual Midsummer party in Hugo's garden was evidence. There was herring and aquavit and dancing around the Midsummer pole. As the evening drew on the little kids were sent to bed while the older ones were bribed with iPads. Then it was time for grilling. The men handled the grill and drank red wine; the women sipped white and cheered them on. Sweden could be awfully predictable at times.

As the entrecotes and corn on the cob changed color, the neighbor across from Hugo said he thought it was a pity that Broman had gone and died in his carrot patch, but at the same time it was nice to have these friendly new neighbors. At which point he raised his glass to the newcomers, who blushed. The neighbor next to the neighbor across from Hugo added that if they were being honest, Broman had in fact been the street's number one killjoy. Additional neighbors nodded in agreement.

The mood was so cheerful and the opinions on poor Broman's many shortcomings so unanimous that the host of the Midsummer festivities found himself telling the story of the garbage can and his many childish thoughts of revenge.

"In some ways it's lucky he died. Otherwise I'd probably be sitting at my kitchen table and muttering to myself still today."

This was met by general merriment and became the start of a lively discussion Hugo hadn't expected. It began when the neighbor next to the neighbor across from him chuckled and said that the juniper hedge plan had been a good one. A solution slow in coming, yes, but it had a certain charm. For long before the junipers cast their shadow over Broman's garden, he would be tormented by the thought of what was to come.

The new neighbors, Alicia and André, had never met Broman; they'd bought the house from his estate. This didn't stop them from coming up with ideas of their own. André was a Volkswagen dealer and had a number of suggestions for what would have been best to pour into the fuel tank of Broman's car to make it feel as ill as possible. Alicia worked at a psychiatric clinic and knew which kinds of medicine one could powder and put into Broman's coffee, and the effects one could expect to see. Some of them were quite amusing.

Hugo's older brother Malte and his Karolin lived close by and were there too. The physician couple successfully resisted the urge to warn Alicia about the dosages she'd just suggested; after all, this was all in good fun.

The rest of the evening continued in similar spirits. Bookseller Runesson was happy to provide literary connections. He began with *The Count of Monte Cristo* but soon shifted gears up to Hamlet: revenge upon revenge until half a royal family kicked the bucket. This prompted a conversation about the poetic differences between a king, on the one hand, and a workplace safety inspector on the other. Everyone but the bookseller was in agreement that a poisoned chalice of wine was not sufficiently creative; that you should take revenge with finesse if you were going to take revenge at all. The bookseller rather preferred to get straight to the point. After all, in the Icelandic sagas, they didn't just prance around pondering what they could plant in the earth on the off chance that they might, a few decades later, wangle some revenge. No, heads rolled on the spot!

This was the moment one of the guests turned to Gunilla Levander from number eight, the parish priest.

"What does the Bible say about revenge? Is God behind us at least as far as spiking Broman's coffee with Rohypnol?"

Gunilla Levander, when sober, was plucky, cheerful, and uncomplicated, but when full of wine, beer, herring and aquavit she took on a different personality. She launched into a lecture, saying that some evidence indicated that Jesus would have voted no to Rohypnol and everything else, but that this theory was primarily based upon Matthew's testimony that one must turn the other cheek if someone slapped you on the right cheek. She made special note of the bit about the *right* cheek. This could be interpreted to mean that we should be forgiving only of those who are left-handed, and that was practically nobody. It was, after all, difficult to deal a blow to someone's right cheek with one's own right hand.

"*I'm* left-handed," said bookseller Runesson, raising his glass.

"You seem to drink just fine with your right hand too," said Pontus Bladh from number ten.

"I've never liked Matthew," said Gunilla Levander. "And the Old Testament is totally on our side when it comes to Broman. Eye for an eye and tooth for a tooth and all that."

"Not an eye for an eye!" said the ophthalmologist.

Thereafter, with God's blessing, each idea trumped the next. The winner was announced during the late-night snack at two in the morning (hot dogs and beer). Housewife Jakobsson was awarded double hot dogs with extra mustard for her detailed plan of how they could have convinced the chairman of the Hells Angels of northern Stockholm that Inspector Broman both rode a Kawasaki and had hit on his girlfriend. Everyone thought it was a pity that Broman was already dead.

Chapter 18

H ugo Hamlin was, out of choice, single and child-
free. He and his headache lingered in bed after
the extraordinarily pleasant Midsummer party, facing
no responsibilities of any sort. It reminded him of his
work hours in general; he came and went as he pleased.
As long as he delivered. And he had been delivering for
a long time. His latest idea, the one about the umami,
had become an ad that played on TVs all over Europe.
A humorous twist on why this particular orange marmalade was an absolute breakfast necessity for anyone
who agonized over the looming day ahead. The thinking behind this message was that we live in a time when
almost everyone has reason to agonize at the thought of
every new day.

Although the worst aftereffects from the night
before hadn't yet relinquished their hold on him, he

got up, went to the kitchen in only his underpants, drank half a liter of milk straight from the carton, and forced down two sandwiches with free marmalade. It didn't make the day seem any less of a threat, but at least he wasn't hungry anymore. Like most Swedish men in residential suburbs on the day after Midsummer, he was *hung-over*.

When his miserable breakfast finally settled, just before lunch, he began to catch up with himself. Hadn't all of his neighbors sat around from late afternoon until early morning, desiring revenge? Regardless of the event. Regardless of anything but the sweet taste of revenge itself.

His condition notwithstanding, the adman got to work.

Revenge as a concept.

Revenge as a business idea.

Hugo was a wizard at packaging marmalade, crisps and lottery tickets better than they deserved. If you could pitch nonsense, you could probably do the same with revenge.

Under his own management.

He had just about one million kronor in the bank but was enamored of the thought of another million. At the same time, it was getting more and more difficult to muster excitement in his work with the firm. Perhaps he could switch gears while he was still on top?

He wasn't out to get revenge on anyone for his own sake; after all, Broman was dead. But weren't there any number of Bromans out there, still breathing and spreading their poison? Who knew what kind of profit they could generate!

Sweet Sweet Revenge Ltd.

That's what his company would be called. Hugo worked on polishing the pitch.

"Do you need to get revenge for an injustice without breaking the law? We're on it! Twelve hundred kronor per hour. Thousands of satisfied customers around the world could have attested to our good quality if only our discretion weren't a point of honor."

The part about thousands of customers wasn't true, of course. Not yet. But it could be.

All that was left was to quit his job. And get a business plan.

"Are you totally sure about this?" said big brother Malte while they were out drinking at their traditional Midsummer afterparty.

He was. In Hugo's mind, subsidiaries were already popping up all over the place. Like La Venganza es Dulce, Rache ist Süß GmbH, La Vengeance est Douce SA, and a handful of others. The company's formal headquarters could be in Stockholm, but the marketing should be local and regional.

Robin at Great & Even Greater Communications had always known that the day would come when Hugo no longer wanted to be part of the firm. Their good luck had lasted for almost twenty years. How many awards had he brought them? Cannes, Berlin, Stockholm, of course . . . and they had come so close to tiny Swedish Great & Even Greater getting the chance to produce an ad for the Superbowl. All thanks to Hugo. To this day, Robin had no idea why they'd fallen short of the mark. Hugo thought it was because of the price tag. Too cheap and the Americans would never get fired up.

The firm's founder had known that there were gears turning in Hugo's mind ever since that moment outside the theater in Stockholm years ago. Great & Even Greater had been a start-up at the time; Robin himself was young and hungry and saw potential in just about everyone and everything. Such as in the kid standing at the bottom of the stairs at the Royal Dramatic Theatre, expounding upon the artistic greatness of a potato peeler. He had painted it gold. He had numbered it. He provided a certificate of authenticity. He referred to Marcel Duchamp. He did all the right things to pitch the unpitchable. Okay, he wasn't successful, but he would be if he were supplied with better tools, thought Robin, as he walked over to offer the kid a job.

The rest was history. The very next day was Hugo's first on the job. After three weeks he was helming his first solo project. After seven months he won his first award in the company's name. And so it went. Until now, and in under a year, the multimillion-kronor contract with the big electronics chain would be up for renewal. And for the first time, Hugo wouldn't be at the table during negotiations.

He didn't want to say what he was going to do, but he promised it wouldn't involve becoming the competition. Robin trusted him, but to be on the safe side he let him go that very day. With a big hug and three months' pay as a thank you.

Hugo Hamlin spent his first day of unemployment in his own kitchen at home in Lidingö. He sat at the table with his laptop, sketching out his marketing plan. At the outset it would take extensive advertising. Preferably along electronic channels, for the social networks seldom left space for understanding, forgiveness, reflection, and other things that stood in direct opposition to his business idea.

The most effective channel would be Facebook. One

whole department within Great & Even Greater Communications was devoted to working on Facebook and its sister networks. They cast a wide net for famous and half-famous individuals in the interest of convincing them to have the opinions the advertising firm and its clients wanted them to have. Hugo actually had nothing to do with that department, but in recent days they had been making a lot of noise after an author hardly anyone had heard of flipped out when asked if he would consider liking a specific brand of ice cream across his social platforms. In return he would receive twenty thousand kronor and as much ice cream as he could eat. The problem was that the author was 1) lactose intolerant and 2) intolerant in general. Now he was raising hell on the theme of how democracy was under threat if we no longer knew who thought what and why.

Hugo thought the intolerant author had summarized the problem of Facebook quite tidily and hoped that a popular uprising might be just around the corner. But since he himself was not a revolutionary but an entrepreneur, he decided that he might as well buy eighty thousand kronor worth of targeted Sweet Sweet Revenge ads all over Europe in the meantime. Hate Facebook. Yay, Facebook!

The next expense item was an office. Hugo needed somewhere to think all his big thoughts in peace and quiet.

He found what he was looking for in the well-to-do neighborhood of Östermalm. A former boutique, seventy square meters plus a kitchenette and bathroom. For four generations the boutique had sold fancy wooden toys to children whose parents suffered no financial hardships. But there was no fifth generation to speak of. What child, regardless of social class, wanted a hand-painted farm with all the farmer's creatures when there were iPads?

Hugo met the former tenant at the contract signing; she was a sad old woman in her seventies. When she saw the name of Hugo's company she expressed interest in becoming his first customer.

"That's fine," said Hugo. "What is it you're looking for, ma'am?"

She didn't quite know. But perhaps her revenge could consist of turning off all the internets that had destroyed both her own life and those of all the poor little children?

This was not the sort of first customer Hugo had hoped for.

"How were you thinking that might work, ma'am?"

The old woman snorted. Surely that was up to

Hamlin to figure out. Why else would she hire him? But this was an honest question. She would give him five thousand kronor in cash if he completed the job to her liking.

Hugo was far too focused on the future to let a five-thousand-kronor old woman stand in his way. He elected to close that door immediately.

"For that amount, I suppose I can come up with a way to turn off your internet, ma'am, should you have any, but no one else's."

Chapter 19

As he waited for the old woman to clear out her toy store and hand over the keys, Hugo went on a tax-deductible business trip to Miami Beach. He sat under a parasol on the shore and ordered umbrella drinks and hors d'oeuvres for himself and his imaginary business contacts. Running a business demanded expenses and revenues. Hugo ate his hors d'oeuvres and was pleased. Now all that was left were the revenues.

When he took possession of the premises he was both tanned and well-rested. Before the first day was over, he had furnished his new office. Nothing fancy: a desk, three chairs, a whiteboard on the wall, a coffeemaker in the kitchen and milk in the fridge. He also discovered a few canned goods in the pantry, possibly ones as old as the woman who had left them behind.

All he needed now was an assistant. Skilled labor not required; all they would have to do was answer the phone and keep potential clients away from the creative mind while simultaneously keeping said clients interested enough for Hugo to get them on the hook at a later date, as time allowed. But that expense item would have to wait until the enterprise got on its feet. Life in Florida had not been cheap.

With that, all the preparations were completed. Still, Hugo held off on the launch. He wanted it to be well into autumn, at least in northern Europe. It had not been lost on him what good spirits he'd been in thanks to the Florida sun and heat. Bitter thoughts of revenge took root more easily in dark days and chilly winds.

Which is just the sort of thing Stockholm is extra good at in November and December. Hugo clicked the Facebook button and launched his campaign when it was three degrees above freezing, with sleet in the air and a fierce north wind that, according to the meteorologists, would make it all the way down to Milan.

Everything started so well! In the days right after his first marketing wave, Hugo received calls and emails from twelve different countries and eighty different people. Most of the messages were sheer madness, of course. Three people wanted their mother-in-law snuffed, one wanted help conquering Albania, and one was stuck on the idea of getting revenge on their own demons.

Seven potential customers would require further effort: they wanted to know more about what the company had to offer and whether results could be guaranteed. Some tried to haggle about the price. Hugo made sure to keep them on the hook.

An eighth interested party, however—Herr Arvid Rössler from the outskirts of Freiburg in Germany— seemed prepared to come to an immediate agreement.

Herr Rössler was a retired high school teacher and had spent his entire working life keeping teenagers under control. He prided himself on his competence as an old-school sort of teacher. On occasion, over the years, this had meant a wallop or two on the ear of an unruly student, exclusively boys.

Anyway, after his retirement he relocated permanently to his summer cottage, not far from the French border. There in the countryside, with a view of the Rhine, he'd intended to live a quiet and pleasant life in the company of his eight Bielefelder hens and his proud Bielefelder rooster. And so it would remain until the day the Lord called him home.

"It isn't the Lord himself that's the problem, I hope?" said Hugo.

Battling God would likely be almost as futile as battling the internet.

"No, no," said Herr Rössler. "It's the next-door neighbor."

"Imagine that," said Hugo. "Next-door neighbors are my personal specialty. Please, tell me more."

The neighbor in question happened to be one of those many hundreds of students Rössler had taught over the years. Sometimes it was a smaller world than one might have wished. This particular specimen was already in his forties. Just as Arvid Rössler had always suspected, he had never amounted to anything. He dragged his feet just as he had in his teenage years, accompanied by his overweight German shepherd. Lived in a caravan. The question was, what did he live on? There were rumors at the village grocery that he had some lottery winnings, but Rössler thought welfare was a more likely story.

Now, it so happened that the possible welfare recipient had a memory as sharp as Arvid Rössler's. The teacher recognized the student—but what's worse, the student recognized the teacher.

"Well, that's a surprise," Rössler muttered. "That lout was hardly ever in school."

Hugo listened with interest, curious where this story would end. But he had to interrupt with a query.

"Is it perhaps the case that this . . . lout . . . as you call him, was one of those who received a wallop now and then, back in school, in the name of education?"

"Yes, he was," Rössler admitted. In fact, there had been occasion for a number of wallops during the three years student and teacher were forced to associate with one another.

"And now he's getting you back?"

"Yes."

"And you want to get back at him for that?"

"He started it."

Hugo shifted his focus; he didn't want to lay the blame on his presumptive client. He said he wanted to know what the neighbor had thought up.

Well, it had to do with the dog, which always ran onto Rössler's property and scared both hens and rooster. Not just because he was a dog, but because the lout encouraged it. A fence likely could have solved everything, but that would ruin the amazing view of the Rhine from Rössler's veranda.

"Have you by any chance spoken with your neighbor about the issue, Herr Rössler?"

Herr Hamlin could bet he had. Again and again.

But the lout merely sneered at him, threatened him, said things like "Perhaps Teacher would prefer I give him back one of his hundred and fifty wallops?"

Arvid Rössler had even called in one of the regional environmental inspectors to come take a look, but the bastard had made sure to keep his dog locked up in the caravan that day.

Hugo took notes as he listened. It was important to get all the facts straight.

Herr Rössler went on to say that it had carried on in this fashion until the other day, when the dog went too far. He caught one of the hens and bit it to death!

"Murder!" Arvid Rössler declared.

Hugo said that a court of law might possibly call it something different.

"But your rage is understandable."

There was no solving this matter over the phone, and it wouldn't be in Hugo's best interest anyway. After all, pay came in relation to hours spent. Sweet Sweet Revenge Ltd. needed to investigate the circumstances on site. Hugo explained that the company did indeed have operations in Europe with plans to expand into the United States and Asia, but that feuds with neighbors were the particular specialty of the Stockholm office—that is, Hugo Hamlin's home office. If Herr Rössler wished to send six thousand kronor as an advance payment, Hugo could arrive at the scene of the crime before the week was out, via a flight to Zurich or Basel.

Herr Rössler did not hesitate to accept and agreed that Hugo could work on a running tab plus expenses.

Whether the lout was indeed a lout could not be determined merely by looking at him. A prejudiced party might, however, see indications in that direction: He had long, stringy hair and wore a faded denim jacket and dirty jeans. He was rather more overweight than his dog.

Hugo had no intention of negotiating or even speaking with him or his German shepherd. He merely studied them from a distance. After keeping watch from Arvid Rössler's kitchen window for six hours, he became witness to how the lout set his dog on the chickens, who fled in every direction.

The evidence confirmed, Hugo walked the property from west to east and north to south, and made a sketch, marking the henhouse in relation to the cottage and veranda. Then he made a careful study of the slope down to the Rhine River and took note of the way the roads and paths ran in the immediate vicinity. With that, he was done for the day.

"I shall now retire to my hotel in Freiburg," he said. "I promise to be in touch within forty-eight hours. Do you find my plan acceptable, Herr Rössler?"

Arvid Rössler hoped it would be.

Hugo first pondered whether he might, with some sort of dam, be able to flood the lout's entire property (speaking of how best to turn off the entire internet). His property was slightly lower than the teacher's, but the topography leading down to the river was, in general, not particularly favorable to this plan.

Once he had dropped the idea of changing sections of the Rhine's course he turned to the main characters, that is, the lout and his dog. Up to this point, Hugo had been thinking along the lines of how best to retaliate against the lout, but what if he went straight for the *dog*? A full-grown German shepherd wasn't the sort of thing you just treated however you liked. Unless, you were, for instance, a wolf?

One flaw in the wolf idea was that wolves are not generally available for purchase. And even if they were, it would have been crucial to find one that could repress its natural instincts to eat up the seven hens and the rooster the moment it had frightened off the dog.

So, not a wolf. What else? Something or someone

that could be mean to the lout's dog, but nice to the chickens.

Hugo's brother Malte had a summer home of his own, not outside Freiburg but rather on the Swedish island of Gotland smack dab in the Baltic Sea. He and Malte had spent quite some time hanging around there during summers. His big brother wanted him around all the time, but Hugo mostly took the opportunity to visit when clumsy Karolin was otherwise occupied.

The island was known for a lot of things—among others, for its large number of sheep farmers. Gotland lamb was world-famous throughout Sweden. And few sheepskins were softer than that of the Gotland sheep.

If there was anything Gotland sheep farmers disliked it was tourists in general and the clever fox in particular. The tourists littered and got in the way, while the fox snuck into the sheep pen at night and grabbed a lamb or two to serve its family for dinner. Night after night.

One of the farmers had obtained a couple of llama-like creatures from Peru; they lived in the pasture and grazed side by side with the sheep. It was hard to find any creature more peaceful than the llama—as long as the fox stayed away. When it showed up, the llama lost its mind and started trying to *spit* the intruder away, and—if that didn't work—it would kick him clear across the island. Hugo recalled all of this from a newspaper article he'd read the previous summer.

One phone call was all it took, and Hugo had the name and number for this farmer. Who answered on the first ring.

His name was Björk and he was very accommodating. And talkative. He began by saying that he had bought a new phone last spring, one of those mobile ones, with no cord attaching it to the wall. Only to discover that no one ever called. Until this point he had been able to imagine that all his friends tried to reach him while he was out with the animals. Now he knew he didn't have any friends.

"This new technology is nothing but crap," said Björk.

Hugo agreed. And steered the conversation towards llamas.

"Guanacos," said the farmer.

This was too difficult for Hugo to repeat.

"Is it true that they protect your sheep from the fox?"

They sure did. Björk had himself read about a big farm on the mainland that was having trouble with wolves and bought three guanacos to help. Once one of them had landed a glob of spit between the eyes of one wolf and kicked another black and blue, the wolves never returned. Björk supposed that what worked on a wolf ought to work on a fox, since they weighed so much less.

And what worked on Swedish wolves and foxes ought to work just as well on a German shepherd, Hugo thought. But how *did* it work, in greater detail?

Farmer Björk responded by telling a story about a fling he'd had as a youth, with a lass from Hemse who had never been able to get used to the sheep smell. Since then he had been to a few community dances over the years, but it seemed like too much trouble with all the showering and cologning and how his clothes had to be washed, or at least brushed off, so he stopped going. He lived alone and it was probably just as well.

Hugo agreed and repeated the question.

This time went better. Lonely Farmer Björk told him that the llama creatures had a flocking instinct; their natural behavior was to adopt the sheep.

"Or the *lambs*, as we say here on the island, but of course I can hear that I'm speaking with a mainlander, might as well say it in a way that will be understood."

What Hugo understood more than anything else was that it took patience to talk to Farmer Björk.

"A flocking instinct?" he said.

Yes, the guanaco would take charge of the flock and protect it with its life.

"No matter the flock?"

"Meaning what?"

"Well, if one was to exchange the sheep for . . . chickens, for instance? What would happen then?"

Farmer Björk considered the question for a moment and said that chicken wire might be one option, but sure, why not, it ought to work.

Hugo thought that the conversation had gone on long enough.

"May I ask what you paid for the animals, Mr. Björk?"

"Ten thousand kronor each," said Farmer Björk.

"May I purchase one of them for double that?"

Nine days later, one of Farmer Björk's llama creatures had arrived outside Freiburg. From Peru, by way of Sweden, to Germany. The castrated male was really getting to see the world. Björk had explained that it was castrated because otherwise it tended to want to mate with the females in the flock.

Hugo pictured a Peruvian llama creature trying to mate with a German Bielefelder hen but quickly shooed the image from his mind. It was too terrible.

While the Swedish adman pounded a pole into the

perfect spot in Arvid Rössler's garden, the teacher wondered what the llama creature's name was. Hugo replied that he'd forgotten to ask the Swedish farmer that particular question. Rössler had named each of his seven hens and his rooster, so it wouldn't do for their guardian to walk around without a name of his own. The Peruvian llama would have to be Mario (after his country's great writer Vargas Llosa, of course). The rooster's name was Pavarotti; he had crowed beautifully when he was young but got a little croakier with age.

A rope was tied around Mario's neck and he was solemnly informed that he was now the boss of seven Bielefelder hens and Pavarotti. Mario tossed his head, and someone so inclined could see in this a nod of confirmation.

The rope was just the right length to allow Mario to walk freely all over Herr Rössler's property but not a step further. Since the hens never left the lot, this limitation didn't bother Mario in the least. For two days, perfect harmony reigned. The lout sat in the caravan along with his dog and wondered what was going on. Had the old man bought a camel? Why?

On day three, he grew tired of not quarreling with his old teacher. Camel or no, the German shepherd was let out with the usual command: "To Teacher!"

The dog was more than ready to do its business; it planned to mess with the birds for a while and round off its sojourn by relieving itself in front of the neighbor's veranda. This typically resulted in extra treats upon returning home. He had no idea what that giant, grazing bird was doing in the garden, but why not scare it out of its wits too?

So thought the dog. To the extent that he thought at all. In any case, this was the last thing that went through his head before he got it crushed by a well-aimed Super Mario kick in the temple. The dog was killed instantly, but Mario gave him another kick that sent the dead animal flying all the way back to his owner's property.

The lout was crying rivers on the other side of the property line, while Herr Rössler was as gleeful as a child. He hummed "The Winner Takes It All" while Hugo wrote out the final invoice at the kitchen table.

Two round trips to Zurich, two round trips from Stockholm to Gotland, animal transport, rental car, purchase of llama creature, rope, sledgehammer, per diem, and forty hours of consulting at 120 euro per hour. In total: 12,800 euro.

"Cheap," said Herr Rössler.

Chapter 20

S weet Sweet Revenge Ltd.'s second job was simpler than the first. A sixteen-year-old Swedish girl was flirting with an exciting sixteen-year-old French boy on Tinder. Unfortunately, she had gone to the United States to visit a friend (and to tell her about the Frenchman) when he messaged her that he had sent "a surprise" by post. Since the Swedish postal service was no longer what it once was (which was the fault of the Danes, but that's a different story), the girl had to pick up the surprise at one of the postal service's designated service centers, in this case a corner shop in the neighborhood where the girl had her legal residence. The corner store sent her a text saying that a package had arrived and had to be picked up within ten days.

But the girl would be in the United States for another eleven. She called the manager of the corner shop, who said that this was out of his control but also that a third party could pick up the package if they brought along a form of ID for the girl, for instance a driver's license. The girl explained that she was on the other side of the Atlantic along with the only form of ID she owned: her passport. Swedish sixteen-year-olds do not have driver's licenses.

The manager of the corner store did not feel this was his problem either.

The girl tried suggesting that she could email a photocopy of her passport to her mother, who could then pick up the package, with the aid of her own ID and the copy of the girl's passport.

The manager of the corner store said it didn't work that way.

How about this? The girl had a tracking number; with this the manager of the corner store could locate the package and put it aside one extra day, instead of sending it back to France the day before the recipient made it home. Just one extra day!

The manager of the corner store asked, rhetorically, what would happen if he made such an exception for every package.

The girl pointed out it wasn't as if everyone demanded this of the manager of the corner store; in fact, she was the only one, wasn't she? To this the manager of the corner store replied that he didn't have time to continue talking to her. The milk refrigerator required his attention.

"And that's where we stand now," said the girl.

"What do you want from me?" Hugo asked.

"For you to kill him, is that too much?"

Hugo felt that it was, but he sympathized with her. What was her budget, and how was she planning to pay?

The answer was music to his ears.

The form of payment was her father's credit card and the budget was essentially unlimited.

Each day, millions of packages are posted this way and that across the globe. Few items take up more space per kilo than the kind of material that is specifically meant to take up a lot of space per kilo for the purpose of filling empty gaps in packages and protecting susceptible products from impact.

If you were by chance to order a package that contained nothing but the kind of material that's meant to take up space while weighing hardly anything—it could potentially turn out to be a very large package that weighs almost nothing and costs very little to ship.

This truth was the starting point of what ensued and demanded one day of Hugo's time. He began by locating fifty private addresses in the immediate neighborhood around the shop he was getting paid to torment. After that he placed the same amount of orders of extremely bulky packing materials from ten different parts of the world. With each order he gave a different fake phone number so none of the recipients could be notified.

He also made an on-site visit so he could see with his own eyes that the total space the corner shop had for packages was limited to two cubic meters behind the single cash register. It would only take the arrival of four of the fifty orders to bring the system to its knees. After eight, the manager would no longer know what to do with himself; after twelve, sixteen, and twenty his will to live would fade more and more. And thirty packages would still be on their way.

This was how Hugo sold the girl on sweet revenge, and for his trouble he wanted forty thousand kronor plus expenses, all by way of her father's credit card.

But she had been looking for more bang for her buck and launched into negotiations. After all, it would be difficult to provide evidence for the loss of will to live Hugo had promised. But a crushed kneecap, for instance, was easier to measure.

Violence was not on the firm's menu, but how about if Hugo also made sure to send one thing and the next directly to the home of the corner store manager and his wife?

Not good enough, according to the girl.

The deal was slipping through Hugo's fingers. But she was far from home and what she didn't know wouldn't hurt her. Hugo wasn't prepared to enact violence of any sort, but that didn't mean he couldn't pretend. He asked for an hour's time to consider.

During that hour he found a suitable video clip online. Someone had set a luxury car on fire while it sat in a parking spot. It was impossible to tell where on earth this car had burned; it could have been Argentina, the Czech Republic—or perhaps Sweden.

Hugo made the video his own and called the girl back to suggest that on top of everything else he would consider setting the corner shop manager's car on fire.

"It's a blue Lamborghini."

The girl did not stop to reflect on the likelihood that a Swedish corner shop manager was driving around in a car worth more than his entire shop. She accepted the arrangement, on the condition that the contracted party would send photographic evidence of the burning car.

Three mornings later, four cubic meters of packages arrived with the post. The manager of the corner shop worked overtime all evening and half the night to make space for the enormous quantities. At one thirty in the morning he was finished. And reasonably satisfied with himself—after all, creativity was the mother of necessity. Or was it that necessity was the inventors' . . . something? In any case, he had filled the large shop freezer with marked-down French fries, which left space in the storeroom freezer for a pallet of paper towels, which meant that the last of the packages could go in the spot where the paper towels had been stored. Then he biked home (a bike was the closest he would ever get to a Lamborghini). He planned to sleep until he woke up on his own the next morning. Elsa could deal with the register.

But poor Elsa called and woke him up at seven o'clock, two hours before the store opened. Where was she supposed to put the thirty new packages from the postal service that had just arrived by truck?

"Thirty?" said the bleary corner shop manager. "Just leave them on the loading dock for now, I'll be right there."

"It's raining," said Elsa.

His third job was a bit more demanding. The father of a Spanish boy contacted him to say that his son had been suspended from his football team for chewing gum during practice. For this, his coach deserved a severe punishment.

Hugo wasn't entirely satisfied with this development. His last client had wished for the manager of a corner store to be snuffed. This current one thought it would be sufficient for his son's tormentor to suffer as much as possible. Insofar as violence was concerned this was a move in the right direction, but it was still several steps past setting rabbits on a spiteful neighbor's carrot patch.

Oh well, perhaps the football coach deserved what he was about to get. And the money was good. Hugo promised he would come up with something that meant plenty of pain.

It took two days of preparations in a suburb of Madrid. Background knowledge was everything!

Thus it happened that the coach in question left his home in Leganés with the aim of getting into his car for the impending Wednesday football practice. On the pavement outside Hugo had placed a round, thirty-kilo chunk of concrete and painted it black and white, making it look remarkably like a football.

At just the right moment, he called out from a distance of sixty meters, uttering a Spanish phrase he'd practiced and practiced.

"*Oiga! Señor!* Could you please send that ball back to me?"

The coach took his mark and aimed perfectly with his right ankle.

Hugo had never heard someone roar so vociferously in pain. In any language.

Five thousand euros in the bank, plus expenses.

PART FOUR

PART FOUR

Chapter 21

Director Hugo Hamlin sat in the office, counting his money. He had done a soft launch with a handful of jobs during the first few months. He'd selected them carefully, with an eye towards learning lessons and getting into the swing of things. To sum it all up, he wasn't satisfied with much beyond all the money streaming in.

Thanks to the contact he'd had with the initial clients and those who might soon be the same, Hugo had come to realize that the degree of legality wasn't of concern to his clientele. It had been part of Hugo's original idea to have the law on his side, but that limited his creativity and demanded greater mental effort. Time was money.

To put it sloppily, you might say that legal equaled inferior and more expensive.

The solution was for Hugo to adjust his moral compass. Unlawful but reasonable, more or less. Those who started shit should get equal amounts of shit in return.

Although it turned out that not even this was in line with his clients' expectations. The proportionality principle, too, was hampered by willingness to pay. People wanted fees to be on par with the amount of damage Hugo could offer, no matter what the law said or how they themselves had suffered previously. It was all about—freely translated from the Bible—eyes for an eye, and teeth for a tooth. People were awfully miserable creatures, the lot of them. Hugo wasn't sure he was any exception.

Big brother Malte popped by for coffee. Hugo happened to share his thoughts. Malte got all worked up at the notion that not only one eye but two must go kaput in a dispute. Beyond that he had no opinions, except that his brother clearly had a screw loose and should also get himself a better coffeemaker. With that, he left his little brother in favor of the afternoon's three cataract surgeries.

Hugo was once again alone with his thoughts. Aside from the aspects of legality and proportion, he was dissatisfied with his own efficiency. It wouldn't be a bad idea to make an addition, in the form of a creative partner. But easier, cheaper, and more immediate would be an office assistant who could answer the phone, reply to emails, and suggest priorities.

His jobs in Madrid, Oslo, Bucharest and Brussels had taken twice as long as was truly necessary, simply because of the need to split his time between the current client and potential future ones. Where could he get hold of suitable reinforcements?

At that moment, two people came in from the street. Up to this point, not a single conceivable customer had arrived by this route; emails and phone calls were the way to go. But there was a first time for everything. These two were a young white woman and an equally young Black man. The woman wished him a good day and said that she and her friend had been the victims of a wrong that they wished to right. They had spotted the shop window of Sweet Sweet Revenge Ltd. by chance. Now they wondered if this business did indeed provide aid in the form of revenge, or whether she and her friend had misunderstood the name and operations.

Typically, Hugo had to reject two out of every three people who contacted him on the spot. Such as the man who wanted to enact revenge on the United States Senate. Or the woman who wanted help destroying an entire breed of dog. It was easy to break contact with these sorts of folks as long as that contact was electronic. But now there stood two real-life potential clients right in front of him. It wouldn't be as painless to wave them off, should it prove necessary. And that was the most likely scenario.

In any case, he asked them to have a seat and give him a brief account of where the shoe was pinching, so to speak.

"Thanks," said Jenny.

"That's kind of you," said Kevin. "Would you like to begin, Jenny?"

She would. But a brief account it was not. She told him about her childhood, her teenage years, and about Victor, whom she had married for the sake of her father. And how her husband had swindled her and danced on her father's grave by stealing her inheritance.

At first, Hugo listened with interest. A high-class art gallery. That had potential. But what was this last bit, about her inheritance?

Well, evil Victor had swindled Jenny so thoroughly that not a single öre was left over for her.

"I was robbed of everything," she concluded. "My childhood, my youth, my inheritance, my life. I have nothing left. *Nothing!*"

Nothing left? Then how did she intend to pay? There was something fundamentally wrong with people. Or did the money belong to the young man beside her?

"How about you?" he addressed Kevin. "Has the art dealer confiscated what you were to inherit from your father, as well?"

"I've never had a father," said Kevin. "And I don't have a mother anymore either, she died of AIDS. But my former guardian—you know who—took me to Kenya and left me for the lions."

Hugo couldn't send them away now. He had to know more.

Kevin's story was absolutely incredible. In the true sense of the word. It was perhaps—*perhaps*—true that he had been left on the savanna to become lion fodder. But the rest of it! That the boy should have been rescued by a local medicine man, adopted, trained as a Maasai, taught to swim among crocodiles, escaped forced circumcision, and more besides.

"Thanks, that'll do," said Hugo.

"But I'm not finished yet. When I got back to Sweden, I met Jenny. It turned out she had been tormented by the same man . . ."

Hugo had already checked out.

"Right, you ran into each other on the street. 'Hi,

I'm Kevin, this guy called Victor was mean to me! Oh, you, too?'"

This was the type of client a future assistant could keep away from him. As if this wasn't enough, the woman had started to cry.

"So you can't help us?" she said.

Hugo couldn't have put it better himself.

"Exactly! I can't help you. Your stories are heart-breaking. But Sweet Sweet Revenge has a responsibility to its shareholders. Your sorrow won't make them any happier. What I mean is, we need to get paid for our services, and if you have—as you say—nothing left, that's not much for the shareholders to split."

Kevin asked who these shareholders were. Hugo said the share register mainly consisted of Hugo himself, but that he was looking forward to going public in the very near future.

Jenny tried to find a way to move forward.

"Wouldn't the principal owner consider working on credit?"

Hugo tried to hide his annoyance. He had three priority jobs on his desk. Two of them seemed very promising: one, a Dutchman who wanted to get revenge on his neighbor; the other, the neighbor, who wanted revenge in return. A fantastic coincidence. Since they remained unaware of one another's intentions, there was every chance Hugo could help them destroy each other while he took all their money. But instead of being on his way to Amsterdam, he was sitting here coddling Little Miss Destitute and her Crocodile Dundee.

"No, that's precisely what he cannot do. I need money in advance in order to sign an agreement. Barring that you may certainly take revenge on whoever you want, however you want, but you'll have to do so elsewhere and without my help."

He wanted at least fifty thousand kronor just to open a case.

"But the money is with Victor Alderheim," said Jenny.

"Bully for him," said Hugo.

"I have a painting to use as payment," said Kevin.

"You do?" said Jenny.

My God! The art dealer's protégé wants to pay with a *painting*! One he made himself?

Kevin had completely forgotten what he took from Papa Ole but had been reminded of it when he opened the backpack to change clothes in the café bathroom.

He took a rolled-up object from the bag; it had been carefully wrapped in paper.

"My adoptive father Ole Mbatian made it. I think

it's lovely! It seems he has a little expressionist inside him, although he doesn't know it."

He unrolled the painting on Hugo's desk.

"He calls it *Woman with Parasol*. Or, I don't know what he calls it, but he wrote *Woman with Parasol* on the back.

"I see," said Hugo.

Enough was enough.

"Now listen here. I don't care if this painting is called "Rocky 2." Can't you two just please go away? Before you arrived I was thinking about hiring an assistant to protect me from people like you, and now I'm wondering if I don't need two. And a padlock on the door."

Jenny was surprisingly quiet after Hugo's dressing-down. Her tears had dried. She looked at the painting she'd never seen before. And looked a little more.

"That's an Irma Stern," she said, without taking her eyes from the painting.

"Irma who?" said Hugo, without actually wanting to know.

"Stern. One of the greatest expressionists of our time."

Now these fools were about to take their fantasies to a new level.

"Worth millions, right?" said Hugo. "Go. Now. Get out."

A piece of art painted by a medicine man on the savanna and one of the greatest expressionists of all time. Simultaneously.

"I'm not sure about millions," Kevin said. "I sold an almost identical one in Mombasa for a thousand dollars so I could afford to fly here. It's no Irma Stern. It's an Ole Mbatian the Younger. Maybe he's got more of them back home. Or back there. Or wherever it is I belong now."

Hugo said that young Kevin was welcome to belong wherever he liked, as long as it wasn't in Hugo's office. And then he repeated his wish—nay, demand!—that they leave.

"And take your Irma with you!"

"Not Irma," said Kevin. "Ole Mbatian."

"Him too."

Jenny stayed put. At last she tore her gaze from the Irma Stern and said that it must be an Ole Mbatian after all, since Irma had died in 1966. But it was a fantastic copy. So precise that it could fool anyone at all.

"If it were a genuine Irma, it would be worth half a million dollars or more."

What had that crybaby of a woman just said? A painting that could fool anyone at all. Out of half a million dollars.

Hugo couldn't help it—his thoughts began to revolve around how best to get this Victor Alderheim to purchase an Ole even as he paid for an Irma. That kind of revenge would certainly cross the line in a legal sense, but it would likely remain within the boundaries of Hugo's moral framework. Alderheim seemed to be of an extraordinarily unpleasant nature. Perhaps to an extent that was worth half a million dollars. Or more.

Jenny and Kevin noticed that Hugo was weighing an alternative to chasing them back into the street. Jenny, who hadn't helped herself to anything ever in her life, helped herself.

"You were saying you needed an assistant? I'm applying for the position. I'm neat and tidy, I'm responsible, and I am always on time to work. I'm good at locking up and opening too. And making coffee. I'm handy with internet connections. I am socially competent, I think. I've never really tried. I don't need much for a salary. Or anything at all, in fact."

Hugo dropped his sudden thoughts of gross fraud and looked at Jenny.

"As long as we take down Victor Alderheim?"

There, he had shown his hand.

Jenny smiled.

Even the fact that the man across from her was considering one thing and the next was a terrific development. Jenny felt that she wanted to say more, something that would tip the odds in their favor, but she didn't know what. Whatever she said next, it had to be the right thing. Kevin felt the same way. They were so close to getting the boss of Sweet Sweet Revenge Ltd. on their side, but close wouldn't cut it.

After a few short but eternal seconds, Hugo Hamlin was done thinking.

"No," he said. "Something is off here. I can feel it. your stories are too good. Not least the last one. Dumped on the savanna, adopted by a medicine man, trained to be a Maasai. The fact that you found one another and then me. And suddenly: a painting worth anywhere from nothing to half a million dollars. I can't take it. You're welcome to come back once you've got your hands on a five-thousand-kronor advance. Thanks for stopping by. Farewell."

Jenny felt that she had gone all in. But Kevin stood up. Not to leave, as Hugo had expected.

"I just had an idea," he said.

He walked past the desk behind Hugo and into the kitchenette. Once there, he opened the refrigerator, where he found nothing but a carton of milk and yesterday's sandwiches. The adjoining pantry was even emptier. Or was it? At the very back were some canned goods.

"Don't touch those, no matter how hungry you may be," said Hugo. "They've been there since this office was a toy factory, or whatever it was."

"I'm not going to eat anything," said Kevin, grabbing a can of corn with his right hand.

He appeared to be judging its heft.

"I'm just going to clear up some doubts. I think it might move this conversation forward."

With canned corn in hand, he went back to his side of Hugo's desk. To the horror of the former adman, he began to undress, removing both pants and shirt.

"What on earth . . ."

But before Hugo was finished being fazed, there stood before him a young Maasai warrior, wearing a *shúkà* and sandals.

"Please follow me," said the Maasai.

Kevin went to the front door, stood on the sidewalk outside, and looked around. He waved Hugo over with his free hand.

"Can't this day just be over yet?" said the adman.

Kevin made up his mind. Fifty or so meters away was a sign proclaiming a parking ban.

"See that no-parking sign over there?"

"Yeah, what about it?" said Hugo. "Just try to find a sign that says parking is *allowed* in central Stockholm. If you can do that, I swear I'll believe everything you say."

Kevin's aim was not to discuss the parking politics of the inner city but—like he'd said—to clear up doubts. And his best idea (his only idea) along those lines was what was about to happen.

He said no more, just aimed the can of corn and threw it. Over the heads of Stockholm pedestrians. Over two passing cars. Between a lamppost and some temporarily hung winter lighting. Fifty meters or more, through the air. And right into the solar plexus of the no-parking sign he'd pointed out.

"Nice throw!" said Jenny.

"*Natumaini kuwa alivutiwa*," said Kevin.

"Hope that impressed him," in Swahili. For dramatic flair.

Hugo stood with his mouth agape, looking at the hateful no-parking sign. It was still shaking.

"My name is Kevin," said Kevin. "Adopted son of Ole Mbatian the Younger. Fully trained Maasai warrior by trade, except for a circumcision that never happened. That sign could have been a charging Cape buffalo. The can of corn could have been my throwing club. In which case, I just saved all of our lives. If you still don't believe me, I ask you to track down a well-balanced spear, for I have more to show you. Otherwise, I too am applying for the advertised position. The two of us, Jenny and I, could share both job and salary."

Now what? Hugo considered the possibility that two of the world's biggest mythomaniacs were telling the truth. The crocodile hunter was apparently for real. The young woman's tears seemed genuine. The medicine man's Irma-whatever-her-name-was fake certainly had its qualities. What if the rest were true as well?

They still had no money. Only the painting.

On the other hand: two free assistants equaled twenty-five thousand kronor plus twenty-five thousand kronor plus social insurance fees in sheer profit each month. It wasn't possible to calculate it like that, but that was how Hugo calculated it. Money was delightful even in the form of costs he didn't have to bear immediately after he'd decided to bear them.

Anyway. He didn't have enough faith in chance to believe it had led Jenny and Kevin arm-in-arm to his little office in Östermalm. It was as unbelievable as a youngster taking an old can of corn from a pantry and using it to strike the exact point he'd said he would strike, from a distance of over fifty meters. In one try.

Fucking canned corn.

Double assistants at the office, neither of whom drew any salary. Taken strictly on its own, that was world-class business economics. But to keep them long-term, he would have to get involved in the Victor Alderheim project, which was worth zero kronor. Or alternately, half a million dollars, depending on how creative Hugo managed to be. There was no in between.

Time to enter into discreet negotiations.

"I can't work on the art dealer full-time," he said.

"That's okay," said Jenny. "We're in no hurry, it's fine."

"Or even half-time."

The young woman looked more hesitant.

"How much can you work, then?"

Not the right time to go lower.

"Maybe half-time. But not right now."

He bought himself time to think by deciding it was time for the workday to be over. It had already involved more than a single day could withstand. Or a whole week, really. But if Jenny and Kevin liked, they were welcome to come back the next morning at nine sharp. Then Hugo would show them the basics of how the office was run, including how to handle potential clients. Freeloading clients like themselves were sent away on the spot.

What to do about that Victor was something they would deal with later. First Hugo had to make a business trip to Amsterdam and back. He expected to return before the week was out. When he returned he expected a report on Victor Alderheim, his strengths and weaknesses.

"Once I've seen that, I promise to apprise you of the job's potential. But I want to make one thing very clear from the start: If, against all expectations, any income arises as this project advances, it will go to Sweet Sweet Revenge Ltd. In full. This may be in the form of money, oil paintings, or canned corn— everything goes to me, because I am covering all expenses. Are we in agreement?"

Jenny nodded. But Kevin was hungry and thinking of the future.

"What do you say to five hundred kronor for a daily allowance? Purely for business reasons, so your assistants don't starve to death."

Hugo had already put down double free salaries. He didn't want to lose them now.

"Two hundred," he said.

"Four," Kevin countered.

Hugo took out his wallet, found four five-hundred-kronor notes and another hundred. He handed them to Kevin.

"Three hundred per day, this will cover the first week. Time to go our separate ways. Well-rested brains do better thinking."

Chapter 22

J enny and Kevin were ten minutes late the next morning; to save money they had walked the whole way—eighteen kilometers—which took three hours and forty-five minutes.

"I'll overlook it this time," said Hugo.

Deducting from their salary was out of the question.

The boss at Sweet Sweet Revenge Ltd. looked at his two new colleagues and felt satisfied. Not every small business owner could keep pace with his rate of new hires.

Hugo kicked off the workday by initiating his assistants in the operations.

The first thing they needed to know was that clients who called on the phone must be treated with kindness and respect, as long as they indicated they could pay their way. And that the revenge they were after was somewhat reasonable. Otherwise, the call should be ended as quickly as possible, so it wasn't tying up the lines for others.

"What counts as reasonable?" Kevin wondered.

Hugo searched his memory for some of the most recent proposals.

"Anyone who is looking for changes in the British line to the throne should look elsewhere."

Kevin nodded and said he thought he understood.

Hugo went on: Those who made it through the first stage of review should be asked to describe their issue in an email message. In Swedish, if they happened to be from Sweden; otherwise, preferably in English. At a pinch—that is, if the client truly had demonstrated that he or she had money—the firm would accept any language. Now including Swahili and Maa, as far as Hugo understood (the more he thought about it, the more satisfied he was with his two free assistants).

Incoming emails should be printed out and archived in the filing cabinet under the desk, given that they lived up to the standards of reasonableness.

"I'm extra good at archiving," said Jenny. "In alphabetical order?"

"Hell no—by financial upsides."

———

The rest of the morning was devoted to coffee breaks and further instructions. Hugo's flight to Amsterdam was to leave just after two in the afternoon. As a final handover, the young man and woman were given keys to the office; they took over responsibility for the business cell phone and were handed one of the company's two credit cards, plus PIN code.

"To be used exclusively for work-related items and according to your best judgment."

They could have a little wiggle room. Leadership was to be trusted, or whatever leadership was. Hugo was excited about what was to come. The thought of revenge had its advantages, but for the first time in several years he truly felt *alive*.

A few days later, the morning paper *The Telegraph* ran the story of a neighborly feud that had gone off the rails. What had begun with a few branches of a cherry tree overhanging a property line had led to the tree in question catching fire at one in the morning, completely out of the blue. What followed was an inexplicably severed fiber optic cable, taking out the internet and TV of the neighbor of the man with the burned-down tree. Twenty-four hours later, the man who no longer had a cherry tree also had no drinking water, for an unfortunate leak on the wrong side of the property line had resulted in two hundred liters of oil in his well.

By the time Hugo took off, the neighbors had learned their lessons well. The first one continued the feud by laying a spike strip in the other's driveway, in response to which the other set the first one's tool shed ablaze, after which the first one shot the other one in the ass with a shotgun. When the police arrived, they caught the one who'd been shot red-handed in the kitchen as he was injecting insecticide into plastic bottles of Coca-Cola. He could not explain why.

All this was going on as Hugo landed at Arlanda Airport in Stockholm, 8,500 euros richer.

When he got back to the office, nothing was as he had left it. The assistants each had a mobile phone. And a laptop. The large window that faced the street was covered by a tasteful, light curtain. The single desk was now accompanied by a conference corner with a table, chairs, and double whiteboards. The wall to the left of the boss's spot was decorated with a poster—a portrait of a woman. In addition, Kevin had both built and published a new website that provided the contact information for the boss and his assistants. Who weren't even assistants anymore. Jenny was chief of financial operations. Kevin was project leader. Fortunately, Hugo himself was still managing director.

Nowadays the firm had a digital client database where potential clients were rated on a scale from one to five, based on the presumed fatness of their wallets. Project Leader was in charge of this assessment.

"How much did all of this cost?" Hugo asked.

"Just a moment," said Jenny, bringing up Excel. "Seventy-four thousand two hundred and twenty kronor, more or less."

"More or less?"

"Well, okay, that much exactly. I was trying not to sound too self-important."

Hugo sank into his office chair. Heavily.

"Any other news? Have we purchased Astra Zeneca? Applied for membership on the UN Security Council?"

No, nothing like that.

"But we did get engaged," said Jenny.

"What the hell are you talking about? You haven't even known each other for a week yet, have you?"

"Eight days."

Hugo muttered something about how this would have to be it for expenses.

"We need engagement rings, though," said Kevin. "Nothing too spendy, but . . . well, even the cheap ones aren't exactly cheap. Could we maybe get an advance on our salary?"

"You don't draw a salary! Or did you change that, too?"

Jenny and Kevin didn't reply.

"How much do you need?"

Kevin smiled. They had bought their extra mattress from a second-hand store in Bollmora, and the owner there stocked everything under the sun. What he had above all were two rings of almost genuine gold for which he was asking two hundred kronor apiece. Not much, but more than the couple's budget allowed. After weekly commuter passes and food in the fridge and pantry, their allowance was gone.

"The two of you sure are expensive, for being free," said Hugo, taking out his wallet.

Jenny said the second-hand store owner had offered a receipt; he was otherwise receiptless by nature. If they wanted, they could call the rings office supplies.

"We do want. Congrats on your engagement, by the way, in case I didn't say that already."

Now, what was leadership again? To be trusted? Well, howdy-do! But there was still something beautiful about the initiative the CFO and Project Leader had taken. The only truly unnecessary investment Hugo could identify was the poster on the wall. It depicted a woman with red hair, blue lips, and big, dark, almost mean eyes.

"Who is she?" he asked.

The painting was called *Head of a Woman*; the original hung in the National Gallery in Edinburgh. The artist was Alexei von Jawlensky. Jenny had found the redhead at the second-hand shop and couldn't help herself.

"A masterpiece, if you ask me. The owner wanted a tenner for her, but I gave him twenty."

Paying double what was necessary was not what Hugo liked to hear. Also, a masterpiece? The redhead was looking at him with her dark gaze. He got the sense that she refused to take her eyes off him.

"Don't you have anything else to stare at?"

Jenny was pleased. Now all three of them talked to works of art.

Chapter 23

CFO Jenny praised Hugo for his work in Amsterdam and said that the company's finances were looking very healthy. So healthy, in fact, that the firm could afford to spend a few weeks on jobs less certain to result in financial gains.

"And you have one of these in the database?"

"Yes, as it happens," said Project Leader Kevin. "I just found one about an evil art dealer here in Östermalm."

Hugo didn't like the idea of working for free. But he couldn't help taking a liking to his new colleagues.

"Where is that report you promised to write up?"

Hugo had been picturing a sheet of A4 with a few bullet points to glance through. But Kevin pulled up what he and Jenny had put together from the digital archive and began to print it out.

Page after page fed out. It seemed like it would never end, and Hugo wondered if the printer was acting up.

"Twenty-six pages," Kevin proudly stated.

"Are you two quite right?"

It had taken the couple two long nights in a row to compile their report. Hugo had never intended to do more than skim through it, no matter how long it was. He had mostly just asked them to write it up so he could head off to Amsterdam in peace and quiet.

"What is there, in these twenty-six pages, that I haven't already heard from you?" he said, feeling as if he had just saved himself an hour's work.

Jenny and Kevin exchanged glances.

"Just the essentials?"

"Just the essentials is great."

"Then I would say we have the key to both art gallery and apartment. When I said he stole everything from me, that was only almost true. I still had the keys in the pocket of my jacket."

This fact was to Hugo's liking.

"So he hasn't changed the locks?"

There was no way of knowing, of course, but Jenny didn't think her ex-husband had the good sense to do that, any more than he did in most other ways.

"Tell me, who is Victor, and what is his greatest interest? His money or his reputation?"

"It says right here," Kevin attempted. "Starting on page eight, we . . ."

"Great, so you know the answer."

Jenny said that the most important factor was not *who* Victor was, but *what*. In short, a pig. A rat. A snake—

Hugo cut her off before she managed to drag further innocent species through the mud.

"Money or reputation?"

"Can't we shoot for both?"

Hugo was on the verge of saying that he would then have to double the price, before he realized what project he was dealing with at the moment. Ugh! Where would it end?

He shook off his negative thoughts. Forward!

"This Irma Stern . . . what relationship does Alderheim have to her?"

"Not Irma Stern," said Kevin. "Ole Mbatian the Younger."

Hugo was aware. But as long as the same wasn't true of Victor Alderheim, they had a potential way in.

Jenny said what she'd already said, that Ole Mbatian's *Woman with Parasol* was a first-class painting and it was amazingly similar to a typical Irma Stern. When Victor was new to the industry, and Jenny was still a child, he had at most been able to point out a

Monet, and then only if given a few guesses and if it had enough water lilies in it.

"But now? After twenty years in the industry?" Jenny pondered.

She was loath to give the pig, rat and snake any sort of credit.

"We should probably assume he'll see that this is an Irma Stern if we put it in front of him."

Then she realized what she'd said.

"I'm sorry, Kevin. That this *looks* like an Irma Stern."

"Thank you," said Kevin.

Hugo was immediately back to top form. Was Jenny saying that the only way you could tell an Irma Stern from the Ole Mbatian painting was the lack of a signature?

She was.

Was she also saying that the price of a genuine *Woman with Parasol* ought to come in around half a million dollars? Or was he misremembering?

He was not. But Jenny had had time to do some more research since then. The least a genuine Irma Stern of this type would fetch was more like a million dollars.

"Or more," she said.

What had Kevin said? Was there a fake Irma in Mombasa as well?

"It's all in the report," said Kevin.

"Just answer the question, please."

Kevin grabbed the twenty-six pages and read aloud from page twenty-one. So, he had brought with him two paintings from his adoptive father's art collection, the ones he could find. If Kevin hadn't succeeded in selling the other one to an art dealer along the way, he wouldn't have been able to afford to get back to Sweden.

This was shaping up to be a good day. First there were the keys, and now this. One piece of the puzzle after the next! There were *two* Ole Mbatians out there, and one could only assume that both were equally likely to be mistaken for Irma Sterns. Ole Mbatian plus Ole Mbatian equaled two thousand dollars. Irma Stern plus Irma Stern equaled two million.

"The painting in Mombasa, is it also a woman with a parasol?"

"No, it was called *Boy by Stream*."

"Is the boy of the same quality as the woman with the parasol?"

Yes, Kevin expected he was. An Ole Mbatian was an Ole Mbatian.

The more Hugo thought about it, the more he wished they also had access to painting number two. What if they could get both into Victor's hands? He could have a friends-and-family discount at half a million apiece. At which point he would sell them as genuine, at which point Sweet Sweet Revenge Ltd.—or, even better, Ole Mbatian the Younger—would pop up to let everyone know what was really going on.

Then the art dealer would be labeled a criminal, or at least an incompetent. While Hugo enjoyed his money.

Once all was said and done, he would treat Jenny and Kevin to a lavish café visit. And maybe even raise their allowance.

"That's all for today," he said. "Tomorrow I'm flying to Mombasa to buy the second of Ole Mbatian's Irma Stern paintings. While I'm gone, promise me you won't splash out more than usual. And preferably less."

All he needed from them now was the name and address of the African art dealer.

"Don't tell me it's in the report," he said to Kevin, who was about to say just that.

Jenny understood that the boss had a plan and wondered if he would share it with the staff. Hugo informed her that she shouldn't bother a creative while he was working.

"I'll tell you when I get home. Now run off and get married or something, in the meantime, you've already been engaged for days."

Chapter 24

M ombasa is a city of a million people on an island of the same name. The city has been a popular place throughout the centuries. Not so much for its great beauty as for what its surroundings could bring to those who were sufficiently enterprising. Like the Portuguese in the sixteenth century. They conquered the region with violence and began to trade in ivory and gold. Only to watch the Arabs come in and destroy their fortune. The Portuguese and the Arabs spent a few centuries arguing over dominion before the British swooped in and put their foot down. The tea-drinking Englishmen identified Mombasa as the perfect place to grow coffee beans. They seized the island in an afternoon and shipped down British farmers, not so much to do work as to put Indians and Africans to work. But the coffee was good.

For reasons both logistical and political, Mombasa was annexed to British East Africa and the whole package was promoted, becoming the colony of Kenya. This all happened without seeking the input of the local population; anyway, they were ungrateful in every way. Instead of seeing potential in an agrarian future, they began to organize in protest against the fact that British settlers were staking a claim on land they didn't own, both in Mombasa and in the Kenyan highlands. Even though the former owners were placed in newly built huts in the bush and offered jobs on the white gentlemen's plantations as compensation, they weren't satisfied. To be sure, the salaries they were offered were non-existent. But what kinds of expenses could someone who lived in a hut possibly have?

The parties had different views on customs and fashions. This led to arguments that led to uprisings that led to bloody war. Two hundred British soldiers and settlers paid with their lives. In the background, twenty thousand members of the native population perished as well.

The British both won and lost. Back home in London, some began to spread the message that it was ridiculous for the Empire to travel around the world, seizing other people's land and basically enslaving those who were there from the start. According to others, these warm, fuzzy feelings for the Black people was communism plain and simple, but the controversial question started to take hold in popular opinion. To the extent that one day, the British had no choice but to allow the Kenyans to rule themselves. On December 12, 1963, the country—Mombasa included—became independent.

In Kenya's second-biggest city you will find history, culture, languages, flavors and scents from all over the world. And exciting people. Including an art dealer not far from the massive harbor of Kilindini, with a Somali mother and British soldier-slash-rapist father. The art dealer understandably had little patience for whites, but in the name of commerce he hid it well.

Therefore he gave a friendly smile when the first customer of the day, a white, a *mzungu*, entered. Hugo nodded in greeting and immediately spotted what he was looking for on the wall.

The oil painting *Boy by Stream* reached—as far as Hugo could ascertain—artistic heights easily matching those of *Woman with Parasol*. Ole Mbatian definitely had qualities beyond the typical.

"What do you want for that one there?" Hugo asked, possibly sounding a little too eager.

Eagerness is not what you want to demonstrate while bargaining in any context. In Mombasa, it's downright stupid.

A *mzungu* with money who knows what he wants, thought the art dealer. This might turn into a lovely afternoon.

"A very good choice, sir. But I'm so enchanted by that painting that I think I want to keep it."

This was not the truth. Just a few weeks earlier, a youngster had come into the store with a rolled-up, unsigned oil painting. Normally the art dealer would never offer more than fifty dollars for something like that. And that was assuming conditions were favorable. Otherwise, more like five.

But this youngster gave a lovely speech about his father's painting and generally conducted himself in a likable way. Plus, *Boy by Stream* looked tremendously similar to an Irma Stern! If he were to scribble on a signature and sell the painting honestly as "a wonderful forgery of one of the great daughters of the continent," the art dealer might get one, two, three or maybe even four thousand dollars for it. Of course, he didn't mention this to the youngster. He did, however, surprise himself by paying the young man the thousand-dollar bill he had pleaded for. Perhaps he was getting soft.

The art dealer intended to deal with the signature bit when he had a chance. In the meantime he hung the painting in the store; after all, it was very nice.

And now this *mzungu* was standing here asking for that very item and none other.

"Why do you have it on display in the store if you don't want to sell it?"

The art dealer answered by not answering, but painted a vivid picture (fittingly enough) of his difficult upbringing, about his mother, about her arthritis and how expensive it was to buy medicine in Mombasa. It was a different story in Mozambique, but of course that was very far away.

"The painting is not for sale, like I said, but five thousand dollars would buy a lot of medicine."

Hugo sighed, sensing shades of Workplace Safety Inspector Broman, but thought it was just as pointless to argue now as it had been back then. Best to pay before the price went up.

The negotiations over, the art dealer was in good spirits. His anxiety about his mother was gone. As he rolled and packaged the painting, he hummed a melody she'd once taught him. He apologized to the client for not knowing all the words, but it so happened that the leading Somali language had neither alphabet nor dictionary. His memory was all he could consult, and as everyone knew, that started to let you down once you were past thirty-five.

The client who had just paid five thousand dollars for a thousand-dollar painting that really shouldn't have cost more than a hundred was not in the mood to discuss Somali linguistics.

"Hurry up, if you please."

Well, well, the *mzungu* was a sore loser. Still, bad winners were worse. Now it was time to show some generosity. The art dealer had a special glass jar under the counter for that very purpose.

"May I offer you a chocolate cream in celebration of sealing the deal?"

Hugo was grumpy. Deep down, this was because he had bungled the negotiations, but he wouldn't admit it even to himself.

"You can keep your chocolates. Or give them to your mother. Maybe they're good for arthritis. But please, speed it up. And call me a taxi. I'm going to the airport."

With that, the art dealer in turn lost patience with his client.

"Call it yourself," he said, putting the glass jar back in its place.

"Very well. Do you know the number?"

"No. But I think it starts with a four."

Chapter 25

*B*oy by Stream lived up to all of Jenny's expectations. It was singularly profound; it depicted a lone Black boy with a luster that took her breath away. The boy was holding a dry stick, about to dip it in the water. His loneliness, coupled with his happiness over such a small thing. The thoughtfulness in the boy's eyes, the fire in his forehead like a mirror reflecting the entire dramatic continent of Africa.

"My father-in-law-to-be is a genius," she said.

"Thanks," said Kevin.

At last it was time for the director to tell them his plan. The project leader was eager to learn how the project would unfold, as was the one who was ultimately responsible for all the financial details.

Hugo had got over being swindled in Mombasa.

Once again, all he saw were possibilities. But he might as well leave the young 'uns in a state of suspense for a little while longer.

"First let's get some food in our bellies," he said, feeling pleased with himself.

After lunch, the trio were back in the office. Hugo asked Jenny and Kevin to have a seat around the conference table. Then he cleared his throat and launched into his explanation.

It was true that Hugo didn't know much about the art world, but he was fully versed in the machinations of the human soul. Thus the trio could rest assured that no art dealer had yet been born who wouldn't jump to pay at least five hundred thousand dollars for a million-dollar painting. Furthermore, now that they had two, the amount could only double.

"We will, however, be best served by pitching them to Alderheim via messenger. All we need is the signature. You'll have to be in charge of that, Jenny."

The CFO looked at Hugo and asked if what they'd just heard was his plan.

A million dollars in the bank. For a plan, that would do. Hugo would have been happy to leave the Victor Alderheim affair behind him once the money came in, but he could tell by Jenny's tepid reaction that she and Kevin needed to see the conned man tortured a little more. That was just the way people were made.

"Was that the whole plan? No sir. Once we've got the money, we'll wait for him to sell the forgeries on, and then we'll reveal the truth. We're filthy rich, or that's mostly just me actually, and Victor's reputation is ruined. I get mine; you get yours. Everyone's happy. Except Victor. And whoever's stuck with the fake paintings, but every war has its victims."

Jenny wasn't as enthusiastic as Hugo had expected. Not at all. Had all his delightful revenge jobs made him too cynical, or was something else going on? Kevin was paging through that damned report.

There had been a few, sporadic occasions in the past in which the great creative mind had been blinded by its own achievements. These all occurred during his first, and extremely successful, years. When enough of what he touched turned to gold, it was as if all humility took a back seat. As if he were invincible. To this day, he shuddered at the memory of how he had forced through a multimillion-dollar campaign for a mobile phone manufacturer that then launched its cute little device, early in the smartphone era, under the motto "Not too smart." That was precisely the problem with the device. That manufacturer no longer existed.

Why was Hugo thinking of this now? Should he have looped in the woman who actually knew something about art at a slightly earlier stage?

"Have you ever, in any context, heard the word "authentication"?" asked Jenny.

"It's in the report," said Kevin.

"If you had kept your damn report shorter than the freaking Old Testament, maybe I could have managed to read it, but by all means. Enlighten me!"

To put it simply, you could say that various authorities all over the world specialized in different artists and became considered trustworthy enough to issue certificates of authenticity.

"To put it simply, that is," said Jenny.

"Let's stick to the simple things. Go on."

It would not be simple to get Ole Mbatian classified as an Irma Stern. It wouldn't even be difficult. It would be impossible.

"The plan falls apart at its provenance."

"Please speak plain Swedish."

"Page twenty-four," said Kevin.

A genuine painting must have a crystal-clear and spotless history, from the artist's hands all the way to the wall in the home of the current owner, with documentation for each change of ownership and the associated receipts in between. Sure, they could sit around thinking up an exciting backstory for the Ole paintings, but who would believe it?

Hugo went cold. *Not too smart.*

"Are you saying that half a million dollars just slipped through my fingers? Our fingers."

"If that's how you'd like to look at it," said the CFO. "Plus the round trip to Mombasa, one night at a hotel, and the cost of *Boy by Stream.*"

Hugo didn't want to hear any more.

"You flew business class, so that's about eighty-two thousand kronor for the trip, lodging, and the painting. It is my unfortunate duty to inform you that this burdens our profits for the current month."

He had embarrassed himself but he was not going to give up. Not yet.

"But if paintings can be forged, can't we just do the same with the provenance?"

Jenny didn't think so. But say they could. Then it would fall apart during brushstroke analysis. This more than anything would reveal Ole Mbatian, unless he didn't just paint like Irma Stern—which of course he did—but also used the exact same brushstrokes as Irma had in her day. Over the years, the inventor of brushstroke analysis had made many a forger unhappy.

"Damn him to hell," said Hugo.

"That's all said and done," said Jenny. "He died in 1890-something."

Hugo said he'd read about the carbon 14 method. Could that be a feasible way?

He was getting desperate.

Kevin wondered how chemical dating of their Ole could prove it was an Irma.

Hugo had no idea.

Jenny advised him to let it go. Carbon dating could determine the age of a painting within about fifty years, nothing more. In this case, it would prove that their Irma Stern artworks had been painted by anyone at any time during the twentieth century or later. Which, of course, they were.

"Ole Mbatian isn't just anyone," said his adopted son.

Hugo was so angry with himself that he took it out on Kevin.

"Can we just agree that Ole Mbatian, in all his glory, is not Irma Stern? And that she is not him?"

Hugo fell silent. He withdrew into himself. He was full of very dark thoughts.

But inside Jenny was a glimmer of hope; she had learned that a brooding Hugo was a thinking Hugo.

And she was right about that. Hugo was thinking that the Victor Alderheim project had two purposes: one was to trick the art dealer out of money for Hugo's sake; the other was to destroy Alderheim's life more generally, after which the firm's staff could sleep easy at night. Or whatever it was they did at night, newly engaged as they were.

Now all that was left was purpose number two. Hugo would need to work for free, but then again that had been a condition from the start. His failure in Mombasa was entirely his own fault; he could feel the frustration.

"Here's what we're going to do," he said. "Instead of making the paintings as authentic as possible, we'll do the opposite."

"As *inauthentic* as possible?" Jenny wondered, thinking that this sounded peculiar.

"Yes. We'll make them as goddamn fake as we possibly can."

There was no longer any money to be made on this project. Only expenses. That pig, rat, snake Alderheim would pay for that.

Sweet Sweet Re-fucking-venge Ltd.

It felt good to swear. Shit!

Chapter 26

Together they hammered out the details. After all, it had proven suboptimal to keep the assistants in the dark about the plan.

Intended target Victor seldom or never went down to the archive in the cellar. Jenny could swear it would look just as it had when she was there before Christmas. Besides the files about works bought and sold, there were easels and other items necessary for the production of one's own oil paintings. This was Jenny's doing or fault. Once, as a teenager, she had gathered her courage and tried to depict her lostness in shapes and colors. Nothing had come of it, as with life in general. Until recently.

Step one of Hugo's plan was for the trio to sneak in at night and rig the Ole Mbatian paintings on easels, so they seemed to be works in progress. Next to them, painted on paper, a number of attempts at imitating Irma Stern's signature. This was, of course, the only thing still left to do before the paintings were complete. Any uninitiated onlooker would come to the immediate conclusion that the cellar was actually a forger's studio.

Kevin wasn't happy about giving away Papa Ole's paintings in this manner, and to the very man on earth who deserved them least of all. But he came to terms with the operation given that it would serve a higher purpose.

Jenny had a few matter-of-fact objections. Creating paintings as good as a real artist was not a crime. Nor was imitating an artist's signature on a piece of paper. It was only when a fake signature ended up on an equally fake artwork that things got dicey.

Hugo had also considered this. But in the days of social networks, there was this thing called the court of popular opinion. If Sweet Sweet Revenge's proud staffers would simply do their jobs right, Victor Alderheim would be sentenced to life by both the people and the global art-dealer industry. Surely this was worth more than a few years in prison for attempted fraud.

"Why not try for both?" said Kevin. "If the part with Papa Ole's paintings is only half illegal, couldn't we throw in something more?"

"Drugs!" said Jenny.

This was the most illegal thing she could think of.

"Porn," Kevin suggested.

Hugo was proud of his colleagues. Naturally they would place a few bags of heroin on the table next to the paintings. Porn was not necessarily equally illegal, but even clear signs of "kinky sex" would aid their cause.

Neither Jenny nor Kevin felt comfortable with the concept of "kinky sex." They themselves had come no further in their development than leaving the ceiling light on one time when they did it. But as a teenager in Bollmora, Kevin had surfed around on various gaming sites, and the step from those to who knows what was never a long one. He therefore had a certain amount of theoretical knowledge concerning items such as remote-controlled vibrating eggs, butt plugs for beginners, and that old standby, the penis pump. Plus things he didn't quite understand, such as chains, canes, masks, and just about anything you could imagine made of leather.

"I can be in charge of getting suitable sex toys," he said.

"You can?" said Jenny.

"Very good, Kevin," said Hugo. "You can have seven thousand kronor for a toy budget, but that must include a blow-up doll."

Which left the drugs. Opiates would be very of-the-day. Hugo had read that the United States was in the process of killing itself by that route. Physicians far and wide were prescribing painkillers for body and mind at a rate never before seen, eagerly cheered on by the manufacturers and their marketing teams. The average life expectancy for men was falling at such a pace that if nothing changed, there would no longer be any men left in 380 years.

"That's sad for the men," said Kevin.

"Almost as sad for the women too, I imagine," said Jenny.

Hugo asked them to stick to the topic at hand. Even better, they should be quiet for a moment, for he was about to call his brother.

Big brother Malte, the now reasonably renowned eye doctor, had always done as his little brother had asked. He also put everything else aside whenever Hugo called.

"Hello, dear brother," said Hugo.

"Hello yourself. How are things? I've got an operation in a few minutes, but tell me what I can do for you."

Hugo had originally planned to pad his request with niceties, but there wasn't time for that now.

"I'd like you to prescribe me a kilo of Oxycodone. And a kilo of Fentanyl."

The eye doctor couldn't believe his ears.

"Have you lost your mind? I mean, *for real*, lost your mind? Beyond the usual Hugo Hamlin style of mind-losing."

"But it's not for me."

"And you thought that would make it better?"

"Half a kilo, then? Four hectograms, that's my final offer. Three?"

Malte was out of time to talk. He was on the threshold of performing cataract surgery. But in short, his objections were grounded in the fact that the medical license he'd put in so much energy to receive would end up in a paper shredder at the National Board of Health and Welfare if he did what his brother asked.

Fortunately, Malte hung up before his little brother had time to get caught up in arguing that medical licenses could be falsified.

So they would have to get hold of the narcotics some other way. Since Hugo had never hung around central Stockholm at night, he had no idea how. Time to involve his staff once again.

"Either of you know how to buy drugs and stuff?"

"Not me," said Jenny, whose history with drugs was limited to the time when she was offered a cigarette at sixteen. She had declined.

"There's an exciting leaf on the savanna you can chew if you need to run a little further than you already have and can actually manage," said Kevin.

The problem was that this leaf was on the savanna, and Hugo had no intention of making another trip to Kenya. He wondered if they thought the owner of the second-hand shop in Bollmora might be of help. Perhaps someone who sold everything from used mattresses to fool's gold engagement rings had some heroin sitting around in a drawer?

He heard for himself how silly he sounded.

"Forget it," he said.

In the absence of what they couldn't get their hands on they would have to use a few bags of flour, with rubber gloves nearby to suggest . . . something. A link to the sex toys, somehow.

When it came to Victor Alderheim's destroyed reputation, the group felt they'd already made it. One important problem to solve was how the long arm of the law would reach all the way down to the Alderheimian cellar. None of the three colleagues could call and tip them off; all calls were recorded. Nor did it seem like a good idea to hire a proxy off a random park bench. The tipster needed to have gravitas and credibility.

Gravitas and credibility, indeed. At the prestigious Bukowskis Auction House in Stockholm there was a department called Private Sales. This was where you could turn if, for instance, you had become too poor for your own way of life and didn't want to admit it to those around you, or even to yourself. To keep from being forced to move into a caravan to die of shame, it was common to take down a family heirloom from the wall—a piece that reached extra great artistic heights and had a price tag to match—and turn to Private Sales. Works of art and money changed hands and the buyer would never know who the seller was. Once the deal was done, of course, a blank spot was left on the seller's wall, but that could be remedied with a white lie or two. "What happened to my Renoir? Oh, I got tired of it, it's down in the basement somewhere. Flowers don't belong on the wall; they look best in a vase."

For this illusion to work, of course, it was crucial for the middleman, Bukowskis, to maintain the utmost discretion. And they did. The firm's entire business idea depended on excessive aplomb and well-maintained credibility. Hugo knew this for certain, because a decade or so earlier, Great & Even

Greater Communications had tried to win Bukowskis as a client. Since Hugo hadn't been in charge of this effort, another firm won, but there had been enough talk about this failure around the office that he had effectively done plenty of homework.

Hugo's plan was for Bukowskis to call the police on their behalf. There could be no better tipster.

Jenny thought this idea seemed smart but tricky.

"If they're as discreet as you say, then won't they be afraid of getting a reputation as police tipsters?"

Hugo nodded. But his time as CEO of Sweet Sweet Revenge Ltd. had brought him fresh insight into the human soul.

"I think I know what it will take," he said. "But one thing at a time."

First they had to fill the cellar with everything that would destroy Victor Alderheim's reputation forevermore. The oil paintings were only the beginning. When the police made their move, Victor would be forced to explain both art forgery and suspected narcotics violations. The evidence of an expert-level sex life wouldn't challenge the criminal code, but the friends' goal was for all of Stockholm to learn about it. And why not the nation? And Europe, while they were at it. Fuck it—the world.

The project still wouldn't bring in any money. But Sweden's leading adman had his pride.

"Victor will never recover from this, if we play all our cards right."

"You're the best!" said Jenny.

"It's not over yet," said Hugo.

He was certainly right about that.

Kevin took the company car for his shopping trip. Besides the sex toys, he was under orders to purchase a kilo of flour and a roll of small plastic baggies. He was so eager to be of service that he hadn't bothered to mention that he didn't have a driver's license. He could, however, drive a car. At least, he could drive the World Wildlife Fund's Range Rover. At least, on the savanna. There was nothing like right-hand or left-hand traffic there, although that was a factor he had to consider now. Right-hand in Kenya and left-hand in Sweden. Or was it the other way around?

After just four blocks and one roundabout in the wrong direction, things were flowing smoothly. And this car shifted all by itself.

After flour, baggies and toys, Kevin got an idea.

A really good one, he told himself. It would mean his breakthrough in the group.

Or eternal rejection.

Kevin made up his mind, parked the car at a bus stop, and took out his new phone. He searched online and found what he was looking for. Only two thousand kronor? He could get that from an ATM.

This would require a couple hours' detour, but Hugo and Jenny would be so proud of him. Right?

"You're a genius, you goddamn idiot," said the adman.

This was just about the finest praise Kevin had ever heard.

What he had done was travel to a farm outside Sigtuna to buy a goat.

"Nanny or billy?" asked the farmer, to avoid any misunderstandings.

"What's the difference?"

"Girl or boy?"

"A girl is fine," said Kevin.

There had to be a limit somewhere.

Chapter 27

Sweet Sweet Revenge Ltd. executed their break-in that night. Or whatever it was they were doing—they did have a key.

The next morning, Hugo waited for everyone to gather before making the crucial phone call.

"Are you ready?"

They were. The phone rang on the other end. Once. Twice. Then, an answer.

"Private Sales, Gustav Jansson speaking."

"Hello. My name is Victor Alderheim, of the Alderheim Art Gallery."

"An illustrious firm. How may I help you?"

"Well, I have a couple of Irma Sterns in storage over here. Or whatever you want to call them, heh heh. I thought you could help me hawk them for a massive amount of money. If you do a good job, I promise you'll get a cut."

Gustav Jansson had twenty years' experience, four of them in his current position. He'd never heard the like.

"Pardon me, but I'm not sure I quite understand. Are we dealing with Irma Stern, or someone else?"

"Irma Stern, definitely. All that's left is the signature, but I'm going to work that out. They're damn good, Jansson, you can rest assured. Maybe we can meet up in my cellar tonight, and I'll show you. How about eleven o'clock, to be on the safe side? I put complete trust in your discretion, Jansson."

Gustav Jansson, who had not wanted to understand what he thought he had grasped right away, now understood completely.

"Mr. Alderheim, you have called the wrong establishment. At this firm we adhere to ethical rules of a different level of dignity than those you seem to represent. I am deeply shocked and I ask you to refrain from bothering us henceforth."

Gustav Jansson had both seen and heard the occasional dubious matter over the years. It wasn't common, but it happened. Up to this point he had managed each time to distance himself before it evolved into something with which he and Bukowskis could come to be associated, even as innocent witnesses.

Hugo knew that Private Sales Representative Jansson was trying to back his way out of this conversation. But he was ready. Now he had to rile him up before it was too late.

In the second that followed, Hugo declared—in the guise of Art Dealer Alderheim—that money does not stink, that Jansson should know this, and that if he didn't he must surely have done things with his mother that no son ought to do, not to mention that in either case his mother had presumably been employed in a very particular line of work. Now, Jansson must toddle on over to the Alderheimian art gallery this very night, where the works by Irma Stern would be completed, with signatures and everything. And also he would be given fifty thousand kronor in cash, in advance, if he promised not to run off and tattle.

"Come on over, you whiny little knob," Hugo concluded.

With that, what had first been doubtful had now become direct knowledge of a premeditated crime. One half of Gustav Jansson was feverishly debating whether there was a way out of this incident after all. The other half wished Victor Alderheim nothing but ill for time eternal.

"Or would you like me to deposit the hush money straight into your bank account?" said Hugo.

That was the last straw. And what if someone was listening in on this call? Jansson knew he had no choice but to call the police.

"What's it gonna be, you fucking twat?"

Within the span of ten seconds, Jansson had been unflatteringly addressed as both the male and female sex organs. It was no longer a matter of what he knew he was obligated to do, but what he would do with pleasure.

The tipster was highly credible. As a result, the raid on Alderheim's art gallery took place that very afternoon. The police seized two suspected forgeries, eight bags of suspected narcotics, a number of fancy sex toys that both glowed and clattered, an inflatable naked rubber woman—and one goat.

PART FIVE

PART FIVE

Chapter 28

O nce a year, the Mbatian family had a reunion. It was organized by the two wives. Six of their eight daughters had flown the nest, but they made the effort to return for the day, to honor their parents, get updates on each other, and celebrate with dancing, food, and even more dancing late into the night.

In recent years, Kevin had been there as part of the family, but not this time. As a result, Ole was finding it difficult to feel cheerful about anything at all.

In the midst of the early dancing, the mailman and his bicycle reached the village. He went to the chief, of course, to greet him politely and say he sought permission to sleep over since it was getting dark. No one biked around the savanna in the darkness. Perhaps a blanket or a bite to eat might be included in the hospitality he was hoping for?

Chief Olemeeli never turned away a guest. Most times that was because he didn't dare. This time it was because the guest had arrived on a bicycle, an honorable form of transportation.

"Yes, indeed it is," said the mailman.

He had an envelope for the medicine man. One with exciting stamps. Looked like it had come from far, far away.

Ole Mbatian was deeply moved by the letter from his vanished son. He read it through twice before interrupting the dancing to tell his double wives and eight daughters that he'd just received a letter from the boy who meant everything.

The boy who meant *everything*? At that, two of his daughters began to cry, another three joined them, and one wife stalked off while the other launched into a tirade.

"Look what you've done, you stupid ass!"

There was something about women Ole would never understand. Kevin was the son God had sent straight from heaven, no middleman necessary, and placed before his feet. The boy who knew nothing about being Maasai and still came very close to becoming the best one of all.

Just three years after his birth on the savanna, he

had already mastered the art of staring down a lion. What you needed to do was walk straight towards the animal at the exact right speed, your eyes fixed on its own. With not a hint of hesitation.

At that point, hesitation would be sparked in the lion, who had inherited the knowledge that an approaching body wrapped in checked fabric meant trouble. It was as if the *shúkà* spoke to the lion and said "I'm a Maasai . . ." and concluded with ". . . come and get me if you dare."

The two-hundred-kilo male did not dare.

Kevin was a master of the throwing club after only two years, including how to account for the effects of different wind speeds. The club-related test of manhood was to encounter a buffalo, the angriest animal on the savanna, and make it reconsider its decision to gore the two-legged being before it. Few creatures, with the exception of the gnu, think less than the buffalo. Only the very best can get a creature who almost doesn't think at all to have second thoughts.

Kevin was one of them.

The final year of education was purely a formality, surviving from migration to migration, the time when hundreds of thousands of zebras and gnus ventured north from the Serengeti. Kevin, like the gnus, had crossed the Mara River without being attacked by crocodiles. The latter did it by sheer chance. Ninety-eight out of a hundred made it through. Kevin analyzed his surroundings. Getting a feel for each crocodile. For who was in which mood. He swam with bow and arrow on his back in case he had miscalculated. Ole almost wished that would happen sometime, because how was the boy planning to shoot a crocodile while swimming? All Ole knew was that Kevin knew.

His beloved Kevin.

After his year on the savanna, the youth were ready for their test, the formal circumcision. Ole knew Kevin would come through that ordeal just fine as well. His father the medicine man would perform it. The knife wasn't exactly dull, but it wasn't too sharp either. It was part of the test, that the procedure should take its time and be felt. Anyone who made a sound while the medicine man worked could look forward to a future as a scrap dealer in Nairobi. At best. Banished from the village, in any case. Those who managed to keep quiet were true Maasai warriors, had taken that last step into the adult world, were free to marry and have children. Preferably sons. Or actually, preferably a mix, now that Ole thought about it.

If only Kevin had spoken more about it with his father, he could have received an alternative treatment. The smith was always happy to brand a full moon into the nape of those who preferred it. The important thing was that you felt pain and didn't show it.

If only he had spoken with his father.

The whole village had searched for him for hours. All they found was what they didn't find: Kevin's backpack and the medicine man's paintings. The boy must have taken off.

Ole's heart broke. But when the letter arrived, it healed itself. Why, his son was in . . .

The one wife continued her tirade; the daughters kept crying. Ole went to the chief to get some peace and quiet.

"Where is Sweden?" he asked Olemeeli the Well-Traveled.

"I've been everywhere," said the chief.

"You have not. But where is Sweden?"

"No idea."

Chapter 29

Up to this point, Ole had been feeling too old or too settled to travel any further than Tabaka or maybe Ndonyo, and even then only during the short rains. Now he was going beyond that, and with a spring in his step.

He knew that Olemeeli's stubborn prohibitions kept them all unnecessarily in the dark about the many new things the kids in the village gossiped about. But what those things exactly were remained to be seen. The smith's sister knew some stuff, but Ole Mbatian would prefer to remain ignorant than listen to her prattle on.

He brought four cows with him and herded them to Narok. Cows as payment. There, at the gas station, worked one of the banished almost-Maasais. He had been watching cars come and go for years and was known for asking where people had come from and where they were heading. He himself had an old Toyota. For one cow, two at the most, he would surely offer to drive Ole the whole way.

"Hello there, Hector."

"Oh, the great medicine man. The man with the dull knife. Have you come to cut off what's still hanging on?"

To think he was still sulking after twenty years.

"No, I've come to ask you to drive me to a special place, for the price of one cow in cash."

You didn't say no to a cow, not if you worked at a gas station.

"Where are you going?"

"Sweden."

Hector saw the cow vanish into thin air.

"Never heard of it. The problem is, it might be across the sea, on the other side of Kilimanjaro. In which case you need a passport."

"A passport?"

"Talk to Wilson at city hall. He's a wizard with papers and stamps and stuff."

Wilson? Another of the failures. It seemed to Ole that this journey was starting off on the wrong foot; he wasn't having the luck he needed.

The head clerk at city hall had completely sat out

the final year on the savanna but submitted to circumcision anyway, because he'd heard somewhere that it pleased God. Just to mess with the others, he had shouted and screamed and sworn while Ole did what he was tasked with doing; after all, he had nothing to lose. Then he swaddled his bloody genitals in fabric, packed his bags, and said he was going to see the world rather than stay put and become as insular as everyone else.

He got no further than Narok. But Wilson knew more than Hector about the world beyond the mountains.

"You need to travel abroad," he said. "And to do that you need a passport."

"All this damn talk about passports."

Wilson said that these could only be issued in Nairobi and to get one, you had to prove that you were Kenyan.

"I'm Maasai," said Ole Mbatian the Younger.

"You're Kenyan as well, and my affidavit and stamps will prove that you exist."

"But I'm standing right here."

For hundreds of years, the Maasai had been crossing the border between present-day Kenya and Tanzania without giving a thought to personal identification or an invisible border. No police on either side had ever dared to ask them to legitimate themselves.

But Ole didn't have time to argue with Wilson about whether or not he existed. He would just have to go along with this passport thing if it was so important.

"Well, get to stamping, then, so we can get on with this."

It wasn't that simple. Wilson's stamps were very special and they had to be treated with respect. It might take a week. The medicine man was welcome to return then with his four cows.

But now Ole Mbatian grew furious. A week for one stamp?

"*Two* stamps, if I may say so."

And incidentally, the medicine man should know that it was much more than just the stamps. This was called *administration*—a very important line of work.

Ole had heard enough.

"You can have one cow per stamp, and a third if you close your office right now, borrow Hector's Toyota, and drive me to Nairobi. For the fourth you must give me cash. Not that I trust paper money, but it's easier to carry in my luggage."

Going against an angry Maasai warrior and medicine man was more than head clerk Wilson had bargained for. After a glance at his calendar he informed Ole that he could shorten the administration time a smidge. From one week to a quarter of an hour. The round trip to Nairobi, however, was a bit more problematic. Who did the medicine man expect would handle the important work at city hall in the meantime?

Ole had seen how a stamp worked; Hector could manage it.

Let Hector handle the stamps? Not on his life. That could lead to sheer chaos.

Wilson stuffed them into his briefcase, both the red one and the blue one.

"Come on, let's go."

"Didn't you need fifteen minutes?"

"I can stamp while I drive."

The next day, a new passport was issued to Ole Mbatian the Younger, with an estimated birthdate.

"A picture of me and everything," Ole said as he flipped through it. "Born on August seventh. That was more than I knew. What's August?"

Wilson felt that it was impossible to tell when the medicine man was and was not joking.

"I have to get home to Narok now," he said. "Safe flight, Medicine Man."

"Flight?"

No one had ever called Ole Mbatian stingy. No one would start now. Besides the agreed-upon compensation for Wilson, the medicine man instructed him to go back to their home village and fetch two more cows as thanks for his good service and steady stamping hand. For the best treatment he should turn to the chief rather than to one of Ole's wives, especially not the first one. Or in fact the other one.

Wilson remarked that the medicine man was more honorable than he'd thought; he thanked him for the tip and wished him good luck on his journey.

Once the head clerk was off, only Ole and the civil servant with the Kenyan passport police were left. The medicine man asked if the officer could direct him to an airplane that was headed to Sweden. He couldn't, and as if that weren't enough, Ole was informed that he needed something called a visa to travel where he wanted to go. These were not merely handed out at the drop of a hat, not for Sweden.

Why the hell was everything so complicated? Ole questioned everything so emphatically that in the end, the civil servant ran out of arguments. And anyway, they were not his own arguments, but those of the Swedish embassy. To get out of standing there and being showered with curses he'd never even heard before, he decided to give the troublesome medicine man a ride over.

"In my opinion, Mr. Mbatian, your reasoning is both rational and clever," he lied, in the interest of getting the old man to shut up. "Please, come with me, I know who you ought to speak with."

Fifteen minutes later, he deposited Ole outside the embassy, thus allowing his day to return to normal.

Within the stately embassy doors, the medicine man discovered a room where about twenty people were waiting their turn. The Maasai did not take a queue number, for he had never heard of doing so. He walked right past all twenty people and knocked on the receptionist's window. Behind it sat a woman who was doing nothing. Ole felt it would be reasonable for her to do something else.

The woman looked up, annoyed. This wasn't the first time a rural visitor had tried to cut in line. But then her expression changed and she opened her window.

"Mr. Mbatian! What an honor. What can I do for you?"

She well remembered the medicine man; she had been a patient of his seven years ago and had been eternally grateful ever since. In contrast to what she'd feared, her five children had not turned into six, seven, or possibly even more.

Ole Mbatian had treated hundreds of women like her and could not reasonably be expected to tell one from the next.

"Nice to see you again," he said. "I remember you very well."

After that he told it like it was: he was planning to pop over to Sweden to see what it was like there, and he had been given to understand that you needed any number of things to do so. He didn't believe any more stamps were in order, however; he already had two.

The grateful receptionist needed to know who he would be seeing in Sweden, and the address of his intended lodgings. She also wanted to see Mr. Mbatian's airline ticket, especially the return one.

Ole shook his head—he was a medicine man, not an oracle. Who could say whom one might meet next, and under which sky one might sleep? The fact that you needed a ticket to fly was news to him, but he wasn't surprised. Since everything else had to be so difficult, why not that too?

This wasn't exactly the response the receptionist wanted. Or, rather: this was the exact response she didn't want. But she had many years of service behind her and knew how things worked around here.

"One moment, Mr. Mbatian, I'll see what I can do."

She disappeared into an adjoining room along with the medicine man's passport. In the span of four minutes she broke at least that many of the embassy's visa rules, after which she returned to the medicine man and handed him his passport, visa and all.

"Anything else I can do for you?" she asked, expecting a no.

"Since you have so kindly offered," said Ole. "I have some cash here. My chief's preferred currency is actually cows, but that seemed impractical now that I'm going to fly and everything. Can you tell me how much this is and whether it will get me where I'm going? Otherwise I suppose I'll have to walk the last little bit."

The receptionist was concerned. What should she do now?

Then the queue behind the medicine man came to her aid. A general grumbling had arisen. How could this Maasai just walk in and be helped straight away, while everyone else had to wait?

She liked her job in customer service at the embassy. The only downside was the customers. It would be nice not to have to look at them for a while.

She placed her "back in a moment" sign in her

window, put on her thin coat, and came around to meet the Maasai.

"Where are you going now?" said the angriest of the men in the queue.

"None of your damn business," the receptionist replied.

The nearest travel agency was right around the corner. The eternally grateful former patient walked briskly, and Ole kept pace with her.

The travel agency found a sufficiently cheap ticket to Stockholm, via Addis Ababa and Istanbul. Once that was paid for, Ole Mbatian's traveling funds consisted of two thousand shillings, which is to say twenty dollars or one twenty-fifth of a cow. This prompted the receptionist to allow the "back in a moment" sign to replace her for a bit longer. The last help Ole Mbatian received from her was in the form of a lift on her moped to Jomo Kenyatta Airport.

Ole thanked her for all her help, kissed her on the cheeks and the forehead, and stepped into the security area.

There he was immediately relieved of the spear on his back and the knife at his side.

"But why?" said the Maasai.

"They can be dangerous," said the security worker.

"Why else would I have them?"

People just got stranger the further he got from home. Ole Mbatian the Younger never went a meter without his weapons! He was just about to say so to the security worker when something further on caught his eye. What was that?

"Oh well," said Ole. "Keep the spear and knife for now, if you must."

And he hurried off towards what he had spotted.

Chapter 30

During his very first encounter with an escalator at the airport in Nairobi, Ole Mbatian made up his mind to stop complaining about everything that wasn't what he'd hoped for, or what he was used to.

Just think—a staircase that did your strolling for you in one direction, while in the other direction you would stand still no matter how hard you walked. Ole had fantasized about having the latter outside his own medicine hut, the one that had been sitting on the small rise on the outskirts of the village for three generations. That way the smith's sister would never arrive.

Although this staircase ran on electricity, of course, which the chief had long ago forbidden along with typewriters and everything that came after. Ole was going to have a serious talk with Olemeeli the not-at-all-well-traveled once he got back home.

His journey continued. Changing planes in Addis Ababa was fine; all he had to do was ask where to go. A situation arose in Istanbul when Ole didn't understand that modern toilets could be separated by gender. All of a sudden he found himself surrounded by angry women as he washed his feet in their sink.

All that came of this incident was that a Turkish airport security worker personally escorted the medicine man to the Stockholm gate, even as he praised the traveler's ambitions to have clean feet.

The medicine man landed at Stockholm Arlanda Airport, where it turned out that the visa in his passport did just what the woman at the embassy in Nairobi had promised. Ole uttered a special thanks to the passport control officer for selecting a black stamp to mark his entry into the country; he already had red and blue. He didn't know quite where they were, but still.

The officer thanked him for the praise, welcomed Ole Mbatian the Younger to the Kingdom of Sweden—and warned him about the temperature. It was not her duty to express opinions about visitors' clothing, but in this case . . . a red-and-black checked cloth in combination with sandals and bare feet was not optimal for the current minus-fifteen-degrees weather.

Ole, who didn't know that degrees could be divided into above and below, shrugged.

Outside the airport, the fabric of his *shúkà* immediately grew stiff, and his sandals slipped around in snow and ice. Fifteen degrees? That passport officer was making things up.

Ole had only experienced something like this once before. One of the most vexing ingredients in his medicine cabinet had the gall to grow just below the glacier atop Kilimanjaro, at an altitude that made you gasp for breath. But the medicine man had his calling, and since the antiseptic moss wouldn't come to him, he would have to go to the moss. And now here he stood, in the same sort of cold, but with neither mountain nor moss.

A kind-hearted passer-by promptly talked Ole out of walking into the capital. It was too far and too cold.

But there was an express train. Which, naturally, you needed a ticket for. Ole skipped that part, and very soon found himself in dialogue with a uniformed man. The conductor of the train informed him that anyone without a ticket had to pay onboard, plus a penalty fee. Credit card or exact change only.

Ole didn't understand a word of what the uniformed man had said in Swedish, and figured it was just as well, since he could guess what the man was after.

When the passenger didn't respond and was dressed in an exceedingly un-Swedish fashion besides, the conductor suspected he ought to switch languages.

"Do you speak English?" he asked, in English.

The medicine man certainly did, but he didn't think it was in his own best interest to initiate any in-depth conversations with the man who wanted the money he didn't even have. A response in Swahili, any response at all, might help. He said what came to him in the moment.

"*Mke mmoja hatoshi, ila ukiongeza mke wa pili hilo nalo ni tatizo la kukupasua kichwa.*"

"One wife is not enough, but two wives are a problem that may cause your head to break."

After thinking for a few seconds, the conductor decided that further argumentation was above his pay grade. He saluted and said in Swedish that the gentleman could keep his money, or—even better—use it to buy a winter coat.

Once he arrived in the Swedish capital, the medicine man needed somewhere to rest up. Sleeping under the open sky was out of the question; the weather in Sweden was too strange to do that.

A hut he could ask to step into was not to be found. This city was larger than he'd imagined. How would he find his beloved boy in all of this? Oh well, rest first. Search later.

He stepped out of Central Station and into the icy air and spotted the word "hotel" across the street. He knew what that was; there was one next to city hall in Narok. Two rooms. Open now and then. A hotel was where you stayed if you didn't want to sleep outside at night and could pay your way.

Now, that last bit. Ole Mbatian the Younger was fundamentally a prosperous man. So he told the woman from whom he attempted to let a room. He had eight hundred cows and over two hundred goats but had been unable to bring them all the way here. Back in Nairobi they had protested even at the sight of his spear and knife—what would they have said about the livestock?

The receptionist was young and had no experience checking in Maasai warriors. No wonder she misunderstood a few key points. What she thought she heard was that he had a spear and a knife and wanted to pay in cows. Or two hundred goats. But she wasn't certain that he had threatened her.

"We are a cash-free hotel," was what she managed to say.

The medicine man said that suited him just fine, since he essentially had no cash anyway. His point was that he wanted to sleep now and pay later. The young woman should not be anxious about this. Ole Mbatian the Younger was his name. Medicine man by trade. Where he came from, you either did the right thing or else you didn't do much more after that.

In order to emphasize this last part, Ole raised his throwing club and smiled. In a friendly way, if he did say so himself.

With that, all doubt was eliminated. The man on the other side of her counter was a lethal threat. He had a spear and a knife hidden somewhere, and he intended to beat the receptionist to death with the club in his hand if he wasn't assigned a room free of charge.

Ole Mbatian's friendly assurances of integrity were received in a manner he could not have foreseen. Instead of showing him to his room, she began to shriek. There was no understanding why, but among the words Ole Mbatian caught were "police" and "help."

PART SIX

Chapter 31

C hristian Carlander studied Spanish between six
and eight o'clock each Tuesday evening, but since
nothing seemed to stick he started again in the beginners' class each autumn. *El perro está bajo la mesa.*
The dog is under the table. Ever since Carlander had
learned to remember what that sentence meant, he had
wondered what it was doing there.

Every now and then, on Saturdays, it was Premier
League with the boys at O'Learys. An inconsistent
tradition. Most recently, only Christian himself and
the manager of lost property had shown up. The company was boring and the match ended nil-nil.

Sundays were for sports on TV: alpine skiing, cross-
country skiing, or biathlon, if the season allowed. He
was, after all, Swedish.

Aside from Swedish lady skiers, most things in life

had been better before, if you asked Carlander. Before the kids moved out. Before his wife left him because he worked too much. Before he got sick of his job and started working as little as possible.

Police inspector certainly *sounded* nice. He'd been one of the top dogs in criminal investigations. But it had been a long time since anything exciting had happened. People didn't even rob banks anymore. These days it was mostly homicide, and nine times out of ten the murdered could have been the murderer if only he'd acted faster. Or else it was cybercrime, and that was more than he could stand. Who left fingerprints or footprints behind online?

On one occasion he'd accidentally said this out loud during a coffee break at the station. His young colleagues protested; it was just that modern-day prints looked different. Before the break was over, they had labeled him a has-been. And rightly so. Carlander had come to terms with it.

Now he was just counting the days to retirement. From Monday to Friday he arrived at work a little after nine, had coffee between ten and eleven, and took an early, long lunch—but made sure to get back in time for the afternoon break. He went home around three: walked a few hundred meters to the metro, one station, change trains, three stations, and up to his one-bedroom flat in Södermalm where no one was waiting for him.

Now and then he had stopped off at a pub along the way. An afternoon beer, two at the most, a couple of evening papers and whatever book he was carrying around. Right now, *One Hundred Years of Solitude*. Carlander had picked it for the title.

On this ill-fated day, the inspector had been a little extra bored, so he left his empty desk even earlier than usual. He decided it was a beer-and-book day. He chose the bar at Nordic Light Hotel, which was within walking distance of the Centralen metro station and three short stops to Mariatorget and his hundred-year solitude back at home.

Suddenly, he was roused from his reading. There was a racket in the hotel lobby. A woman raised her voice, mentioning the word "police."

Fourteen days from retirement. Carlander knew exactly what awaited him in the form of paperwork and other unnecessary tasks if he got involved. So he stuck with his beer and his book.

But the racket kept going, now involving both "help!" and "save me!" The inspector sighed. He guessed that there was a tipsy CEO demanding a larger room. He should go break things up before his colleagues had to respond. After all, God help him, he was a police officer for a little while longer. And besides, he was—to be perfectly honest—still on duty.

It was an unusual sight. The tipsy CEO was wearing neither suit nor tie. He was wrapped in a red-and-black checked cloth, was wearing sandals without socks, and held a wooden club in his hand. Many signs indicated that he wasn't even a CEO.

Inspector Carlander held up his badge, announced himself, and asked what was going on. He spoke in English, without quite knowing why. There was something international about the man in front of him.

Ole Mbatian was pleased. Now he would receive help with this difficult woman. Not that they needed to arrest her; a proper reprimand would suffice.

"Thank you, kind officer, for arriving so quickly," he said, trying—as tradition dictated—to give him a kiss on each cheek and one on his forehead.

But Carlander didn't want any kisses. He shoved the Maasai off and appeared to be preparing himself to grab him somehow. Arresting Ole when the woman at the reception desk was the ridiculous one? The medicine man had no choice but to wallop the officer over the head with his club.

"Ouch, dammit," said Inspector Carlander, falling onto his bum.

He scrambled back up but was so woozy that he had to sit down on a chair.

Now more officers were coming through the door, a man and a woman.

"What's going on?" asked the woman.

"Assault on a public official?" Inspector Carlander suggested from where he sat with one hand on his forehead.

By the time Ole had finished wondering about the advisability of using the club on the woman as well, she had wrestled him to the floor.

Chapter seventeen, paragraph one of the Swedish Criminal Code clearly states that a person who threatens or practices violence against a police officer should be sentenced to prison for a maximum of four years or, if the crime is minor, to fines or prison for a maximum of six months.

The uniformed officers recognized the formerly competent criminal investigator and asked if he intended to press charges against the apprehended party. Carlander wasn't feeling very well after his blow to the head and said he mostly just wanted to go back to his book and his beer and that he would consider their question in the meantime. For the moment, couldn't they just bring the man in?

Ole Mbatian was naturally charming when he wanted to be. And he had been relieved of his club. He explained to the young female officer that this was all a misunderstanding. When Ole went to embrace her colleague out of gratefulness, his throwing club had happened to bump into the colleague's forehead. The whole situation was amplified by the woman behind the reception desk losing her mind when Ole wished simply to discuss price and currency.

Sergeant Appelgren was indeed young, but she was sufficiently good at her job to bend the rules a bit when reality came knocking. She could have guessed from miles away that this incident was a direct result of culture clash. But that didn't mean that she could ignore the fact that a respected colleague had been struck down.

She informed the Maasai that he would be released from the handcuffs she'd placed on him, given that he promised not to embrace her out of gratefulness as well, that he remained calm all the way to the detention center, and that he stopped calling her "Young Miss Officer." She was a sergeant and her name was Sofia.

Ole didn't know what a detention center was, but he was satisfied with the explanation that if you happened to scuffle with a police officer you might end up there and be given a bed and some food as punishment. The medicine man nodded in approval. That wasn't quite how people were punished on the savanna.

"My name is Ole Mbatian the Younger. In this sort of context, where we have achieved an almost familiar atmosphere, it will do to call me simply Ole Mbatian."

Sofia asked what sort of business Ole Mbatian had in Sweden and learned that he was looking for his son Kevin, the first-rate Maasai warrior. At least among those who had never actually graduated.

There was no time for any further discussion in the back seat of the patrol car. It wasn't a long trip.

Kronoberg Remand Prison has spent over a century being where it is, on Kungsholmen in Stockholm. On average, about twenty-five worrying elements are checked in there each day, every day of the year; a few more than average on Christmas Eve and a few fewer on a Tuesday evening in November. Somewhere in between on a day like this one, mid-week in February. Anyone who has worked as a prison guard for long enough will have soon seen and experienced everything. Truly, everything.

Except for a Maasai warrior–slash–medicine man.

"Private room," Ole Mbatian observed. "Why thank you."

The guard had rules to follow, for instance the one dictating that every delinquent must exchange their own clothes for the detention center's green trousers and shirt. But this particular specimen refused so emphatically that it was heard all the way down the corridor and reached the ears of Sergeant Sofia. She spoke with the guard, said that the Maasai appeared to be a most peaceful sort, and—above all—the *shúkà* he wore was so thin and almost transparent that there could be no room inside it to conceal objects. The prison guard sighed and acquiesced to the sergeant and the medicine man. He had already argued with his wife earlier that day; further arguments were more than he could handle at the moment.

Dinner was served in the room. Macaroni with sausage and juice. After he had eaten, Ole summoned the guard to tell him that he didn't want to be disturbed unless it was urgent—he intended to recover from his long journey and wasn't planning to leave until the next day.

"I understand," said the guard, although in fact he kind of didn't.

Chapter 32

Ole Mbatian enjoyed a good, long sleep in his cell. When he woke up, he was hungry again. He asked the guard if a bit more food might be arranged before he went on his way.

Breakfast was already laid out in the common room; the guard on duty felt it would save time if the medicine man were welcome to visit it. He went off to check the peculiar man's status in respect to restrictions. On the way he ran into Inspector Carlander, who had just spoken with the prosecutor. The Maasai could take his morning meal wherever he preferred.

Breakfast didn't look like it did back home, but Ole Mbatian was satisfied. There was bread, he recognized that, and cow's milk in a pitcher, there was no mistaking it even if it did look oddly thin. Next to the milk was a bowl of what looked like small, withered, pale brown leaves from the baobab tree. What could that be? And jam. Why, hard-boiled eggs as well.

Ole studied the establishment's only other guest, hoping to watch and learn. The guest filled a bowl with the pale brown leaves, poured milk over them, and added a dollop of jam. It looked funny—some of the leaves bobbed on the surface, while others sank.

"Excuse me, my friend, these brown leaves you just poured milk over—is that something you intend to eat?"

The addressed party didn't bother to respond. Partly due to the fact that he was angry because he had been arrested the day before in his art gallery and accused of a variety of crimes of which he was innocent. And partly because the person asking was both foreign and Black. Victor Alderheim was of the opinion that foreigners in general, Blacks in particular, and also feminists, liberals, Green Party members, Social Democrats and homosexuals posed a threat to the nation he wanted to save.

He couldn't think of a single reason to speak to the native in the room. Who was speaking English, to boot.

"Learn Swedish if you want something from me."

Snubbing, after all, was not the same as conversing.

Ole Mbatian didn't give up. He finally had someone

to talk to besides the smith's sister and folks who had nothing to teach him, and he wasn't about to be deterred by a simple snub.

"Please excuse me, but you remind me of one of my wives in your morning mood."

With that, the conversation had begun.

"One of your wives? Do you have two?"

Victor immediately regretted saying anything, but it was impossible to hide his curiosity.

"I had planned on a third as well, since the first two only gave me daughters. But One and Two disabused me of that notion, you might say. It all worked out in the end, though, for God sent me a son. He came straight from heaven. Now, I see you are eating these leaves—I thought as much. May I have a taste?"

Ole took a seat across from Victor Alderheim, who, for a moment, was speechless with surprise.

"Why the hell would I let you taste my cornflakes?"

"Oh, is that what they're called. Well, that's how it works back home. Everyone shares everything; it makes no difference."

Enough was enough. Victor Alderheim announced that he didn't speak to Black people unless it was absolutely necessary, and he didn't expect it was in this instance.

"So shut your mouth, if you please."

Ole Mbatian burst out laughing.

"Where I'm from, a man who doesn't speak to Black people won't be able to say much."

But sure, he could keep his mouth shut if the angry man wanted him to. Ole Mbatian knew few people who were as good at being quiet as he was. One time he didn't say a word for four months in a row. Of course, this was due to the fact that he had no one to talk to; he had been out on a terribly long walk to search for a heart medicine that was said to bloom next to the big lake called Nyanza, the one the uneducated referred to as Victoria. The lake, that is. Not the flower. That was called something else. Pink flowers. Half a man high, more or less. He never found it.

During the harangue that was meant to serve as proof Ole Mbatian could be quiet, the art dealer had an opportunity to take in this troublesome person's attire. He was wearing the same red-and-black checked cloth Victor had seen the natives wearing as they walked along the road in the hour before he dumped Kevin. Did everyone dress the same down there?

"Could you pass me the jam?" said Ole Mbatian. "I'm sorry, I just said something again."

He had prepared his own bowl of what was called cornflakes as he was going on about how quiet he could be. Now all that was missing was the preserved red berries.

"Are you from Africa?" Victor Alderheim asked, as he handed over the lingonberries.

"No, Maasai Mara. But as long as we're speaking even though we weren't supposed to, may I ask what sort of business you have here? For my part I have been getting some rest and warming up my body. Soon I'm going to set off to look for my son, Kevin. The one from the sky. I don't suppose luck would have it that you know where he is?"

It seemed quite unlikely, of course. The city was far too big. But Ole Mbatian couldn't think of a better plan than querying his way forward. Plus, it kept the conversation going.

Victor was startled. *Kevin.* A coincidence. After all, his Kevin had been dead and eaten up for ages.

Stupid question, incidentally.

He said he didn't know any Kevins.

"And the reason I'm here is because someone is screwing with me! As if I would make counterfeit paintings or fuck goats!"

Ole Mbatian said he was sorry that the man had been accused of things he hadn't done. That might explain why he was so angry. The part with the goat sounded extra unfortunate. The smith's sister back home had certain similarities with a goat, mostly appearance-wise, but that wasn't the same thing at all.

The medicine man liked the mixture of leaves, milk and jam. He helped himself to another bowl. He'd always had a healthy appetite.

"By the way, what kind of paintings is it you don't counterfeit? I have a couple of fine paintings myself, from a dreadfully long time ago. Or had, rather. Kevin, that scoundrel, took them with him when he came here. He didn't want to be circumcised. Which is understandable, in retrospect."

Victor Alderheim had the vague sense that the number of coincidences was getting to be excessive. The man appeared to come from the region where Victor had left Kevin to die. And God had sent him a son by that very name, one who later stole paintings from his father, *paintings*, of all the things Victor knew one could steal from one's parents. Not alcohol, not money, not his Social-Democrat father's gold watch. *Paintings*.

"Hope he didn't throw them away, because they're very fine, did I mention that? Yet they soon will have been rolled up for almost a whole lifetime. Back home, paintings aren't suitable to hang on the walls, because they're made of cow dung and will burn a hole right through just about anything, given the chance."

"The paintings are made of cow dung?"

Victor Alderheim was finding it difficult to follow the native's chatter. From circumcision to dung in the span of a few seconds.

"No, the walls are. The paintings were made of paint by a woman who visited the village when I was just a wee little fellow."

The medicine man chuckled again. He had completely forgotten to introduce himself.

"Ole Mbatian the Younger. Medicine man by trade. Village champion in club-throwing. Two wives, eight daughters, and one son, Kevin, but I already told you that. I'm here to look for him. Oh, never mind, I already told you that too. Not *here* here, but in the country of Sweden."

The art dealer was done with his cornflakes and turned to preparing an open-faced sandwich with slices of hard-boiled egg and a pink string of something on top, whatever that was.

What was about to occur was Ole Mbatian's very first encounter with Sweden's national open-faced sandwich topping: caviar in a tube, brand name Kalles Kaviar. No self-respecting Iranian would ever even think of calling Kalles caviar, but it has been a Swed-ish tradition since 1954. Half cod roe, the other half sugar, salt, tomato puree, potato flakes and preserva-tives. Into the tube and out onto the sandwiches of tens of thousands of Swedes each morning. Preferably in the company of a hard-boiled egg, as the art dealer was preparing right before the Maasai's eyes.

"If I know you, there's no point in asking for a bite of what you're holding in your hand, is there?" said Ole Mbatian.

It was worth a shot.

Victor Alderheim had far too much to process to say no this time. Circumstances were on their way to be-coming extraordinary.

"By all means," he said, passing his untouched sandwich across the table.

The Maasai, as pleased as he was surprised, took a bite of the Hönö bread, egg and Kalles as Alderheim continued to mull.

In an initial interrogation with the police, he had been shown photographs of what they'd confiscated from the cellar. Besides the goat, the fake drugs and the sex toys there were two paintings with *African* motifs. A woman under a parasol and a boy by a stream. And hadn't the boy been wearing a *red-and-black checked cloth*?

Alderheim tested the waters.

"They're saying I counterfeited Irma Stern. Is that a name you . . ."

"Dear, sweet, Auntie Irma. You're counterfeiting her? No, that was what you said you didn't do. Oh my, this sandwich is delicious."

The art dealer's heart may have stopped for a second.

"You've met?"

Something big was happening. But what?

"It was many years ago. She came to the village, got sick, recovered, thanked Dad, made portraits of me and Mom—and left."

Many years ago. Well, anything else would have been out of the question. Portraits . . . ?

"Were you by any chance sitting by a stream when she painted you? Was your mother under a parasol?"

Ole chuckled a third time. He'd never heard such a lucky guess. Or two.

Victor's mind was reeling. Kevin and Kevin had to be the same person. The fake Irma Stern paintings were authentic. The police thought Victor owned them, even as he was sitting here feeding the real owner.

Feeding him Kalles Kaviar.

"And now you've come to Sweden to find your paintings?"

"Not at all! I'm looking for my son."

"So . . . the paintings aren't important?"

Ole considered the question. As he recalled, Auntie Irma had been a comfy sort of lady. She often patted him on the head, in a motherly fashion. Had a nice smile. And made beautiful paintings.

Her creations had stayed rolled up in Ole Mbatian the Elder's third hut, the one on the hill, for as long as he lived. When Ole Junior took over, he brought out the artworks for the fire festival every year. As extra decoration. That was it. The villagers had got it into their heads that he was the artist, and why not let them think so? A medicine man had to protect his reputation as being something special.

But then Kevin took the paintings with him when he fled circumcision. It was unclear why, but the reason didn't matter. Nothing was of any importance besides Kevin himself. One could only hope they ended up on a proper wall eventually. That they could bring happiness to a few more viewers and a little more often. Ole had no concerns beyond this.

"No, they're not important," he said.

"Then perhaps I could purchase them? I'm an art dealer and I love the cheap and simple. A hundred dollars for the pair, what do you say?"

How much was a hundred dollars in livestock

again? The suggestion reminded Ole Mbatian of the chief's stubborn refusal ever to do anything new. And how many *cards* would it be? One of the many things he'd observed up to this point on his journey was the small plastic cards. It was a form of payment, and yet it wasn't. The buyer always seemed to keep the card, but the seller never got upset about it.

It remained to be seen how exactly this worked, but even the crazy receptionist at the hotel had refused not only livestock on credit, but also cash—that is, dollars. Perhaps Ole could demand a card or two for the paintings, to be on the safe side. One or two, in that case?

No, the medicine man knew how many chickens equaled a goat and how many goats equaled a cow. If he gave it some thought, he could probably manage to translate all of that into dollars as well, but that was where he drew the line. And anyway, the method of payment wasn't the problem right now. Kevin had taken the paintings with him. And he was missing. There were no paintings to sell.

The medicine man got an idea.

"If you help me find my son, you can *have* the paintings."

Now things were shaping up to be as fantastic for Victor as they were problematic. There was no way it would end well if he and the native tracked down

Kevin together. The kid must have put the paintings in the cellar to frame him. That goddamn brat. What had Victor ever done to him?

There was no reasonable way Kevin could have grasped what he was doing when he did it. Now Victor would have to take over ownership of the paintings *before* the little brat and the native were reunited.

Victor held out the sandwich once more.

"Have another bite, Mr. Mb . . . Mbth . . . Mr. Africa. And please tell me more about Irma Stern."

The second bite was almost better than the first. Ole swallowed and gave an account of his meeting with Auntie Irma when he was a child. She had been treated by Ole's father, Ole Mbatian the Elder, and stayed for several months until she was well again. She left the two fine pieces of art behind as a gift.

"Would you like to see pictures of Irma and me?" said Ole Mbatian.

"What?" said Victor.

"No, how silly of me. Why, the photographs and the letters are in the hut, and that's not here."

While Ole prattled on, Victor Alderheim managed to catch up with himself. The deal *must* be closed here and now, or else it would be too late.

"Fantastic that you want to donate your Irma Sterns to a poor lover of art, but I simply can't go along with that. And I'm afraid they won't let me out of here for a long time yet, so I don't know how I can be of any help in your search for . . . Kevin, was it?"

The medicine man understood. On the other hand, it seemed like dollars no longer cut it, at least not at the hotel.

"May I ask what that pink stuff is that comes out of the blue and yellow tube? It certainly elevated the flavor of both egg and bread."

"You know what?" Victor Alderheim had a brain-wave. "You can have my whole Kalles Kaviar sandwich with egg as payment for the paintings!"

The native had already eaten up a third of it; two million-dollar paintings for the last two-thirds seemed fair.

"But what if I don't find Kevin and the paintings? Then I'll have nothing to offer and you will have paid for something you never received."

Unlike Ole, Victor Alderheim knew that the paintings were somewhere in the police station.

"Aw, well, if it happens it happens. Just the *thought* of owning them makes me happy."

Now it was Ole Mbatian's turn to mull. It would

have been easy to simply give paintings to someone who would appreciate them. But to *sell* them? That was making a business deal out of it, and in business one must take no prisoners. A sandwich struck the Maasai as too cheap.

"Well, there were *two* paintings," said Ole.

Victor Alderheim was quick to respond.

"You're absolutely right. I'm authorized to make another sandwich, exactly the same. Egg and caviar. You can have that too, okay?"

In just a few seconds, the offer had doubled. Ole Mbatian was pleased. As he munched on what was left of the first sandwich, Victor assembled the second.

"Not as much butter underneath this time," Ole said with his mouth full. "And caviar all the way to the edges, please."

Once the Maasai had eaten up the Irma Stern paintings, Victor wanted to get their agreement down on paper. While he tried to formulate the handover on a napkin, the medicine man told him more about how grateful Irma Stern had been after Ole Mbatian the Elder saved her life, and that was why she first painted his first wife under a parasol and then his son—that is, Ole—playing by a stream. Well, not exactly playing; she sat at her easel and asked him to stand as still as possible with a stick in his hand.

Alderheim needed to get a better grip on the native's name.

"How is Mb . . . Mbth . . ."

"Mbatian," Ole said, as clearly as he could. "First an 'm,' then a 'b,' and then the rest is obvious. And what might you be called?"

"Victor Alderheim," said Victor Alderheim.

The angry man was easier to remember. Although he wasn't as angry by this point. That could change; Ole wanted to know more about his relationship with goats.

"Back home we use goats as currency and for milk production. For sex and so forth, we prefer to stick to our women. And they to us. That's just who we are. Do you have differing thoughts on the matter? Perhaps the goat is of a more accommodating nature?"

Victor Alderheim was too focused on what he was doing to become angry again. He had just finished with the napkin, upon which only the signature of the native was missing. *Lord, let him know how to write.* Victor didn't know if they knew how, in Africa. Some of them, sure, but out there in the jungle?

"Well, Mr. Mbatian. In keeping with Swedish tradition, I thought we could both sign this little document as a way to remember today's business deal."

Ole said that where he came from, a man kept his

word; if he didn't, he seldom grew as old as he might have hoped. But sure, the medicine man could offer up a signature. He had practiced it as recently as a few days ago, when he was getting his passport.

"A passport is something you need if you're going to travel a long way," he stated.

Chapter 33

The men in the breakfast room at the remand prison were interrupted when a third man entered the room. It was Inspector Carlander. He had arrived at work earlier than he had in a long time, hoping to forestall a report on the assault of an official. He knew what sort of work such a report would mean, and—above all—how much glee his colleagues would exhibit during their coffee breaks if they learned that the experienced investigator had been struck down by a slightly aged Maasai medicine man.

Thirteen days until retirement. Now it was time for harm reduction and a smooth crossing of the finish line.

"Why, look, it's the police officer from yesterday. How's the noggin? If only there were any left, you could have had a bite of my sandwich as a balm on top of the balm I see you have already put on your head. Egg with caviar from a tube."

Before the inspector could say anything, Victor Alderheim stood up and rounded the table. His face was red; something about Carlander's arrival had set him off.

He couldn't let anyone intervene now. None of his alleged crimes mattered, as long as he could take possession of the paintings he had just purchased. He grabbed the Maasai's arm, thrust the pen into his hand, and pointed at the napkin.

"Sign!"

But too much was happening at once for Ole. The angry man appeared to be returning to his old self again. The medicine man paused, pen in hand.

In a loud voice directed at Carlander, Alderheim announced that he would plead guilty to everything if necessary, except some goddamn phone call in which he allegedly turned himself in. The goat was his, the flour was his, the sex toys were his—but above all, the two paintings were his!

"I'll confess to anything, as long as you give them back. They're authentic! And they're mine! Ask this native here! They're mine!"

Victor Alderheim demanded to be released immediately; there was nothing illegal about having paintings in one's own cellar. He was an art dealer, for Christ's sake! But before anything else happened, this lunatic here had to put his name down on the napkin.

"Just sign it, goddammit!"

Inspector Carlander had a headache from being hit in the head with a throwing club the day before, and it was only made worse when someone shouted and tried to boss him around.

He planted himself between the Maasai and the loudmouth.

"I don't care where you stick your dick in your own time, but in this building you will calm the hell down, is that clear? Otherwise I'll go get the taser."

He would not be doing the bidding of this goat-sex man.

Ole Mbatian dropped the napkin issue; his good word would have to suffice. He wanted to leave now. "If you will excuse me, Angry Man and Police Officer, I'm going to set out to look for my son. Could you please fetch me my club before I go? I promise not to hit anyone in the head with it, including this angry fellow, although I know that such things can cause a change of mood in anyone."

The inspector could not comprehend how the Maasai knew he was free to go. That decision had only been made a few minutes earlier, when Carlander informed the prosecutor—whom he'd known for over thirty years—that he wasn't going to file charges for violence against an official. The prosecutor said he understood.

"Please come with me, Mr. Mbatian. your case has been terminated. But the throwing club shall remain in our care; it's what we call "forfeit" around here."

Now they had taken his knife, spear, *and* throwing club from him.

As Ole Mbatian and Inspector Carlander left the room, Alderheim continued his oration. The medicine man didn't understand why. If he hadn't done you know what with the goat, he had nothing to be upset about, and if he had, then really the goat was the one who had the right to complain.

On their way through the corridors, Inspector Carlander thought about what he had just experienced. Did the goat-fucker and the medicine man have something in common? Like the very paintings that had been confiscated along with the sex toys and the animal?

In a different time, before Inspector Carlander had mentally clocked out of his job, the case of the forged paintings in the art dealer's cellar would have been right up his alley. His boss had made an attempt in this direction the previous morning, but Carlander claimed a dentist appointment. No one in his right mind would take on an investigation of this scope two weeks before retirement.

But now the situation had rather changed. Curiosity had sunk its claws into him. The break room had kept him up to speed.

"Mr. Mbatian, you will soon be perfectly free to go," he said. "But first I'd like to have a brief conversation with you, if you don't mind?"

"It's hard to know that ahead of time," said Ole Mbatian.

Christian Carlander managed to surprise his boss along the way. He stuck his head in and said:

"Hello, have you already put the goat-fucking case on someone else's desk? If not, I can take it."

"You go ahead and take it, Carlander," said his boss.

In fact, it had been assigned to that idiot Gustavsson. Who had kicked things off by calling in sick. To think that Carlander, of all people, would come to the rescue. Would wonders never cease?

Chapter 34

Inspector Carlander asked Ole Mbatian to have a seat on one side of the empty desk; he himself sat on the other side.

He began by saying that he was investigating a raid at the gallery of an art dealer suspect, which had taken place two days earlier. The thing was, there had initially been a rather lengthy list of actionable items against the man, but one by one they had fallen out of play.

Carlander really had no reason to be going into detail about this case in the presence of the Maasai warrior. But in brief, the fact was that the goat who had been discovered in the cellar, looking confused, did not appear at this juncture to have been subjected to sexual violence. Or even cruelty to animals in a more general sense; it had been supplied with both water and carrots to munch on if it liked. However peculiar it might be to keep goats in your cellar, there was no criminal charge to be applied in that matter. The confiscated heroin turned out to be nothing but flour, and it was certainly not illegal to have or wish to have exciting sex, so all that was left was the alleged art forgery. Which was, to be sure, damning enough. If it had in fact happened—this point suddenly seemed unclear.

"Mr. Mbatian," said Carlander. "What do you have to say about these two photographs?"

He placed them on the table; one depicted *Woman with Parasol*; the other, *Boy by Stream*.

"What do you want me to say?" said Ole Mbatian.

"Do you recognize the paintings?"

"I sure do. They were once mine. I just sold them to the man with the goat. Got a better deal than I first understood, because he's probably still yelling and screaming if someone hasn't made him stop."

"They're *yours*?"

Imagine having such poor hearing.

"No."

What Carlander meant was that if the paintings had *previously* been under Mr. Mbatian's ownership, before he sold them, how could he prove this? And what connection did Mbatian have to Victor Alderheim?

Ole Mbatian said he had no connection at all to Victor Alder . . . something, and that this was probably just as well, considering the other sorts of relationships that man appeared interested in building.

"But you were conversing during breakfast?"

"Yes, a little. At first he didn't want to talk to me because I'm Black. He thought I should keep my mouth shut. At which point he became cheerful before becoming surly once again. One of the most trying people I've ever met. What was it you wanted to know?"

The inspector almost didn't know anymore.

"How you're acquainted," he said.

"But we're not."

Carlander went on:

"He said those Irma Stern paintings were in his cellar and he didn't know how they got there. Do you know?"

"Not a clue. Ask my son, if you can find him. I'm going to look for him myself, as soon as you let me go."

"Your son? What's his name?"

"Kevin."

"Kevin Mbatian?"

"Sure. Or just Kevin. He was sent to me from heaven."

Interrogator Carlander had conducted strange interrogations before, but in every other instance the interrogated party had been high as a kite. What had he got himself into?

"Where can I find Kevin?"

Ole Mbatian looked at Inspector Carlander without a word.

"Oh, that's right," the inspector corrected himself. "You intend to search for him. Do you have an address, Mr. Mbatian?"

"If I did, there would be no reason to search."

The inspector regretted his question.

"This Kevin—do you know his personal identity number?"

Personal identity number? Thought Ole Mbatian. *What a strange phrase.*

"Nine," he said.

"Nine?"

"First, eight girls."

"It's just that Swedish personal identity numbers consist of ten digits. Or twelve."

"By how many wives?"

Carlander felt it would be best to start again at the beginning.

"What I'm interested in first and foremost is those paintings. I thought you said they were painted by Irma Stern. How do you know that?"

"I was there when she painted them."

"Can you prove that?"

"Why?"

Inspector Carlander didn't quite know. The truth was, of course, that no one had claimed they were genuine; no one had tried to sell them as such. No one had tried to sell them at all. Alderheim himself denied any knowledge of anything, including the goat. He said he hadn't called Bukowskis, he denied having bought any sex toys, he maintained he had not filled a dozen plastic bags with flour while wearing gloves. Now, though, he'd changed his tune on all points except the phone call. He was audible from all the way at the other end of the corridor, through double doors. He was standing in the common room and ranting about how he demanded to see first his paintings and thereafter a lawyer.

Meanwhile the Maasai had confirmed that the paintings had been his, prior to being sold to Victor Alderheim, even though the two men had never met before. The phone call to Bukowskis had not been recorded. Perhaps it would be possible to find out where the goat had come from, and it would almost certainly be possible to trace the sex toys. But why dig deeper into legal transactions? If only that bastard hadn't changed his tune, they might have had something to take a closer look at. But now there hadn't even been a break-in. A quick search in the databases for Kevin Mbatian brought up zero hits.

With that, Inspector Carlander's sudden fervor for his job was over. The easiest thing for everyone would simply be to drop the case that perhaps had never been a case to start with. Especially easiest for Carlander himself.

"Then I will take this opportunity to thank you, Mr. Mbatian, for taking the time to answer my questions."

"By all means."

Twelve and a half days left. And then Christian Carlander would be free. To reward himself for the day's thorough investigative work, he decided to take the following day off.

PART SEVEN

Chapter 35

South Africa was too small for Irma. Not to mention Cape Town. She wrote an angry letter to a friend, describing how unpleasant it was, for a woman used to the metropolis of Berlin, to live in a provincial bubble where everyone knew everyone else and closed newcomers out.

What's more, of course, the entire continent of Africa lay at her feet, if only she turned to face north. And she did.

For a number of years her artistry thrived, nourished by her constant travels. An oceanside village in Kwa-Zulu-Natal was her first stop. She made friends wherever she went, with no regard for the boundaries of the era. While other hotel guests tossed their dirty clothes into the laundry baskets, Irma sat down with the young washerwoman. They became friends; the washerwoman invited Irma to her wedding.

Her journey through Africa continued. This way and that. Senegal, Zanzibar, Congo . . . the artist met folks of high and low standing along the way. After the washerwoman, Rosalie Gicanda, Queen of Rwanda, posed for her. And an Arabic priest. Two men. A Bahora girl. A naked girl with oranges.

Flowers too had a life of their own in Irma's world. Gladiolas, delphiniums, white lilies . . . she set form, color and inner beauty to an entire continent. Madeira became extra dear to her heart. "Sunshine and bright colors and beautiful children with big, dark eyes," she wrote in one of her many travel letters.

Her expressionistic treasure trove only grew. It so happened that during her early years in Cape Town, a buyer, who felt sorry for the mediocre young woman, handed her thirty pounds and took one of her works with him.

A hundred years later, when the mediocre woman was long dead, that painting turned up at the prestigious auction house Bonhams in London. By then the price had gone up.

From thirty pounds to three million.

Chapter 36

Irma Stern's travels through Africa are well documented by way of her many letters. In contrast to her paintings, they were not artistic masterpieces, only strong attempts: "The images fell into my lap as ripe pears fall to the grass in the autumn." But a short period of her journey can be compared to a blank spot on a world map from the end of the century before last. Anyone who tries to retrace her life and travels will encounter only silence for a whole year in the early 1960s. At that point she was over seventy, weakened by her diabetes, and nearing her end. But there was so much more to discover. Such as Congo, yet again. And after that—what?

The letters to medicine man Ole Mbatian the Elder fill the gap. Irma took a riverboat from Kinshasa all the way to Kinsangi. From there she walked on feeble legs until she got a ride on a bus and then a train into Uganda. Bus again; train once more.

Her illness grabbed hold of her somewhere east of Kampala and settled like a blanket over her diabetes-ravaged body. Her fellow travelers noticed it more than she did. Rumors began to bubble up in the rail-car. Lassa fever? Yellow fever? Dengue? Zika?

When the diagnosis was determined to be a mixture of them all, the court of popular opinion decided to pull the emergency brake and dump the white woman in a ditch. She was herded out with canes; no one wanted to touch her. Her suitcase followed her into the ditch; all it contained was art crap, nothing worth stealing.

And there the life called Irma Stern likely would have ended, if not for a cowherd who happened by with his emaciated livestock. He fetched a donkey and cart and took the dying woman to the local medicine man.

Ole Mbatian the Elder was well-known from the highlands of Chyulu in the east to Kisumu in the west. The woman had a fever, was likely diabetic, and complained of muscle aches during the times she was alert.

The medicine man took out his mixture of mint, gum acacia, and a sesame plant that previous generations had dubbed Devil's Claw. The mixture had been in the medicine cabinet a long time, would it still work?

Three months later, Irma was back on her feet thanks to Ole Mbatian's herbs, his knack for keeping the hut cool, and three glasses of papaya juice per day.

To thank him for saving her life, she painted portraits of his first wife under a parasol and his eldest son by a stream. She didn't sign them because they weren't hers—it was Ole Mbatian who gave her the opportunity to paint them by saving her life.

She attached two sincere letters, one to each painting, in which she expressed her deepest gratitude.

And headed west. Fever-free, but increasingly bothered by her diabetes.

Just before she died, sixteen months later, she sent a third letter of thanks from Cape Town, the provincial bubble that had grown into itself.

She died a hero. Seen by an entire art world. Her home became a museum. The price of her works doubled. And doubled again. And increased fivefold on top of that.

PART EIGHT

PART EIGHT

Chapter 37

Swedish winters are cruel. Not least for someone who clothes his body with a *shúkà* and his bare feet with sandals. It was minus-four degrees Celsius on the front steps of the police station when Ole Mbatian the Younger said farewell to nosy officer Carlander with the bandaged forehead.

Ole found that the cold wind that struck him outside the police doors kicked his brain into gear. Up to this point, he had been absorbed by the goal of getting out into the fresh air; now he reminded himself of the task at hand.

Standing there unsure whether he should go to the right, the left, or straight ahead was not the best way to retain his body heat. So what should he do?

Kronoberg Remand Prison had a security guard permanently stationed outside the lobby, one hired from a private firm. The place locked up every imaginable type, and it wasn't unusual for acquaintances or acquaintances of acquaintances to show up and make a scene. The guard on duty was named Pettersson.

Ole understood that the man stationed outside the door rather than inside it wasn't a member of law-enforcement leadership. But he was wearing a uniform and, like most people, was likely susceptible to flattery.

The Maasai approached him. Better too much than too little.

"Good day, Mr. Chief of Police. I wonder if you have by any chance seen my son Kevin? I think he lives here in the city somewhere."

From security company temp to chief of police in one second. Pettersson was instantly eager to lend a hand.

"What's his name, besides Kevin?"

"Besides? He's pretty tall, younger than me."

The information that the missing son was younger than his father wasn't much of a clue.

"Do you have his personal identity number? If you do, we can look up his address."

For the second time in ten minutes, Ole Mbatian had been asked the same peculiar question.

"Well, I know it's not nine."

Temporary guard Pettersson was getting the feeling that this conversation might drag on for a bit, and he became anxious about standing in the cold and talking to the half-naked Maasai.

"Shall we step into the lobby while we chat?"

"This isn't about locking me up, is it?"

"Certainly not!"

"Then that's fine."

Inside the doors, Pettersson said he needed more leads in order to have a decent chance of helping the gentleman look for his son.

Ole considered this. He gazed out at the street and the broad sidewalk through the large windows. All the while, people were passing in both directions. If one of them happened to resemble Kevin, perhaps it might be of guidance to the police chief or security guard.

Not that man, running by in some sort of tights. White of skin and red of cheek. Looked like he was in a hurry.

Not that woman, pushing a cart on four wheels in front of her. Still whiter, without red cheeks. And the wrong sex.

Definitely not whoever she had nestled down in the cart. Kevin would never fit.

The medicine man kept looking, gazing to the right and the left as temporary guard Pettersson began to lose interest. They couldn't stand there staring at the sidewalk until every one of the God-knows-how-many residents of Greater Stockholm passed by. And a half a million tourists on top of that.

"Listen, sir," he said, and was immediately cut off.

"There, maybe!" said Ole. "See those three over there, in a line, coming this way?"

"Oh, please . . ."

Life as chief of police was not at all what Pettersson had imagined.

"The one in the middle has the same color skin as my Kevin. And me, now that I think about it. He's the same height and age. Not as me, but as himself."

Jenny, Kevin and Hugo came closer.

"That's exactly what he looks like," said Ole Mbatian.

There are about ten thousand people named Kevin in Sweden. A quarter of them live in or near Stockholm, among about two and a half million other people that are named something else. Locating the correct Kevin wouldn't be easy for anyone. Not knowing his last name, address, or personal identity number wouldn't make it any easier.

The best way to find him might be to put a notice in one of the city's big newspapers, or in all of them.

This was what Ole Mbatian had done. Without being aware of it himself.

The four most important newspapers in the capital city reported on the incident at Nordic Light Hotel, where a police inspector got walloped. The editorial teams treated the matter differently, however. In the *Daily News* one could read, in an out-of-the-way corner, that an older man was suspected of minor assault on a public official after a scuffle in a hotel lobby in the central part of the city. The *Express* was more blunt:

"Maasai Warrior Runs Amok at Hotel."

The publication of the *Express* article was preceded by a discussion of media ethics in the newsroom. On the one hand, the arrested party's ethnicity was not relevant. On the other hand, writing "a man in his seventies" would provoke an unreasonable number of questions in the reader, given the photograph that showed someone wearing a red-and-black checked cloth and sandals being hauled off by police in the middle of winter.

They decided to handle the matter by calling the arrested party a Maasai warrior, after the editor-in-chief determined that this could be considered a profession like any other. Furthermore, there were enough Maasai warriors that this one could not be considered singled out (which would be in violation of Swedish journalism law). After all, each Maasai warrior was free to practice his job anywhere in the world he wished. The issue of whether the Maasai had truly "run amok" was not put to further discussion. Some things sounded too good to resist.

The result, for the *Express*, was more single issues sold in one day than at any other time in the past seven years. Meanwhile, *Dagens Nyheter*, to no commercial benefit, prioritized the story about continued disorder in the British Parliament.

Jenny saw the front pages posted outside the newsstand she and Kevin passed on their way to the bus. She poked Kevin in the shoulder and pointed. Her boyfriend looked at the headline and photograph.

"Dad!" he said.

They opted for a taxi, rather than a bus, to the office. When they arrived, Jenny and Kevin kept talking over each other and it took a minute for Hugo to understand what was going on. And another fifteen seconds to get a grip on the situation.

"They arrested him for assaulting an officer. That means Kronoberg. Ten minutes away. Come on!"

The reunion of father and adopted son was an emotional one. The son begged for forgiveness; the father hugged him and said he would be silly to expect anything else. They spoke English with one another; Swahili and Maa were best left to the savanna.

Temporary guard Pettersson looked on. And decided to drop his plans for a career in the police when he heard what he heard.

"Beloved Kevin! No one will cut your willy without your consent. *No one!*" said the man in the red-and-black checked cloth.

"Thank you, Dad, thank you!" said the youngster.

Chapter 38

O le and Kevin hardly had time to finish hugging before a young woman entered, discovered the Maasai, and walked over to introduce herself. Behind her was a cameraman.

"Hello. I'm Magda Eliasson from TV4. I understand you are Ole Mbatian, could we have a word?"

The medicine man did not know what TV4 was, but he certainly liked to talk.

"Sure we can, of course."

Also, "Magda Eliasson" sounded fun to say.

"What do you want to talk about, Magda Eliasson? I'm a medicine man by trade. If you become pregnant too often and find it troublesome, Magda Eliasson, I'm your man."

The TV reporter said she wasn't suffering from that particular malady, but she wanted to speak to

Mr. Mbatian about who he was, where he came from, and what had happened the day before at Nordic Light Hotel.

She took out the microphone and nodded at her colleague to begin filming.

"I understand that all charges against you have been dropped. Has there been any police violence?"

Ole Mbatian was struck by a guilty conscience. But it was important to tell the truth, even when it felt uncomfortable.

"I confess I happened to strike down a policeman, but it was under special and unfortunate circumstances. Furthermore, I must say that he was awfully easy to drop. The blow I dealt him wouldn't have taken down a pygmy antelope. Whyever one might wish to do that."

The reporter hadn't got quite the answer she was hoping for. But she tried again.

"And after that? Did the police retaliate?"

"After that we chatted for a bit and then they offered me dinner. Macaroni, it was called. Have you ever tried that, Magda Eliasson?"

The TV4 reporter dropped the topic of police violence; it was too difficult to combine with the served-up macaroni. So, what was the angle on this piece, if any? Might as well start over again.

296 · JONAS JONASSON

"Tell me, what are you doing here?"

By "here," she meant Sweden.

"Nothing in particular, I probably would have left by now if Magda Eliasson weren't holding me back."

"What about up to this point?"

"Up to this point I have been given a comfortable bed to sleep in, after the wonderful dinner. And breakfast in the morning, pale brown leaves in milk with jam. Sweet, but good. Also, I did a deal for two sandwiches with a caviar named Kalle, a clever swap indeed if you'll allow me to place my humility aside for a moment, Magda Eliasson."

"A deal?"

"Long story. It started with a bite. But plenty wants more. I put two oil paintings from my past in the pot and got double sandwiches in return. Her name was Irma. Pleasant lady. But sickly. Dad saved her life. My my, it was so long ago."

Ole was in a chatty mood now. Besides the fact that he'd found his Kevin, the best part of the trip was that he seemed to be meeting so many people to talk to, in contrast to his lonely hours, days, and sometimes weeks on the savanna.

The TV4 reporter had come for a different reason, but she was well aware of the story of the goat-sex man and his forgeries. Instagram, Facebook and Twitter had seen to that. Had he and the Maasai done art deals in jail?

"Irma Stern, I understand. So, the paintings you mentioned are authentic?"

"What do you mean, authentic?"

"I mean, they were painted by Irma Stern?"

"Who else would paint an Irma Stern painting? Are you not feeling quite well, Magda Eliasson? It can't be the heat—that disappeared somewhere around Istanbul."

The reporter fumbled for her next question. It was more unclear than ever what this story was about. Was it about the Maasai or the guy with the goat? Maybe a bit of both. She would have to keep asking questions and then edit together something that could be broadcast. Best-case scenario.

"So you and the jailed art dealer know each other?"

"The art dealer?"

"Victor Alderheim."

"Oh, him. No, we don't. We just spoke for a while even though he didn't want to. I never figured out whether he was angry because he had sex with goats or because he didn't."

"But the paintings . . . you said your friend Irma was the one who made them. What is the connection between . . . er, the goat-sex man and her?"

"None, as far as I'm aware. Except for the paintings, of course, but that one is brand new. Why, at
first he said he knew nothing about them. Then he
wanted them so badly that he not only gave away his
own sandwich in the deal but made me another one.
Back home on the savanna, we call that the art of ne-
gotiation. Oops, there I go placing my humility aside
again."

"So the Irma Stern paintings belong to you?"

What was wrong with Swedes?

"Didn't I just say I sold them to him?"

Jenny, Kevin and Hugo were listening. Befuddled. Be-
wildered. Bedeviled. Hugo's mind was spinning fast-
est of all.

It *was* Irma Stern who had painted the Irma Stern
paintings.

For a reason as incomprehensible as it was unpleasant, Ole Mbatian the Younger had traded them for two
sandwiches. And the man who owned them now was
the one man on earth who deserved them least.

This whole thing had turned out to be the greatest
failure Sweet Sweet Revenge Ltd. had ever seen. Hugo
Hamlin's greatest failure in every category, including
the golden potato peeler. They had destroyed the art

dealer's reputation, but in return he had come to possess paintings worth millions.

Hugo didn't know if the worst part was that the medicine man had sold the paintings from under his nose; or that he had sold them for two sandwiches with Kalles Kaviar; or that he had sold them to Victor Alderheim, of all people.

But Hugo wouldn't give up. There were signs of hope. Such as, for example, that the Ole Mbatian paintings had changed artists and in doing so had increased a thousandfold in value. For the time being they were in the extremely wrong hands, but if that detail could be changed then Hugo's fortune would be made. They could share, incidentally. There was plenty for both unpaid colleagues and Maasais and then some.

Hugo decided that the newly formed quartet should regroup. He checked Jenny and Kevin into one guest room at his home in Lidingö, and Ole Mbatian into the other.

The adman called a meeting in the dining room; they certainly had a lot to talk about and a horrendous development to hinder. But they still had to eat. They could order pizza.

"Not pizza," said Kevin.

"Hamburgers?"

"Better."

Kevin began by telling his adoptive father about his former life in Sweden. After all, the Maasai believed that his son had been delivered by En-Kai, and Kevin had never disabused him of the notion, mostly because he thought there might be something to it. Or perhaps it was the other way around: Ole Mbatian was a godsend to him. Now he was afraid that Ole Mbatian would lose faith when he learned that his son had not come straight from heaven but had previously lived a worldly life.

But the medicine man's faith in God was stronger than that. What a waste it would have been, to hold onto such a fine boy for so many years. Of course he had been down and back before.

Indeed, and his first time on earth hadn't gone so well. The father he had back then was not actually a real father, but something called a guardian. And he was none other than Victor, whom Ole had of course met while in custody.

"The angry man? The one with the goat? Then we're basically family! If I'd known that, I would have kissed him on the forehead."

Kevin was glad he hadn't. Not only was the angry

man angry, he was a *bad* person. God had missed the mark that time, which was perhaps why he'd started over with Kevin and sent him to the savanna.

Ole nodded thoughtfully. That could be.

Hugo was getting impatient. He wanted to move things forward, get straight to the point. Their task was to destroy Victor's reputation—they'd done a good job of that thus far—but also, now, his newfound wealth.

"We're out to get revenge on Victor," he said.

"Thrilling," said Ole Mbatian.

The Maasai was well-acquainted with the concept of revenge. It could be sly; you had to remain on guard. Ole recalled a time many years earlier when eighteen of the village goats vanished overnight. The youngster in charge of watching them had fallen asleep on the job. Everyone knew that it was thieving Miterienanka from the neighboring village who had come by. Chief Kakenya gathered a large and duly armed delegation from their own village. They killed the thieving man, burned down his village, and took back the eighteen goats plus another thirty who no longer had anywhere to go.

Hugo thought this sounded like a rather harsh reaction, but it wouldn't serve his purposes to say so. "Scary story" would have to suffice.

The medicine man nodded.

"It was just a bit of a letdown to find the eighteen goats were back when we got home. They had slipped out through a hole in the fence because the grass was greener on the other side. After their meal they got homesick and came back."

Hugo didn't want to hear the rest. He guided the conversation back to the present moment and continent at hand.

Ole was happy to be of service. Revenge sounded like a nice change of pace; it had been too long.

"Will you come home with me afterwards?" he asked Kevin.

His adopted son felt ill at ease.

"I just got engaged, Dad."

"What's that?"

"I'm getting married."

"To how many women?"

"One, to start with."

"To me and no one else," said Jenny.

Ole Mbatian congratulated them both. He said he would understand if they chose Sweden over the savanna, even if it was cold beyond all reason. It explained why Jenny was so pale, along with just about everyone else. But couldn't they give it some thought?

Kevin loved his adopted father more than ever.

"We'll see how it all turns out. But first we need to make sure justice is served."

Hugo was pleased to hear that Kevin was getting back on topic.

"That's right. The first thing we should try to do is get your paintings back from the angry man."

Everything ground to a halt.

"But he bought them from me."

"For two sandwiches," said Hugo. "That doesn't count."

"With caviar," said the medicine man.

"Cod roe, sugar and potato flakes," Hugo corrected him.

"A deal's a deal."

Curtain.

Darkness.

What were they supposed to do now?

The only thing Hugo was certain of—one hundred percent—was that Ole Mbatian was not going to change his mind. This happened on occasion, in the ad business: a client could be objectively wrong yet lack the ability to change their mind. When this occurred, the adman had to do it for them.

Hugo's plan had been, from the start, to make two counterfeit paintings appear authentic. Complications ensued. Circumstances changed.

The new plan had been: get two counterfeit paintings to look like forgeries under production. Circumstances changed. Complications ensued.

Coming up with a fresh idea in this case meant getting the now *authentic* Irma Stern paintings to appear as unauthentic as possible. This would demand a reverse authentication. A shattered provenance. Whatever words Jenny was showing off with this time.

So thought Hugo.

Six kilometers away sat Victor with his goat, thinking the same thing. But the other way around.

Chapter 39

Two days after the news of the paintings was made public, thanks to tasteless stories of sex toys, drugs and goats all over the press and social media, the art world was roiling with excitement. Two presumed Irma Stern forgeries! How it happened was unclear, but the media had got their hands on the police photographs (it wasn't unclear to those involved: the current list price dictated five thousand pre-taxed kronor per image to Officer X from Newspaper Y). The photographs were of high quality and it seemed as though their motifs were extraordinary. If they had not been made by the artist herself—and it seemed highly unlikely—then people wanted to know more about the forger. Among the most vociferous participants in the debate was a high-profile member of the Swedish Academy in Stockholm. He was famous for his opinions that art transcended rape and the breaking of both rule and law. The most interesting aspect of this case—according to the member of the academy—was consequently not the alleged forger's alleged drug dealings or what he had done with his goat, but how he could have achieved such luster in his counterfeits.

The main character of this artistic worldwide drama had been freed and was back in his art gallery. A few minutes earlier, a police van had come by to return two Irma Stern paintings, four large boxes of sex toys, and one goat. The bags of flour had vanished somewhere along the way.

Victor tried to refuse the goat and the sex toys, but the carriers wouldn't let him.

"They're on our list, you can't pick and choose. Please sign the delivery slip."

To maintain a modicum of control over the goat, they had put it on a leash. As soon as Victor signed the document, one of the carriers handed him the leash.

"Have a nice day, sicko!"

The carrier's colleague, in the meantime, was carrying in toys and paintings with their easels and stacking them all inside the door. On his way back, he spit on the ground at Victor Alderheim's feet.

The men in the van took off. Victor noticed someone had written something in white paint across his two big shop windows:

PER on one, and VERT! on the other.

He hurried inside, goat and all, and locked the door.

Stockholm's most prominent pervert sat in the kitchen of the six-bedroom apartment to gather his thoughts. At first it didn't work at all, because the goat was bleating for food and drink. One liter of water and four apples later, it turned out that the goat wasn't potty-trained.

So someone had broken into the gallery, gone down to the cellar, and rigged up paintings, sex toys, pretend heroin—and a goat.

This someone had to be Kevin, the former ward whom Victor had also thought was "former" in every sense.

But why would he have done this? And how had he come across the paintings? Via the Maasai man in prison. Who had presumably run into the youngster there on the savanna in the middle of the night and saved his life. Indeed, their kind stuck together.

The Maasai was named Mb-something and claimed that the paintings were his. But more importantly, he claimed they were authentic—and Victor had bought them for a Kalles Kaviar sandwich apiece. Without a receipt, as luck would have it. What with the police inspector's entrance and the hubbub that ensued, the napkin was never signed.

Now he had to tread carefully. If he was dealing with two authentic, yet-undiscovered Irma Sterns, he would be financially home free. In which case it couldn't have come at a better time; the gallery's accounts had become an increasingly sad story since that old devil Alderheim died. No one had better luck than him when it came to buying low and selling high.

Speaking of the old man, the Alderheim name was ruined—a goat and a few other things had seen to that. But names could be changed, and Victor had done it before. Incidentally, he was fine being called both PER and VERT if he must, as long as he had millions in the bank. Quite a few millions, as it seemed.

With them he could put his twenty-eight-year detour as an art dealer behind him. He would have enough for both paid love encounters and effecting real-world change. Exactly how he would do that he hadn't yet figured out; it had all happened so quickly there at the end. Maybe he would track down the revolutionaries from his past (the ones who weren't in the slammer, that is), and on the strength of his age, cleverness and capital place himself at the top of the hierarchy.

Victor had hated the clientele of Alderheim's art gallery from his very first day. It was as if proud nationalism no longer had a place there. Old Man Alderheim bragged about what a broad selection of art he carried. "We have *everything*," he used to say. Everything but anything that meant something, Victor thought.

Alderheim's prided itself on being a leader in the Scandinavian art world, but beyond a lone Carl Larsson in one corner, there was nothing there, on Victor's first day, to remind one of the soul of the Swedish people. The Larsson painting was a tribute to a traditional Christmas celebration in rural Sweden, totally free of Kurds, Afghans, and other such half-people. Yet it remained unsold. Victor was sure this was the fault of the social-liberal government and had nothing to do with the fact that he'd doubled the price to do justice to Larsson.

Beyond the Scandinavian, the gallery offered a broad assortment of European sculptures, Asian porcelain, and antiques from every corner of the world. And above all: that bloody modernism.

As the years went by, Victor learned more about the art trade than Jenny knew or would have liked to admit. He hated Irma Stern, of course, but understood her commercial value. She was—almost sixty years after her death—hotter than ever. And he was aware (unlike Hugo Hamlin) that his *authentic* Irma Stern paintings needed to be so in the eyes of the experts as well. It wasn't enough for a confused Maasai in Stockholm to say they were.

The leading Irma Stern expert was in New York. But things had to be done in the right order. Other tasks were more urgent. The most urgent of all was tied up next to Victor's stove, peeing on the floor.

Chapter 40

Background knowledge was everything. The day after Ole Mbatian's astonishing appearance in Stockholm, Hugo assembled his lodgers in the living room. To start with, he wanted to know all about Irma Stern's connection with the medicine man.

Ole, who considered himself extremely forgetful, said he remembered it like it was yesterday. He immediately followed up by proving that this wasn't quite true. He wasn't sure if he'd gone through his test of manhood before Irma showed up. Back then, a Maasai warrior-to-be didn't have to live under the open sky from long rain to long rain before his circumcision; it was enough to encounter a lion on the savanna and win the fight. A boy who lost wasn't given the final test. Or an honorable burial.

In any case, the Maasai recalled how Auntie Irma

had painted him by a stream. He had to sit there poking a stick into the water for almost an entire day.

"Boy by stream," Jenny said reverently.

In Hugo's world, this was bad news. Any proven connections between Irma and Mbatian were harmful to the cause.

"Do you have any lovely mementos of those days left back home?" he asked insidiously.

He was hoping for the opposite.

"Oh, yes. My father had a camera—no one else in the village had one. They still don't. We're not known for adapting new things. That's because we have a half-toothless numbskull for a chief. I have a lot to tell him when I get home, about escalators and so forth."

"Escalators?" said Hugo.

"Yes, it looks like an ordinary staircase, but it moves all on its own in either one direction or the other. Just think, walking and walking and getting nowhere. Kind of reminds me of the chief, actually."

Hugo gently interrupted the Maasai, saying he believed he did know what an escalator was. What he wanted to know more about was Ole's father's camera.

"Well, he used it to take photographs, which he developed himself in the medicine hut. I got to be his assistant. I recall one time as a little boy I tasted the developer, which I should not have done. Lucky Dad was the man he was—he saved my life. If you ingest such a thing you must neutralize it with arrowroot and—"

But Hugo was too impatient to find out what sort of concoction Ole Mbatian had used to save the life of his son.

"That's fine," he said.

It wasn't, though. Each piece of news was worse than the last.

"According to Murphy's Law, those photographs must still exist, right?"

"I'm not familiar with that law, but each image has been saved. Dad photographed me and Auntie Irma down by the stream."

Well, goddammit. If there were photographs of Irma Stern painting a boy by a stream, an expert would have to be both blind and reality-challenged not to assess the painting as authentic, even if sixty years had passed. Ole Mbatian's photographic archive must disappear. Immediately!

But Hugo didn't know whether he could trust the proud Maasai. Best to keep him partially in the dark about the details.

"It would be so fantastic to see those pictures.

Would you be comfortable with letting me go down and get them? Then we can sit here and look through them together."

It wouldn't be cheap, but this was war. Hugo couldn't stand the fact that they'd just made Victor Alderheim beyond rich. Revenge had been achieved in the sense that the art dealer's reputation had been destroyed. Now said revenge just needed to be made sweet. It felt like a tough nut to crack.

"That's fine," said Ole Mbatian. "But it's a terribly long journey."

Hugo said he was aware.

"As long as you're there, why don't you bring back Irma's delightful thank-you letters to Dad as well? They're in the same drawer."

Letters too? Hugo cursed inwardly. Irma Stern might as well just come back from the dead to confirm everything in person.

Now, a strange white man couldn't simply march into Ole Mbatian's village, ask directions, and take with him the medicine man's belongings. He might end up with a spear or two through his body.

"Perhaps it's best if I come along," said Ole Mbatian.

"But Dad! You just got here!" said Kevin.

Hugo did not like the idea of moving between continents with the unpredictable Maasai as a travel companion.

Jenny came to his rescue. She had read in her boyfriend's adoptive father's passport that his visa was valid for no more than a single entry into the Kingdom of Sweden. If he went home and came back, he would have to apply again, and no one knew how that might turn out, given that he now had a police record.

"Too bad," said Hugo.

They arrived at an agreement: Ole Mbatian the Younger would call Civil Servant Wilson at city hall in Narok to ask him to travel to the Maasai village a half-day's journey away to prepare the chief for the upcoming visit from a white man.

"Hello there, Wilson. It's Ole."

"The medicine man?"

"The Kenyan. You made that happen with your red stamp, or maybe it was the blue one."

"Both, actually."

"I'm calling from . . . that country. My memory, you know. Sweden! I need a favor from you."

"Just don't ask me to close city hall, I almost got fired by the mayor last time."

"I was going to ask you to close city hall."

Before the conversation was over, it had cost the medicine man yet another cow. Oh well, he had plenty to spare.

Wilson was already on his way to the village. That just left Hugo.

"Shall I explain how to navigate the last little bit?" Ole Mbatian asked.

"Please do."

How else would he find his way?

According to Ole, it was complicated. He could ask for directions to find the road to Narok; there were even signs. The difficult part started once he got there. It was most important that Hugo did not take a left at the intersection where the post office used to be, but continued on to the next one.

"How am I supposed to know where the post office used to be?"

"No, you're *not* supposed to turn there."

Kevin interrupted the adman and his father before anything went off the rails.

"Wouldn't it be better if I sent you a link with the coordinates, Hugo?"

So it would, and so it was.

"Just think, I lived in my village for an entire life

without knowing that it has coordinates," said Ole Mbatian. "Let's not tell the chief back home, he would ban them."

The toothless one seemed less and less well-traveled with every passing day.

Chapter 41

Victor Alderheim was not particularly digital. Or social. He didn't have any personal accounts on Facebook, Instagram, or Twitter. He did, however, regularly visit online forums, where people who shared his worldview exchanged both information and thoughts.

There were threads about almost everything. Such as conflict between true nationalism and liberalism. The general public had such a ridiculously hard time understanding that strong nations were not built by the raising of hands. But the laughable notion of "one citizen one vote" had, during the past decade, bitten itself in the ass. While traditional politicians, traditional media, and state-controlled television continued to walk hand in hand towards the abyss, people were silently mobilizing. Like in Victor's preferred forum: those who knew what was what told the masses all they ought to understand. This had already begun dismantling the liberal fag-democracy in basically every country in Europe. The developments in the United States and parts of South America showed promise as well. The post-communist democracy in Russia was already history, while in China they had never even pretended to have one. That fucking Irma Stern ought to have been sent to a prison camp there as punishment. Now, instead, she was about to make Victor a multimillionaire, which could be considered punishment enough.

The right forum threads made him feel like he had things in common with other people, even if the level of discourse was seldom as high as he might wish. To find sufficiently intellectual stimulation, he turned to the National Library. He who searched meticulously through the shelves would find the nuggets of gold he was after. Such as Paul Schultze-Naumburg's extraordinary *Art and Race*, in which the author alleged that only Aryan artists could create culturally advanced works. In his argument against rebellious art forms he compared specific modernist paintings with carefully selected photographs of people with developmental disorders. Schultze-Naumburg was of the opinion that

the only correct traditions were the medieval and clas-
sical Greek ones. Modernism was mental illness, not
art. Alderheim thought more than once about making
a post with book recommendations, but to do so he
would have to register on the forum, and he didn't
want to do that.

That Victor himself would become a hot topic on
the forum was not a development he could have pre-
dicted. Thus far, the free discussion there was serving
the purposes of the revolution, so he could let it go.
But Christ, how people exaggerated. Alleged sex with
goats was not something you could get away with.

The plus side of his character assassination on social
networks was that it had some influence on the traditional media and prompted them to push some boundaries. For instance, TV4 actually allowed the phrase
"goat-sex man" to be used in their feature on the
Maasai. He really should have sued, but he had gained
so much for his trouble. Such as the medicine man's
name. *Ole Mbatian the Younger.* And the fact that the
stupid bastard stood there on TV and confirmed that
he had sold his paintings to Victor. There—his signed
contract!

And incidentally, the animal was out of the way. It

had taken a certain amount of brainpower to get rid of it properly. He couldn't simply tie Sweden's most publicized goat to a lamppost in downtown Stockholm and walk away. He would have been branded a whole new dimension of animal abuser the very next day.

Nor could he drive it into the country and sneak it into the nearest paddock. It was February. The paddocks were full of snow and empty of animals.

His solution was to sell the damn thing. Victor knew nothing about the current market value of a goat, but he feared it was worse than nothing. He formulated a classified ad in the right place online: "For sale: goat and five thousand kronor. Price: one hundred kronor."

After two minutes, he received a response from a taxi driver in Solna.

He wanted to know if the goat already had a name; if not, he planned to name it after his mother.

"Go right ahead," said Victor Alderheim. "I'm sure that'll make her proud."

With the goat gone, the authentication of the Irma Stern paintings was top of the Alderheimian agenda. The expert in New York, one Dr. Harris, was not easy to get hold of. From the start, he communicated via his secretary's secretary. After two rounds of emails,

Victor was allowed to deal with the secretary herself, who informed him that she would shortly be bringing this matter to the doctor's attention.

Alderheim hated the American Irma Stern expert's guts before he'd even got hold of him. But he needed a thumbs up from the arrogant man. And he wouldn't get one unless he did his homework first.

PART NINE

Chapter 42

A four-wheel-drive rental car awaited him at Jomo Kenyatta Airport, its steering wheel on the wrong side. The Brits had really colonized this country with a vengeance.

The GPS on Hugo's phone led him on a four-hour journey through the Kenyan countryside, followed by another two through the Kenyan savanna and bush. Whether he passed a post office that was no longer there along the way, he had no way of knowing.

Ole Mbatian's village was strikingly similar to what he had imagined. About forty mud-and-wood huts, each with four straight walls and roofs of dried palm grass. All of them within a pole fence that protected them from the wild animals at night. Even the buffalo in its best of moods could otherwise be a danger to life and limb if it got the bright idea of scratching its back against one of the fragile hut walls. The wall would collapse, a sleepy Maasai family would rise from the wreckage and meet the gaze of the beast. A buffalo was to a human more or less as the llama creature was to the German shepherd. Things would be sure to start off on the wrong hoof.

Ole Mbatian's three huts were on the other end of the village, next to the fence. In hut number one he lived with his first wife; in hut number two, with his second, and—most of the time—up on the hill in hut number three with Kevin, the paintings, and his collected apothecary.

The medicine man had warned the adman against simply storming into any of the huts without first announcing his presence and drinking tea with the chief. He could converse about whatever he liked, of course, but Ole recommended avoiding any questions about why there were no teeth in the chief's mouth. On the other hand, it wouldn't hurt for Hugo to happen to say something positive about Ole.

"Such as?"

The medicine man didn't know, just something small. Like that he'd brokered peace between people or saved someone's life. It wouldn't be true in the strictest sense, but there were deeper, more philosophical ways to see things. Who knew? Perhaps Ole had saved the life of that art dealer by selling the two paintings. He'd been so angry he might have burst otherwise.

Hugo privately thought that he himself had just about suffered a heart attack on account of that sale, but he nodded. A medicine man on a long journey would only benefit from having his position in the village affirmed now and then. Otherwise he might find someone else at his post on the day he returned.

Hugo politely greeted a few of the villagers and was about to ask after the chief's hut when he realized which one it was. It was the largest one, located in the center of the village. It could very well have been a four-room home. With a two-roomer right next to it.

Outside the large hut, three women were crouching down and washing clothes, each with a basin full of water. Hugo guessed they were wives one, two, and three. He asked if they knew where the chief was, but there was no need for them to answer, for at that very moment a half-toothless man came out through the opening.

The toothless man eyed the white man up and down.

"Good day. How can I help you? I'm the chief. My name is Olemeeli the Well-Traveled, son of Kakenya the Handsome and grandson of Lekuton the Bold."

Hugo said he was Hugo Hamlin, son of Erik Hamlin the drunk and grandson of Rurik Hamlin who had been stationmaster in his time. A job for the courageous; each day one had to keep from being run over by a train.

Olemeeli was impressed by the guest's family tree, and it didn't hurt that Hugo said he was a chief himself, over a tribe called Sweet Sweet Revenge Ltd. Ole Mbatian was a guest of honor there, ever since he had . . . brokered peace between Israel and Palestine and saved the life of . . . a man of very great worth. Potentially.

The chief didn't know who Israel and Palestine were or why they had been enemies, but he thanked Hugo for the information about the medicine man's doings.

Deep down, Olemeeli was happy the troublesome medicine man was off somewhere else; he was the only one who dared, thanks to his position, to act obstinate with his chief. To be sure, the knocked-out teeth incident was fifty years in the past, but not only was Olemeeli well-traveled, he also held a grudge.

He did not, however, share any of this with the guest from afar. He said that Ole Mbatian was missed, and that it was good to hear he was well and that his talents were flourishing.

It was getting on towards evening. Hugo wanted to make his return trip as soon as he had completed his errand, but he knew that he had to be patient. Olemeeli announced that the two chiefs would drink to success before dinner. Then the guest could choose which wife he wanted to sleep with that night. Two of the three had already expressed interest; the third might be open to persuasion.

Hugo feared both stages of the evening. But life had taught him not to be tormented by anticipated misfortunes ahead of time but to take them as they came. The first one was what he and the chief would drink to their mutual successes. Ox blood?

No—rather, an eighteen-year-old Glenfiddich. The chief poured them each a glass.

"My father and grandfather made their toasts with fermented goat's milk, but I'm well-traveled and happened to get a taste of this in my relative youth. This was during a field trip to Loiyangalani way up north. I was attacked by an electrical outlet in the wall and passed out. All they had to do was pass the drink under my nose and I woke right up again."

Olemeeli took a sip without first offering a toast—anathema in Sweden. Hugo thought perhaps this wasn't part of Maasai culture, or maybe the chief was simply thirsty. The adman followed his lead as he listened to the rest of the story.

Immediately after the outlet accident, something even worse happened. Olemeeli got his left index finger stuck in a typewriter and broke it in two places. It hurt something awful and the local medicine man suggested that Olemeeli should not merely sniff the golden-brown liquid, but also drink it.

"And that was that," said Olemeeli.

Because, what a flavor! It filled his mouth and soul in a way the future chief had never before experienced. It was as if it had been sent to him directly from En-Kai.

Hugo didn't know what En-Kai was; it sounded like God, or maybe heaven. But he did know Glenfiddich, and although it wasn't as smoky as he would have wished, there was no ruling out that both God and heaven might have had a finger in that pie. After all the trials and tribulations of the last twenty-four hours, it was as if his whole body was startled back to life.

"En-Kai," he said.

After the second glass, Hugo wondered where the chief had got hold of the magical drink. Because surely it wasn't the same bottle from his time up north?

No, there was a liquor store in Nairobi that offered delivery service. They grumbled when Olemeeli wanted liquor driven to a village in Maasai Mara, a six-

SWEET SWEET REVENGE LTD · 331

or seven-hour drive from the store, and they grumbled a little more when he wanted to pay in livestock. But after a few days' negotiations, the puzzle pieces fell into place. Now they came once a year in a lorry, dropped off crates of Glenfiddich, and received cows and goats as thanks for their trouble.

"One cow for every two boxes. Or six goats. Like I always say: they can't count in Nairobi!"

Which left the question of which of the wives Hugo would spend the night with. But that problem solved itself. He fell asleep with his left cheek on the dinner table after seven courses and most of a second bottle of whisky. The chief put two blankets over him and assigned an underling to keep watch.

At breakfast, Olemeeli thanked him for the previous evening and added that his head was pounding so badly that he actually missed his medicine man. Hugo wouldn't go so far as to say that he missed Ole Mbatian, but he agreed about the pounding.

After an omelet, mixed fruits and coffee, he thought it was time to get down to business. Olemeeli beat him to it.

"I understand that you're a big deal back home, Chief Hugo. Unlike the *mzungu* who was here and left two days ago."

"*Mzungu?*"

"Your colleague, Chief Hugo. The one who took the medicine man's belongings. I must say, however—just between us chiefs—that the colleague was not a pleasant experience. I'll leave any potential punishment up to you. I've always been of the opinion that chiefs ought not step on each other's feet."

At first, Hugo understood nothing. Then everything.

Victor Alderheim had beat him there. And Ole Mbatian's phone call had helped him.

Chapter 43

Victor had traveled the route before. Stockholm— Nairobi, rental car, making tracks straight to the middle of nowhere. He took the same flight as he had five years earlier, but he really hit the gas for the last few hours, so it was still light when he arrived. Because of course he had to ask his way to the goddamn medicine man's village, starting from the spot where he had once dumped Kevin. Once Victor got to the village, he planned to track down those pictures the medicine man had mentioned, the ones of him and Irma together. He had his pockets full of bills to help him along the way. If there was anything the locals understood, it must be dollars.

With the help of double goatherds (just imagine) he found himself in Ole Mbatian's village even faster than he could have hoped. There he was welcomed as if they expected him. Simply inconceivable. He hardly had to clear his throat before they carried out all the evidence in a box and put it in the back of his car.

Victor had hoped for a blurry photograph of the Maasai in the red sheet, along with Irma. That would be enough to answer all questions about the authenticity of the paintings. What he received instead was a treasure he couldn't even have dreamed up.

All that was left was to snub the chief, who seemed to think they should sit there chatting half the night. Idiot!

While the old man disappeared into the hut to fetch some sort of hocus pocus for them to toast with, Victor took the opportunity to leave. Without saying goodbye.

He slept a few hours in the car, halfway to Nairobi, and was on his way home again by seven o'clock the next morning. Somewhere in the sky above Egypt he passed Hugo heading in the other direction. Neither of them knew it. Any more than they knew anything about what awaited them.

Chapter 44

Victor Alderheim needed, once and for all, to find someone to look at the paintings and evidence. And to say: "These are authentic goods." This could be none other than Dr. Frank B. Harris of New York, the world's leading expert on Irma Stern. His word was law—literally, according to a series of paragraphs in the American legal system.

As it happened, Dr. Harris was deeply religious and of a high moral standing. His social circle was mainly populated by two Supreme Court justices, a Republican senator and the Archbishop of New York.

For several days, the leading topic of conversation in Dr. Frank B. Harris's Manhattan office had been the two presumably counterfeit Irma Stern paintings that had shown up at the home of a man who apparently had sex with animals. All of this likely would have been possible to shake off if the published photographs of the aforementioned paintings hadn't suggested that they were masterpieces rather than forgeries. Or both.

Dr. Harris felt that he needed to know who had painted them, if indeed it had not been Irma Stern herself. On the one hand, it was inconceivable that she had. On the other hand, for the past day or so there had been rumors online that the alleged owner claimed the works were authentic. Not that the doctor spent time on obscure internet sites or on social media in general. But he did have colleagues, including two secretaries. Who in turn had assistants. Simpler folks socialized in simpler ways than did the doctor himself.

Dr. Harris had no desire to meet the Swedish zoophile. Unfortunately, it would be impossible to avoid if he wanted a closer look at the paintings. And he did. He must. What's more, the man who had sex with animals had contacted his office to ask for help.

The doctor was at a loss. He needed to buy time, so decided to bounce the horrible man between his secretaries for a few days.

Meanwhile he called his friend the archbishop, who in turn contacted his childhood friend and mentor, the former archbishop of Buenos Aires. Things had gone really well for him since last they spoke. He now lived in a massive house in Rome after having been offered the job as boss of everything.

Pope Francis was as happy to hear from his friend the archbishop as he was concerned about their topic of conversation. He firmly believed that he already had plenty of sex-related nuisances to deal with. Oh well, the Lord continued to give him crosses to carry. All he could do was grin and bear it.

The question his friend posed was as concrete as it was infernal:

Was it advisable for the friend's friend to associate with, and perhaps even shake hands with, a man who copulated with animals?

In fact, it really was not. Such a sin must be repudiated at all imaginable levels and in all imaginable ways.

But what if there might be a greater purpose, for instance the possibility that one might be able to give the world two new, extraordinary paintings by a great artist?

The Pope sought answers in the Bible, where else? Certainly, Psalms did say "depart from evil, and do good." This was not a signal to fraternize with persons who, according to Leviticus, should be punished by death. But in Romans 12, it said "do not be overcome by evil, but overcome evil with good."

Confronting the horrible man was the right path.

338 · JONAS JONASSON

The Bible was great in the sense that it often contradicted itself. You could choose whatever fit best in a
given situation.

"Tell your friend he can travel to see the lost
Mr. Alderheim in Stockholm, and shake his hand if he
must, but at the same time he must take every measure
to bring him to rights, he must overwhelm him with
goodness."

So it came to pass that Dr. Frank B. Harris, with the
indirect blessing of the Pope, landed at Terminal 5 at
Stockholm Arlanda Airport early one morning, where
he was met by one very eager Victor Alderheim.

"Dr. Harris? It's an honor to welcome you to Sweden."

"He has told you, O mortal, what is good; and what
does the Lord require of you, but to do justice, and to
love kindness, and to walk humbly with your God,"
said Dr. Frank B. Harris.

"What now?" said Victor Alderheim.

One silent journey from the airport to the capital city
later, Dr. Harris was sitting in the lost man's kitchen
with the alleged Irma Stern paintings on the table in
front of him. He gave thanks to the Lord that there
were no goats in the room.

The doctor studied the paintings minutely for over

half an hour but was deeply enamored of both works after ten seconds.

"Well, what do you say?" Victor Alderheim asked at last.

When the doctor didn't respond, Victor took out the evidence he'd gathered in Africa.

What a treasure trove! Black-and-white pictures of Irma painting the child by the stream. *That* child, of course. And her letters to the man who had apparently saved her life.

Dr. Harris looked breathlessly through the photographs. The American expert's eyes filled with tears at the sight.

And the letters—definitely penned by the great artist! No one spelled as badly as she. No one else placed their periods and commas so incorrectly. And, on top of that, the handwriting: when Irma wrote, the recipient had to guess at every fourth word.

But the one who guessed right, and moved the punctuation around, would also discover a beauty to her words. Such as in the letter to the medicine man who had saved her life, in which the aging woman thanked him for the chance to live a little longer.

It was established beyond all doubt that what lay on the table before Dr. Harris were two previously unknown late Sterns.

"Who owns the paintings, in God's name?" he said. He found himself thinking too much of the Pope.

"I do, of course," said Victor. "In my name."

"Can you prove it?"

Prove it? Victor's excited tension turned into a moderate rage.

"How is that relevant to the appraisal? You just confirm that the paintings are authentic, and I'll deal with the rest."

Until this point, the terrible man who had sex with animals had remained calm. But now Dr. Harris felt he was getting a glimpse of the man's true nature.

"Even Paul the Apostle felt remorse. You ought to consider the same, Mr. Alderheim."

Who was this fruitcake they had shipped across the Atlantic?

"Soon I will feel remorse for having invited you here. Just tell me what the paintings are worth, and I'll drive you back to your plane."

Money, Dr. Harris thought. A constant threat to piety. Humanity had been on a downhill slide ever since the advent of mercantilism.

"I will sign a certificate of authenticity and give an estimated value, but only to the owner of the works. Judging by the photographs and letters, this person was one Mr. Ole Mbatian in the sixties. It is not my responsibility to guess, but if I permit myself the freedom, I would guess that Ole Mbatian is dead. In that case, one might reasonably assume that the ownership transferred to his children and perhaps grandchildren, given that there are no letters of sale along the way."

Victor wanted to strangle the American. But that bastard would probably be delighted at the chance to meet his maker. Instead he pulled up a video clip he'd saved from TV4, in which a man named Ole Mbatian the Younger, apparently the son of his father, announced that he had sold the paintings to "the goat-sex man."

"And that's you?"

"Yes," said Victor. "That is, no, that is, yes."

After all, no one wanted to be the goat-sex man, but more important things were at stake here.

Dr. Harris studied the clip again.

"There is clear circumstantial evidence," he said. "May I then just ask you to produce a copy of the receipt."

Dr. Harris lifted his briefcase into his lap as if to put inside it what he would soon hold in his hand.

"That's not how it works in Africa," Victor attempted.

"Have you purchased two probable Irma Sterns without a receipt?"

"Jesus Christ."

"Therefore I tell you, people will be forgiven for every sin and blasphemy, but blasphemy against the Spirit will not be forgiven."

"Huh?"

"Matthew 12:31."

It was impossible to get anywhere with the religious nut of an American expert. Victor had planned to drive him to the hotel, but the weather was so bad he was happy to let him walk. As an alternative to a good-bye, Dr. Harris repeated his conditions.

"In a few days I'm going back to the United States. Before I do, I intend to visit Moderna Museet and a few other places. Judging by Irma Stern's letters, the masterpieces were owned by Ole Mbatian the Elder. I accept that Ole Mbatian the Younger inherited them from him. I judge these men to be the original owners of the works. To produce the certificate you have requested, Mr. Alderheim, I want evidence for each new owner after them and up to you. The television clip about the goat-sex man, that is to say, you, God forgive you, indicates that no change in ownership has taken place in recent decades. Which means I must get in writing what was said on TV. Amen."

Now Harris was mixing God up in what he said again. It threw Victor off.

"What are you saying?"

Dr. Harris was only human; he was under pressure. He tried to express himself in a worldly way but felt the Pope looming over him. What he wanted to say was that spoken words were all well and good, but in this case, it was necessary to have them in writing. When his brain mixed up the Writ with the Word, it all came out wrong.

"This is he who hears the word, but the cares of the world and the delight in riches choke the word, and it proves unfruitful."

"Do you have a screw loose, Dr. Harris?"

The doctor tried again.

"Make sure that you get Ole Mbatian's signature on a transfer-of-ownership document."

"But you already said that."

The snow was coming down in clumps. The snow-plows had not yet begun their work.

"Now, don't slip and fall, Dr. Harris."

Where should Victor begin? He had not only to find a Black medicine man in snow-white Stockholm and get him to sign his name on the correct paper, he also had to protect what he'd already achieved. After all, he was in possession of two paintings potentially worth millions and the almost unparalleled evidence of just how authentic they were. Even the evidence itself was a cultural treasure with monetary value.

What he also had was a front door that Kevin, with or without a companion, had come through without even damaging the lock. It was thirty years old and apparently could be forced with a yawn by anyone who knew what he or she was doing.

A new lock. Now.

Then it would be time to find the Maasai. Should the bizarre American authenticator have time to head home, then so be it. There was a flight to New York every day; all he'd have to do was go after him and shove the evidence down his throat, preferably along with the New Testament.

A new lock? No.

The average locksmith in Stockholm was, like the average Stockholmer, active on social media. A place where one could, in contrast to traditional media, find out the actual state of things. Accordingly, it had been firmly established that the state of things inside the art dealer's door was beyond disgusting. The four goats (one can easily become four when the truth gets out) were involuntarily in the company of both lambs and calves. It was said, but not confirmed, that the art dealer also had a cage with a hamster inside. No one wanted to know more. Everyone wanted to know more. Enough people knew what they knew, that Victor Alderheim's best bet would have been to move to the other side of the globe, or to another planet had that been feasible.

The long and the short of it was that the first three locksmiths refused to help him. The fourth was more defensive and might have time next autumn.

Victor would have to find a makeshift solution. For it was clear that Kevin had forced his old lock without even leaving a mark. It was almost as if he had a key of his own.

While Victor drilled and installed a hasp and a sturdy padlock, his thoughts returned to the key. They didn't take him as far as Jenny, but they did go so far as to wonder whether Kevin might decide to try again. The first time, the kid had—among other things—placed two paintings in his cellar, at which point the police arrived and accused Victor of forgery. Who would place two authentic Irma Sterns anywhere but on their own wall or in a safe?

Conclusion number one: Kevin didn't know what he was doing when he did it.

Conclusion number two: If Kevin had been watching TV or had found the Maasai, he would have wised up since. And he might try again. In this case to steal back what he'd given away.

Victor had installed the hasp and padlock on the inside of the door. From the street side, there would be no reason to suspect that this was anything but the same easily forced door as last time.

Victor Alderheim didn't know of anyone more gifted than he.

A long day was nearing its end. The art dealer was back in his apartment, sitting on the same chair Dr. Harris had sat on while he alternately studied the paintings and made references to God. Time to open the day's mail, which consisted of a single envelope. From the Tax Authority.

Five years and three days after the former guardian had reported Kevin missing and presumed dead, the decision had been made.

He had been declared deceased.

Too bad it wasn't true.

Chapter 45

While Hugo was in Kenya drinking whisky, Jenny and Kevin set about entertaining themselves and the Maasai to the best of their ability. First, Moderna Museet.

The two youngsters had already hit it off, of course, but it had all happened so fast. Each affirmation of their sudden feelings was, therefore, to their benefit. For instance, an encounter with Sigrid Hjertén, one of the few female Swedish representatives of expressionism. In one of her works she had placed a lady of the fancier persuasion on a balcony overlooking a bustling Stockholm. Down below were horse-drawn vehicles, streetcars, social encounters and commerce. In the foreground was the woman on the balcony, which had an extra-high railing, as if she were a prisoner in her own social situation.

Kevin thought the work was like a rendezvous of expressionism and the yet-to-be-invented feminism. Jenny knew what he meant. Her feelings for her boyfriend were affirmed every day.

"Why does she look so grumpy?" said Ole Mbatian.

After the museum, Jenny suggested they visit Skansen, Stockholm's renowned open-air museum. There one could look at interesting animals and historical buildings. Ole said he had already looked at plenty of animals over the years. When he found out that some of the historical Skansen buildings were several hundred years old, he was merely annoyed. It reminded him that no hut back home had stood for more than four years without collapsing and having to be rebuilt.

The Skansen plan was a bad one from a number of perspectives. It was still below freezing outside, and Ole Mbatian had no intention of abandoning his *shúkà*.

Perhaps an indoor shopping center might be just the thing? Ole thought that sounded good; there were a few purchases he wanted to make. Above all, he needed a new set of weapons. They'd confiscated his spear and knife way back in Nairobi. The club had made it all the way to Sweden, but now the police were holding it simply because it happened to land on a forehead belonging to one of them.

Jenny and Kevin suggested a trip to Mall of Scandinavia—over two hundred shops, restaurants and experiences spread out over one hundred thousand square meters. All the international brands you could think of competed for visitors there: luxury clothing, interior design, electronics . . . you could even purchase an electric vehicle on the spot, if you liked.

This last bit did not impress. Ole Mbatian assumed that an electric vehicle required electricity, which would render it useless back home in his village. Chief Toothless had more than a few things to answer for when the day came.

But a few articles of clothing under his *shúkà* wouldn't hurt. The medicine man wasn't the sort to complain, but the cold certainly did nip at one's skin.

Even though Jenny and Kevin prevented the purchase of any weapons, the shopping center was a success, not least thanks to all the escalators. Ole simply had to try going the wrong direction on one to confirm his hypothesis. Fascinating! No matter how much he walked, he got nowhere.

You couldn't tell to look at him, but underneath his

shúkà he now wore both long johns and a thin tur-
tleneck. On his hands were a pair of black gloves in
real leather. Ole knew what gloves were, of course, but
he'd never worn any before.

"The black really brings out the checks of my
shúkà," he said in admiration.

"You're very stylish," said Jenny.

Which left footwear. The medicine man didn't want
to seem backwards like his chief, but while gloves felt
cozy, shoes made his feet feel trapped. He wanted to
keep wearing his sandals, but he would consider socks
as long as the weather insisted on being the way it was.

Sandals with socks? Speaking of stylish . . .

The salesperson at the shoe store saw the face Jenny
made but found a way to make a sale. She pointed out
that even the Wall Street Journal had addressed the
question of whether it wasn't aesthetically reasonable
after all, to wear socks with sandals. To accompany the
outfit in question she recommended burgundy ones
with a pair of black Birkenstocks. It just so happened
that she had both in stock.

The medicine man nodded. His current light-brown
sandals not only slipped about, they also clashed with
his new black gloves. Ole didn't want to have to walk
around feeling ashamed while he was in Sweden. If
Mrs. Salesperson didn't think Mr. Wall Street Jour-

nal would take offense, he was ready to make a deal. Should any uncertainty arise, perhaps they could call him and ask.

When Hugo got back home again, he gathered Jenny, Kevin and Ole Mbatian in the living room. The Maasai had his gloves on, inside as well as outside. Furthermore, he was sporting a watch on his left wrist. Kevin had found it at the second-hand shop in Bollmora for next to nothing. Ole had gazed so jealously at the watch, and for so long, that his son gave it to him. Included in the gift was an introductory course in how to read the hands. Papa learned quickly.

Hugo recounted his meeting with the chief, their all-but-ritual drinking, and the next day's excruciating headache and realization that Victor Alderheim had already been there and was now sitting on both the paintings and the proof of their true value. Hugo turned to Ole Mbatian, a faintly detectable chill in his voice:

"Did you tell Alderheim . . . the angry man . . . that there were photographs of you and Irma on the savanna?"

Ole understood that this was something he could have avoided, but of course there had been no way to know this during his breakfast of caviar in a tube.

"It's true that the angry man bought my paintings. What's done is done. But taking things that don't belong to you . . . Do you know what we Maasais call that?"

"No?" said Hugo.

"Theft."

Did Hugo sense an opening here? He pointed out that, with their provenance, the paintings increased in value. The international attention, along with the previously demonstrated pricing trends for Irma Stern, would likely lead to their valuation at over two million dollars.

"How much is that?" Ole Mbatian wondered.

"How much what?" Jenny said.

Kevin made a conversion.

"About two thousand cows, Papa."

"Oh my!"

Had the medicine man absorbed what a grotesquely massive amount of money was on the line? Hugo cautiously inquired whether it might be a viable path for Ole Mbatian to challenge the sale after all.

"What do you mean?"

"Say that you never sold the paintings? That he misunderstood you."

"Misunderstood me?"

Now Hugo had really lost it. The angry man had certainly understood; he'd gone from angry to ridiculously happy in the blink of an eye. Then, of course, he'd swung back in the other direction, but that likely had more to do with his personality. The deal had been perfectly executed. Hugo need not worry about any misunderstandings.

The Maasai and the adman did not inhabit the same world.

"What I mean is, should we allow ourselves to *claim* that he misunderstood? Then maybe we can get the paintings back, and exchange them for, say, two thousand cows."

Ole Mbatian shook his head. Said was said. Sold was sold. Anyway, who was going to herd two thousand cows all the way home from Sweden? Poor cows, by the way, in this weather. Put some gloves on their hooves, at least.

Back to this again. When was the Maasai fact and when was he fiction?

No matter how lamentable their situation, Kevin couldn't help feeling proud of his father for keeping his word. Hugo was mostly annoyed. And Jenny, empty.

The medicine man wanted to make one thing clear.

Like he'd said, sold was sold. Just as stolen was stolen. For the latter, the art dealer—the angry man—deserved a proper upbraiding. Preferably in the Maasai fashion.

"The Maasai fashion?" said Hugo.

Kevin explained the anthills. For a minor infraction, the guilty party's head must stay there for fifteen minutes or so. For more grave ones, a half hour or more.

Now, it wasn't easy to find an anthill in Greater Stockholm, and anyway it would have been frozen solid in the present season. Still, Hugo wanted to know where on the scale the medicine man would locate the crime in question.

"If only we could get back what belongs to us, fifteen minutes would do nicely," said Ole. "But if he's ornery and we add in all the other messes he's made, then the other extreme might be of interest, if you ask me. Which you just did."

"The other extreme?"

"Where you tie the thief's hands behind his back, push his head into the anthill, and walk away."

As an alternative to the anthill, the Maasai suggested that they arm themselves with whatever they could find in Hugo's garage and pay a visit to the art dealer to give him what-for.

This was not a plan the others could agree to. Certainly Alderheim deserved a little of everything, but if Ole Mbatian took the lead, no one would have any control over the level of punishment. Probably including the Maasai himself, who already seemed to have dropped the issue. While the others pondered their next step, he sat there fluttering his glove-clad hands in the air, except for those moments when he took yet another look at his watch to tell them what time it was. Absent? Present? Situationally aware? Who could say.

Hugo felt that his brain wasn't keeping up. He cursed the whisky. Its remnants seemed to be sticking with him even two days later. Alcohol and double intercontinental flights—quite the combination. He wasn't getting sick, was he?

Ole nodded in recognition when the brown drinks came up. He, the chief, and Glenfiddich had, by tradition, a meeting each Thursday after sundown. The gist was that the chief talked nonsense and the medicine man corrected him.

"Around nineteen hundred hours, I imagine," he said, indicating his fine watch. "Or seven, as we say."

The meetings between chief and medicine man were followed by a follow-up the next morning, in which they helped each other recall what they hadn't been able to decide the night before, since they were never in agreement.

"Between ten o'clock and ten thirty. More or less. Maybe eleven. But no later o'clock than that."

They could not challenge the sale; Ole refused. They couldn't track down the art dealer to demand that he return what he'd stolen; Ole refused to do that unless he was allowed to teach Alderheim a lesson at the same time. This, in turn, was something the others couldn't go along with, despite the apparent lack of anthills. Even though on the savanna, you risked losing your life even if you hadn't stolen any goats.

Hugo needed to think. And catch up on his sleep. Perhaps in reverse order. There was something up with his body. He asked the others to stay away until he told them otherwise. It might take a day or two.

While Hugo rested and considered the future, the Maasai, the half-Maasai, and the ex-wife of the big baddy amused themselves by going sledding at a children's hill nearby. They ran into Hugo in the kitchen now and then.

"Don't you want to come out sledding with us?" said Kevin. "You can't work all the time."

"It's quarter past two," said Ole. "Fourteen and fifteen."

"Thanks, but no thanks. And thank you for the time, Ole. Now I know."

He took his coffee cup and went back to his bedroom one floor up. There he found sufficient peace and quiet to focus on how things actually were and how they ought to be. The image of a Maasai wearing a *shúkà*, gloves, and sandals on a sled would inevitably drag him right back to surreality.

In the midst of all this, what Hugo had sensed was on its way broke out. He became feverish and developed a cold. He, the only one of them who hadn't spent all day, every day tumbling around in the snow. There was no justice in the world.

It took three days, a lot of sleep, and even more ginger ale for the internationally renowned creator to find his way back to himself, and also to a new path forward. Or, rather, a new-*ish* one. It wasn't until that weekend that he felt both healthy and like he was done thinking.

He had to win over the Maasai, which meant he had to choose his words wisely. Hugo called another general meeting and began by turning to Ole Mbatian:

"You sold *Woman with Parasol* and *Boy by Stream* to Victor Alderheim, and you don't wish to remedy that. Am I correct thus far?"

"I've never eaten such delicious sandwiches," said Ole Mbatian.

"And all the photographs and letters from before still belong to you?"

"Theft," said Ole Mbatian. "Give me a throwing club, an anthill, or both, and I'll take care of the rest."

Hugo hadn't given up the idea of proportionality in dispensing revenge.

"We can't allow that," he said. "I know how you feel about theft, but what would you say to breaking in to steal things if you already own what you steal?"

The Maasai considered this. It would be like going to the neighboring village to retrieve one's own goats.

"With the important distinction that we're not going to kill anyone this time," said Hugo.

"And that we actually do own the goats in question," said Jenny.

The adman was ashamed that he had needed several days to figure out that the group must start over from square one with another night-time visit to Victor Alderheim's place. He blamed his cold. Or the fact that he'd unconsciously put the planned solution off to the last minute because the risk was that what had to be stolen back wasn't in the gallery on the ground floor but in the apartment one floor up. Perhaps under the pillow of a sleeping Victor Alderheim.

A high-risk project, to put it mildly. But once the

paintings were conclusively upgraded to authentic it would be too late. Unauthentic paintings could still, by way of winding paths, end up where they belonged. The Maasai notwithstanding.

So: another visit to the art dealer tonight. No, Sunday night—that was when the city was at its quietest. If the art dealer was as stupid as Jenny had suggested, or preferably even a little stupider, he wouldn't have changed the lock yet.

Chapter 46

I t was a far sight from free, the web camera Victor
Alderheim had mounted to the wall diagonally
above the door of his gallery. But it was an investment
that might pay for itself several thousand times over.
The camera responded to light and sound and delivered the recorded result to its owner. It could even film
in the dark, which was a good thing considering that
the Swedish winter essentially consisted of just that.
Not to mention that a thief would hardly try to strike
in the few hours in the middle of the day when you
could see more than just your hand in front of your
face.

On the first night, the camera remained in the same
state of rest as its owner, one floor up.

But on night number two, Victor got a hit. A
four-minute-and-thirteen-second recording—between

02:05:30 and 02:09:43. The clip was delivered, as promised, to the app on Victor's phone.

The art dealer watched the film from the previous night with both fascination and fear. He recognized the tall man at the back of the group—the Maasai! In front of him was a man he couldn't identify. But second from the front: Kevin! That Kevin. Victor's dead former ward. He had known it, and yet not. How could he be alive when he was dead?

The only thing that brought him relief was that Kevin was apparently the Maasai's son. That took care of the paternity question once and for all. That plague-ridden mother of his had been so stubborn in her claims that Victor had taken a test to shut her up. Later on, she had used it against him. Couldn't she see that they didn't even have the same color skin?

In the negotiations that followed, the mother promised not to make a big deal of it as long as Victor took over responsibility for Kevin until the boy's eighteenth birthday.

That was an easy promise to make; after all, she was going to die soon.

Unfortunately, she'd turned out to be craftier than Victor had thought. On tottering legs she dragged him along to the office of family rights, where, facing the gallows, he had gone along with things that he was later unable to simply ignore. The alternative had been a court of law, and that was worse. As Victor understood it, all lay judges were members of the Green Party or other horrible things. Plus they would have dragged the boy into the mess.

So that's how the Bollmora and pizza delivery situation came to be, until the kid was of age. Followed by the realization that his problem wouldn't go away until it literally went away.

The one-way ticket to Africa had been a good idea. If only those lazy lions had done their job. You couldn't trust anyone or anything in this world; not even the wild animals were wild enough.

Kevin's presence during the attempted break-in was no surprise. But *Jenny* in the lead, with a key. How on earth . . . Of course!

Victor had been too busy emptying her bank accounts to think of her pockets. She had, of course, locked and unlocked that same door every day since she was a child.

This time her key didn't matter, because no matter how hard she tugged at the door it resisted, thanks to the hasp and padlock on the inside. He was her intellectual superior. Which was not news at all, but it was a refreshing confirmation.

Which left the question of how Jenny and Kevin had met each other.

Bollmora, Victor realized. Obviously!

And who the strange man was.

Yeah, who the hell was he?

A few pieces of the puzzle were still missing, but most had slotted into place. Of course Kevin and Jenny had rigged the trap in the cellar; it was revenge for Victor's being goal-oriented to an extent they couldn't tolerate. Kevin brought the paintings from Africa; Ole Mbatian followed him but didn't make it in time, and the dumb kid broke into the cellar of the art gallery. At which point the even dumber Maasai sold what Kevin had already stolen from him. To Victor! For a sandwich. Well, two.

Moving on, there was no way to rule out that the news had traveled all the way from Kenya to Sweden and that Jenny and Kevin were now aware that Victor had not only the paintings they had so kindly handed over, but also the materials necessary to establish their provenance.

The art dealer was ahead in this game. Kevin and Jenny had scored a minor victory in causing all of Europe, and possibly the world, to believe that he had sex with goats. But for enough money, the world could believe whatever it wanted about what Victor did with every species in existence.

All he had to do now was get the Maasai to sell the paintings in writing as well. After all, this was what the crazy American and his god had demanded. It was frustrating. On the other hand, it was just as well— without proof of ownership, the paintings would be difficult to sell; at the very least they would go for a much lower price.

Until now, Victor hadn't dared to believe that the Maasai would stand by his word.

Again, until now.

For now the medicine man had to choose between doing so and getting Kevin, Jenny, the stranger, and himself locked up for burglary and whatever reverse burglary was called in the book of statutes.

This would all work itself out.

If only he could find the Maasai.

Chapter 47

Aslight dip in his mood, a rather more substantial cold with a fever. But still. If he hadn't taken so long to work out that they needed to break into Alderheim's place again, the bastard wouldn't have had to barricade himself in. Hugo devoted the greater part of Monday's breakfast to pondering whom he liked the least: the art dealer or himself.

Meanwhile, Ole Mbatian inspected Hugo's toaster and pondered product development. It seemed that toast with a fried egg, where the egg was fried inside the toaster, had a shortcoming: the egg ran off the bread before it could congeal. What if you laid the toaster on its side?

He didn't complete the investigation; after all, toast with an egg couldn't compete with the brown leaves and jam from prison. Caviar that wasn't caviar wasn't too bad itself.

Jenny and Kevin could tell that something was off about Hugo after their most recent setback. It would probably be best to let him grieve in peace for a while. Another trip to the shopping center, perhaps? To buy cornflakes and lingonberry jam for the medicine man, and a tube of Kalles. They could browse the waffle irons, tabletop fans, coffeemakers and other exciting things that ran on electricity. And ward off Ole's attempts to buy another knife. And explain that spears were not for sale. Maybe they would let him get a wooden club, if they could find one.

For the sake of good manners, Jenny invited Hugo to come along. Instead of responding, he became lost in thought.

Until very recently he had run a company with a brilliant business idea: to make money off people's desire to harm one another. One hundred out of one hundred people were victims, now and then, of a wrong. Fifty out of one hundred wished to do wrong in return. Ten of those could afford to pay for it. If only one of these ten made it official, then Sweet Sweet Revenge Ltd. had future prospects practically brighter than one could calculate.

Globally, the biggest revenge-seekers were states and terrorist organizations. The states seldom blamed anyone else; the terrorist organizations called themselves something other than what they were. What they had in common was that they didn't represent competition for Hugo. Rather, he considered his competition to be, for instance, the Italian Mafia. Therefore it was crucial that in his marketing strategy he emphasized that his methods remained within the boundaries of the law. After all, this was not the top priority for Cosa Nostra. The fact that Hugo had ended up in alignment with their principles after his very first job was a different matter.

Subsidiary branches in a number of cities was already part of the plan. First, London. No one was better than two Englishmen at becoming enemies over basically nothing. Over whose turn it was to use the dartboard at the pub. Over which football team one should support, actual quality notwithstanding. Two Brits couldn't even agree on the simple question of whether or not they were part of Europe.

Then Berlin. In many ways, Germans were like Swedes. Everything in order, arrive on time for meetings, stick to the rules—both written and unwritten. When someone's toes were trodden upon, the reaction was as expected. So it had been for as long as anyone could recall. Even Hansel and Gretel retaliated with a vengeance. When the evil witch expressed malicious intent, reasoning with her was out of the question— instead, they burned her up.

After Great Britain and Germany would come France. Not because it was the most lucrative market; the French were far too skilled at getting revenge on their own, preferably in groups. But Paris had a certain ring to it. If something didn't exist there, it didn't exist at all.

He'd already been to Spain and back. The concrete football revenge had become a news item down there. According to *El Diario*, the coach had suffered fractures in eighteen separate bones in his right foot. Hugo struggled his way through the article with the help of a translation app. To think that something as simple as a foot could have eighteen bones inside.

Once Europe was conquered, the United States would be on deck. For this, Hugo would need a proper business plan with analyses of strengths, weaknesses, feasibility and threats. One complicating factor was that if you scratched someone's car in America, you might—in accordance with the American definition of self-defense—get a bullet to the head in return.

All in all, the future had been looking bright when Jenny and Kevin stepped into Hugo's office. Since then, a quixotic medicine man from Kenya had intervened. If the American punishment for scratched paint was a bullet to the head, what might it be for a man who sold two multimillion-dollar paintings for an equal amount of sandwiches with fake caviar from a tube? When Hugo had explained in desperation what was so unreasonable about the deal in question, the guilty Maasai had pointed out that there had been hard-boiled egg in addition to the caviar.

For the moment, Sweet Sweet Revenge Ltd. was a shambles. After the failed break-in attempt, the great creative had no idea what to do. All he knew was what he *wouldn't* do: accompany Jenny, Kevin and the walking disaster on their shopping trip.

"You all go ahead. I'm staying home."

The Clas Ohlson everything-under-the-sun shop offered a wooden mallet for 79.90; it was thirty-three centimeters long and made of oak. Ole Mbatian weighed it in his hand and nodded. His son paid with a plastic card that said "beep" when you held it against a little box with buttons on it. Ole observed that the "beep" was the payment itself. This, if anything, was product development in comparison to the herding of four cows all the way to Narok.

Not far from Clas Ohlson was a grocery store that carried both cornflakes and lingonberry jam. After this purchase, the medicine man was in a cheerful mood; he swung his new club jauntily while Kevin carried the bag of food.

"Perhaps I should buy something for the folks back home," Ole mused. "There's a lot to choose from here."

He nodded towards a shop that sold gold and silver jewelry.

Jenny lit up.

"A necklace, perhaps?"

The medicine man shook his head. That wouldn't work; unfortunately there were two wives.

"Two necklaces?"

Smart! Jenny had great insight into how women worked.

"Indeed, I happen to be one myself."

It was Fanny Sundin's first day on her own as a salesperson at Hellgrens Gold. She was well-prepared; she'd shadowed her more experienced colleague for a whole week. She'd learned all about the different types of customers—which ones sent signals that they wanted to buy, which ones took some extra care, which ones were only there to look. She also knew where the alarm button was located on the floor, in case the unthinkable happened.

Then the unthinkable happened.

In stepped a tall Black man in a red-and-black checked cloth and only sandals, in the middle of winter. In one of his glove-clad hands he held a wooden club. He didn't even have time to utter the obvious "this is a robbery" before Fanny hit the alarm.

Ole was disappointed. He had been planning to pay with Kevin's credit card for the first time in his life, the one that said "beep." But the woman behind the counter decided to cry instead of sell. When Ole tried to pat her cheek with his gloved hand, she switched over to screaming worse than the receptionist at the hotel on that first day. The receptionist had refused to accept cows or cash; this one didn't want to take a card. Ole didn't understand how Sweden could function if no one wanted to accept payment.

A few minutes earlier, Jenny and Kevin had sent the Maasai into the shop on his own; the two of them planned to sit nearby with an ice cream each. Both of them thought this was a good idea, for several reasons. Jenny wanted Ole to select necklaces on his own; that

372 • JONAS JONASSON

was the proper way when it came to gifts for those you love, no matter how many wives you happened to have. Kevin had observed his father's curiosity about everything they didn't have in the valley back home. Letting him conduct a financial transaction by electronic means would make him feel proud. And Kevin would be proud of him.

Then the alarm went off.

Kevin and Jenny exchanged glances. They put down their ice cream and headed towards the racket.

How many people had already gathered outside the jewelry shop? Fifty? A hundred? It was almost impossible to crowd their way through. Ole Mbatian was having the same issue on the other side of the throng. He felt that he had no more to accomplish in the shop; kissing the salesperson on both cheeks and her forehead was out of the question. But where had all these people come from? And why all this noise?

Robbing a jewelry shop is not recommended. If you truly must do so, and intend to escape the police, you probably shouldn't choose Sweden's largest shopping mall as the scene of the crime. Especially not on this particular day. Not one but two police patrols were in the immediate vicinity of the mall when the alarm went off. The most senior of the four officers took charge, leading himself and his three colleagues through the sea of shoppers until he spotted the suspect in the door of the shop.

"Drop your weapon and get down on the floor!" the self-appointed commanding officer shouted as his three colleagues crept up behind him with guns drawn.

"Not this again," said Ole Mbatian.

Jenny and Kevin managed to make it through the throngs from the other direction. But what should they do now? The atmosphere was threatening, and Kevin's skin was as Black as that of his adoptive father. He thought he would be wise not to jump in and put things to rights. He conveyed this decision to Jenny using only his eyes. At which point he retreated.

Jenny thought she looked sufficiently Swedish to avoid being shot on sight; her gender, too, might have a mitigating effect. But she didn't have time to step in before everything went in a new direction.

One of the three cops behind the commanding officer suddenly lowered her weapon, engaged the safety, and approached the suspect.

"Ole, for God's sake," she said.

The medicine man lit up.

"Why, if it isn't Young Miss Officer!"

"You promised not to call me that."

Chapter 48

Ole Mbatian got another ride to Kronoberg Remand Prison—not necessarily to be locked up, but the matter had to be investigated. The prosecutor on duty would at the very least have to weigh in on whether the Everything-under-the-sun shop's item number 40-7527, a wooden mallet weighing 492 grams, could be considered a weapon.

Christian Carlander was on his fourth-to-last workday. Or whatever you'd call it. When the superintendent stuck his head into Carlander's office, he was flipping paperclips into a wastebasket. He had hit the mark two out of three tries.

"Hey, Carlander. Keeping busy, I see. your buddy the Maasai is back. Just robbed a jeweler's."

"What the hell?"

"Nah, I'm exaggerating. But you need to have a chat with him before we put him back out on the street."

It was two thirty in the afternoon. Which meant it was time to rest before he went home. But of course he couldn't say this.

The superintendent briefed his former best investigator, then invited Ole Mbatian into the room and walked off with a smile full of Schadenfreude.

"Welcome back, Mr. Mbatian," said Inspector Carlander.

Ole had already realized that he wasn't about to be locked up for nothing. He was looking forward to another nice chat. There was no reason to keep the conversation shorter than necessary.

"Thank you, thank you," he said. "Although now I've forgotten your name. I'm bad at names. When I was young I had a friend, Mzwaga Kit Chiu Wakajawaka, which was downright impossible to remember. Although I did recall it just now. How odd."

"Inspector Carlander," said Inspector Carlander.

"Oh, that's right. What can I do for you?"

Indeed, what could the Maasai do? In the very best case he would go away, of course. Then Christian Carlander could do the same, at which point he would only have three days left.

"Tell me what happened at Mall of Scandinavia."

"All of it, or just the last part?"

Ole was hoping for "all."

"The last part will do."

"I went into a shop to buy a necklace. Or two. Coming home to two wives with one is not the sort of thing you can get away with."

Carlander mused that he had come home far too often with no necklace for his only wife. Now she was remarried.

"And?"

"I must have frightened the saleswoman with my wooden club, because there was quite the hullabaloo until Sofia arrived and cleared up the misunderstanding."

"Sofia?"

"Young Miss Officer, but please don't call her that."

Carlander nodded. Sergeant Sofia Appelgren. Bright and eager. Just like Carlander himself, once upon a time.

"But didn't we keep your club here?"

"Kevin bought me a new one. From someone called Ohlson, I believe. Like I said, me and names."

"So you've found Kevin?"

"Otherwise he couldn't have been there shopping with me."

The Maasai had no patience for rhetorical questions.

"Perhaps you can tell me how those paintings ended up at Victor Alderheim's place? Last time you said that Kevin probably knew."

Ole Mbatian considered the question. For some time now he had understood that Jenny had a key to the home of the angry man; they had used it to try to break in and steal back what belonged to them. But luckily, this was not what the inspector had asked. He still didn't know exactly how the paintings had ended up in Alderheim's cellar in the first place. He suspected that the key had been used once before, but what you didn't know, you didn't know.

"Did I say that? Well, a person says a lot of things. Once I said so much that the man across from me asked me to shut up. That was the angry man, by the way. Alderheim. Unpleasant fellow."

Three days and the rest of this conversation left before retirement. Christian Carlander swore to himself he would fight to the end.

"I would like to meet Kevin," he said. "By way of information, as we at the Police Authority call it. Do you think you could ask him to come by tomorrow morning? Ten thirty? It's getting late, and I have a number of things I need to deal with."

Such as Gabriel García Márquez and two beers, followed by three metro stops. Or maybe one beer would suffice; it was Monday, after all.

"I certainly can," said Ole Mbatian. "Ten thirty is the same as half past ten."

"I know. Well, thank you for this conversation, Mr. Mbatian. Can you find the way out on your own?"

Before Ole could respond, Carlander realized it wouldn't do to send the medicine man wandering alone through the police corridors. From experience he knew this could end any which way.

"I'll walk you to the lobby," he said.

Chapter 49

The art dealer wasn't as stupid as he was horrible. He read on his smartphone that the Maasai had caused a scene—again. As a result, Victor Alderheim suspected he knew where the man was currently located, so now he was waiting outside Kronoberg Remand Prison in his Mercedes AMG S 65 Coupé, purchased fair and square with what had once been Jenny's money. Hopefully that tiresome Dr. Harris was still in the country. There was still time.

The medicine man had gone in and cleared out a jewelry store. Initial reports said robbery, but after fifteen minutes the word "misunderstanding" appeared in the newsfeeds for the first time. Victor didn't believe for an instant that the Maasai was guilty. Anyone who was that clueless about the true value of objects would probably be more likely to rob a paperboy. Thus he had good reason to hope that the man he was looking for would come tumbling out of the jail any moment or hour, with that checkered curtain around his body. And anyway, he certainly didn't have any other bright ideas about how to find the bastard.

Kevin had departed the scene of the crime that wasn't a crime scene back when the police thought they were dealing with a robbery. He had come to the lamentable conclusion that the color of his skin would not have a calming effect on the police officers with their weapons drawn. At least not during those first, critical seconds.

A few seconds later, Jenny followed his lead once she realized that the danger was over because one of the officers had recognized their Maasai.

So both of them were still unknown to the police, as was Hugo, while Ole Mbatian was more known than ever.

Presently the adman and Kevin were sitting at an Asian restaurant not far from Kronoberg Remand Prison, with a decent view of its entrance. Meanwhile, Jenny had snuck over to wait for Ole. Their joint assessment was that she had the greatest chance of blending into the environs as an innocent next of kin, no one worth remembering.

Unfortunately the Maasai was accompanied by a police officer. Jenny tried, by way of eye contact, to get Ole to understand that they shouldn't know one another right there and then. It didn't work.

"Why hello there, Jenny," he said, revealing half her identity.

To think that just about everything he said and did was so wrong.

The inspector politely said hello to the Maasai's friend but couldn't come up with any immediate reason to ask who she was more specifically.

"Then I'll see you tomorrow," said Carlander. "Ten thirty. When you have Kevin with you."

"Half past ten is great," said Ole Mbatian.

During the short walk from the jail to the restaurant, Jenny wondered if Ole Mbatian was quite sound of mind. Had he promised that *Kevin* would come talk to the inspector? What was he thinking?

She was so upset, and he was so calm, that neither of them noticed a strange man approaching from behind. It was already getting dark.

Hugo and Kevin watched from the restaurant as Jenny and the medicine man crossed the street. They also registered the shadow behind them.

"Who could that be?" said Hugo.

"Just as long as it's not the man I'm sure it is," said Kevin.

The Maasai and Jenny had no sooner taken seats at the table before the stranger came in and positioned himself near their table. Ole immediately recognized the letter-and-photograph thief, the one who needed to be taught a good lesson.

"Well, look at that," he said. "Are you here to give me back what's mine? Otherwise I have a lovely new throwing club to show you."

The art dealer ignored the Maasai's implied threat, but it did have the effect of causing the conversation that followed to be conducted in English. Hugo wasn't quite sure what was happening.

"Can I help you?" he said.

"Yes," said the man. "My name is Victor Alder-heim."

"Oh no," said Hugo.

"That's an excellent assessment. If I may take a seat, I'll explain."

"I'd rather you didn't."

Victor Alderheim sat down.

"Hello there, Jenny," he said to his ex-wife.

He said it with a smile. She didn't respond.

"And hello to you, Kevin. Did you get homesick in Africa?"

His former ward didn't respond either. There was something deeply unnerving about Alderheim's confidence. What did he know that they didn't?

Ole Mbatian honestly believed that the art dealer was there to give back what didn't belong to him. In which case he would let bygones be bygones. No point in fighting when it wasn't necessary.

"If I've understood correctly, you dropped by my village back home and happened to take my lovely photographs of Irma Stern and her equally lovely letters, is that true?"

Happened to? Victor Alderheim felt that the medicine man had just insulted his intelligence. Who *happened* to drop by a ramshackle village on the African savanna? He had gone there and taken what he wanted as a result of sheer strategy and aptitude.

When the art dealer didn't reply, Ole Mbatian went on in a conciliatory tone:

"It's easy to accidentally take things. One time during the annual fire festival I happened to take a young woman behind a bush. Before I discovered this myself, one of my wives did it for me. This was both lucky and unlucky at the same time. Where were we?

Oh yes, you have something that belongs to me and I want it back. Now, for example."

Victor Alderheim ignored the medicine man and turned to Hugo.

"I'm here because the Maasai needs to sign a transfer-of-ownership document. I mean, not you, Kevin, the other one. As soon as that's done, I'll be on my way."

He placed a document and a pen on the table in front of Ole.

Victor Alderheim was just as loathsome as he'd seemed in Jenny and Kevin's tales. In that sense, Sweet Sweet Revenge Ltd. had taken on the right case. There wasn't much else to be happy about here. Hugo still assumed that a good offense was the best defense.

"As spokesperson for Ole Mbatian the Younger, I can tell you right now that he will not sign anything without consulting an attorney."

"I didn't catch your name, Mr. Spokesperson."

"That's fine," said Hugo. "Still . . ."

Ole Mbatian read the document. He recalled that the angry man had tried to create a similar one during their breakfast that time. As if the word of a Maasai warrior wasn't sufficient. Oh well, one had to remember: different cultures, different traditions. Back home in the valley payment was made with livestock.

Here, they called the police when you wanted to pay at all.

"This paper elucidates the circumstances of ownership surrounding the two paintings one or several of which you were kind enough to place in my cellar."

"Like I said," Hugo began. "As the spokesperson for . . ."

This was as far as he got before Ole Mbatian signed the paper.

"There we go. Time for the other part. I want you to give back what's mine, and you want to remain in possession of your good health. Don't you?"

Victor Alderheim had prepared himself to win a tough match in overtime; he had his trump card on his phone. And then that stupid fucking Maasai just went and signed his name without Victor even having to whip it out. Alderheim grabbed the document and put it back in the inner pocket of his jacket.

Hugo's existence, which absolutely could not have got any worse, did just that. All while Ole waited for his photographs and letters to be returned.

"Well?" he said.

Did the native honestly believe he was going to get back what belonged to him? Victor racked his brains for an appropriate response. His starting point was: Not on your life! Now he had the transfer of ownership. The paintings were his, once and for all; even the American expert would agree. If he could sell them *along with* the stolen items, he could count on several million extra.

"You can forget what belonged to you, you dumb Maasai," he said, rising from the table.

Halfway to the door, he turned around to say farewell. Circumstances had allowed him to save the best for last.

"I know it was you who broke into my house with a goat, some bags of flour, and so on. And I know you tried again last night."

As he said this, he took his phone from the breast pocket of his blazer with a smirk, then put it back again.

"And now I even have the medicine man's signature. In the event that I *happened* to bring a thing or two back from Africa with me, seems to me like that's compensation for the mess you made. If you argue, I'll go to the police. And they'll lock all four of you up."

Then he turned and walked away.

Ole Mbatian considered himself to be a fundamentally peaceful man. This explained why he had taken a conciliatory tone with the art dealer and thief. Just like Western doctors, he preferred to fix people rather than break them. Then again, he had no Hippocratic oath to live up to. Only his pride. He made up his mind and rose from the table.

"If you'll excuse me. My club and I have something to see to. Be right back."

But Hugo didn't want to add another disaster to the series. He jumped up from his chair and managed to get between the Maasai and the door.

"For God's sake, Ole, stop! You can't club Alderheim in the middle of the street!"

"Why not?"

"Because the biggest police station in Sweden is seventy meters away."

The medicine man lowered his club. There was a little too much truth in what the adman had just said. The Swedish police had already tangled with him twice and probably would do so again, given the chance. Teaching this particular lesson could wait.

Meanwhile, Hugo had time to consider the advantages in letting the Maasai loose on Alderheim. *Within reason*. While Ole's throwing club talked to the art dealer, he himself could dig for Alderheim's phone and delete what needed deleting.

The medicine man sat down. He realized that he was hungry and caught sight of sticks where he should have found a knife and fork.

"What's this?" he asked.

The waiter came to the table and wondered if the lady and gentlemen had finished considering what items on the menu might best suit them. Up to this point, he had not been able to serve them anything other than two glasses of water with slices of lemon.

But this was no time for food. Alderheim must certainly be on his way back to his art gallery, or at least he would get there sooner or later during the evening. Hugo said that he would like to pay for the previously delivered waters, but that the party had discovered this establishment served Asian cuisine, which wasn't what they had in mind, so they would look elsewhere.

"But thank you anyway."

The waiter apologized that the message "Asian cuisine" in large letters on the restaurant window had been insufficiently clear. He promised to raise the matter with his boss. With that, he wished the party a pleasant evening; the water and lemon slices were on the house.

Victor Alderheim had a few minutes' head start on his pursuers, but on account of Kevin's general ignorance of traffic laws, they caught up to him. Choosing to go the wrong direction on one-way streets can be devastating. Or, as in this case, it can be a real time-saver. Suddenly they spotted the art dealer ahead of them. Apparently heading right where they expected him to go.

Jenny kept Kevin company in front; Hugo sat with the Maasai in the back and explained his plan.

"When Alderheim stops and gets out of the car, we do the same. On my cue, you can give him a mild whack on the head with your lovely club, as I try to get his phone out of his jacket pocket."

The Maasai thought the man deserved more than just a mild whack.

"Halfway mild," Hugo compromised.

He could see the advantages. He wasn't about to say so to Ole, but this might give him the chance to fish that damned bill of sale out of Alderheim's inner pocket as well.

"Wait for my cue, though, okay? We need a window of time with no witnesses."

"A halfway mild whack on the head, on your cue," said Ole Mbatian. "No one is better at dealing a halfway mild whack on the head than I am. Just ask Inspector Carlander. Hey, I remembered his name!"

"Are you sure about this, Hugo?" said Jenny.

Victor Alderheim did not discover that he was being followed. He never looked in the rear-view mirror when he drove; for him, there was only forward. Anyway, he wouldn't have seen anything but two headlights just like all the others among the twinkling lights of the dark capital city.

When he was basically where he was going, the art dealer cruised around for a few blocks in search of an available parking space, until he decided to temporarily commandeer a spot reserved for the Ethiopian embassy. He just had to dash inside to make a copy of the proof of ownership, the photographs and the letters; then he could track down religious nut Dr. Harris. If his god was good enough, the doctor was probably in his hotel room after a day of rolling around in modernist rubbish someplace.

The Alderheimian parking decision came as a surprise to Kevin, with his lack of experience. He slammed on the brakes sixty meters away, at a loss about what to do. Alderheim had almost arrived at the door to his art gallery.

"Hurry!" Hugo said to Ole Mbatian as he climbed out of the car.

The Maasai asked himself whether the word "hurry" could be considered the cue Hugo had mentioned. Because they *were* in a hurry, there was no time to discuss the matter. Ole Mbatian made up his mind and acted accordingly.

Sixty meters is nothing for a several-time village

throwing club champion. But unlike the original, the Clas Ohlson model made a whining sound as it flew through the air. Thus the intended victim had time to turn his head in surprise one-tenth of a second before the club reached its target. This explains why the blow struck him in the temple rather than the back of his head.

"What the hell did you just do?" Hugo exclaimed.

"I acted on your cue. But that whack was not quite as halfway mild as I'd intended. At least now we have plenty of time before the thief gets up again."

Plenty of time was in no way an accurate characterization. To be sure, the art dealer was deeply unconscious outside his own door, and no one was passing by on the sidewalk just then. But for how many more seconds would this be true? There was some activity outside a restaurant across the street. The only reason no one there had discovered the unconscious man was that parked cars blocked their view.

Hugo ran up to the knocked-out art dealer, with Ole Mbatian strolling behind him.

By the time the medicine man arrived, the adman had already nabbed the victim's phone. But Alderheim was sleeping partway on his stomach; it was hard to get at his inner pocket.

At the same time, Kevin rolled up with the car.

While Hugo dug for the confounded bill of sale, and Ole Mbatian admired the mark on the letter-and-photograph thief's right temple, Jenny hopped out and joined the group. Ole must not forget his throwing club! After all, both the original and the replacement were known to the whole police force. Leaving one of them behind, next to an unconscious man, would be tantamount to pleading guilty.

Ole considered Jenny's words. He had no desire to pay a third visit to the police station. On that note, he picked up his weapon from the ground, reached up, and clubbed away the video camera above the gallery door. That done, he went to the car, took an item from the sack of food in the back seat, came back, and dropped a glass jar of lingonberries onto the sidewalk, right before the nose of the sleeping man.

It splashed onto Hugo, who was just about to ask what the medicine man was doing when the lights came on in the nearest stairwell. Someone was on their way out. Hugo abandoned his search for the bill of sale: Everyone in the car! Now!

If the elderly woman and her poodle had come out of the building next door just a few seconds earlier, she would have discovered, among other things, a tall Black man with a club in one hand and a busted security camera in the other. The man was dressed in a red-and-black checked cloth and sandals instead of a winter coat and boots. At his feet lay another man, more traditionally dressed, but highly untraditionally asleep on the freezing-cold sidewalk—apparently knocked out by the man in the cloth. The older woman had poor eyesight, but only someone who was truly blind would have failed, later on, to provide an accurate description of the suspect.

But now all that was there to be discovered was the unconscious man and the lingonberries. The woman recognized the victim as the horrid art dealer everyone in the neighborhood gossiped about, and she wasn't surprised to find that someone had laid him out. Nor was she even particularly frightened, in fact. The Lord giveth, and the Lord taketh away.

Still, she wasn't about to let him freeze to death on the street. She would have to interrupt her evening stroll with the dog. The woman called 112.

It was thanks to Jenny that the throwing club did not remain beside Alderheim. And this prompted Ole Mbatian to think another couple of steps ahead. First, there had been the security camera. Then, the mark on the thief's temple. It was impressive. The police would wonder what had caused it.

"Now that they've got the lingonberries, they won't have to wonder," he said. "So perhaps I can keep my new club in peace and quiet."

Hugo didn't know where to start. Ole Mbatian deserved a good scolding for releasing his weapon without awaiting Hugo's authorization. And he deserved praise for the strike. And for the camera and lingonberries. The second and third action might as well cancel out the first. Now all he had to do was get into the phone and clean up what oughtn't be there.

"Twelve zero four," said Jenny.

"What?"

"The pin code for the phone. I set it up for him. December fourth. I figured he could remember his own birthday. He always forgot mine."

Alderheim had *two* downloaded files. One was the one he'd bragged about at the restaurant; the other was a brand-new video that showed the art dealer being felled by a club to the temple, followed by a razor-sharp sequence in which the city's most renowned adman rummaged through the unconscious man's pockets, followed by a Black man in a red-and-black checked cloth picking up the club and . . .

That was the end of the video.

What didn't make it in was how the Maasai first

bashed in and took the security camera, and then dropped a glass jar of lingonberries on the ground before the sleeping man. But still, the evidence would be overwhelming. Impossible to deny. Hugo carefully deleted everything he could delete: the videos, the email notifications and the app itself.

"Slow down if you see any water anywhere, Kevin. We have a telephone to get rid of."

"And a broken security camera," said Ole.

There was water everywhere in and around Stockholm, except for their present location in Roslagstull.

"Could that be a good substitute?" their chauffeur said, pointing ahead and to the left.

What he had spotted was a garbage truck, likely performing its last job on this late afternoon. Hugo ordered his chauffeur to slow down; he rolled down his window and managed, from a distance of several meters, to bury the Alderheimian telephone in the maw of the garbage truck.

Ole handed over the camera and asked Hugo to repeat the move if he could.

Score, again. The medicine man was impressed.

"I wonder if there isn't a little Maasai inside you."

"Let's hope not," said Hugo.

Chapter 50

The trip home to Lidingö was so charged with adrenaline that they made it all the way to assembly in Hugo's kitchen before Kevin gave voice to the thought he assumed everyone else was thinking too.

"How bad did your club get him, Papa? I hope Alderheim isn't lying there and—"

"Dying?" said Ole. "I don't expect so. A buffalo would have shaken its head and walked off."

Jenny remarked that that pig, rat and snake Alderheim might as well be akin to a buffalo too, but she didn't find herself quite convincing. Victor had been *awfully* still, there on the ground.

Ole Mbatian searched for new ways to reassure the group. He recalled that the temple is where you should hit chickens before you chop their heads off. The chicken will be out like a light, but if allowed to keep its head while unconscious—as, of course, the art dealer had—it will wake up after a while and stumble off.

Hugo pointed out that there were some differences between a chicken brain and an art-dealer brain; Jenny muttered that she wasn't so sure. Kevin was assigned the task of following the latest news on his phone, in case there were any items about a knocked-out art dealer in Östermalm.

After this bewildering engagement with Victor Alderheim's health, Hugo changed the subject. The adman began by thanking everyone involved for their efforts outside the art gallery. Time, in contrast to most other things, had been on their side. This increased their chances of getting away with it from zero percent to more than that.

Moving on, Hugo apologized—they'd been in such a rush that the bill of sale remained in the victim's inner pocket. When the art dealer woke up, he would still be holding all the trump cards, minus the videos of their attempted break-in.

On the other hand, there was no risk that Alderheim could identify Hugo or any of the others as assailants or phone thieves. After all, he'd been clubbed from a distance of sixty meters.

"It doesn't matter much that he *knows* it was us.

He won't stay knocked out forever; he'll be angry as a hornet now and suffering from a headache. He's welcome to it."

"It's not quite an anthill," said Ole. "But it's close."

Kevin took in the latest news on his phone, and let out an "oh my." Followed by an "oh no."

"What is it?" Jenny asked.

"Alderheim isn't knocked out anymore."

"That's what I just said," said Hugo.

Kevin read aloud.

"'A middle-aged man fell victim to a grave assault around four thirty this afternoon in downtown Stockholm. When the ambulance arrived on the scene, the man was unconscious. He suffered cardiac arrest in the ambulance and the paramedics were unable to revive him.'"

Hugo went perfectly cold.

Jenny buried her face in her hands.

"Did someone die?" said Ole.

Indeed, Victor Alderheim had been knocked out with the help of Clas Ohlson. The blow fractured the bone at his temple, just above his right ear, and the underlying artery burst. If one wishes to survive a brain bleed of this sort, it's much better to be at a hospital when it happens rather than on a wintery sidewalk in down-town Stockholm.

The bleed increased the pressure on the art dealer's brain as he lay there. Function after function ceased; slowly, the blood supply to his breathing center was strangled. By the time Alderheim ended up in the ambulance twenty-three minutes later, it was already too late.

PART TEN

Chapter 51

Now things were getting serious for real. The revenge they had just achieved did not seem sweet at all, and it could get even worse. A halfway mild whack on the head was the sort of thing you could get away with, but now they were talking murder. Or at least homicide. Or at the very least, involuntary manslaughter.

Ole Mbatian enjoyed learning new things on his journey.

"I'm familiar with murder, and homicide must be murder but not on purpose. But involuntary what now?"

"Manslaughter. Like homicide, but even less on purpose," Jenny said.

Ole Mbatian weighed the import of all three.

"I'm leaning towards homicide," he said.

Hugo blew up. He said that it didn't seem Ole Mbatian understood what a serious situation they were in. They were all sitting around being murderers, every one!

"Homiciders, don't you think?" said Ole. "Or man-slaughterers."

Jenny and Kevin were sitting next to each other, feeling the exact same feelings: relief, satisfaction, deep concern and incredible guilt all at once. Hugo was getting off easier, in an emotional sense: he managed to keep full focus on how they would get out of this. Ole Mbatian the Younger had seen worse. His main issue at the moment was the realization that they no longer had any lingonberries to accompany the corn-flakes they'd bought. He considered asking the adman whether there were any eggs to go along with the caviar in a tube that was in the fridge for tomorrow morning, but something told him that question could wait.

Hugo's creative mind was working hard. It was one thing that Sweet Sweet Revenge Ltd. had devoted a lot of time and money to a loss-making project. Now the case was closed, which left them to make sure everything would end up as bad as it was, rather than getting much worse.

"Right now the most important thing is for Jenny, Kevin and me to remain unknown to the police."

This reminded Ole Mbatian that he had a message from Inspector Carlander. He and the inspector had agreed to meet at the police station along with Kevin the next morning.

"We decided to meet at ten thirty, if I recall correctly. It's possible that I don't recall at all, but I don't typically recall wrong once I remember."

Much of what the Maasai said took twice as long as necessary.

"Ten thirty is the same thing as half past ten," Ole went on. "I promised to show up with him."

"Not on your life," said Hugo.

"A man should keep his word," said Ole.

Chapter 52

Inspector Carlander stuck a TV dinner into the microwave. It was actually too late for Salisbury steak with mashed potatoes. It was past ten at night, but he needed comfort food.

As his retirement approached, he found himself returning ever more often to what he'd actually accomplished, mixed with a guilty conscience over what, during recent years, he had not bothered to accomplish. Furthermore, he'd skipped Spanish for the past week. It was like he couldn't see the value in it or anything else. If a Spaniard turned up he could say his *El perro está bajo la mesa*, that the dog was under the table. But what if it wasn't? Or what if it was a cat? Or, for that matter, what if the Spaniard turned out to be Portuguese? Or, worst of all, if the bastard knew English?

Carlander was aware that his musings verged on depression. Three days of work left. And then what? Even more Spanish? Why?

The phone rang. At this hour? The superintendent!

"Hello, did I wake you?"

"No, I'm eating Salisbury steak with lingonberries."

"Interesting."

"How's that?"

"Someone killed the goat-fucker today. With a jar of lingonberries."

"Am I a suspect?"

"Oh, lay off."

Until very recently, Carlander had had reason to close the case of the portrait-counterfeiting art dealer. Good reason, in fact. For one thing, it wasn't illegal to paint in the same style as a world-renowned colleague. The law-twisting part only came in if you attached that colleague's signature and tried to sell the paintings under false pretenses.

And Alderheim had not done so.

For another thing, it was suddenly entirely possible that the paintings were authentic, and that meant there weren't even any malicious intentions of which to suspect Alderheim.

For the third, fourth and fifth things, there was

nothing illegal about sex toys, bags of flour, or keeping unusual pets in the cellar.

There was a sixth aspect as well. Among the few charges Victor Alderheim continued to deny after admitting to everything else, was the idea that he had ever called Bukowskis. If the trustworthy representative for Private Sales had been fooled by a prank caller, who was it and why? Apparently someone who wished Alderheim ill; Carlander imagined that there might be a few of those around.

Still, on the final line of his equations, Carlander had written: Close! There was no apparent crime upon which to hang this mess.

Until very recently.

For now Victor Alderheim was dead. What's more, he'd been killed outside his own art gallery, brought down with the help of a jar of lingonberries.

The Maasai who said he had owned the paintings but had randomly sold them to Alderheim had directed the police to his Swedish son Kevin to find answers to the question of why the paintings had suddenly turned up in a Stockholm cellar. Kevin, for his part, had neither surname nor personal identity number, at least not that his father the Maasai knew of.

Until very recently, Carlander would not have found it more than vaguely interesting to meet Kevin and ask a few questions. The conversation would take place the next day at ten thirty. This was in conflict with the morning coffee break, but sometimes you had to grin and bear it.

Until very recently, again.

For now there was a murder to prop everything up.

Carlander tossed the Salisbury steak, the mashed potatoes, and—above all—the lingonberries into the bin, untouched.

Chapter 53

To say that Hugo slept on it would be an exaggeration. That night, he didn't get much sleep at all. But still, it was enough to see things with sufficient clarity. There was not a chance that Kevin would be able to explain to Inspector Carlander how the Irma Stern paintings ended up behind the closed doors of the premises where the owner was found dead a few days later. It was just as easy to rule out that he could deny knowledge of all of this, since his father the Maasai had been kind enough to direct the question to his son. The same Maasai who would sit at Kevin's side during the questioning. An armed grenade would have felt safer.

"I want you to listen to me carefully," he said at breakfast.

"Can you pass the caviar in a tube, Kevin?" said Ole Mbatian.

Hugo gave the medicine man a look, and Kevin another, before he went on with what he had to say.

Both Ole and Kevin must *immediately* leave the country. And head straight to Kenya. Without visiting Carlander. If the police didn't have conclusive evidence already, they would need someone who provided incorrect answers to their curious questions. Without those, they might, in the best case, tire of the matter after a few months or a year.

"You have to stay there until things calm down."

Kevin nodded sadly.

"What about me?" said Jenny.

She wasn't about to export her husband-to-be and end up alone.

Hugo realized in that instant that *all three* troublesome elements could vanish to another continent that very day. With that, he might be on his way to getting his life back, to starting over from the moment before Jenny and Kevin stepped into his office with their stories.

Getting. His. Life. Back.

So why wasn't he satisfied?

Immediately after breakfast, just hours before their departure, Kevin realized that he didn't have a valid passport. His old one had expired a few days earlier.

Hugo swore. Couldn't something at some point just go smoothly for once?

Still, it might be okay. First a new passport for Kevin; after all, you could get provisional ones in just an hour or two. Then they would have to stay far away from that inspector until they were on the first flight they could find out of the country. From that moment on, and until the end of time, Hugo planned to have nothing to do with art in any form.

The adman put Kevin in a taxi, destination passport office, while the others packed their bags and the car. When the passportless one had completed his errand, he would call to be picked up.

Hugo thought extensively, and mostly cleverly.

But he wasn't infallible.

The one thing he didn't know, apropos the decision he'd just made, was that if you needed a new passport for a same-day departure you had to go to the passport police at Arlanda Airport, not the passport office in the city.

The second thing was that the passport office shared a wall with the police station where a certain Inspector Carlander was sitting, on his third-to-last workday, and waiting for a visit—from Kevin and his father.

The third thing Hugo didn't know was that you

can't provide proof of identity with an expired passport alone if you need a new one. Kevin didn't know this either, but that was of less significance for what was about to occur. Or, to put it another way:

Things went so badly anyway that it didn't make a difference.

As Kevin stepped into the passport office to take care of business, Hugo briefed everyone else. They would, as mentioned, immediately make their way to the medicine man's remote village on the savanna and remain hidden there until Hugo got in touch to let them know that the danger had passed. If they did as he said, they would successfully get away with murder, homicide, or involuntary manslaughter, whichever the prosecutor elected to call it.

Jenny and Kevin had already resigned themselves to the fact that they must emigrate, but Ole Mbatian thought there were alternatives to simply fleeing.

"Such as?"

"Back home we have a saying."

"Oh, really?" said Hugo, who had no desire to know.

"We like to say it's better to act than to react."

Jenny lit up.

"We say that in Sweden too! Fantastic."

"It sure is," said Hugo. "That changes everything."

"It does?" said Ole Mbatian.

He understood neither rhetorical questions nor sarcasm.

The medicine man went on.

"The last time I involuntarily manslaughtered, we gave ten kilos of dried meat and a spare tire to the policeman who was sent to the scene. I don't think he cared much about the meat, but the tire was almost new. He closed the inquiry and it hasn't been opened again in the forty years since."

The adman asked if Ole had just suggested they contact Inspector Carlander with a bribe.

"That's the word I was looking for."

Hugo was certain that no spare tire in the world could make Carlander forget what he might potentially know. Now it was about keeping him from knowing it in the first place. The best way to avoid that was to keep him uninformed. And the best way to keep him uninformed was never to meet him.

Just then, the business phone rang. Jenny answered.

"Hi, it's Kevin. I'm waiting for Inspector Carlander. He wants to meet with you and Ole too."

"But you were going to the passport office!"

"That's where they arrested me."

Chapter 54

The meeting between Ole Mbatian, Kevin and Inspector Carlander was scheduled to begin at ten thirty. According to Hugo's original plan, they should by that point have started on their journey to Arlanda and out of the country well before Carlander realized what was going on.

Now, it happened to be about ten twenty when the alarm went off at the passport office and Kevin was arrested. And it was almost ten thirty on the dot when he was brought through the doors of the police station–slash–remand prison.

Carlander was already in the lobby to meet the Maasai and his son. He was more than a bit surprised when the son showed up with handcuffs but without a Maasai.

"What's going on here?" he asked the two colleagues who were shoving the delinquent ahead of them.

"Suspected fraud or forgery or something," said one of the officers. "Was trying to obtain a passport on improper grounds."

He didn't know much more than that, nor did he want to. His job was just to get hooligans off the street. That was enough for him.

But Carlander had put in years on the job. Once he'd ascertained that Kevin was Kevin, he said:

"Remove the cuffs. I'll take responsibility for this guy."

His colleague shrugged. If old Carlander wanted to land himself in the shit, that was his problem. He did as the inspector said, handed over the suspect's passport in a sealed bag, and went on his way.

Carlander invited Kevin to his office.

"Would you like anything to drink?"

Kevin said he was just fine and could hear for himself how silly that sounded.

The inspector asked the young man to tell him what was going on, to explain why he had arrived at their meeting accompanied by handcuffs instead of his father the Maasai.

Kevin told him.

He came to the passport office to renew his passport. He provided his old passport as identification. The alarm went off. He was arrested.

That was about it.

Carlander gave a *hmm*. He took the passport from the sealed bag and opened it.

"Kevin Beck," he said. "Not Mbatian."

"I'm thinking about changing it."

"I see you have a personal identity number as well. Look at that, twelve digits."

Kevin was a little confused, but he sat quietly as the inspector typed at his keyboard.

"I'll be damned."

Kevin wondered what was going on.

"I see here that you're dead."

Chapter 55

Shostakovich apparently once said that only some-one who still has reason to hope can feel despair. That was about where Hugo found himself. Everything seemed to be over. There was no more than a small chance that any of them would make it past this. Not least considering the material Hugo had to work with. And here he was primarily thinking of the Maasai.

But curling up to die was not an option. Not yet. In the car on the way to the police station, he made one last attempt.

"Ole, I know you greatly value the truth."

"That's true," said the medicine man.

"Still, I'm going to get down on my bare knees and beg you."

"You're going to get down on what now?"

"My knees. I'm going to beg you to lie as much as

you possibly can to Inspector Carlander. Don't try to bribe him. Just lie. As much as you can."

"Well, you said it. On your bare knees."

There was no need to beg Jenny. She was sitting in the passenger seat, quiet and sad. Imagining what awaited them. When they were almost there, though, she managed to speak.

"Do you have any tips, Hugo? For how best we can lie?"

He didn't, actually. But still, he said:

"Victor Alderheim is dead? God, that's terrible. You'd be hard-pressed to find a nicer person."

Jenny nodded. The question was, which was worse? Life in prison, or saying that?

Hugo dropped Jenny and the Maasai off about a block from the police station he so strongly disliked. He wished them luck and asked if Ole understood how important it was to say anything but the truth on this particular day. The medicine man nodded. It might be exciting to try something new.

After Jenny and Ole signed in at the lobby, they were led to a waiting room, where Kevin was already seated.

"Where's the inspector, then?" said Ole Mbatian. "The one whose name I almost remember?"

"He'll be here soon. I've only spoken briefly with him so far."

"How did you end up here?" Jenny asked.

Kevin didn't quite know. First he had queued at the passport office, and then he queued a little more. When it was his turn, he produced his old passport and asked for a new one. Then he was informed that he needed another valid form of ID. He said he didn't have any, the woman at the window typed something on her computer—and then the alarm went off. The doors closed, two guards arrested him, the police arrived, and . . . well, it wasn't a long journey to the police station.

"But you don't look arrested," said Jenny.

"That's all thanks to the inspector. He says it's not possible to detain dead people. According to his computer, I'm in that category."

"I thought it was the art dealer we killed," said Ole Mbatian.

Jenny shushed him and asked Kevin to continue.

When Carlander was finished sighing over what he'd just discovered about Kevin, he said it was time to get to the bottom of this, once and for all. He wanted to immediately summon not only Ole, but also his friend, the one he'd met so briefly in the lobby the day before.

"He said that anyone who was a friend of Stockholm's resident Maasai must have something to contribute. He even knew your name, Jenny."

"I know. Ole was kind enough to share it with him. Then what happened?"

"Then he said it was time for his break. And he brought me here."

A moment of silence ensued. It was interrupted by Kevin:

"What did Hugo have to say about all this?"

"That we should lie as much as we can," said Ole Mbatian. "Not bribe, just lie."

"But how?"

Apparently, Ole listened more than one might expect.

"The angry man is dead? Oh my God, that's awful. He was such a good and lovely person."

Chapter 56

The morning coffee break was over. Two and a half days left until retirement.

"Everyone's here, I see. Please, step into my office."

Carlander began by pouring a glass of water for each of the three across the desk, and one for himself, as was his routine.

"Cheers, and welcome," he said, and voilà, he had fingerprints for all three.

Not that the inspector had any particular suspicions, but now that was done.

Carlander's main goal for this meeting was to find out how the oil paintings by Irma Stern had ended up at Victor Alderheim's place. The art dealer himself seemed to have no clue, and the former owner, Ole Mbatian, had referred the question to his son, Kevin.

But to discuss this without first talking about the latest developments would be too odd.

"Victor Alderheim is dead," he said, and saw three stony faces in a row.

"God, that's awful," said Jenny.

Part of her felt that way. Two other parts felt something else.

"A lovely man," said Ole Mbatian.

His entire being meant the opposite.

Kevin said nothing. Carlander sensed that something was a little off.

"Why don't we start with you Kevin, could you tell me what your relationship to Alderheim is, or rather, was? Your father Ole said at one point that I should ask you how those two oil paintings ended up in his cellar."

"He was my guardian for a number of years," Kevin said quietly.

Oh dear. Carlander had sensed wrong. Clearly the boy was upset. What the inspector had worked out so far was that Kevin's last name was not Mbatian, like his father, but Beck, like his deceased mother. She had been dead for seven years; Kevin himself had been reported missing just over five years ago—and declared dead a day or so after he returned to Sweden. The one who reported him missing must have been his former guardian. Who was now dead himself, for real. And Carlander had just thrown this in poor Kevin's face. He offered his condolences and apologized for his clumsiness.

What was the plan again? Kevin thought. Lie as much as possible.

"How did he die? Was he sick?"

"No, he was a victim of grave assault. We don't yet know by whom. The indirect cause of death seems to have been a blow on the temple with a glass jar. He was attacked outside his gallery."

Then Inspector Carlander was struck by something he'd noticed much earlier when he was considering the Alderheim case. He hit a few keys on his computer and his vague mental image was confirmed.

"Alderheim was divorced. His ex-wife's name is Jenny Alderheim. There are quite a few Jennys in our country, but a long police career has taught me to dig where I stand. Would I be correct in guessing that it's you?"

He looked at Jenny, who nodded.

"My beloved Victor," she said. "He didn't want me anymore."

Ole Mbatian had never lied before, except to his

wives, his children, the chief, and the smith's sister. It seemed like fun.

"There was nothing but good in that man," he said.

Carlander turned his gaze on the Maasai.

"Didn't you call him 'unpleasant' last time?"

"But that was *then*, my dear Inspector."

"It was yesterday."

"There you go. It reminds me of a girl from my youth, the girl from the hut next door. For a long time I thought she was only prickly and troublesome, but then one day we were married. This isn't a terrific example, now that I think about it, because the prickliness and troublesomeness remained. What I think I mean is that you should have been there with me and the art dealer at the restaurant after the last time you and I met. We had such a wonderful time. And so much fun! They had sticks to eat with, can you imagine? We shared a hearty laugh over that."

Two and a half days.

Carlander backed up to his original question. He was done grieving Alderheim's death on behalf of the others.

"Exactly how did those paintings end up with the now-deceased?"

He looked at Kevin, who, in the midst of this unfolding nightmare, took a certain amount of inspiration from his father Ole. Speaking first and thinking later sometimes worked for him. He decided to try the same thing.

"Victor was like a father to me. He took care of me, gave me an apartment in Bollmora, and often surprised me with pizza. Each time he came, we would sit there for hours, talking about art. The last time, if I recall correctly, the Grünewald-Hjertén couple came up. The pair of them endured quite a bit of criticism in their day. For him, because he was an expressionist and a Jew. For her, because she was an expressionist and depressed. In fact, they lobotomized the Hjertén woman so she would think the better of things. But she died instead."

"Please answer the question," said Carlander.

"What was it? Right, I brought the paintings with me when I came home from Kenya. I wanted to surprise Victor and hid them in the cellar when he wasn't looking."

This was the best idea he could come up with.

"So you entered the art gallery when neither he nor anyone else was looking, you went down to the cellar, put up two paintings, and left, still without being discovered?"

Kevin could tell this didn't seem plausible. Not until Jenny added:

"Meanwhile I distracted Victor with my own issues. He had started talking about increasing my alimony, but I didn't want his money—I wanted him. We were discussing that as Kevin snuck in and out."

"How much was he paying in alimony?"

"Nothing."

"And that's what he wanted to increase?"

"Well, it would have been hard to decrease," said Ole Mbatian.

Two and a half days. Soon, only two. The inspector soldiered on.

"Victor reported you missing, presumed dead," he said.

"Well, could he have presumed anything different?" Kevin said, searching frantically for a reasonable way to continue.

"En-Kai," said Ole Mbatian.

"What's that?"

"The Great God. Kevin came to find himself. What he found was me and the Great God. Through Him, you can be born again. But you must leave the old ways behind."

Kevin was on board now.

"So I called my guardian and said farewell. I might have said farewell to life, but I meant my old life, the person I was *before.*"

"Victor was inconsolable," Jenny recalled.

"And how are things between you and En-Kai these days?" the inspector inquired.

"Thanks for asking. I suppose things have developed into more of what you might call a friendship relation. I feel comfortable wandering between worlds."

"I would like to emphasize, in this context, that En-Kai does not demand circumcision," said Ole Mbatian.

"Oh, is that so," said Inspector Carlander.

Two days. And a bit.

"So, Mr. Mbatian, you encountered Victor Alderheim yesterday afternoon, after you and I had our meeting?"

"First the inspector, then the art dealer. What a super afternoon."

"Kevin and I were at the restaurant too," said Jenny. "A pleasant time, like he said."

Inspector Carlander took out the document he'd just received from his superintendent.

"And during that pleasant dinner, you signed this?"

"Dinner, lunch, or something in between," said Ole Mbatian.

The inspector said that the medicine man could call their gathering whatever he liked. The important part now was the bill of sale. Had Mr. Mbatian signed it, or was the signature a forgery?

Ole looked at it and spoke the truth for the first time in a while.

"Sure, I signed it. I was happy to! Or maybe not happy, exactly, but we Maasais keep our word. Paper and pen seem unnecessary. But when in Rome. If brown leaves with milk is on the menu, so be it."

"Leaves?"

"Cornflakes," said Jenny.

Could the inspector muster the strength for another round? He must.

"After this early dinner—or late lunch!—Alderheim went to his art gallery and was killed just outside it. Where were you all at that point?"

"Please, Inspector," said Kevin. "We only just found out . . . what time did this horrific event take place?"

"Sometime in the late afternoon or early evening. He can't have had time to do much else between eating and dying."

"Then I expect we were on our way to Lidingö," said Jenny, regretting the words as soon as they had left her mouth.

"What were you doing there?"

Yes, what were they doing there?

Ole Mbatian decided to buy the other two some time.

"En-Kai is love and the sun, did I mention that?"

"What?"

"He lives in Kirinyaga, the mountain he created with his own hands. Many people believe that in the beginning of time he married the moon goddess Olapa, and they had Gikuyu and Mumbi, the first two people, who in turn had nine daughters, can you imagine? I only had eight, but then again, I'm no god. Just a medicine man."

"What does this have to do with anything?"

Kevin was done thinking by now.

"Victor loved pizza, you know, he would surprise me with it back home in Bollmora. There's supposed to be a wonderful pizzeria on Lidingö, right by the water, so we were heading there."

Hugo talked about it nonstop, but Kevin refused to go. Pizza: never again.

"But hadn't you just eaten?"

Ole Mbatian had a certain talent for this.

"Eaten? Inspector, have you ever tried to eat with sticks? I was as hungry after the meal as I was before it."

"So you went to Lidingö and ate pizza?"

"No," said Jenny. "We changed our minds and went home to Bollmora."

"And now here we are," said Kevin.

"Why did you need a new passport?"

"My old one had expired."

"Are you planning to travel somewhere?"

"We're thinking about going to Kenya with Ole. If you allow it, of course, Inspector."

Three days from now they could do whatever they liked. But in the meantime . . . he needed to know more. But what?

Right, in Alderheim's jacket pocket the police had discovered an old boarding pass for flights from Nairobi to Frankfurt to Stockholm. Kenya was, of course, Ole Mbatian's stomping ground. Could Kevin or Ole explain what Alderheim had been doing there, especially while, as far as Carlander understood, the two of them were here?

Kevin had really got into the swing of lying.

"It was so unfortunate. I called Jenny from Nairobi and asked her to tell Victor I would be on my way home as soon as I scraped together enough money for the ticket. Of course, I didn't know at the time that he thought I was dead. He got all worked up and came down to see me and lend a hand. Before he got there,

I was already here. I managed to sell Papa Ole's gold necklace in Kenya, and that's how I got the money."

"Gold necklace?" said Ole.

He'd never owned such a thing. But then he realized that nothing was for real anymore.

Jenny leapt in to distract the interrogator.

"One of the best things about Victor was his big heart and his spontaneous ways."

It felt dreadful to say.

The inspector missed the bit about the necklace. He was lost in his thoughts about the time his ex-wife got so upset with him because he didn't meet her at Arlanda when she came home after a fourteen-day conference in New York. Perhaps someone who flew to Africa and back on a similar errand had healthier ideas about how to nurture a relationship.

Carlander recommended that Kevin contact the Tax Authority and ask them to return him to the realm of the living. In the meantime, he should avoid trying to get a new passport, because he'd probably be arrested again.

Then he suggested that this informal questioning could be over with.

"Just one more thing. When you snuck into the cellar with the paintings, Kevin, did you by any chance see a goat?"

"No."

"Or any inflatable naked rubber women? Bags of what looked like heroin?"

"No."

Carlander didn't want to prolong this meeting any further. Next up was lunch, afternoon coffee, and a quick visit to the pathologist. If he kept the coffee break on the short side he would have time to make a list of suspects as well. He wouldn't rule out including one or more of the people in his office right this second.

"With that, I'll say thank you for this enlightening conversation. I will be delving deeper into the circumstances surrounding Victor Alderheim's death, and I would like you all to remain available for follow-up questions."

"Of course," said Kevin.

"Absolutely," said Jenny.

"It will be a pleasure to be of assistance," said Ole Mbatian the Younger.

Chapter 57

Hugo was sitting in the car two blocks from the police station. It wasn't likely that any of the three would be released, but it was still possible. At least temporarily. In which case, they knew where he was waiting.

No more than half an hour had passed, but it felt like an eternity. Would Kevin and Jenny manage to keep Hugo out of it in all the interrogations? He wasn't as worried about the Maasai. He couldn't tell Lidingö from Bollmora, and he probably didn't even know Hugo's name, or at least nothing past his first name. Then again, that would be bad enough.

His phone rang. Had the police found him already? It was Malte.

"This isn't a good time. I'm busy. Can I call you back?"

His big brother didn't listen.

"She kicked me out," he said.

"Who?"

"Karolin. Who the hell do you think?"

This was a conversation Hugo really didn't want to have. And certainly not right now. Malte went on:

"Can I stay with you tonight?"

As if there weren't already enough people staying at his place.

Malte and Karolin had met in a hospital corridor eight years earlier. She was a doctor as well, an ear, nose and throat specialist. In this way, she and the eye doctor really completed one another.

Karolin already had a house on Lidingö, not far from where Malte had grown up. After three years, her boyfriend moved in, and there he stayed. It wasn't all that important to get married, and kids could wait.

The years passed. Their relationship had lost its spark, but it worked. Malte and Karolin had sort of merged together, and on the whole it felt pretty good.

Thought Malte.

At which point Karolin went to Sundsvall for a conference and hooked up with a urologist. The world's funniest and most cheerful urologist. She came straight home to Malte and told him. She suggested that he move out, for everyone's sake. After all, the house was hers. She strongly preferred that he pack his bags at once, because the urologist was coming by after work. It might be awkward for all three of them to hang out on the couch, watching *Solsidan* and eating popcorn. Didn't he think?

"A urologist?" said Hugo.

He didn't know what else to say.

"I don't have anywhere to live now, Hugo! Don't you get it? She kicked me out!"

"Yes, so you said."

At that moment, he spotted Jenny, Kevin and the Maasai walking towards the car. All three of them. It was like a mirage.

"Like I said, I'm swamped here. But of course you can stay with me. The couch in the living room is free. You know where to find the key. See you later."

Hugo was certain that a greater miracle was not possible. Jenny, Kevin and the medicine man were all sitting in the car.

"How on earth? What happened? What did Carlander say?"

"That we should remain available," said Jenny.

"Available?"

That was the last thing they would be.

None of the three had been remanded, or even officially named a suspect of any crime. And Hugo himself remained under the radar.

But they had no way of knowing what Carlander would find as he continued his murder investigation, which had likely hardly even begun. Like, for instance, the medicine man's fingerprints on the lingonberry jar, Hugo suddenly realized.

"I sleep with my gloves on," said Ole. "I took them off for a moment while we were chatting with the inspector, the one whose name is something. I thought someone who wants to appear as innocent as a leopard cub would do best to show his bare hands. But during the lingonberry affair they were where they were."

Imagine that, another minor miracle. Of course, that didn't mean there was any reason *not* to stick to their original plan: Jenny, Kevin and the Maasai would vanish to Kenya as soon as possible. Their top priority, the next morning, would be to convince the Tax Authority of Kevin's continued and ongoing existence.

"By the way, we've got another problem on our plates. Karolin kicked Malte out."

"Who's Karolin?" said Jenny.

"And Malte?" said Kevin.

"That's a lot of names," said Ole Mbatian.

Chapter 58

Inspector Carlander's third-to-last afternoon at work turned out to be the most intense in many years. He began by visiting Victor Alderheim—or rather, Pathologist Eklund—in the morgue. Not that Carlander expected to learn more than he already knew, but this was what he had always done back when he actually did his job, and old habits die hard.

The cause of death, of course, was listed as a brain bleed that had robbed Alderheim of his ability to breathe.

"Respire or expire," said Eklund with a smile.

Carlander had never liked him.

"And what was the cause of the brain bleed?"

"Blunt trauma to the head. With an object. A jar of lingonberries, I'd say. Felix brand, raw sugared,

410 grams. Our friend here has lingonberry spatter on his face and in his hair."

"Why Felix raw sugared in particular?" Carlander asked, falling into Eklund's trap.

"Well, how should I know? Will you never learn, Carlander?"

Just over two days left.

The meeting was a waste of time; he gained nothing but a bad mood. The inspector was bolstered by the thought, though, that he had likely had his last ever dealings with a corpse, not counting his own, when his time came.

Carlander skipped his coffee break to make it home well before his workday was officially over. He took a cup of coffee to his office and started on a list of suspects, together with possible motives.

First there was the unknown spontaneous violent actor X. No one planned to assault someone with lingonberries. Nor did anyone walk around town with jars of lingonberries in their pockets. Thus X must have been grocery shopping right before the spontaneous act, for instance at the store a few hundred meters north of the crime scene.

On his way home, X caught sight of the goat-sex

man, whose very existence upset him. He looked for a weapon in his recently purchased groceries, perhaps ruling out a cucumber and a loaf of syrup bread, figuring that the jar of lingonberries had better heft.

In this case, X's fingerprints must be among the shards. Perhaps he had even cut himself.

X might still be hard to track down. See above: A spontaneous perpetrator. Likely not a habitual offender. But in any case, the store would have statistics on the number of jars of lingonberries sold on the afternoon in question, and they probably had security cameras on top of that. If X had in fact shopped at Hemköp, that is. There was a Coop down by Sveavägen too. And a 7-Eleven across the street. And another hundred shops in the vicinity.

Carlander decided, for the moment, to put X on the back burner.

Person Y, from Alderheim's circle of acquaintances, was a possibility, but there was no way of knowing anything about that circle before the technicians had reconstructed the victim's life by way of his emails, texts, multimedia messages, WhatsApp, Instagram, Facebook, Twitter, and all the other asocial channels Carlander knew far too little about.

After X and Y, he would turn to the victim's next of kin. That was to say, his ex-wife Jenny and his former ward Kevin. They had seemed honestly dismayed over Alderheim's death, and there was no direct motive in sight. The divorce was legally final, the division of assets was complete. Jenny had nothing to gain from her ex-husband's death. And if the motive was to be found in the bill of sale that had been found in Alderheim's inner pocket, then wouldn't it have been preferable not to leave it there?

What about Ole Mbatian? He was certainly good at hitting people in the head. But not with lingonberries. And if the motive was the paintings, he could have simply not sold them in the presence of everyone over a pleasant lunch, dinner, or something in between just a few hours earlier.

For the time being, X seemed more likely. Or possibly Y.

Chapter 59

Malte was in a sorry state. After a restless night on Hugo's sofa, one of the first things he did was call the eye clinic and quit, effective immediately. His employer was taken aback.

"What on earth? What's going on? Do you want a bigger salary? We can make that happen."

It wasn't the salary. Malte had been blind not to see what was coming, and the blind shouldn't be eye doctors. He had seven months of overtime saved up and said he would use it to offset the notice he was required to give according to his contract.

Still, Hugo's now-unemployed big brother took comfort from his conversations with the medicine man. These had begun on that very first night, while everyone else was still moaning and groaning about something, it was unclear what, an activity they returned to right after breakfast the next day.

Ole Mbatian told Malte all he knew about how unpredictable woman was. Sure, you could loan her out on special occasions, if she didn't have anything against it, but this must never happen behind her husband's back!

For his part, as it happened, he got a double dose of all these problems. First one was peevish because he slept at the other one's house; then the other one was the same when he slept at the first one's house. Then things calmed down for a while before taking a new turn. His wives had got on the same page somehow and asked him to move up the hill to the third hut. If you didn't know any better, you'd think they had grown tired of him.

It was nice for Malte to hear that someone else could be cast off too. But he and Ole had more in common: for instance, an affinity for healing people. The medicine man thought the eye doctor demonstrated an amazing breadth of his relative knowledge, considering what limited scope he'd had in his practice. Malte thanked him for his praise and explained that in Sweden, one first became a medicine man of all sorts of things before specializing. What was Ole's specialty, by the way?

Ole Mbatian considered the question. He was outstanding in many ways, but most renowned for his ability to help women who didn't want more children to avoid just that.

Malte was eager to learn the Maasai's contraceptive recipe right away, but that was where Ole Mbatian drew the line. It was a bottle of the medicine man's secret concoction, which one had to drink each time one ovulated. He called the prescription *inatosha*, which means something like "that's enough" in Swahili. Anyone with their senses of smell and taste intact could guess their way to some of the ingredients, but it was a big step from there to a perfected medicine. A quack in the next village had once tried to copy *inatosha*. He undercut Ole by half but didn't even put bitter melon in his mixture.

"Before the long rains were over, he'd made himself two hundred enemies among the women of Maasai Mara. Two hundred! That's a very different story from my two back home. And your one, now that I think about it."

"I don't even have my one left," said Malte.

In light of Ole Mbatian's experiences, this no longer seemed so terrible.

Chapter 60

The work of a modern police detective no longer depended on door-knocking or hiding behind someone's curtains. Today it was all about technology. Involuntary investigation leader Carlander requested, and received on his desk, an initial report right around time for morning coffee on his penultimate day.

Thus far the most interesting part was what the technicians had *not* found, either on the victim or in his apartment: a phone.

It was beyond the realm of possibility that a businessman in Stockholm wouldn't have a smartphone. The technicians had confirmed its existence by way of a quick search. The mobile phone subscription both existed and was available for review.

Alderheim had hardly called anyone in several weeks. Didn't he have any friends? For surely none of the three locksmiths he'd called, to no avail, would fit in that category. Apparently none of them had installed the padlock on the inside of his front door.

And by the way—a padlock? Who or what was he afraid of? Perhaps the person who had painted PERVERT in meter-high letters on his windows.

Carlander had no time for further pondering; his favorite colleague was coming through the door. It was forensic technician and IT expert Cecilia Hulth, best known for breezily getting into phones, tablets and computers that were impossible to get into.

Among the few things Hulth couldn't hack was a missing phone. Still, she was able to tell him what it had been up to during Alderheim's final hours of life. It was all to do with the placement of the 4G towers, and the mobile provider's logbook.

She gave a report to her investigation leader.

"The phone was located on Kungsholmen, near the police station, in the hours before the art dealer died."

Alderheim had been too. So far, Carlander saw no red flags.

"Then it traveled to the neighborhood where the art gallery is located."

Still logical.

"From there, it went to Högdalen."

"What did you say? What did it do there?"

"It stopped making contact with outside world."

The correct answer was, it had gone up in smoke. The garbage truck traveled from Östermalm to the municipal incineration plant in Högdalen, which was about ten kilometers south of central Stockholm. There it was dumped, along with a few tonnes of household waste, and lay at a depth of five meters among potato peels and used coffee filters until it was all burned up.

Hardly anything can survive a temperature of 960 degrees Celsius. Not potato peelings, not coffee filters, and definitely not mobile phones.

Hulth went on to say that Alderheim must have been an odd duck. He had not a single contact listed in his phone. Nor was there much of interest in his email inbox. But there was a little. One round-trip ticket to Nairobi, very recently.

"I'm aware of that," said Carlander.

Beyond the ticket, there were a vast amount of ordered and confirmed pedicures from known high-end prostitutes.

"Pedicures?" said Carlander.

"A rose by any other name," said Cecilia Hulth.

Dammit. Carlander had just been saddled with another interrogation.

"Anything else?"

"A brief exchange with an American art expert in New York, or rather, his secretary. It seems Alderheim wanted to get his forgeries declared authentic."

Carlander didn't bother to inform the forensic technician of the forgeries' presumed genuine nature; it no longer had any bearing on the situation.

"Anything else?"

"Well, just this one incoming call in the past week. From an anonymous prepaid number. One minute and twenty seconds long."

The inspector knew that the government was considering banning anonymous phone cards. Given that the issue had been relevant for fifteen years by this point, it couldn't be ruled out that a decision might be made any decade now. This was of no help to him at the present moment.

"Anything more?"

Cecilia Hulth was notorious for always having a little bit more.

"We haven't been working on this more than a day or so, Carlander. What do you expect? There were faint fingerprints on the lingonberry jar, but nothing that matched the three you gave us. On the day of the murder, no lingonberries were sold in any of the three nearby grocery stores. That makes it pointless to look through their security tapes. If you like, I can dig deeper in the emails. He could have deleted something, after all. It's typically possible to recreate those things, although it's a little tricky. Actually, it's a lot tricky."

The inspector wanted to be done with all of this by seventeen hundred hours the following day, at the latest. If Alderheim hadn't bothered to delete his conversation with the high-end prostitute, what else did he have to hide?

"Forget it. I want you to dig up the numbers and names of everyone who threatened Alderheim on the big hate-and-threat site."

"Everyone?"

"About five hundred posts, maybe three hundred different threats. Can you have a list ready for me in an hour?"

Since Hulth and Carlander had known each other for twenty-five years, she had no qualms about asking the inspector whether the Maasai's blow to his head had done more harm than it had seemed at first.

"Pick three of your five hundred and I'll see what I can do."

The fact was, it was part of the hate-and-threat site's business idea to protect their accounts at any price.

Not even Cecilia Hulth could get in through a back-door. But a chain was only as strong as its weakest link. She had a contact on the inside. It typically cost fifteen hundred kronor per IP address, but it would work.

With one and a half days left to retirement, the alleged forgery turned murder or manslaughter by an unknown perpetrator began to grow beyond what the soon-former inspector could handle. For the past day his breaks had been all out of whack.

Carlander selected four of the worst threats from the hate-and-threat site and sent them to Hulth. Then he approached his boss and made an attempt to dump this case on Gustavsson, who would have been in charge from the start if only he hadn't been faking a cold. But the superintendent's response was that the goat-sex man sat where he sat in Carlander's lap, dead or no.

"Just find the perpetrator, you have a few days."

"One day, to be precise," said Carlander.

"One and a half."

Carlander realized that his afternoon coffee break, too, was canceled. He decided to track down a certain person in town for a discussion about foot care.

She called herself Lola, but her name was Elsa-Stina Lövkvist. He found her in the hotel lobby, just where the forensic technician suggested he look.

At first Lola was clueless about everything, but once she realized that Carlander wasn't out on a morality errand she transformed into Elsa-Stina and began to tell it like it was. Alderheim had been a regular client of her special variety of foot care for several years. He wasn't a pleasant one, but nor was he worse than many others. Still, Elsa-Stina had had enough when she read about what he did with goats in his cellar; there was, of course, no way of knowing what sort of diseases this might transmit.

"Is it possible that you called Alderheim from a prepaid mobile phone and spent one minute and twenty seconds telling him he was no longer welcome?"

Elsa-Stina hadn't timed the call, but she confirmed that this was an accurate description of the situation.

Beyond this she had no information of value. She had cared for his feet at least a hundred times. At no point had they chit-chatted before, during, or after the session.

"Was he married?" she asked.

"They got divorced a while ago."

"Give the ex-wife my congratulations."

Carlander promised he would. He stood up, took

both Lola and Elsa-Stina's fingerprints with him by way of the plastic bottle of water he'd offered her, and said there were other jobs than pedicurist out there, but that he otherwise didn't want to interfere.

"Goodbye then, Lola."

"Goodbye to you," said Elsa-Stina.

Chapter 61

Kevin headed for the Tax Authority offices in the neighborhood of Södermalm, where he had to wait an eternity for his turn. He didn't want to get Hugo a parking ticket on top of everything else.

But at last he was able to meet with a caseworker who introduced himself as Kjell and asked the young man to have a seat.

"Hi Kjell, my name is Kevin. I hope you can solve my problem quickly, because my parking meter is about to run out."

Kjell promised to do his best and asked how he could be of service.

"The thing is, I'm dead. Could you please bring me back to life?"

Kjell responded that this type of errand was best

handled by Jesus, but of course no one had spotted him around for some time.

"Perhaps we could begin with your providing some ID," said Kjell. "And an obituary won't cut it."

Kjell was the type of guy who liked to have some fun at work.

Kevin could provide his passport if Kjell promised not to hit the alarm. The caseworker said he had only pushed it once during his eighteen years at the Tax Authority. That client had provided not a passport but a hand grenade. Sad story in a lot of ways.

With the help of his passport, Kjell brought up all the information about twenty-three-year-old Kevin Beck. He nodded and said that the rumors of this client's formal death had not been exaggerated.

"But I see, of course, that you are you, and there is a lot to suggest that you are alive. The problem is, you must prove it beyond all reasonable doubt before I can do anything. Your passport is expired—do you have any other form of ID?"

Kevin did not.

"What about a driver's license?"

"I don't have a driver's license."

"So who parked the car?"

Goddammit, Kjell.

"I was in a hurry. It's hard to bring charges against a dead man, is it not?"

Kjell smiled and said death had its advantages. Besides, he was a caseworker with the Tax Authority, not a traffic cop.

"But I do need a formal witness statement from a relative who can, in turn, positively identify themselves. Judging by the information on my computer, there aren't many to choose from. But you have a father. Might he be close at hand?"

Ole Mbatian? What could his word be worth?

"I don't see any Ole Whatever-you-just-said listed on my screen, I was thinking first and foremost of Victor Alderheim."

Kevin felt thoroughly muddled.

"For one thing, he's not my father, and for another he's dead. *Dead* dead."

What had started out as an interesting matter had become even more intriguing to caseworker Kjell.

"The fact that Victor is your father has been proven beyond all doubt. I understand you might not have been very close throughout your life; the fact of paternity was determined when you were fifteen. Parents who need that much time to think it over are seldom the most attentive sort. I see that you haven't exactly grieved yourself to death, if you'll pardon the choice of words."

Was he saying Victor was Kevin's father? For real?

"Whatever the case, he no longer exists. It was even in the paper."

Caseworker Kjell nodded contemplatively. He said that one couldn't believe everything one read in the paper but admitted that if the death had occurred recently the Tax Authority computers might not have been updated yet. They had no direct link to the morgue.

"So what do we do now?" said Kevin.

Kjell had no idea.

"Come back tomorrow. I will have figured something out by then. Feel free to bring your next of kin, to the extent that they exist."

458 · JONAS JONASSON

Chapter 62

S olving an unsolved murder in one workday re-
quires the existence of a known suspect and for the
only missing piece to be evidence sufficient to prompt
the guilty party to confess by seventeen hundred hours
that same day. In practice, this meant that Carlander
needed to get either Kevin Beck, Jenny Alderheim,
Ole Mbatian the Younger, or all three to crack. The
problem was that the inspector had no idea why they
would do that. The relationships between all involved
were muddy, but none of them had an obvious motive.
Nor did the fingerprints that had been lifted from a few
shards of the lingonberry jar match any of theirs. Or
foot-care specialist Lola's, for that matter.

Thus the prints belonged instead to perpetrator X.
Or grocery store worker Z. Since X hadn't bought
his lingonberries in any of the three closest grocery

stores, at least not immediately prior to the crime, it was pointless to look for him by way of the shops' security cameras.

But what if one assumed X lived in Högdalen—then what? Perhaps he came driving down Birger Jarlsgatan and caught sight of the man he and many others already hated and threatened on the hate-and-threat forum they frequented online. In this case there could have been no mistaking him, for the subject was standing directly outside the gallery windows upon which someone had painted PERVERT.

The man from Högdalen stopped his car; perhaps he even found an available parking spot, although that seemed far-fetched. Then he climbed out, opened the trunk to grab a wrench or some other weapon, and for lack of other options ended up with the jar of lingonberries in his hand. He snuck up behind Alderheim, aimed for his skull with the jar, maybe said "Take this, you goddamn . . ." at which point Alderheim whirled around, causing the jar to strike him more unpropitiously than intended.

With an unconscious PERVERT at his feet, X discovered the victim's mobile phone and took it with him. Why? Out of panic? Because Alderheim had managed to capture an incriminating photograph? Whatever reason the man from Högdalen preferred—he took the phone, went back to his car, and drove home.

Carlander was a bit ashamed. This wasn't the proper way to handle investigations into murder or manslaughter. Then again, he had historically apprehended more criminals than had got away. The inspector convinced himself that he had delivered. He wasn't doing so anymore, but still.

Or maybe he was? The Hulth was back with information about the people behind the four worst hates and threats from the hate-and-threat site.

Vaguely suspect poster number one called himself Uzi1970. His real name was Lennart Helmersson and he lived in the forest outside Jukkasjärvi, thirteen hundred kilometers north of Stockholm. This was where he'd posted from. Lennart was an electrician and had a wife and two grown daughters. He had no criminal record, but for the past five years he had been plagued by an onerous, unsettled debt to the Enforcement Authority. This might explain why the majority of his posts involved suggestions of what one ought to do to the Enforcement Authority's offices in general and its staff in particular. He'd been a member of the forum since just after being saddled with the debt. Over the years, Uzi1970 expanded his hatred to encompass others as well.

His threats against the goat-sex man could be summarized as a series of opinions on what should most preferably be shoved up the victim's rear end in the interest of administering justice. Lennart Helmersson was not particularly imaginative; he went back and forth between a baseball bat and a hockey stick in a total of seven separate posts.

Carlander was unsure whether either of those objects would fit in the space suggested, but that didn't matter—in contrast to the fact that Uzi1970 lived north of the Arctic circle, where it was dark around the clock at this time of year. People had become embittered for lesser reasons.

"Nope, not him," said Carlander. "Next."

Vaguely suspect poster number two called themselves Everyonemustdie. The profile picture suggested it was a man, but the account traced back to one Helena Segerstedt, who lived on Centrumslingan in Solna, less than twenty minutes from the scene of the crime.

"A pretty negative view of humanity, that everyone must die," said Carlander, but he thought there might be something to it. "What do we know about the lovely Helena?"

"Animal-rights activist. One conviction after far too frequent and long-winded threats against a particular mink farmer in Blekinge. Seven years ago. Has since learned how not to cross the line. Or not. She wants to emasculate Alderheim. Literally. Expresses it a different way each time, five times in all, but the common denominator is that his dick has got to go."

It was difficult for Carlander to recalibrate. He had got it into his head that the perpetrator was a man. What was wrong with people? One wanted to shove things up his rear; another wanted to snip off the dangly bits next door. After a moment's consideration, he decided that Helena Segerstedt would have used organic lingonberries as a weapon, and that at the very least she would have kicked the crotch she was so obsessed with. For the time being, she too was ruled out.

"Vaguely suspect poster number three, please."

"Lives in Buenos Aires. Want to know the address?"

"Number four, please."

Number four was HellHell84, an alias that was rather hard to interpret. Perhaps it was simply an homage to hell. The man behind it was named Linus Forsgren, thirty-eight, a single churchwarden with no criminal record who lived on Trollesundsvägen, south of the city. No skeletons in his closet, but he was the most industrious poster of the four on the hate-and-threat site. A member since 2009 and still going strong.

"Any obvious pattern in his posts, historically?" Carlander asked.

"In general it seems he wants anyone he turns against to be gravely tortured."

"Does he want to kill?"

"Nah, just gravely torture. Twist a knife around in some intestines and so forth."

Carlander reflected that you could die from less than a knife to the gut. Like a jar of lingonberries to the head.

"Trollesundsvägen, where's that?"

"In Högdalen."

Chapter 63

Kevin brought his father Ole and his girlfriend Jenny to vouch for his identity in the presence of the caseworker at the Tax Authority. He thought Jenny might make a difference. Ole was less of a sure bet.

It took up quite a bit of the morning. Caseworker Kjell elected to consult a colleague in Karlstad, an expert in extra-complicated matters of the national registry. In essence, what they needed was a sworn testimony from a brother, sister, mother, or father. There were no siblings in this instance; the mother had been dead for many years; the father had just followed her example.

The colleague in Karlstad attended the meeting by speakerphone. Around the table at the Tax Authority in Stockholm sat Kjell, Kevin, Jenny and Ole. The latter was in a bad mood because Kevin had made him leave his throwing club in the car.

"Don't come crying to me if they start fighting and I can't object."

"Your club has objected plenty for the time being, Papa. But thanks anyway."

Kjell wanted to know more about the witnesses and their relationship with the subject. Jenny was just about to respond when the medicine man budged in line. He was done sulking; now he wanted to declare that no one could swim among crocodiles like his Kevin.

Neither Kjell nor his colleague in Karlstad understood what this had to do with anything. The Maasai said that if they would just provide a river full of crocodiles, they would see.

Kjell asked his colleague about the current crocodile level in Klarälven. The colleague, who did not have a sense of humor, replied that they would do best to focus on the woman.

Jenny introduced herself as Kevin's girlfriend and said that they hadn't known each other terribly long, but it was long enough to have become engaged, and she could both promise and swear that he was who he said he was.

It's impossible to keep any secrets from the computers of the Tax Authority. Kjell, who thoroughly enjoyed having fun at work, suddenly had a lot of fun when he determined that Jenny had previously been married to Victor Alderheim. The caseworker quickly calculated that Kevin's future wife was thus also his stepmother.

There came a sigh from the speakerphone on the table. The colleague in Karlstad had been cast from too traditional a mold of authority to laugh at such a serious matter. Or at matters in general. Furthermore, he knew his Greek mythology. According to which, Oedipus married his own mother. Next thing you knew it would turn out that Kevin was the one who had just killed his father.

No one around the table in Stockholm caught on to the dramatic train of thought in Karlstad. Kevin suggested they call upon the passport officer from Arlanda Airport, the one who had recently let him into the country. That officer must, after all, be able to attest that he was the person he said he was. Perhaps based on that information, the Tax Authority could assume he had not become anyone else since.

"If we all hold hands and pray to En-Kai, perhaps we'll have a vision," said Ole Mbatian.

This wasn't something he actually believed would happen. He just wanted to be included in the conversation.

Whether it was En-Kai, the passport officer, the potential crocodiles in Klarälven, or the spirit of Oedipus that was the final straw, Kevin and the others never knew. But suddenly the expert in Karlstad declared he'd heard enough. He asked Kjell if they shouldn't just decide in Kevin's favor before one of them went bananas.

"Good idea," said Kjell.

For lack of other next of kin, Jenny got to sign a document in which she solemnly swore that the expired passport she was shown was identical to the same passport that had been valid a few days previously. Ole Mbatian asked where he should sign and was informed by Kjell that it wouldn't be necessary. Armed with the signature and a James Bond quote, he extended his right hand over the table to Kevin.

"'You only live twice.' Use your second chance wisely."

Kevin thanked him and promised to do his best.

Chapter 64

Abreakthrough with four hours left to retirement! Christian Carlander felt a thrill of work-related joy he hadn't experienced since . . . well, since when? Was it 1991, when he and his wife were in Torekov on vacation? He had just forgotten their anniversary and she spent the first two days expressing her dissatisfaction with his character. At which point, on day three, he was miraculously called home to Stockholm for a double homicide at a nightclub.

The inspector sent a car to HellHell84's place of work to pick him up and deliver him to Carlander.

Linus Forsgren's plans for the afternoon were to grease the hinges on the cemetery gates. Eight gates times four hinges makes thirty-two. It would take some time.

When he had seven and a half gates left, two police officers showed up, asked if he was who he was, and asked him to come with them, in such a tone that the hinges didn't even matter anymore.

It happened so fast that Linus Forsgren didn't have time to be afraid before he was sitting opposite Inspector Carlander in the police station in Kungsholmen.

"You know why you're here, don't you?"

Linus Forsgren did not.

"What would you say if I said HellHell84?"

Linus Forsgren's eyes went wide. He said he didn't know what the inspector was talking about.

"I'm talking about how you like to torture people, isn't that so?"

The churchwarden was living his worst nightmare.

Carlander went on to say that there was evidence Linus Forsgren was the same as HellHell84 on Sweden's biggest hate-and-threat site, and that the latter, which is to say the former, had wished death upon a certain art dealer with a possible predilection for four-legged creatures.

"And just think—your wish has been granted."

Now Linus Forsgren appeared to be crying. He said that this was all a terrible misunderstanding, and that he certainly neither threatened nor hated people. He was a servant of God, a churchwarden in a lively and life-affirming congregation.

When the churchwarden attempted to deny everything yet again, the inspector said that he respected his response, but the problem was that the hatred and threats had been formulated by the account of Linus Forsgren and published from a computer that belonged to his church.

"So I won't trouble you any further. However, I must get to the bottom of this and I have no choice but to call in all the priests, deacons, choirmasters, organists, and educators from your church. I promise to be very tough on them so we can find out which of them hacked your account."

At that point, Linus Forsgren confessed.

And began to cry for real.

Chapter 65

Had it not been for a damned churchwarden conference, Carlander could have solved the murder-or-manslaughter case on his very last day of work.

With Linus Forsgren still in shock as he faced the possibility that everyone at church would come to know him as HellHell84, Carlander dealt the fatal blow. He shared with Forsgren the date and time of the homicide on Birger Jarlsgatan and recommended that he confess his whereabouts at that time to avoid being locked up for murder.

To Carlander's surprise, Forsgren's despair was interrupted. Was the officer suggesting he was guilty of killing someone? That was impossible.

Linus Forsgren emphatically declared that he had an alibi, that he had been standing on a stage in Gothenburg and delivering a lecture on biodegradable methods of keeping weeds out of gravel paths *at the very moment* he was supposedly smashing a jar of lingonberries into the head of Victor Alderheim in Stockholm, 470 kilometers away.

Carlander wasn't born yesterday. Crime suspects in a state of desperation could make up just about anything. "I definitely didn't rob that bank last Wednesday, I was with my dog at the time, just ask him." It was pitiful enough, directing inquiries to one's own dog or cat. But what man with even a shred of good reason intact would lie about a whole conference? That was practically like saying "I can't be the murderer, because at the time in question I was playing in the World Cup final." Few things were easier to confirm.

Linus Forsgren was surely guilty of a lot of things.

But he hadn't killed Victor Alderheim.

"Thanks, I'm out," Carlander said to his boss at one minute past five on his very last day of work.

But the superintendent didn't feel like letting him have a pain-free goodbye.

"You're not getting off that easy, Christian," he said with a smile.

He only called Carlander by his first name when he was about to get personal.

"Cake and bubbly and the whole kit and caboodle

await you in the break room. Everyone will be there soon, except for the ones who are out nabbing hooligans."

"I'll be goddamned," said Carlander.

"But we have a minute or two. Tell me about the man from Högdalen. It was a close one, from what I heard. Forsgren, was that his name?"

"I thought I had him," said Carlander. "It all seemed to track right up until we got to the crime itself. Then that bastard claimed to have been at a churchwarden conference in Gothenburg at the same moment he supposedly whacked Alderheim in the head with his jar of lingonberries."

"And?"

"I checked it out on the spot, so to speak. And learned that four hundred churchwardens from all over the country were in the audience, and could act as witnesses in Forsgren's favor. As if that wasn't enough, the whole thing is on YouTube."

His boss smiled and said that churchwardens could be a sly bunch. Carlander was amazed at the whole phenomenon. What even was a churchwarden conference? Who the hell arranged such a thing?

In any case, it was now several minutes past five and the boss wanted to wish his longstanding colleague good luck with his pigeon-feeding or however he planned to occupy himself.

"How's the Spanish going, by the way?"

"The dog is under the table and won't leave."

"Huh?"

Carlander asked to be spared from explaining. He returned to the previous topic and asked that the case of the goat-sex man and the lingonberry jar not land in the archive quite yet. It was back on Gustavsson's desk now, wasn't it? Carlander had already carefully investigated four suspects from the leading hate-and-threat site. All that was left for Gustavsson was the other four hundred and ninety-six.

"Do I detect a certain amount of Schadenfreude here?"

"Definitely. If I know Gustavsson, he won't make it through the four hundred and ninety-six entries before the statute of limitations runs out."

"There is no statute of limitations on murder anymore."

"I know."

The superintendent mused that perhaps he had the colleagues he deserved. He stood up, rounded his desk, and said it was high time for cake and celebration.

"Your very last coffee break at the station."

It felt strange. For many years, Carlander had escaped his job to go to morning or afternoon coffee,
with lunch in between. What would he escape from
now that he no longer had a job? He supposed he
would find out. For the escape must go on.

Chapter 66

Tragically unaware of the fact that the greatest threat to their future freedom had just retired, Jenny and Ole Mbatian went to Mall of Scandinavia to shop for necessities ahead of their move or escape to Kenya. Kevin had been assured he would receive his new passport within the next few days.

First it was time for double silver necklaces at Albrekts Gold.

"Should I go in, or should you?" said Ole.

"I'll do it," said Jenny.

After that, Ole very much wanted a couple of extra throwing clubs of the Clas Ohlson variety. The model had its downsides—it made an unpleasant sound as it sailed through the air—but there might, with some effort, be something there. Ole knew his brother Uhuru would appreciate the gift.

Last but not least, the Maasai had asked to bring some cornflakes and lingonberry jam. Milk—from goats or cows—was something they already had in abundance back home.

The world is so large, and yet so small. Just as Jenny was putting four jars of raw sugared lingonberries in her cart, she found herself standing eye to eye with someone she recognized.

"Inspector Carlander? What are the chances?"

Ole Mbatian didn't always understand everything that was going on, but at that moment he joined up with Jenny, the cart, and the inspector. He had six boxes of cornflakes in his arms, and he quickly placed them on top of the jars of lingonberries. There was no reason to give the inspector any ideas if they could help it.

"Yes, what indeed," said Carlander. "Once again, allow me to express my condolences for the fate of your ex-husband."

"Hard to process," said Jenny. "How is the murder investigation going?"

An anxious question, but she had to say something.

"It's not going at all, you might say. I retired yesterday, and my successor is looking for suspects on the big hate-and-threat site. But it's no easy job, not when you've got an unknown perpetrator of a spontaneous crime. You shouldn't get your hopes up."

"That's too bad," said Jenny.

"The art dealer was a fine fellow," said Ole Mbatian. "I miss him."

Another general meeting at Hugo's. Under the leadership of Jenny, for the first time. She told them about how she and Ole had run into the now-former inspector, about the medicine man's lightning-fast maneuver that kept Carlander from seeing what he absolutely must not see, and about the conversation that ensued.

"We're not suspects anymore, if we ever were in the first place. So why do we have to flee to the savanna?"

"It's nice there," said Ole Mbatian.

Jenny was sure it was, and she would be happy to visit, but the question was, why did they have to flee?

Hugo had no immediate response. Suddenly the cardinal reason the Maasai and the others had to leave was something other than sheer survival. The idea was that, once they left, everything would go back to normal for Hugo himself. Sweet Sweet Revenge Ltd. could start anew and go back to making money.

Jobs awaited. As recently as the day before, a well-to-do widow in Seoul had contacted him. She was careful to point out that she was of the posh sort and lived in one of the city's most fashionable retirement homes. Now she had learned from the home's director that her one-point-nine kilo Pomeranian would not be allowed to remain on site, the reason being that the other residents were scared of it. Accordingly, the widow wanted Hugo to scare the director to the tune of twenty-five million South Korean won. The dog could, of course, have done so for free if it had even a shred of talent for such a thing.

Now, twenty-five million won wasn't as much as it sounded like—converted to euro it was about twenty thousand. Still, this was enough for Hugo to scare just about anyone to death.

But he hesitated, partly because killing in general must not become a habit, and partly because Hugo had his hands full trying to clean up the current situation. He declined the widow's offer and said he was fully booked. Which, in a broader sense, was entirely true.

If they all stayed in Sweden, what would happen? Jenny and Kevin no longer had any incentive to work for free, but perhaps they would work on commission? Malte the unemployed eye doctor was now part of the equation. Big brother could probably live on his assets for a year or two, and if he had nothing better to do Hugo could train him in the art of revenge.

But how much fun would that be, really? Hugo had known from the start that revenge as a business idea had intrinsic growth potential. If someone stepped on someone else's toe, the wronged party felt that the toe-stepper ought to lose their whole foot. At which point the newly footless party wanted the guilty one to lose their head. There was definitely money in this, but it certainly wasn't a meaningful contribution to a better world. Even less so than umami-flavored marmalade, in fact.

"Can't I come with?" Malte suddenly said, turning everything upside down.

"Come with?" said Hugo. "Where to?"

"Kenya. What is there for me here?"

Kevin had said almost nothing all day long. He elected not to accompany Jenny and Ole on their shopping trip, muttering that he had things to think about. Jenny thought she recognized this feeling; sometimes a person needed to withdraw. What was more, her dear Kevin had just gained and lost a father within the span of a few days, but in the opposite order.

In any case, now he had something to say. Hugo hoped it would spark some ideas, because he felt generally out of sorts. Was he so badly off that he didn't want to get rid of the three worrying elements? Or did it have something to do with Malte, who wanted to go along to Kenya? Hugo would be left behind, all alone, with no one to hang out with but all the clients who wanted each other dead.

"Victor Alderheim is dead," said Kevin.

Was that all he had to contribute? Hugo said that he'd read something along those lines in the paper.

"At the time of his death, he had considerable assets," Kevin continued. "Including two genuine Irma Sterns."

"Right, thanks," said Hugo. "So?"

Kevin had arrived at the idea he'd been brooding over all day.

"Shouldn't his only begotten son inherit all that?"

PART ELEVEN

PART ELEVEN

Chapter 67

One advantage to Victor Alderheim's departure from life was that his son Kevin got to learn new and exciting words and phrases. Like for example death certificate, genealogy report, estate executor, estate beneficiary and estate administrator.

Kevin had the Tax Authority on his side; formally, there was no doubt. But in Sweden, everything surrounding death was highly regulated, including who bore financial responsibility for any unpaid rubbish hauling bills, in the event that the deceased hadn't settled such debts from the other side. And up to this point it had never happened.

The long and the short of it was that Kevin had a lot to do in order to get all the formalities squared up. Jenny helped, while Hugo sat at home and pondered the meaning of life.

Given all the money that was about to rain down on Kevin, it did not seem likely that he and Jenny would elect to stick around as colleagues at Sweet Sweet Revenge Ltd. Not even if their boss raised their allowance or went so far as to give them a salary. No, they would go with Ole Mbatian to Kenya. The worst part of all was that if they went, Malte would too.

Hugo devoted a few more thoughts to his financial situation. He recalled his agreement with Jenny and Kevin. Sweet Sweet Revenge Ltd. had taken on the case of Victor Alderheim pro bono, given that any resulting proceeds would go to the firm. For a long time it appeared that there would be nothing but costs. But now what? Hugo certainly couldn't demand to be given the inheritance, or even part of it. Truth be told, it didn't feel right to demand anything at all. They had killed Kevin's biological father, and that was not the sort of action you sent an invoice for.

While Hugo spent time with his thoughts, the medicine man and the eye doctor were enjoying each other's company more and more. They developed an afternoon tradition: sitting on Hugo's sofa and talking about the art of healing with a bottle of Glenfiddich to keep them company.

Malte recalled from his medical training what had

been said about natural remedies and what reasonable amount of respect one ought to have for them even without the benefit of scientific evidence for their capabilities. After all, plants were often full of various phytochemicals or secondary metabolites. But Malte didn't know much about how exactly they worked, either on their own or in combination with each other.

"I've been given to understand that the chemicals in medicinal plants function catalytically and synergistically to arrive at a combined effect in which one plus one is meant to equal three. Can you tell me more about that, Ole?"

"No, I can't."

Ole Mbatian liked the eye doctor very much, but sometimes he was unnecessarily complicated.

After two glasses, the thing that always happened when Ole Mbatian got too close to a bottle of Glenfiddich happened. He became sentimental. For the umpteenth time, he expressed his deep sorrow that his son would not follow in his footsteps when it came to his career. Kevin had fallen from the sky too late to grow into his medicinal inheritance. It had been necessary to prioritize the Maasai warrior training; after all, without it he could not be sent to the savanna to pick herbs and roots. Not if his community wanted him to return, and they did.

His brooding intensified partway through the third glass. Here he sat with his eight daughters and the son who was anything but a medicine man. It was impossible to say exactly how old Ole Mbatian the Younger was; the information in his passport was not to be trusted—his date of birth was something he had winged along with Wilson with his stamps in the car on the way to Nairobi. But he wasn't getting any younger. If only circumstances had allowed, he would have handed everything over to the next generation and entered retirement.

But now, instead, he would be forced to die at his post. He couldn't stand the thought that some amateur from one of the neighboring villages would take over his position and make a living off his good name.

Malte nodded and offered his sympathies.

Hugo was listening from the floor above. Fully sober.

Thinking. Creating.

Without really knowing it, he had begun to build his own future, and that of those around him. Bit by bit.

Chapter 68

The deceased art dealer's assets would have fallen to the Inheritance Fund, if not for the fact that Victor Alderheim had a son who, at the last moment, rose from the dead and in doing so switched places with his father.

It took time to finish the estate inventory, but when that was done it was Kevin's turn to call a general meeting.

Jenny and Ole were on one side of the kitchen table; Hugo and Malte were on the other. Kevin was on one end; in contrast to the others he was standing up, and he wore an expression that none of them had ever seen before. He seemed . . . focused. Solemn.

"My dear friends," he began.

But straight off the bat he changed his mind.

"Let me start over. My dear Jenny. I know we're engaged. But are you sure you want to marry me?"

Jenny smiled lovingly at her boyfriend.

"You know I do."

Kevin did know, but he needed to hear it again in the face of what was coming. He reached for her hand, gave it a kiss, and went back to his solemn self.

"That's done. The next point on our agenda is how recent developments have affected our collected assets. Because that's how I see it—that all of us here around this table share in solidarity the costs and proceeds that have so suddenly arisen. Anyone of a different mindset?"

Hugo sensed a trap, imagining that it would be no surprise if the costs exceeded the proceeds, according to the famous Murphy's Law. But in that case, let it be so. You didn't kill people, even by mistake, only to cash out.

Kevin took the brief nods around the table as confirmation and launched into his financial report.

First, the property and the business. Victor managed to destroy quite a bit during his years as owner. The real estate, consisting of one place of business and one apartment, was valued at thirty-two million kronor. It was held by a limited company that was insolvent thanks to the art dealer's ill-advised investments in nationalistic nineteenth-century art. The inventory consisted of one hundred and twenty national-romantic works with a combined value of one million two hundred thousand kronor, purchased at twenty times that. The property was mortgaged rather beyond what was actually allowed. Preliminary calculations indicated there would be approximately zero kronor left over once Kevin was done cleaning up, with Jenny's help. The numbers would have looked a little better if only Alderheim hadn't given himself fringe benefits in the form of a quarter of a million kronor's worth of foot care per annum.

"I cared for my feet in a basin at the airport in Istanbul once," Ole Mbatian recalled. "Didn't cost more than a telling-off."

Kevin left his father Ole's interjection unremarked.

"We have a few sporadic, private expenditure items as well. It seems Alderheim rented the apartment from his own company. This rendered him personally responsible for refuse-collection service, among other things."

Twelve days had passed from the point of Alderheim's final payment, just before his death, to the point at which Kevin became authorized to cancel any further collections in his name. This left twelve three hundred sixty fifths in outstanding fees. Given a yearly cost of two thousand four hundred kronor, the accumulated debt lay at just over eighty-eight kronor.

"Is that all?" said Hugo.

It wasn't.

"There is an additional flex fee. Each subscriber must pay one krona and seventy-five öre per kilo of rubbish; this is meant to ensure that customers won't throw stuff away just for the hell of it. Unfortunately, Alderheim must have done that very thing, because he owed thirty-six kilos' worth in fees."

Hugo imagined that this was a reasonable estimate of the collected weight of sex toys with chains, bags of flour, crumpled easels, and perhaps a banana peel on top.

"Thirty-six kilos at one and seventy-five?" said Jenny.

Kevin nodded. That made sixty-three kronor in addition to the original eighty-eight.

"Is that all?" said Hugo.

"Essentially, yes."

"But aren't there a couple of newly arrived expressionist works in addition to all the national-romantic stuff?"

Yes indeed. Kevin had almost forgotten. The Irma Stern paintings, with the accompanying letters and photographs, were the property of private citizen

Victor Alderheim. As recently as the day before, the involuntary son had it listed at Sotheby's in London, with the asking price starting at eight million one hundred thirty thousand pounds sterling.

"All in all, that's about a hundred million Swedish kronor," said Kevin.

"Minus one hundred fifty kronor for the rubbish," said Jenny.

"More or less."

Hugo, who had just declined the job in Seoul, tried to calculate how much this was in South Korean won, but there were so many zeroes that he lost count.

Kevin's financial report, along with the suggestion that they should divide things up equally, was the jolt it took for the pieces of the puzzle to fall into place in Hugo's mind. He thanked Kevin for the report and said that, with the permission of the others, he would take charge again, because he had just seen the light.

The group consisted of a medicine man who longed to return home, a former eye doctor who longed to get away, two new lovebird multimillionaires who didn't need to long for anything in particular because they had each other, and an adman who until just now had been lost but suddenly knew exactly what his future held.

"Ole, my dear friend."

Hugo felt like this was overdoing it a bit, but there was something special in the air.

"I want you to pack your throwing clubs, gloves, boxes of cornflakes and whatever, and go home—by way of London."

"London?" said the medicine man. "I've heard good things. Where is it?"

"The rest of us have a property to sell, and some rubbish to clean up—it might take a few weeks, but we'll see you on the savanna as soon as possible."

Chapter 69

By listening with one ear as Malte and the medicine man exchanged experiences in the living room in Lidingö, Hugo had come to understand the potential value of a professionally packaged medical operation in Kenya. Apparently Ole Mbatian couldn't explain his medical abilities in a clinical fashion, but it was perfectly clear that he'd attained better results than others. He had a stellar reputation. Or, as it was called in Hugo Hamlin-ese: a strong brand.

Now that brand was about to go to the grave. Ole wanted to retire, and there was no younger Mbatian to take over, since Kevin was medically insufficient. In Hugo Hamlin's world, this was like owning and shuttering the Adidas brand just because the boss got a little too old.

Ole's name and good quality meant that he dominated the market in large swathes of Maasai Mara. But according to Ole, on the other side of the border stones, in what was called the Serengeti, was a medical dunce who would not hesitate to attempt a takeover. His name was Kamanu, and he couldn't tell a cold from a broken bone.

One man Ole Mbatian had come to respect almost as much as himself, however, was Hugo's brother Malte. He wasn't a medicine man in the true sense of the idea, and he was too white of skin to be pitched as an authentic Mbatian—not to mention that he spoke neither Swahili nor Maa.

But Kevin had everything Malte lacked. And Malte had everything that Kevin lacked. But there was one thing that neither of them had: a good head for business.

That belonged to Hugo.

Chapter 70

Considering the global attention surrounding *Woman with Parasol* and *Boy by Stream*, Sotheby's elected to sell them as a pair, along with the letters and photographs. In an unusual move, the auctioneer introduced one of the motifs in person—the boy by the stream—just before bidding began.

"I would like to extend a warm welcome to Mr. Ole Mbatian the Younger."

Hugo had a knack for advertising. Ahead of the auction, he spent three days drilling the medicine man in the correct things to say.

The event was broadcast live online. The audience on site and all over the world got to hear about the medicine man's meeting with Irma Stern, how he had posed by a stream for her when he was just a boy, how his mother did the same under a parasol, and the circumstances that led to the creation of the paintings in question.

So far, all was going according to Hugo's plan. But then there was the medicine man's preference to keep talking once he'd got started. Thus the world also learned that Ole Mbatian the Elder's first wife, the one under the parasol, was the angriest of the three, and they also heard about the reasons behind that anger: her spouse's many shortcomings. Additionally, Ole thought it would be fitting to explain how an escalator worked, that livestock was an unwieldy form of currency, and that time was running out for circumcision as a test of manliness. He was just about to launch into his views of a caviar called Kalle when, to Hugo's relief, he was cut off by the auctioneer. Ole was kindly shown to a front-row seat. Ten minutes later, the auction was over.

The paintings, and their accompanying cultural treasure in the form of photographs and letters, went for a sensational twelve million and ninety thousand pounds.

One hundred fifty million Swedish kronor.

Just over fifteen million dollars.

Seventeen and a half billion South Korean won.

Fifteen thousand cows.

PART TWELVE

PART TWELVE.

Chapter 71

April, May, June

When the political leadership of Nairobi decided to run a new high-voltage line between Lolgorien and Talek, it ended up awfully close to the borders of the valley where Chief Olemeeli the Well-Traveled ruled, and which he seldom or never left. The chief viewed this operation as an act of war. He rode his bicycle over to argue with the workers about running their lines elsewhere. To his horror, he discovered that there was already electricity there; light bulbs glowed everywhere he looked. The power came from a diesel unit; after all, it takes electricity to make electricity. Olemeeli tore an iron bar from the hands of one of the workers and managed, in a single blow, to sever the cable to the unit.

It was a move as enterprising as it was stupid. The four hundred volts in the cable grabbed hold of the iron bar—and of the man holding it. Olemeeli's heart did somersaults inside his body before it stopped permanently.

There weren't many people who grieved the chief's death. He'd had only weak support to start with, and over the years it had done nothing but grow weaker thanks to his decree banning electricity. The only woman on the village council had argued for washing machines, stoves and bathrooms. When she added the future potential of Netflix, she got all the men except the chief on her side.

Since Olemeeli had decided his vote was the only one that counted, the powerlessness lasted until his death. Now the question was what his successor, his oldest and only son, thought about the matter. Or not. For the son had discovered some feelings he could have for other men rather than for women, and in light of said feelings had found a perfectly delightful and like-minded fellow in the village. They shared a secret that could bring five to seven years in prison as long as they stayed in Kenya, or life on the inside should they flee to any neighboring country. Rumor had it that you could love whoever you liked in South Africa, which was a four-thousand-kilometer walk through enemy territory away. It would definitely be worth it, but of course this also ruled out inheriting his father's position.

For the first time in nine generations, then, the next chief would be selected by a vote of the village council. Majority ruled. Six men and one woman meant a total of six and one half votes, so it couldn't result in a tie.

In the midst of all this, the popular and much-missed medicine man returned. His name was already being floated in the village council as a potential new chief, and he was called for an interview. During the interview he said he was planning to build an escalator to the medical hut on the hill (or, rather, from it). A little while later, after it had become clear to the council what an escalator was, they all realized it required electricity. And that there would be power left over for other things. Like for example washing machines and—most importantly—Netflix.

Thanks to his vision of an escalator, Ole was elected the new chief by a vote of six and a half to zero. From that moment on, his name would be Ole Mbatian the Modern.

So many good things happened one after the next in the life of Ole Mbatian the Modern. The silver necklaces he'd brought from Sweden for his two wives had a magical effect. While one kissed him on the cheek, the other pointed out in a kind voice that this was the first time he'd shown either of them any appreciation, and late was better than never. If he happened to be in the neighborhood of her hut some evening soon, she might consider letting him in.

Ole officiated the wedding of his son Kevin and Kevin's Jenny. A big moment for all three of them. The chief realized he liked confiding in his daughter-in-law about the technical aspects of a relationship. After all, she was the one who'd picked out the necklaces for his wives. What did Jenny think about his continuing to give them nice things on occasion between the short and long rains? He had a lot to pick from now that the electricity was flowing. Dishwashers, refrigerators, toasters . . .

Jenny said that the chief was thinking along the right lines, but wrong. As she understood it, he had half a century's lack of appreciation to catch up with. But kitchen appliances fell under the category of useful items, not presents.

"Vacuum cleaners?"

"Think again, father-in-law. Carefully."

Ole thought again.

"Earrings?"

"You're a fast learner."

At first there was general suspicion of the new medicine man. To be sure, Kevin was a Mbatian, one who had come straight from heaven besides. But everyone in the valley knew his story. En-Kai had sent him down in a totally unfinished state. He wasn't a warrior; he knew only one of the three proper languages and nothing about the healing powers of nature. The predecessor had lamented his son's medicinal shortcomings to Olemeeli each time they gathered over a bottle of Glenfiddich, and it wasn't as if the villagers didn't have ears to hear.

But now Ole Mbatian was the chief. He said that his son had learned everything and a bit more during his travels. To such an extent that he gathered disciples around him. Or one disciple, in any case. A *mzungu* named Malte.

And Kevin wasted no time in proving himself. He arranged to import Cape aloe from Lesotho to treat bacterial infections. It was said to have anti-inflammatory properties. Exactly how true that was didn't matter so

504 • JONAS JONASSON

much, because Malte secretly enhanced the concoction with the proper amount of antibiotics. The results were sensational.

What had once been Ole Mbatian the Younger's specialty, medicine to counter excessive births, became the specialty of his successor as well. Ole's very effective mixture was time-consuming to produce; neither Malte nor Kevin could have found the right ingredients on the savanna even if they'd known what to look for. Their new recipe was as secret as the old one; only the medicine man and his assistant knew the details: tomato soup, basil, garlic, and one contraceptive pill per dose. In its crushed form, the pill looked surprisingly similar to the refined powder of the baobab fruit.

"A daily dose of vitamin C is essential to attain the best results," Kevin might authoritatively inform his current patient. "With the help of En-Kai, we expect that your seven children will not increase further in number. Make sure to love the ones you already have even more."

"May En-Kai bless you," said the patient.

"How would you like to pay?" Malte asked. "Credit card, PayPal, dollars, or livestock?"

The brains behind this setup were named Hugo Hamlin. His newly launched, Nairobi-based company was called Sweet Sweet Health Ltd. His business idea was to commercialize medicine both natural and science-based at the same time. He hired his big brother as the medical expert.

Malte had to fight for one week to attain physician status there. Each day he visited a contrary woman at the licensing board, the one who held the power and the stamps in her hand.

She was called Almasi, and in all her rigidness was really quite adorable. Malte found himself drowning in her eyes.

"Miss Almasi, the anterior chambers of your eyes are in perfect balance," said the ophthalmologist.

"What a lovely thing to say," said Almasi. "I think."

The step from this compliment to allowing herself to be invited to dinner was not a long one. The next evening, she returned the favor. And the day after that, all the stamps were in their proper places.

Since then they had been a couple on a trial basis. Almasi took a leave of absence. Malte bought an electric car. One reason for this was that Chief Mbatian the Modern had had the savanna's first rapid charger installed in the village. Another was that the formerly so staid eye doctor had discovered that he felt young again each time he violated the speed limit (from Nairobi to the savanna in three hours and forty-four minutes). He felt even younger when he pushed the limits of the Hippocratic oath. Calling contraceptive pills vitamin C was merely a different sort of way to serve his fellow humans. Or so he told himself.

Chapter 72

July, August, September

Hugo's ambitions to use medicine to take over all of Maasai Mara and the northern part of the Serengeti had one shortcoming: Kevin couldn't be in more than one place at the same time and he couldn't treat more than one patient at a time. The solution was to expand the medical hut, with three treatment rooms in a row. When it was up and running at capacity, all patients were seen by the medicine man, before two of the three were passed along, one to Jenny and one to Malte. Each patient was given ten minutes to explain what was wrong, and then the medicine man and his assistants had a confab outside the hut—in Swedish, to be safe. This was followed by Kevin spending one minute per treatment room to hand out his prescription, with Malte or Jenny right behind him to take payment.

Their efficiency tripled, but Hugo wanted more. Perhaps frustration would have eventually taken hold of the creator if it hadn't been for the escalator and what it led to.

In the strictest sense, it led to the expanded medical hut on the hill. Or away from it. Kevin's friend, the Norwegian from the World Wildlife Fund (the one who had taught him to drive a car), took a picture of the escalator and posted it on Facebook, with a caption pointing out which direction it led. At which point someone shared it. At which point someone shared the share.

Hugo mostly stuck to the capital city, but he happened to be in the village delivering some medicine when the first tourists cautiously approached to have a look at the escalator. A white man? Could he have something to do with the escalator?

There were four tourists in all, two men and two women. One of the men introduced himself and the group. They came from New Zealand and were actually out on a six-week art tour of Europe.

Paris, of course. Rome. Florence. Madrid. London.

The goal of their trip was to enjoy what they already loved, but also to challenge themselves. Leonardo da

Vinci was, after all, Leonardo da Vinci. Monet and Seurat brought peace to the soul, and the expressionists kept the viewer awake and alert.

They had imagined the trip's challenges would consist of postmodernist and abstract art. None of them had any inclinations in that direction, but oh well—in for a penny, in for a pound.

Suddenly it showed up on Facebook, a picture of the most remarkable installation piece imaginable: An apparently fully functional escalator in a Kenyan village in a remote valley between bush and savanna. One that led in a counterproductive direction.

It was so unique that all the art lovers' plans were turned upside down. They canceled London and rebooked. And now they were here.

"Can we just walk into the village, or is there an entry fee?"

Hugo Hamlin needed three seconds to consider.

"Thirty dollars per person, or one hundred for a group of four. Half price for children under twelve."

Chapter 73

October, November, December

Hugo was so inspired by the escalator installation that he launched a reorganization. Kevin and Malte would have to handle the medicine man industry themselves, along with Almasi. Meanwhile, Hugo appointed Jenny as artistic director of what was to come.

She traveled around Africa to buy up some of the best contemporary African art. She had a generous budget, and the results followed suit.

She arrived home with furniture from Mozambique that was constructed of the remains of what could be found on military battlefields. And with Francis Bacon–inspired South African women in blue. And Nigerian creations woven from the trees and roots provided by nature. And much more besides.

It turned out that modern African art could not be collectively pigeonholed. It rebelled against war, post-colonialism, environmental destruction, and views of women—anything that stood in its way. Controlled and regulated by no one, neither in color nor shape.

Hugo allowed the exhibit to blend in with the fenced-in Maasai village in such a tasteful way that village life itself became part of the artistic whole. All while Chief Ole Mbatian the Modern had a receiver installed on the top of a nearby hill to provide Wi-Fi to the entire valley. That is, it was free until Hugo discovered it. After that, the villagers continued to surf for free; everyone else had to pay according to the following fee schedule: three dollars for one hour. Ten dollars for five hours. Twenty dollars for one full day.

Maasai Mara's leading and only permanent art exhibition brought in between two and four thousand dollars per day. Included in the entry fee were examples of the contemporary African artistic expression; for ten dollars extra, you could take a walk in the wrong direction on the escalator installation.

It was an immediate success. But that did not mean that the commercial director of the exhibition, Hugo Hamlin, was satisfied (he seldom was). The former adman always strove for more, without necessarily spending too much money in his pursuits. Accordingly, he called the artistic director to a meeting. He noted that the exhibition was lacking in tribal masks and suggested that the chief's wives could produce such items behind a hut where no one would see them. By temporarily burying the masks in the ground, and fertilizing them with iron-rich water, they would become two centuries old within a week.

Jenny shook her head. But Hugo didn't give up. He had more ideas.

"What about Irma Stern's unfinished work, then?"

The artistic director's pulse increased for a moment, before she realized what he was talking about.

"And where is this unfinished work?"

"I was thinking you could make one."

Jenny promised Hugo that when they had the time she would remind him all about provenance and authentication. But she didn't enjoy being the constant naysayer. She wanted to give him *some* small thing.

As a result, five weeks later Hugo would reveal the exhibit's latest addition, which was placed on a pedestal next to the escalator.

Laid Bare, a golden potato peeler. Which was purchased, the very next day, by an American tourist for eight thousand dollars.

Kevin and Malte's operation reached new heights right alongside the art exhibition. The former eye doctor's girlfriend permanently took over Jenny's role in the organization. She spoke Swahili, had the right skin color, and agreed with Malte and Kevin that medical results were more important than the truth.

Meanwhile, there was whispering in the wings. Kamanu, the medicine man on the other side of the border stones—the man who, according to Ole Mbatian, couldn't tell a broken bone from a cold—felt that his way of life was under threat. In a short time, his roster of patients had shrunk by half. And he was still better off than several of his colleagues.

To be a medicine man was to have power. To be a medicine man without patients, however, was nothing but a disgrace.

Kamanu arranged an emergency summit with fifteen other medicine men from Maasai Mara and the Serengeti. He was of the mindset that there must be a way to bring down the threatening medicine man monopoly in the region. Those with the least painful joints were practically slaloming their way between local medicine men in order to go all the way to the man who seemed able to cure it all.

514 • JONAS JONASSON

The others were in agreement.

After a brief discussion, it was decided that balance must be restored. But also that this couldn't be achieved with arguments of a purely medical nature, because just about every single one of the damn patients was healthy again after a visit to Mbatian's boy and his henchmen.

The solution would have to be a change of focus. The sixteen medicine men had vague suspicions that witchcraft was involved—just think of how rumor said that the boy had fallen out of the sky. Who could say for certain that he hadn't come from the other direction?

There was no proof of witchcraft, or even any clear indications, but where there was a will there was a way.

One of the sixteen wronged medicine men in the group had a background that included four years at the university in Abuja. There he had learned how the internet worked. In the past, rumors of witchcraft and other serious matters could take months, sometimes years, to travel sufficiently far. Now every goatherd walked around with his nose in a smartphone, even in the valley where the backwards-striving Chief Toothless had ruled until very recently. Research suggested that general levels of intelligence were suffering in countries that had become obsessed with the internet in the past twenty years. The corresponding effect among goatherds on the savanna was that the number killed by wild animals had increased from two per year to ninety-six. It was, of course, impossible to protect goats, keep an eye out for buffalo and rhinoceroses, and watch *Game of Thrones* all at the same time.

The Abuja medicine man's point was that they ought, for the common good, to start and spread a rumor on social media, one that would play to their own advantage. This rumor should seize on xenophobia and cultural decay.

He was the only one who fully understood what he'd just said, but when Kamanu nodded, the others did the same.

As a consequence of the medicine men's meeting, it was soon possible to follow a cautiously growing protest movement against what Almasi, Jenny, Hugo, Kevin, Malte and Ole had built up along with the villagers.

The movement went by the name "Save the Maasai Kingdom." There it was alleged that *real* art took its inspiration from the Maasai warrior's shield or spear, the Maasai woman's bridal dress, headdresses for various purposes, necklaces and ornamented bowls. The incorporation of foreign elements from Nigeria, South

Africa and Mozambique was an abomination. The latter especially: everyone knew what Mozambicans were like.

Furthermore, the movement claimed that escalators on the savanna were a threat to the Maasai culture that went back centuries. And there had been a Scandinavian potato peeler of gold as well. And worst of all: it was said that artworks from Somalia and Egypt were on their way. If no one put a stop to this, everyone on the savanna would soon be speaking Arabic. Or some European language; there were indications in that direction too. "Save the Maasai Kingdom" knew that the medicine man was assisted by a *mzungu*.

Kamanu and his fifteen conspiring colleagues could not attack Kevin Mbatian on purely medical grounds. But they could attack what surrounded him. The escalator and the artworks that were said to represent various different parts of Africa were, in reality, the manner in which ill-willed colonizers planned to re-enslave the Maasai soul, orchestrated by a medicine man who was possessed by evil spirits. In short, burn it all!

Now, social networking wasn't as well-developed in Maasai Mara and the Serengeti as it was in many other parts of the world. The medicine man's revenge on Ole

Mbatian and his crew might instead be comparable in effect to planting a hedge of juniper with the goal of blocking the sunlight for one's neighbor's carrot patch years later. But the hedge was planted. And it was watered every day.

Still, the conspiring medicine men's plan was doomed to fail. At least from a broader perspective than a slowly growing juniper bush. For, historically, modernism has an unfailing ability to rise again. The difference between this and a phoenix is that the latter recreates an identical copy of itself. When art rises from its own ashes, no one can predict what will happen.

Chapter 74

January, February, March

Chief Ole Mbatian decided that the only woman on the village council would be given a full vote.

The smith protested. He was primarily afraid of women in general and his own wife and sister in particular, but as his main reason he offered that the group might break even when voting on important principles. Ole Mbatian the Modern had introduced majority rule instead of making all decisions on his own.

The chief took this to heart and solved the voting issue by removing half a vote from any member of the council who was a smith by trade.

That same evening, Jenny Mbatian admired her father-in-law's courage.

"And by the way, you're on your way to becoming a grandfather," she revealed.

Ole Mbatian the Modern was absolutely thrilled.

"A grandson!" he exclaimed.

But Jenny and Kevin had already been to Nairobi for an ultrasound. Growing in Jenny's belly was a future medicine woman.

"She's going to be a Maasai warrior too," said the pregnant one.

Ole took it better than either he or Jenny could have expected.

"Well, modern is modern. Have you decided on a name?"

"Irma."

Epilogue

Fifteen months after the incident on Birger Jarlsgatan, Inspector Gustavsson had investigated twenty-five of the remaining four hundred ninety-six suspects on the hate-and-threat site. But that didn't mean he was any closer to solving the murder mystery. For a new thread appeared early on, on the theme of "the goat-sex man got just what he deserved." The result was three hundred new suspects.

"Shouldn't we close this case now?" Gustavsson asked his boss.

"No," said the superintendent.

He found it amusing to watch Gustavsson work.

Gustavsson's predecessor, Christian Carlander, began his retirement days by doing two things. One: quitting his never-ending course in beginners' Spanish, and two: finishing the García Márquez book he'd begun while he was still working on avoiding his job.

Those boxes ticked, life no longer had any purpose. Carlander realized that after *One Hundred Years of Solitude* he had to look forward to a hundred more. Or pull himself together.

He elected to do the latter and applied to a study group in Contemporary International Politics and Development. He didn't know why that was the group he chose—perhaps because the educational association had squeezed it in between one about ceramics design and another about finding yourself through healing.

The group leader, a phlegmatic former social studies teacher from Örebro, couldn't get a word in edgewise. The woman who took over was named Juanita; she was Spanish, divorced and had a fiery temperament.

From Spanish classes to a Spanish woman, Carlander thought. Someone up there had a sense of humor.

Juanita declared within the first few minutes of the first meeting that everything was going to hell. She based her argument on the man named Adolf, saying that what had once happened in Germany had nothing to do with the Germans, but that it would happen again and start somewhere else.

"Again?" said Carlander, mostly because he wanted

Juanita to keep talking. She had beautiful lips, and they were even more beautiful when they were moving.

The phlegmatic leader tried to regain control, offering all due respect to what might have happened ninety years ago but saying that he wished to return the conversation to more recent times, and preferably the present.

"Yes, *again!*" said Juanita, as if the phlegmatic man didn't exist. "There's always a next time, for everything. People don't remember any further back than their noses can reach!"

A beautiful nose, too, thought Carlander, trying to think of something to say that might prompt her to go on a little longer. But Juanita didn't need his help.

"Just take all the goddamned presidents."

She rattled them off. There was the supposed leader of the free world who was whipping up "us-versus-them" sentiments on Twitter. There was the one in the most populous country in the world who had declared that the most important function of art was to serve the nation and the party. There was the one who had taken over the country with the threatened rainforest and begun his term as president by shuttering the country's ministry of culture and assigning a former porn star to watch over the nation's cultural and moral attitudes.

"Porn star?" said the phlegmatic man, who had lost control of his group before he'd even tried to start having it.

But Juanita had already switched continents and arrived at the president of the allegedly democratic superpower who had created his own internet alongside the one that already existed.

"Why?" said Carlander, suspecting this was a dumb question.

He had to get hold of himself. Until very recently, his life had been over. Now he was sitting across from a woman so vivacious that the air seemed to crackle around her. What might happen if they had dinner together?

Juanita answered Carlander as she looked at the phlegmatic man.

"So he can pull the plug on the real internet once the truth gets to be too much for him and his agenda."

Carlander nodded. And tried to look deep. Whatever use that was, if the Spanish woman kept looking in a different direction.

"It seems democracy as we know it is under threat."

That didn't sound so dumb!

Juanita moved on to Central Europe, where some were starting to rewrite their own histories, chase disapproving universities out of the country, rearrange their supreme courts, and supply films with warning labels if they didn't live up to the government's new, patriotic demands.

"As if a film wasn't fine art, but a pack of cigarettes," said Carlander.

Now she had discovered him!

The two other members of the group said nothing. The phlegmatic man felt steamrollered, but at least he had brought the conversation (or the monologue) into the present day.

"Do you know what the worst part of all is, Börje?" Juanita addressed the phlegmatic man.

"My name is Bengt," he said.

Juanita had no time for details. She was far too eager to announce what the worst part of all was: Us-versus-them politics was spreading through the world like poison! Insignificant political parties that wanted to overthrow society, ones that no one had taken seriously before, were spiffing up their party platforms and helping themselves to power in this new zeitgeist. This way and that.

"Soon they will have taken over entirely—mark my words—and then we're back to the thirties! They start by censoring art, then architecture and the media, and soon enough everything else is just waiting its turn!"

By this point, Juanita's cheeks were almost as red

as her lips. Carlander thought they better hurry up and have dinner if she was right about the looming end of the world. He felt that he must, to this end, say at least one good thing before the leader brought this evening's session to an end.

He searched inside himself and happened to think of the art dealer who had fallen victim to an evil jar of lingonberries the year before. What was her name again, the woman who had created the two paintings in his cellar?

"That sounds dreadful," he said, just as he recalled her name. "A censored Irma Stern, for instance, would be a great loss for the world."

Juanita's agitation was derailed.

"You know art?"

She had discovered him for real!

"What would humanity be without it?" Carlander said, figuring that he had a lot to read up on before their first dinner, should he manage to take things that far.

Juanita accepted the invitation as soon as his first attempt after the second study-group meeting.

After that came another dinner.

And yet another. With an overnight stay.

The Spanish woman was not all fire and politics.

Her laugh was heaven-sent and she had a lust for life that Carlander had previously thought existed only in the movies. She laughed hardest of all when the former police inspector, before their third dinner, confessed that he could hardly even spell the word expressionism. All was fair in love and war, right? And in saying so, the coming war wasn't foremost in his mind.

The study group met its demise when Börje, whose name was Bengt, stopped showing up, just like the two nameless members who never contributed to the conversation anyway. That left Carlander and Juanita. They decided to continue group-studying on their own, preferably in Carlander's bedroom. After six weeks she said it for the first time, but not the last:

"*Te quiero.*" I love you.

"*El perro está bajo la mesa,*" Carlander replied.

Thank You

Most of all I want to thank my publisher, Sofia Brattselius Thunfors, and my editor, Anna Hirvi Sigurdsson at Piratförlaget. You have read my simple declaration of love to fine art again and again (and again!) without tiring (either that, or you hide it well). Your work has made such a difference to this book.

Next, I thank my early readers: Uncle Hans (who in his later years has become a kind critic), my buddy Rixon (who has always been just that) and my big brother Lars. For the sake of familial harmony I'd better thank my brother Martin as well, although he still hasn't read a single line.

The most fun to thank is my fellow author Sara Lövestam for her knowledge of Swahili. In turn, she has involved Bakari Mngazija and Aisia Nyirenda and family (not least Papa Robert!). To them I say not only thanks, but *asante sana*.

Thanks too to the experts who have given advice and pointers along the way. Art expert Mikael Karlsson, Master of Laws Sten Bergström, former police officer and security expert Björn von Sydow, IT security expert Jonas Lejon, physicians Erik & Lotta Wåhlin, and—not least—the slightly clandestine expert Joakim. I have listened to what you told me, considered it—and, in the end, done what I thought was best for the story. A novel should above all be worth reading rather than true.

Thanks too to my agent Erik Larsson at Partners in Stories, who managed to sell *Sweet Sweet Revenge Ltd* to half the world before there was even a manuscript.

There's room for a few more thanks. One of them goes to all you readers who send cheers from Pakistan to Canada and just about every country in between. Your greetings make me feel just as happy and proud each time.

I have saved my very last thanks for you, Irma Stern. I have taken poetic license in making just a few things up about your fantastic life, but *nothing* in this book is truer than your artistic greatness. You died in 1966, but you will be with us until the end of time. As long as the patriots don't take over and ban you.

Jonas Jonasson
Stockholm, August 2020

A Note from the Translator

O ne of my favorite parts about translating is doing miniature forays into research. It happens every workday. I'll spend a few minutes getting more background on a cultural item. To give a generic example, perhaps it's some pastry enjoyed with coffee during *fika*: Does it have an already-accepted translation in English? What are its ingredients, and is there something similar that's already familiar to American readers? Is a *pepparkaka* close enough to a gingersnap? Opinions vary. Even my own opinion varies, depending on the day and the context.

Or perhaps I'll spend some time tooling around a neighborhood on Google Maps to get a feel for where the main characters in a novel spend their days. That was certainly the case in this book, as I imagined the sequence of events that led our heroes to traverse central Stockholm—from a meal at the Asian restaurant near Kronoberg Remand Prison to the lingonberry incident outside the gallery on Birger Jarlsgatan and their subsequent getaway back to Lidingö. While I am moderately familiar with Stockholm, during this project I also had occasion to visit environs I've never visited in person, as I followed the road from Nairobi to Narok and on into the Kenyan countryside.

The best research forays of all, though, are the ones that turn into deeper rabbit holes—times I want to learn some minute details about an aspect of everyday life in Sweden, for instance. This is when I find myself digging into the websites of various municipal or national authorities, comparing their typically sparse English-language information pages with the much more informative Swedish versions, hoping to find a matching term to pluck out and use in my document.

Perhaps the most unusual rabbit hole I went down during this translation was the one about garbage. The paragraph that prompted it involves household waste—such as potato peelings and coffee filters—on its way to an incineration plant in greater Stockholm. It's only a minor plot point, yet I wanted to know: How do Stockholmers separate their garbage and recycling? Is composting required by city statute? Was the truck hauling the waste a garbage truck or a more specialized compost truck? Thus, a visit to the website of the Stockholm Municipal Council's Waste Management Plan.

I didn't find my answer there, but I wasn't out of options yet. Another enjoyable part of my job is the opportunity to build a relationship with an author and to ask questions about an unfamiliar word or something I want to understand more fully than the given context might allow. In this case, as I put it to Jonas Jonasson in the email I sent him, "I ask partly because it will affect word choice but also because I'm curious." In his response, he described his personal experience of Stockholm garbage separation and collection and answered my many other questions gamely and helpfully. And for that, and the chance to work with Jonas Jonasson's novel, and the chance to share a few thoughts on translation with you, reader, I am grateful. Happy reading!

—Rachel Willson-Broyles

HARPER LARGE PRINT

We hope you enjoyed reading
our new, comfortable print size and found it
an experience you would like to repeat.

Well – you're in luck!

Harper Large Print offers the finest in
fiction and nonfiction books in this same larger
print size and paperback format. Light and easy to read,
Harper Large Print paperbacks are for the book lovers
who want to see what they are reading without strain.

For a full listing of titles and
new releases to come, please visit our website:
www.hc.com

HARPER LARGE PRINT

SEEING IS BELIEVING!